Novallia

By Brenda Nolan

Table of Contents

Chapter One...3

Chapter Two 23

Chapter Three...35

Chapter Four...45

Chapter Five...59

Chapter Six...75

Chapter Seven 97

Chapter Eight...106

Chapter Nine 118

Chapter Ten...134

Chapter Eleven...160

Chapter Twelve..191

Chapter Thirteen 204

Chapter Fourteen 219

Chapter Fifteen 237

Chapter Sixteen 274

Chapter One

Family Matters (Thedford City, 1886)

Each step of her boots on the cobblestone sounded like the tick of a clock. The puddles were not deep but enough to soak the bottom of her skirt as she ducked into the alley. Clutching a book to her chest, Nola remained close to the wall waiting and listening for the drunkards behind her.

"Check over there." The male voice was deep and grated. "The little strumpet couldn't have gone far." Stood frozen, Nola could hear three different sets of boots on the road. "Where ye' you hiding at, love? We just want to talk to you. There is nothing much to fear." One of the three men tried to coax her out.

"Nothing at all," a second voice much too close, pricked her ears. "We just want another look at those pretty eyes and that shiny hair."

Sidestepping from the corner, Nola knew she had to run. There was one mile between her and home, but it was no ordinary mile. That distance would take her out of the alley, across Falkenstein Avenue, past the less reputable pubs, over the bridge by Darlington Avenue before finally the Capstan District. If she were lucky the trio would give up their pursuit long before Darlington. There were well-lit streets near the clock tower. Nevertheless, the returning click of her heels alerted the pursuers.

"Over here!" The yell rang out. Nola hiked up her thick skirt with one hand and clung to a book with the other. She could run like the wind, but the men from a nearby pub were still following her.

"Get her!" One of the young men shouted. Another was gaining distance and not more than twenty feet behind. Too terrified to cry out, Nola hurried on. A carriage crossed her path at the end of the alley. Still, she knew that the side roads could be just as dangerous as the alleys.

"Where did she go?"

There was no time to think. Nola's concern was the one man at her heels. Thankfully, her ability to set aside emotion granted her clear thinking and controlled fear. She was not afraid of the men, at all. She was simply hyperaware that it was in her best interest to escape them. With a flick of her arm, she sent her book flying backward. The connection was loud as pages fluttered through the night, but it was not enough to slow him down.

Without the book, she hurled all momentum forward. Another side street was just ahead but it was two more blocks to Darlington Avenue. Glancing up, she could see the peak of the clock tower looming above the rooftops. Being the third-largest clock tower in the city, it offered a great deal of light to the streets below. Still, at the rate she was running, she was not going to make it to the safer side of town.

Just in front of her, a large service door opened. A worker stepped into the alley. Sighting opportunity, Nola dove around.

Immediately, the man in pursuit collided with the unprepared stranger.

"Ay, mind where you're at!" The stranger yelled as both the men scuffled and came to their feet. However, brief the struggle it put just enough distance between them that Nola looked up at the clock tower once more.

"Get back here!" The man yelled, returning to the chase. "We just want to talk, pretty lady."

The glow of Darlington Avenue was just in the distance. The smell of the slums was behind her, and the scenery had become less depressing. Windows were lit, streets were cleaner, and no debris lined the roads. Still, strangers pursued her. The river rushed close by. It wasn't long before the alley would end, and Darlington Avenue would open up. The dominating clock tower stood safely on the other side of the bridge.

Where the narrow road expanded at the river's edge a group of young men stood huddled over a burning barrel. There were four of them. Thankfully, they looked familiar.

"What's this here?" A seated man asked as Nola continued at a full run toward the bridge.

"Hey!" One of them stood out and came toward her. "Nola, is that you?" Her cousin Davey called in a tone that should not have been as comforting as it was. Without pause, she ran, knowing that the convenient group would prove upsetting to her pursuers. Like a jolt of electricity, Davey's fist shot out, hitting the closest man.

Instantly, the stunned man had been slammed to the cobblestone.

"Luke?" Nola turned around, surprised to see Davey's younger brother in the group. Davey passed off the bottle in his hand and faced the other two men. Taking a swig from the bottle, the younger brother finally recognized Nola. "Luke!" Shock gave them both a pause.

"Get out of here!" Luke, the thinnest of the group, came around the barrel just as another buster reached the end of the alley.

"Run home, Nola!" Davey yelled.

She did not take time to argue. Nola heard the other men rile up to face her assailants, but she would not turn around to watch as

4

the standoff began. Darting across Baggerty Bridge, she high-tailed it to Darlington Avenue, breathing a sigh of relief only when the clock tower rose high above her. Still, her feet were swift carrying her past two streets of shops and three streets of houses until reaching Capstan District. Only then, she quit the pace and began to reclaim composure.

Knowing it wouldn't take long for her cousins to catch up, she cautiously delayed the walk home. It took a few minutes, but her suspicions were correct. A glance behind revealed Luke's silhouette under the streetlamp.

"Wait," Luke called just before they reached the house. "Don't you dare walk in there and let Mum know you were out this late!" Through the shadows, his tall lanky form was easily recognized. "Who were they? What did they want?" Looking through the trees, Luke made sure that no one was around. "Why were they chasing you?" His narrow frame and thick dark hair depicted his youth perfectly. "More importantly, what were you doing out and across the bridge?"

"Pardon me?" Nola huffed, finally having caught her breath. "My whereabouts are my business. I have no idea who those vagrants were. And ...welcome home, dear cousin."

"You're twisting my meaning ...and thank you." Luke watched her shoulders rise and fall with every exaggerated gasp of breath. "Tell me what happened."

"I lost track of time, which is all. I went to the library and lost track of time. A few drunkards tried to rile me up. Davey took care of it, end of story."

"Did you miss the big blooming clock bell?" Coming up to the porch, Luke looked back to the road.

"Where is Davey?" Nola asked.

"Probably dumping a body in the river." Luke chuckled.

Glancing over nonchalantly, he checked for wounds or marks on her skin. "Are you hurt?"

"No," she answered aware of his concern. "And you better not say a thing to your mother about this."

"Once Mum sees Davey's knuckles all swollen and bloody, she'll corner us all until she gets an answer."

"Where is he?" Nola waited, staring at the road until she saw a few men walking their way. There was no sound of concern in her voice, she knew the elder brother would be fine. Davey's stocky frame stood out like a stag among fawns. He may have been the same height as his friends, but there was no mistaking the reliable brawn. "Good, he's alright." Nola sighed with relief. "I did not want to tell Aunt Dottie that he was arrested."

"It would have been your fault." Luke looked her up and down twice. "It's nice to see you. I hadn't intended to see you until the morning. Now, tell me what happened!" Even as Luke tried to force an answer, Nola watched Davey, the elder of the brother's, walk up to the house. There was a shared glance between the eldest and youngest, but it was less than friendly.

"Davey... I'd like..." Nola tried to thank him.

Davey turned on her like someone threw kerosene in a blaze. "You nuisance! If Mum finds out you crossed the bridge, she'll start hauling all of us in at night." Quickly, he wiped the blood off his lip. "Luke, you better think of what to tell Mum."

"Tell her what?" Luke was more annoyed than before. "I don't know what happened."

"Make something up ...and quick." Davey left the thinking to his younger brother. "I have to be to work in five hours."

"You aren't going to ask her what she was doing way over there?"

"What was she up to?" Drawing back for a moment, Davey considered just how long Luke had been away at university. "You really don't know, do you?" Davey's blue eyes seemed to glow in the moonlight. With light russet hair and handsome features, he was easily approached by women of his age. However, to Nola, he was as friendly as a cactus up a horse's ass. "It turns out that our little prissy princess has a genuine lack of morals. She has developed a shitty sense of superiority as of late."

"What does that mean?" Luke questioned.

"Watch your mouth, Davey." Nola kept her voice to a whisper, but she was still careful of her words. "I have nothing to be ashamed of. I will not have you speaking as if I have."

"What have you been up to then?" Luke was far more curious than before. "And for the last time, who were those men?"

"I have no idea." Nola nearly lost her temper. "All I know is they came out of the shadows asked me what I was reading and started after me when I tried to walk away." Her shoulders tensed up as Davey shook his head. "I wasn't about to take time to make their acquaintance."

"You expect us to believe that?" Davey asked.

With the unmistakable sound of a window being drawn open, they stopped talking. All three heads lifted as if the heavens themselves opened wide, with a foul temper. "What are you three rambling on about out here?" Aunt Dottie slid open the second-floor window and peered down at the porch. "Do you have any idea what time it is? Get in here before you wake the neighborhood!"

"I think it's time we bought someone a chastity belt," Davey pushed past Nola and walked into the house.

"There is no need to be vulgar," Nola hissed at Davey. "Come up with one hell of a good excuse," the elder brother whispered before entering the house. "If you don't, you'll be on a leash for the next month."

"Luke, is that you? It's about time you came home," Dottie called curiously. "Nola, get up here and stop making such a racket." Davey had already entered the house by the time Dottie's window had closed. Nola's admiration for her cousin's quick fists faded as she followed him into the house.

"Nola!" Dottie called from the top of the stairs. "What on earth are you doing out this late?"

Wishing she had the library book as an excuse, Nola came to the foot of the stairs. Davey, eldest and breadwinner, walked into the kitchen. Dottie stood above her, silvery strands of hair curling down around her shoulders. The crutch under one arm seemed to annoy her as well as the late hour. Still, she looked more like an angel than a harbinger of punishment.

As if she needed a savior, Luke interfered. "It's alright, Mum." He was at the stairs beside Nola. "Mrs. Laghterly asked us to help find her dog."

"Mrs. Laghterly? Is she the elderly woman across the way?" Nodding to the east window, Dottie appeared very confused.

"Stop," Nola whispered to Luke under her breath.

"That's the one," he answered quickly, raising his hand to scratch the back of his head.

"Did she come all the way over here for your help?" Dottie asked the younger of her two boys.

"No," Luke continued easily. "Davey was already out... The boy's found out I was home, and we were just sitting around when we heard her calling."

"Just stop," Nola hissed under her breath, looking down at the
floor.

"Well, in that case, I have nothing to worry about then." Dottie placed her crutch further away from the steps. "I just wish we could get the money back from that big fancy school you graduated from." Turning on the wooden knob of the crutch, Dottie hobbled back to her bedroom. "They did a horrible job of teaching you how to lie." Luke's cool demeanor changed slowly as his mother spoke. "That mangy mutt has been dead a year now."

Unable to hide her snicker, Nola whispered, "I tried to tell you."

"God Damn you," Luke stated loudly. "You could have been a little faster," Luke whispered at the bold woman.

"Well now, you had best prepare to get up early," Dottie hollered back over her shoulder. "You're going to have a busy day rinsing soap out of that dirty mouth." Long after her form was gone, Dottie could still be heard. "And I wouldn't make any plans for the next while. No one is leaving this house unless I know exactly when, where, and why! I'm too old for anything to happen to you three."

"Yes, Aunt Dottie," Nola agreed.

"Davey," the old lady called. "Davey?" All three of them waited to see if Davey would answer. However, the house fell silent until Dottie limped back into her bedroom and closed the door.

"You fool!" Nola shook her head. "You can't just come back after being gone so long and expect nothing to have changed."

"Excuse me, for trying to cover your scrawny little ass."

"Where did you get such a mouth? Did they teach you that at university?"

"Yes, and then some. Now, what were you doing over the bridge?" Luke asked.

"None of your business." Curtly, she turned to head up the stairs.

Ignoring the creaking hallway and the shuffling blankets in Dottie's room, Nola walked directly to the small window across from her bedroom door. All the excitement had made her far too annoyed to sleep. Pulling back the thick green curtain she peered down to the road below. She had been given awkward glances and a few direct stares from the strangers across Baggerty Bridge, but never had she been chased.

A small glint of light across the road caught her attention. In that split second, she saw him. Nola backed away from the curtain and into the darkness. Across the road, a tall and unmistakable form stood in the shadows of a large tree. A long black coat covering much of his pristine shirt. If not for the moonlight reflecting his eyes one may not have noticed him at all. She could tell instantly from the long expensive coat and glimmer of gold on his finger. Nola took a step closer to the window, knowing she was perfectly safe under his watchful eyes.

In his hands, she could see the library book that had been thrown at the men in the alley. As soon as they made eye contact, the dark figure stepped back into the shadows and disappeared into the night. The single moment lifted Nola's stomach to her chest. For weeks she had tried to catch a glimpse of him. The one night she ended up in trouble, he followed her all the way home.

***

"What is all this?" Luke asked as he walked into the sweet-smelling kitchen.

"This is breakfast." Dottie held the most beautiful smile beneath sprinkles of flour. The kitchen was filled with tarts, hotcakes, and ham. With a single crutch beneath her arm and the other leaning against the wall, it was obvious that Dottie had gone to great lengths for the meal. "You didn't think a graduated ...Mister Luke Ellis would be eating oats and honey now, did you?" Her choice of words conveyed all pride.

"You didn't have to do any of this, Mum." Luke walked up, kissed her plump cheek, and picked up a tart between his fingers. "They're good," he whispered while chewing.

"Now, I know you didn't lose your manners at that fancy school. Sit down and take a plate." Her silver hair was pulled-up in a bun and her apron looked as messy as the kitchen.

"Not unless you sit down with me." Luke pulled out the chair behind her before grabbing a few hotcakes with his fingers.

"What's all this?" Nola came into the kitchen, drawn by the delicious smell. "Aunt Dottie?" There was no mistaking her surprise. "What are you doing up?"

"Making my son a home-cooked breakfast." Her eyes, faded by time, still held a bit of sparkle as she gloated. "Come on, dear. I've made plenty for you too."

"Why don't you sit down?" Nola offered. Seeing the chair, Nola reached out to Dottie's arm and took some of her weight as they hobbled to the chair. "You could have awakened me. I would have been glad to help."

"Nonsense, we all know how late you were out last night." The old woman smiled.

"I'll get that plate." Trying desperately to ignore the subject, Nola took the spatula from the frying pan and flipped the bacon. Luke glanced up at his mother curiously, but her gaze stayed on the magnificent food she had spent hours preparing.

"I haven't cooked like this in months." Dottie continued to smile. "A simple pot of coffee for Davey and maybe a honey biscuit here or there, but neither of you two children eat anything." She watched Nola prepare a healthy plate of food. "I've gotten lazy over the last while."

"Did Davey leave already?" Luke took another cake and a few strips of bacon.

"Oh goodness, he's gone well before the sun gets up. That boy is still one of the hardest working men God gave."

"He's gargantuan compared to when I left." Standing up slightly, Luke poured a full cup of tea into Dottie's cup.

"They have him working six days a week building that bridge over the Delmar River and half a day on Sundays." The left side of her skirt hung heavily on the chair, vacant where her leg should have been. Dottie had become used to wearing long dresses that covered her single shoe. However, everyone knew about the missing limb.

"How long do they expect it to take?" Luke asked.

"They have been saying another six months since the project began. With any luck, I'll live to see it finished."

"You're not that old."

"I feel it." She nodded her head as Nola brought her a plate. "Now as for you, young lady, what have you got to say for yourself?"

"In regard to...?" Nola's voice trailed off.

"You know very well what I am talking about. My body may be decaying but the senses are still sharp." Trying to maintain a gentle voice, Dottie buttered the cakes Nola served. "How do we get you to stop running around all hours of the night ...getting your dresses all muddy," Dottie huffed as she spoke, "You must be needing something we don't already have!"

"I could use a carriage," she answered with honesty and bold courage.

The coffee burned Luke's chin and wrist as he coughed a bit out. Taking a cloth, he wiped his face and watched Dottie's expression change slowly. Somehow, she maintained a kind temperament.

"You do not need a carriage. You need to be home and in bed." Dottie gave no room for leverage in her tone.

"The books I study are far older than the usual lot. They are not lent out by any library." Unemotional to the obvious upset of her aunt and cousin, Nola continued. "Not only that, but several are restricted to registered students. There is only one caretaker that allows me inside, after-hours. He grants me as much time as I need to read." With sincerity and conviction, she added, "It would be ridiculous of me not to take advantage of the opportunity."

"You do not need anything at that time of night. Your education has been well taken care of by your guardian." Dottie held the argument.

"Lord Graelohr?" Nola gave a disapproving headshake. "He allows me to study language, art, music, and etiquette," she gave the list with a disheartened tone. "My interests lie outside of the feminine norm."

"We have pushed her education," Luke added to the discussion. "Her continued interest is commendable."

"Davey said, you have been going over to that big house again." Without looking away from her plate, Dottie managed to bring the room to a silent halt. "Is that true?"

"Yes," Nola answered.

"What big house?" Luke glanced from his mother to his cousin. "You mean ...Graelohr Manor?"

"I don't go inside," Nola spat out quickly.

"You don't go inside, that's a relief." The sarcasm in Luke's voice was unmistakable. "What are you doing then, spying on your benefactor?"

"Of course not." Setting down the maple syrup jar with a thud, Nola plopped down in a chair. "I couldn't possibly see him from the road."

"Oh dear," Dottie put her hand to her chest. "Nola... you cannot be outside a man's house in the middle of the night. Do you realize what people will say?"

"Wait, wait hold fast." Luke, slightly bewildered, set down his fork. "What do you do?"

"There is a park bench on the opposite side of the road. I sit beneath the streetlamp and read until the lamplighter comes around to put it out." Flipping a hot cake, Nola shrugged her shoulders.

"A park bench, till nearly midnight?" He paused as if trying to reach his own conclusion. "Why would you ever sit there? It's over a mile and halfway through the worst of the city. Can't you just read in the parlor?" Watching her stuff a large portion of cake into her mouth, Luke continued to wait until she was finished chewing. Only then, Nola took another bite. "Aren't you going to answer me?"

"No. She won't," Dottie spoke, sighing heavily at the mess around her. "Nola no longer answers anyone's questions. She believes she is a woman of the modern age. She comes and goes as she pleases."

"And you let her?" Luke was astonished.

"Oh, dear. I don't let her," Dottie restated the words with a stern tone. "However, I can't rightly go running around after her. Can I?" She looked down at her crippled form.

"Well, you won't be sneaking out while I'm here." Luke poured a second cup of coffee and stood up from the table.

"What a fantastic idea." Dottie wore a sweet smile. "Since you have so much energy to stay up all night long and create a ruckus on the back porch, perhaps you have the stamina to keep her in the house for a change."

"No." Luke shook his head instantly, aware of the blooming implication. "No! I start my job in a few days. I am not about to sit in the hall all night." Dottie simply smiled at him and nodded. "No," Luke stated again. "I have few priceless nights of freedom."

"I understand," Dottie sighed. "If Davey couldn't keep her home, I can only imagine how much trouble it would be for you."

"Entrapment is not going to work, Mum. You're not baiting me by using that old trick."

"I would consider no such thing," she defended herself.

Nola stood up, obviously annoyed at the conversation. "I must hurry." She left the dirty dishes in the basin. "Leave this here for when I return, I am only helping Miss Peetz for an hour this morning. Tomorrow, I will be at the school all day."

Reveling in an obvious false sense of security, Luke surmised, "See, she has to work all day tomorrow. No need to worry about her running out tonight. Besides, I have a few people to meet up with."

"Yes, Davey and I were sure of the same thing. Weren't we, Nola?" Dottie kept her sweet smile. The woman always managed to make her point without ruffling any feathers.

"My leaving did not bother you last night, Aunt Dottie. It was Luke and Davey that woke you up."

"I fear for you." Dottie's honesty brought Nola to turn back around.

"Please, don't." Kissing the top of her aunt's forehead, Nola left for the morning.

"Davey couldn't keep her home?" Luke asked as soon as she left the house. "How hard could it be?" His tall thin frame stood at the window watching his oddly quiet cousin walk toward the street.

Dottie grinned with satisfaction knowing her youngest son could not refuse the challenge.

***

With Luke Ellis returned, the house was a buzz for hours. It seemed like everyone from the baker to the Ferrier came to visit.

Dottie could hardly stay awake at the end of the day. It was fortunate Nola resided with them. Her Aunt could not have managed the evening meal on her own after such company. The young men, however, were still hyper and chatty. They had been all evening. Both Nola and Dottie knew they were working up to more drinking out on the town.

"Don't even ask me about Christine." Davey lifted his dinner fork toward Luke.

"I wasn't going to ask," Luke snickered. "I simply wanted to know how Annabelle was doing. Curiosity," he assured them all. "Mild curiosity..."

"Mild curiosity?" Davey laughed and put another hunk of chicken on his fork. "You haven't asked me about a single person since you been back. Now, the first name you bring up is Christine's sister."

"She's a nice girl," Luke tried to deter the conversation.

"What is so wrong with him wanting to know about Christine?" Dottie asked with a yawn. "She was a very nice girl."

"I wasn't asking about Christine!" Luke raised his voice defensively. "The last I heard, Annabelle had come down with something serious and was being seen by different doctors." He flipped over the mushrooms on his plate and rolled them in the gravy.

"Right," Davey continued to chuckle. Dottie nearly laughed at the boys teasing each other, again. "She was cured of that last winter. You've been home since then." The elder brother shook his head with a smile.

"Good," Patting his chest as he swallowed his food, Luke looked down at his plate. "I'm glad to hear it."

"I think she's still available," Dottie offered quickly.

"No," Nola chimed in quietly, gazing out the dark window. "Annabelle got married just a few months ago."

"Not her," Dottie whispered. "Christine..."

"I didn't ask about..." Luke sat upright and lifted his palms. "Did I ask about Christine?"

"You were meaning to..." Davey began.

"Did I?" His smile grew. "Did I say one word about Christine?" From the side of the table, Luke held his eyes on Davey. The elder brother, at the head of the table, returned the stare with much more humor.

"Alright, you didn't ask." Davey could not quit his smile.

"I know, I didn't ask. You would know if I had asked." Luke straightened his shoulders and sniffled with a tough expression.

Knowing he couldn't eat another bite Luke pushed his plate away. "So, ...how is Christine?"

Instantly, Luke broke his stern expression just before Davey came out of his chair. Dottie barely had time to grab her glass as the table was pushed aside. Instantly, Davey had Luke pinned to the kitchen floor. Despite personalities and over twenty years each, they were still the same children that would fish and hunt together.

"Boys!" Dottie cried out. Coming to the rescue, Nola pulled Dottie's chair away from the skidding furniture with her aunt still in it. "No roughhousing! Take it outside!" The mother's warning was sincere.

Nola enjoyed watching the boys argue and tease each other.

However, she did not have the same reaction of laughter and smiles as the rest of them. She wished to laugh at the boys like Dottie but felt numb to their games.

"Davey!" Nola yelled as Luke got in two open-handed slaps on his big brother.

"Weak, little college boy," Davey grabbed his fist.

"Weak?" Luke asked with wide eyes. Wriggling his wrist out of the firm grasp, he closed his fist on the next hit. Davey barely turned his jaw with the impact, and Luke knew he was in trouble. "Lord, you smell horrid!" Trying not to inhale the twelve hours' worth of sweat, Luke turned his head.

"You shouldn't have said that." Davey's evil grin was forewarning enough for Dottie.

Waving for assistance, the old woman huffed at the young men tormenting her last nerves. However, having missed the boyhood commotion, the mother hid her amusement. "Nola, get me out of here before they rid me of my last leg."

"Davey, get out of the way!" Nola yelled.

The only motion he took was to lift his hands above his head and remove his putrid shirt. The smell spanned the room, forcing Nola to scrunch up her nose. "Move, you big ox!" She watched as Luke tried to avoid the descent of the disgusting linen toward his face.

"Davey!" Picking up her crutch, Dottie clubbed him over the head as soon as the shirt was rubbed in Luke's nose. Nola smiled slightly at the mother's reaction.

"Ouch, Mum!" He reached up to hold his head. "What are you doing?"

"Put your shirt back on! I told you to take it outside." Dottie scolded as Nola helped her into the hallway. "If you break one single thing, I'm going to tan it out of your hides." The warning was firm.

"Yes, Mum," Davey answered as he grabbed a fist full of Luke's dark hair.

"I'm going to bed," Dottie waved her hand down at them as she leaned on Nola and the crutch.

"Goodnight," Luke grunted beneath Davey's balled fist. Luke gave a valiant return and Davey groaned in exaggerated pain. A second later both men raced through the house to take the fight outside, laughing the entire way.

"Shut the door behind them, please?" Dottie placed her hand on the banister and began the long climb up the stairs.

"Alright, I'll be right back to help you."

"I can drag myself up the stairs." She alternated her weight between the crutch and the banister. Her round cheeks and big eyes seemed to have aged in that single day. "I would be grateful if you were to take care of the kitchen." Nola nodded her head and ignored the grunting and groans from the grown men in the yard. She closed the door as Dottie climbed another stair. "I know I don't need to ask. You do it every night."

"Is there anything else I can do?" Nola was hoping the woman would suggest any little item just to see the familiar small grin.

"Not unless you can promise me you will stay in tonight." Dottie glanced at the young lady, but the returned blank expression was enough of a refusal. "No, I guess I can't get you to promise me that. You do not lie." With a grin, she shifted her weight and gained another step. "Good night then, dearest."

"Good night," Nola whispered. After a moment, she headed back into the kitchen.

The window held her focus. She could only hope the men would leave right away. It was a long way to the library.

The moon was rising, and the sky was clear. Setting the dishes in the basin, Nola glanced out the window to see Davey walking away from the house. As usual, his friends would be waiting for him at the tavern. Leaning forward, she considered telling Luke that she intended to leave.

"Are you ready?" He called from directly behind her.

"Good gracious, Luke!" She jumped at the sudden voice. "You startled me."

"Apologies, and I don't give a rat's ass." He clasped his hands together and rubbed his red knuckles. "Are you going to get ready?"

"Ready for what?"

"The library, I'm going with you." He swayed back and forth in a playful manner.

"Hardly," she shook her head. "Would you please put the table and chairs back?"

"Why not?" Lifting the edge of the table, Luke put it back in place. "I won't sit on a park bench and spy on the high-and-mighty Lord Graelohr, but I'm willing to read a book or two."

"Absolutely not," she refused. "You look like you have been put through a meat grinder."

"Then you are not going," he warned solemnly.

"I have to clean the kitchen." Nola turned away from him. It was one thing to disobey but another thing to disappoint.

"I really want to go out tonight. If you want to go to the library, let's go. If we do not, I'm going to be stuck here all night."

"You are not going with me, not tonight, not ever." She did not even look over her shoulder while working. "You are here for a week, maybe two. How much difference do you think you can make?"

"About fourteen days' worth," he answered coolly. "Davey's mentioned your infatuation with Lord Graelohr... how you look for him everywhere ...follow his habits." Nola seemed surprised but for only a moment. "You are not allowed to bother him."

"Did you know that he pays for everything, even your tuition?" For once, Nola had Luke engaging in a conversation about the mysterious benefactor.

"Yes." Luke cleared his throat, praying to avoid torturous inquiries.

"What else do you know?" Nola turned around, knowing that Luke would not lie. Eyeing him like an eagle, she waited. Finally, the inevitable sigh escaped his chest. Luke cleared his throat and began stacking the utensils on a plate. "Is he related to me?" She asked the question quickly, knowing he had little patience for the old subject.

"Nola..."

"Do you know?" Sincere curiosity was in her voice.

"No," he shook his head gently. "I don't know if you are related."

"Do you know why he supports us?" Again, the same shake of his head answered the question. Frustrated without any new information she added, "What do you know?"

"I know that I don't want to have this conversation again, and...I do want to go have a drink with the boys." He could see her disappointment instantly. "Now, can we mosey on over to the library? If we hurry, I can still meet up with the boys?"

"You're not needed, Luke." She returned to her chores with the same aura of indifference. "Be off with your tavern boys. I'll be fine."

"Nola, let me take you. You can study and be back before turning into a pumpkin." His offer was not even appealing. "It's still late enough to ruffle Mum's feathers a bit." Luke stood waiting for a reply, but silence was all he received. "Alright," he turned around and began to exit the kitchen. "You're sure?" Again, Nola did not respond. "Then I'll read in the parlor until you head to bed." Still, she would not say a word. "Thank you, by the way, this will be a fantastic fun-filled evening." His sarcasm was easily ignored. Tapping his fingers on the frame of the door, Luke turned and left the room.

"I disagree," she sighed.

***

Curtains of thin vanilla lace lined her vision. There was an ancient wooden dresser with a large oval mirror against the wall. Beyond that, soft white candles stood on pedestals. However, the illumination of the gray stone room came from circular glass bulbs dangling from the ceiling. Everything was clear, but still very dreamlike.

It was the sound of footsteps that caused her to move back behind the thin curtains. As transparent as they were, she somehow felt safe. Nola watched him walk into the room and over to the dresser, but he was no ordinary man. So large was his frame, she felt like a child in comparison. Seeing him in the room triggered her memory. The dream had occurred several times before, but each time was slightly different. Lord Gavin Graelohr was surreal in every way. No man could be so tall, no shoulders could be so broad, and no eyes could be so alluring.

Slowly, he began to pull the dark jacket off his shoulders revealing the starched shirt that stretched over his massive frame. Within the reflection of the mirror, he seemed to look directly at Nola

...though her reflection was not there. His hair was as black as the night, barely hanging above his eyes. He paused and turned toward the presence of her dream-like view through the golden curtain.

Facing him directly was enough to shake her from her restless sleep. Nola sat up from her bed, feeling her heart pound in her chest.

It was simply another dream. She had to talk to him. She had to know why every time she closed her eyes he was there. Throwing the covers off of her legs, she placed her feet on the hardwood floor. It only took a moment to throw on her gown and quietly step into her boots.

The house was quiet. Dottie slept soundly, filling the hallway with gurgles of light snoring. Davey's door was closed, and she was not too worried that he would catch her. Luke's room was beside hers and before the top of the stairs. For once, she was going to have to tiptoe down the hallway.

Light on her feet, she entered the hallway, listening briefly at Davey's door across the way. Sure, that he was not yet home, she hurried down the hall. The banister that guarded the stairwell began just outside her door. Careful not to step on the creaky floorboards, she made her way to the top step. So fast and light were her steps as she came to Luke's door that she didn't see the small thin wire that crossed from his doorknob to the railing of the banister. The ring of a bell on the other side of the door scared her half to death.

"What are you doing?" Nola asked as Luke opened the door. "Are you trying to wake the whole house?"

"Yell at me? Where do you think you're going?" His eyes were barely open. His shirt twisted around his chest.

"Luke?" Dottie called from her bedroom.

"It's me, Mum." Holding his finger to his lips, he silenced Nola. "Go back to sleep." They both waited for several moments until Dottie's bed creaked and groaned under the weight of her settling back down. "Get rid of the boots and go back to bed." Luke warned her in a whisper. "This isn't the only trap set for you."

"What are you going to do if you catch Davey?" she asked with pure annoyance in her voice.

"I'll probably laugh." Pointing back down the hall toward her bedroom, he waited for her to turn around and start walking. "Don't try it again," he warned.

Closing the door to her room, Nola walked over to her window and plopped down in her chair. The hazy glass showed much of the city, but there were too many obstacles to see either the clock tower or anything on the other side of the river.

Knowing that sleep was as likely as snow in July, she sat in the chair and stared at the stars. Davey had chopped down the tree outside her window earlier that year. Unwilling to wake Dottie a second time that night, she resorted to concentrating on the dream.

Breathing deeply, she recalled every detail of the room she had seen. It was the same room she had dreamed of many nights before. The same color curtains, the same old mirror, and the same strange light, however this was the first time he ever turned toward her. Wanting desperately to reclaim the vision, to see and hear the same details, Nola breathed deeply and closed her eyes. Knowing that sleep would fail her, and escape was unlikely, she wrapped a shawl around her shoulders and settled in for the long night.

***

"It is one thing for the children to fall asleep in class, Miss Valerian." Miss Peetz stood over the desk with her hands on her hips. "It is quite another for you to doze off at yours!"

"I understand," Nola began stacking her papers, ignoring the irate woman before her. "I'm sorry, it won't happen again."

"It won't happen again?" Miss Peetz placed her hand to her forehead. "This is the second time this month already and I'm not even going to recall how many times it happened last month."

"I apologized," she restated, coming to her feet. There was no remorse in her tone. Nola could not see herself to blame for the boring lectures and endless unimportant rambling of the schoolteacher.

"Perhaps you should consider an earlier evening schedule when I need you the next day?" Miss Peetz remained where she stood, preaching like a holy guru.

"Perhaps we should end this conversation," Nola warned. It wasn't often that she reacted to her emotions. However, Miss Peetz's self-righteous stance was quickly etching her exhausted nerves. "I am quickly becoming annoyed with your advice."

"It is being given in anger," Miss Peetz sighed heavily. "When I ask for your help, it is because I need your help! It embarrasses me when the students see you dozing off!"

Picking up her coat, Nola realized how irritating the woman's sermon was. It would have been too easy to retaliate. The teacher would have surely taken any criticism to heart and ignored any useful suggestions. Instead, she wrapped the coat around her shoulders and half-listened to the rest of Miss Peetz's endless gibberish.

"Nola?" Davey stood in the doorway. "Excuse me, the door was open."

"Yes, Mr. Ellis, we were just finished with our conversation." Miss Peetz nodded at Nola and returned to her desk.

"What are you doing here?" Nola asked, not half as bothered by the confrontation as Miss Peetz seemed to be.

"Walking you home," he answered. "Why?" she asked outright.

"Because I told Mum that I would." He looked over Nola's shoulder at the expression on the teacher's face. "You fell asleep again?" Turning into the hallway, Nola closed the door behind them.

"Her lectures are nothing more than a lullaby."

"You didn't say that ...did you?"

"Of course not," she scoffed. "She is too fragile for an actual response." The temperature difference was vast, still Nola did not react to the sudden chill. "I find it's best if I speak very little except for compliments and direct yes or no answers."

"Are you sure you're not a man?" There was a chuckle in his voice. Holding on to the sack of tools over his shoulder, Davey held his arm out in front of her before she stepped into the street. "Don't you even look where you are going?" Peering down both sides of the road to absolutely no traffic, she glanced up at him.

"There is no one coming."

"There could have been." Davey stepped into the road and crossed the street. "You don't even look."

"There was no one coming," she restated.

"You have to be more careful. Be aware of what could happen." The entire time he spoke, Davey was looking around at the people, dark alleys, and carriages. "Mum has already lost one child."

"He was not her child." The clear and stern tone to Nola's voice stopped Davey immediately.

"She gave her husband and her leg to try and save Esteban." He stepped closer and glared at her. "She was more his mother than the woman that gave you two away." The words cut deeply. Nola stood where she was for several moments as Davey continued down the sidewalk. "Keep up," he warned.

Cursed with a perfect memory, Nola envisioned her brother's curly hair and precious eyes. They had been passed from orphanage to orphanage before Aunt Dottie and Uncle Arthur came to find them.

Never had Nola felt such joy as when she and Esteban were finally given a home.

"Nola," Davey called. "Keep up," he warned again.

The night before had been long, and the day had been more than troubling. Setting her sights on the comforts of home, Nola sped up her pace. If she were feeling hungry, then Davey must have been starving. No doubt his appetite and long hours were fueling his temper.

"I'm grateful to your mother...and father," she offered quietly behind his back. "I didn't mean to insult them."

"I know," he stated quietly. "But you don't realize how every move we make will affect her. Without us, she would be lost." Nola wanted to ask if that was the reason he was not married, but she knew he would not answer. The moment they reached the small houses of the Capstan District the world seemed a lot quieter. Davey slowed his pace as their house came into view. The small white two-story home looked pristine compared to the places he had been working nearby. "Do you think she's got supper on?"

"If not, it will only take me a few minutes. The butcher's son was going to drop off a chicken today. He's been good about deliveries as long as we keep doing their wash."

"Is it costing anything more?"

"No," Nola answered.

"Davey!" A man called from one of the yards. "Are you heading up the card game tonight?"

"Yeah," Davey answered resituating the tools over his shoulder. "You got my money yet?" There was a clearly smug expression on his face.

"Good afternoon, Miss Valerian." The other man nodded his head. "I trust your cousin is squeezing his pennies as much at home as he does at the tables."

"Good afternoon," she replied.

"Go on," Davey instructed her. "I'll be there in a few minutes."

The house was as warm as a kettle on the stove. It was common for them to come home to the fire roaring, but Dottie had obviously had a particularly cold day in the house. Her smile was unending as Nola hung her coat in the closet.

"Oh good, you're home. Did you have a nice day?" Dottie asked underneath the blanket that drooped over her leg.

"I fell asleep during one of Miss Peetz's lectures." Taking an apron off the wall, she tied it around her waist. "It earned me an additional lecture."

"You didn't talk back to her, did you?" Dottie asked, adjusting her knitting needles on top of the blanket.

"No, I stayed quiet for most of it." Tying the ends of the apron, she stepped into the parlor. "Did the boy drop off the chicken?"

"Yes, but I was just getting around to start it." Dottie began to pull the blanket off of her lap.

"Please," Nola held up her hand. "Let me. I've been meaning to try a new recipe for a while now."

"I could help," the old woman insisted.

"Not at all," Nola shook her head. "Davey's in a good mood. My making dinner will keep it that way until he goes out again."

"You've never worried about keeping him in a good mood before." There was a hint of curiosity in her voice. "Why the interest now?"

It was not in Nola's character to lie. However, sometimes the truth brought on more questions. With a gentle smile, she stepped over to Dottie and placed a quick kiss in her hair.

"You like it when the boys are happy. Just relax and keep me company if you wish. I'll start the chicken," she answered.

Nola walked down the small hall and entered the kitchen. The pans were stacked on a shelf above the counter, and she grabbed the biggest kettle and pan. Her intentions were to fry up the chicken, but as she looked at the plucked meat in the sink she stood back. The chicken had not been quartered or cleaned. With a heavy sigh, she stood over the sink. It sickened her to think of what she had to do.

Grabbing the largest knife, she looked down at the pink slab of meat.

Just the idea of the bones breaking and the organs inside brought the nausea to a boil. Breathing only through her nose, she rested her arms against the counter. It was a job she did not want to do, but she was not going to waste time being concerned about it.

"What's wrong?" Davey asked, bringing the smell of his twelve-hour workday into the kitchen. Before she had a chance to complain about his state he stepped over to the sink. "Get the potatoes going, I'll cut up the chicken." Pulling the meat out of the sink he began to wash up.

"You're unusually pleasant this afternoon," she commented. "I didn't have to worry about seeing you sneak in the house at two in the morning." After making the comment, he washed his face and dried it off with the towel. "You stay home. I stay nice. It's as simple as that." Without commenting further, Nola started the fat frying and the water boiling. She was not about to admit her firm plans to leave that evening.

Chapter Two

History and Acquaintances

The house was fairly quiet as Dottie snored gently. Davey had gone and Luke was silent for over an hour. Nola paced the floor, looking out the window and waiting for the right opportunity. It was well past ten o'clock, but there was still plenty of time to make it across town. No doubt Luke had devised a plan to keep her in the house. Still, she had to find a way to the manor, mesmerized as a moth to flame.

Nola considered the consequences of her actions. Davey would be in a foul mood again once he learned of her expedition. Dottie would lecture, and Luke would tail her like a dog. No matter. It was well worth the punishment. The library was her destination, but Graelohr Manor called her.

Nola's benefactor, Lord Gavin Graelohr, was the most mysterious man in Thedford City. Mainly, because no one seemed to know how or where he received his title and luxurious property.

Obviously, the most qualified bachelor in the surrounding areas, Gavin Graelohr was a financial prize. There had always been rumors about his wealth and political connections. Nonetheless, it was his electric lit house and various travels that intrigued people the most. India, China, and America were the least fantastic of his destinations as far as most heard. Some say he had been from Havana to New Zealand in just the past year. Honestly, no one knew him well enough to say anything other than gossip. However, it was substantially more than rumor and curiosity driving Nola. Not only was Lord Graelohr the estranged guardian, but there was a connection. He was the alluring man of her dreams, quite literally as of late. A driving force beyond Nola's comprehension was always enticing her closer. Her most recent and realistic vision held all attention.

Unable to withstand her confinement any longer, Nola placed her shawl around her shoulders and headed toward the door. Her steps were light, and her heels barely touched the wood. She opened the door carefully, looking for anything that might alert Luke. Entering the hallway, she tiptoed silently. The sudden clearing of his throat turned her attention to the stairs. There he sat, coat and hat on, waiting patiently.

"I was wondering how long it was going to take you," he whispered. "Are you ready?"

Annoyed, Nola kept her voice low, checking Dottie's room for any movement. "You are not going with me."

"Then you'd best go back to bed." The arrogant expression on his face was annoying. Looking back at her room, she glanced toward Davey's door. "He's still out. If we leave now, we might get back before he does."

"Shh," she hissed. Nola could not imagine another night cooped up in her bedroom, but Luke was the last person on earth she wanted to tag along. Even if she did meet any trouble in the slums, he was neither aggressive nor fast enough to do anything about it. He was simply an annoyance. Still, he was the only one between her and the front door.

"Alright then," Luke stated as she sighed and headed toward the stairs. "I knew you would see things my way."

"Just don't talk," she whispered as they hurried down the stairs.

"Not likely. I'm somewhat of a talker."

"I know," Nola responded sharply. Taking hold of the door, they left the house in a hurry.

"So, what is the agenda?" Luke walked backwards as he spoke. "Do we head to the library and look at restricted books, or spy on the eccentric Lord Graelohr from a park bench?"

The noise of the day had subsided and the people of Thedford had begun to rest. Granted, there was the occasional glimpse of people closing up their houses for the night or a few on their way to work a late-night job. For the most part everything was quiet.

"You're ruining this," Nola whispered.

"Ruining what?"

"The sound," she answered. Luke spanned the location, clueless. His blank expression was all she needed. "The river, the wind, the leaves... When you exchange words with children all day these gentle sounds are particularly pleasing."

"That actually makes sense," Luke agreed. "Are we to walk the whole mile without talking?"

"If you think you can," she answered with a grin.

"Ah, you have developed a sense of humor." He chuckled. "Seriously though, why this urge to haunt Lord Graelohr? Do you think spying on his house in the middle of the night will get you anywhere?"

"I have questions and I want answers." There was a curious tone to Nola's voice. The wind seemed calm, but Luke pulled his jacket close around his chest. "I want to know if Lord Graelohr and I are related, why he has taken on financial responsibility for our family, and why..."

Luke cut off her repeated curiosities. "He's not going to tell you anything. You've only seen the man three times in your life, Nola. He hardly leaves opportunity for interrogation."

"That is why I am creating an opportunity."

"Do you think he will come outside for a midnight chat at the park bench?" Luke chuckled at his own question.

"I hope, someday." Her honest admission puzzled him.

"You're serious?" Luke's smile irritated her. "You really expect him to see you out there and come talk to you?"

"Why not? I have no time during the day and the manor lights are always on for as long as I have seen. It is possible he will notice me." The water had risen under the bridge, but it was moving too slowly to make a lot of noise.

"It's possible he'll have you arrested and put in an asylum. Nola, spying on a man's home is not acceptable." With his hands in his pockets, Luke kicked a pebble off the bridge into the water. The closer they came to the center of the city; the more anxious Nola was to reach her destination. "What are you reading at the library?" Luke changed the subject. "These ...restricted books you are looking for, what is in them?"

"See, this is why I don't want you to come. I don't want to answer these questions."

"Wait," Instantly, Luke grabbed her arm and pulled her into the shadows as soon as they crossed the bridge. "Be quiet." It was off in the distance, but definitely the sound of a struggle. A single groan was heard and then the quiet cheer of a crowd. "You'd better go home," Luke whispered leaving her on the side of the road and walking toward the alley with the commotion.

"Luke," Nola called. "Luke?"

"Go home!" He stated as quietly as he could. Lowering his head, he peered around the corner and into the alley. He could hear Davey's name being called, but he could not see why. Starting off down the alleyway, he stopped only when he felt the tug of Nola's small hand.

"Don't go down there," she warned. "It's Davey," Luke said.

"Even if it is Davey, you're just going to get yourself hurt." Luke was not afraid of a fight. "I learned more than Philosophy and Geometry in school, Nola. Davey wasn't there for me." Ignoring her warning, Luke continued to the group of men. "Go home." As they drew closer, they could see that Davey was not the one in trouble. Nola had no intentions of listening and followed her cousin closely.

Surprisingly, they had stumbled upon a back-alley gambling fight. Davey was unable to knock out his huge opponent. Taking another hit to his midsection, Davey retaliated with a jab to the brute's head. His russet hair was darkened with sweat, and his lip was covered with blood. The other fighter took another swing, throwing himself into Davey's midsection. With no effort, Davey shoved the man away and hit him square in the jaw with one fist and then the other. Around them the crowd cheered quietly, setting wagers on the winner. The eldest Ellis brother was fighting for money and sport, again.

"Come on." Luke grabbed her arm and started hauling her back to the bridge.

"Wait, we can still go. He can obviously handle himself."

"I'm taking you home, then I'm coming back to make sure he doesn't get what is left of his brain bashed in." Angry and frustrated, Luke hauled her alongside him.

"He's going to win," she explained calmly. Just as she said the words, the men began a small uproar. She couldn't see him but knew that the fight was over. "Have you ever seen him lose?"

"No, but you should never have seen him fight. Mum would kill us if she knew you were out here for this."

"Hey!" Davey's enraged call came from behind them. The two of them turned around, waiting for him to escape the small crowd. "What in hell are you doing?" With two other men in tow, Davey came down the alley toward them collecting his winnings on the way.

"I was taking her to the library! What in hell were you doing?" Luke was irate. "You fight for scratch, still?"

"I was doing it just for fun," he answered, glaring at Nola. "Then, money started to roll in as a perk." He nodded his head to his cousin. "You talked him into taking you across town?"

"No," Nola answered. "I was going, regardless. Luke offered to keep me company."

"Is that right?" Davey asked.

"That would have been the perfect time to lie to him." Luke turned to Nola.

"I swear, you two haven't got a clue between you." Davey folded up his money and stuffed it in his jacket pocket. "Take her back," he stated angrily with his eyes glaring at Nola. "I don't give a damn what you do after that, but you aren't going to condone her actions before moving across town and leaving us to deal with her."

"I was trying to find a solution," Luke argued.

"The solution is to leave things as they have been!"

"Right," nodding his head, Luke understood his meaning. "Because you've done so well being in charge of this family."

"Watch it, little brother," Davey warned.

Nola could bear no more. She looked back at the clock tower and wondered how many nights would pass before she could finally get into her routine of solitude and silence. Luke's return had been a blessing for Dottie and a pleasantry for Nola, but it was wreaking havoc on her normality.

"I am not a child that has to be dealt with," she whispered. Turning on her heels, she left them both to argue without her.

Walking across Baggerty Bridge, heading in the wrong direction was the most agonizing part of her evening. The clock tower helped to light up Darlington Avenue, but it did nothing to ease her depression. Unsettled to return to her confinement, Nola continued to the small houses. All the while, she endured the nagging desire that drove her nightly.

***

A third night at home had passed, a third night without rest. She had always had trouble falling asleep. However, the condition was worsening. If she closed her eyes for more than an hour at a time it felt like a success. Still the hour would pass, her eyes would open, and she would be acutely aware of every sound in her house.

With a heavy sigh, Nola turned to her side to face the window and the pouring rain. Her thoughts scattered everywhere. For one moment she would be thinking of taking the approaching teaching job, and the next she was wondering how often Luke would visit once he took his new job across town. It was exhausting, and infuriating.

One moment she was tired from the last few days and the next she was too deep in thought to consider sleep. Then, there was Gavin. Lord Graelohr always came to her mind. Annoyed once more, she tossed onto her back and stared up at the ceiling. Even if she could not force her body to rest, she could force her mind to focus. Closing her eyes, Nola dove deep into her past. Apprehensively, she recalled the first time she ever saw Lord Graelohr and the last she saw of her uncle and beloved brother.

Nola reached into the depths of her memory, far away from the little house in Thedford. Aunt Dottie and Uncle Arthur, as she had come to call them, had given them a home and a family, but the true bond Nola and Esteban felt about each other could never be breached. They were obedient and kind, but their love did not span to the Ellis's. Fortunately, Dottie and Arthur ignored their indifference and treated them as lovingly as their own.

Wealth was of no concern for the insane murderer that stopped their carriage in the dark of night. He simply demanded Esteban. Her mind recalled every detail of the carriage blazing through the forest as Arthur Ellis tried to outrun the maniac. She could not deny that the stranger seemed familiar, like a distant memory. However, any link she may have felt vanished as the carriage tipped on its side as it was driven off the road. Tossed and battered, the family scurried away.

Alas, Uncle Arthur had been shot and pinned underneath the carriage. What Nola remembered next was the stranger turning his horse around and heading toward them with a long sword drawn and ready. Seeing the man ride directly toward Esteban, Dottie grabbed the four- year-old and tried to hide him behind her. With one dreadful slice, the man removed Dottie's leg and young Esteban's head. The strength of the memory brought the terrible sound of her own scream to mind.

A heavy sigh tore from her chest as Nola recalled how the man turned his horse toward them for a second time. The steel of his blade shone in the moonlight. Thankfully, the fanatic never reached them. Somehow, Lord Graelohr stood in the road. His own sword at the ready, the stranger faced Lord Graelohr, but their blades never touched. Without knowing how or why, the stranger fled back into the forest. It was as if the night swallowed him whole.

Instantly, Lord Graelohr was there. He went to Dottie's side, tying her severed thigh with a ripped piece of skirt and covering Esteban's body with a blanket from the carriage. There was too much fear for any of them to move. However, once Arthur had drawn his last breath and the carriage was somehow upright, the Lord turned his attention and focused completely on Nola.

It was disturbing at first. She could not make heads or tails of the situation, but the moment became frozen. As Nola gazed up at the tall stranger, noting his dark hair and even darker eyes, a humming sound rose in her ears. The intense sound pulled her attention directly to Lord Graelohr. She almost lost her balance, leaning against the nearest tree for stability. Nola's head tilted upward, and her eyes closed... still seeing, but from the stranger's perspective. Her aunt still cried, her cousins stared up in terror, and she herself leaned on a sapling no more than a few feet away. There was no sound, smell, or feeling. The vision itself had a colored tint, as if the night were not so dark.

"My name is Gavin Graelohr," he whispered, causing the yellow-gold veil to lift along with the buzzing sound in her ears.

Nola couldn't stand the memory any longer. Shaking her head, she opened her eyes to reality. The rain still pummeled the window, the house still settled in the wind, and her mind still refused to let her body rest.

Finally, unable to sleep and unable to stay awake, Nola rubbed her forehead with her hands. The restlessness was misery. Again, she flipped onto her side with a heavy breath. By the time she had her pillow fluffed exactly right, there was a quiet tap at her door.

"What is it?" she whispered, popping the door open just a crack. Luke peered into her room.

"You alright?"

"I'm fine," she answered shoving the end of her pillow further under her head.

"If you toss and turn anymore, your bed is likely to fall through the floor." Opening her door slowly he stepped into her room. His shirt was hanging below the waist of his pants. It was obvious that she had awoken him. "Here, drink this."

"What is it?"

"Whisky." The answer was simple. "It smells like tonic, burns like hell, and tastes like shit, but it will get you a little shut eye."

"No... thank you." The refusal was made with a little room for negotiation. "I don't think I should."

"Go on. I know you haven't been sleeping, lately." Luke uncorked the bottle and handed it to her. "One good swig is all you'll need."

Nola took the drink. The bottle felt lighter than she expected, and over half of the liquid was gone. With one annoyed look at Luke, she tipped the glass bottle up and let one large gulp of liquid fire race down her throat. Gasping for air, she sought to cool the sensation.

"How can you drink that?" She coughed as Luke chuckled.

"It takes a bit of getting used to." Luke had a drink as well.

"Ugh, it's putrid... like drinking kerosene..."

"That would have been my next suggestion," he whispered.

When Nola looked up in confusion, he decided to ease her mind. "I'm fooling you." Tilting his head downward, he recapped the bottle. "You alright then?"

"Better, I hope." The answer was honest. "Thank you."

"Sure," Luke answered. "Just try to get some sleep." Placing his hand on the door, he turned back to face her. "Don't tell Mum about this. You know how she hates liquor in the house."

"Right," Nola agreed. "I'll keep quiet." No more than ten minutes after Luke left, she felt the effects of the drink. Her mind became foggy, her hands became heavy, and her eyes began to close. The thick edge of constant thought had been worn down letting her descend into a restful sleep.

**

Dottie set her knitting needles down on her lap as Davey opened the door. It was well before noon, and he had only been gone from the house for a little more than an hour. There was no reason for him to be home so soon. At first, Dottie merely glanced at him, but as the oddities added-up she grew curious.

"Well, this is a surprise." She tilted her head and took note of the bruises that were barely noticeable that morning. "I'd like to know why you are home so early, but mostly I would like to hear that you haven't lost your job."

For Nola, the air instantly felt different in the house. It was not immediate, but more like a breeze of clarity blowing in from the open door. The day seemed brighter, the colors of the room seemed twice as vivid, and the air felt as if it had been charged by a storm.

"Mother," Davey stepped into the room and cleared his throat. He looked worried, as if carrying unwelcome news. However, before he could say another word Nola came to the edge of her chair.

The sensation she was experiencing was not unknown. It was the same elation she experienced each night outside the library. With complete assurance, she peered behind her cousin waiting to see the strange guest.

"We have company," Davey announced. "Nola, please remain seated," he whispered in reaction to her blatant stare at the guest.

There he was, standing in their doorway. Lord Gavin Graelohr bowed his head as he entered the house. Had he overlooked the gesture, he could have knocked his head on the top of the frame.

However, his height was not his only notable feature. Lord Graelohr was quite possibly the most covetable man Nola had ever seen.

Standing in front of her, there was not a chance of putting his corporeal perfection out of her mind. A perfect smile set the canvas. His hair was more than fashionable with thick dark waves, and his stature dwarfed Davey's embarrassingly. Yet, it was his eyes that stole her breath. Enthralling, they were a deep and dangerous brown, darker and more captivating than she could have ever thought possible.

"Good morning," the distinguished gentleman spoke with subtle eloquence.

"Lord Graelohr, welcome." Dottie tried to get up, placing a lot of weight on the arm of her chair. "Please, make yourself at home."

"Don't trouble yourself, Mrs. Ellis." He moved across the room to her side. "There is no need for either of you to get up."

"Would you like to sit down? I'm afraid I will put my neck out if we are to talk like this." Her smile was gracious and heartwarming.

When Gavin took to the chair nearest her aunt, Nola realized how happy Dottie became. Her eyes warmed over him as if he were a saint in a pinstriped suit. Slowly, Dottie reached her hand out to pat Gavin's, a gesture she did not fully understand. "It has been a long time, Lord Graelohr."

"Please, Dottie, we go back too far for you to call me that."

"Of course," she nodded her head and smiled. "I suppose we do."

"How have you been?" He leaned toward her as if he were a long-lost son. His age was considered for a few seconds. He was far more civilized than Davey, but he could not have been five years his senior.

"We've been well." Once the answer was given, she looked up at Davey. "My eldest has become a man of good reputation, my youngest has just graduated university, and Nola is considering a teaching position at the school."

"You have much to be proud of." Gavin's dark eyes glanced at Davey and then briefly at Nola. Politely, he returned his attention to Dottie. "And you... how have you been?" The old woman's smile did not fade.

"I'm tired," she answered with a gentle nod. "Though very glad you have come to see us."

"You know I cannot stay long."

"Yes," she answered, "But you are here now. Tell me, what brings you to visit?" Their sentimental gaze was bewildering to both Davey and Nola.

"It has come to my understanding that your children are aware of our financial arrangement." He again glanced at both Davey and Nola. Curiosity drove Davey to move closer into the room. "Questions have arisen, and too many people are becoming aware."

"This is a problem." Dottie sighed, agreeing with the knowledge.

"Well, I cannot have questions." Gavin stated plainly.

"And we cannot have answers," Davey spoke, leaning against the wall beside Nola's chair.

"I have seen you as the man of this house for many years, Mr. Ellis. My interest in your family has been reduced to a simple monthly stipend considering how well you have managed."

"We could do without your money," Davey's tone was slightly rude.

"Davey," Dottie warned.

"It's alright," Gavin hushed her gently. "I respect his honesty." Again, he soothed her with a touch of his hand. "Permit me to speak?"

"Of course," she answered. Placing a single hand in his pocket as he rose, Gavin again took up nearly all the space in the room.

Subdued by his unnaturally faultless features, Nola stood silent.

"Is it your choice that I leave this family and your good mother in your hands?" he asked, holding his hands behind his back.

"I would prefer it." Davey stood as tall as he could, answering without a doubt.

"Done," Gavin answered. "Under one condition..."

"Which is?" Davey did not see how his folded arms made him look smug.

"Miss Valerian remains my ward and begins attendance at Phillmore College next semester, remaining under this roof."

Nola could not bring herself to lift her jaw. The amount of confusion was endless as she listened to the proposition. Her eyes glanced over to Dottie, then to Davey, then finally Lord Graelohr. "I don't understand." Nola could not hold back her words.

"You will," Gavin answered. "But first, I have to have Davey's word on our agreement."

"Why?" Davey asked.

Reaching up a single hand, Dottie drew their attention. "No son, I'm sorry but you cannot have that answer," Dottie whispered softly.

"Davey, you will own everything; the house, the carriage, the horse, and the responsibility." Gavin breathed through his nose, waiting patiently for a response. His wide brow and thick jaw held his face emotionless. Regardless of her curiosity, Nola was surprised to see Davey pause at the offer.

"My father adopted Nola over ten years ago." Davey continued to lean on the wall but took on a more relaxed tone.

"Nola came to live with you over ten years ago. Nevertheless, I am her legal guardian." The admission was followed by a few moments of silence. Nola sat dumfounded looking to Dottie for answers but there were none.

Davey stated plainly, "We have appreciated your years of generosity." He tried to sound grateful. "However, Nola is a part of this family and I have been responsible for her. She intends to teach at the local school." Nola could not comprehend the strange and subtle kindness she felt for Davey at that moment.

Gavin placed his large hand on Davey's shoulder and smiled proudly, "I am entrusting her to you as she always has been. My role as her guardian will remain distant. My expectation is for Nola to further her studies at ...convenient hours." Lifting his right hand, he waited for Davey to take it. "Do we have an agreement?" Davey contemplated the offer for only a moment before lifting his hand to shake Gavin's. "Good. My attorney will be by next week with a few papers for you to sign as well as Miss Valerian's entrance papers for next spring."

"And what of my role?" Dottie asked, sitting back in her chair. "You've relinquished me from a mother to their burden."

"Nola still needs you," Gavin returned to the chair by her side. Mindful of her manners, Nola stood up and bowed politely.

Her eyes remained on Gavin and Dottie, but she waited for them to acknowledge her. When at last Gavin looked up, she was almost distracted by his chiseled features.

"Are we related?" she asked, knowing it was the most essential truth she really needed.

"No." The word was firm. "We are not blood relation in any manner." Her mind whirled at his answer forming new questions every second.

"I have much to ask," she warned him fairly.

"I am sure that you do, but you will not have your answers today." Reaching into his coat pocket, Gavin withdrew a book. "Your late-night travels are dangerous," he said as he handed her the familiar book. Looking at the cover, Nola realized it was the copy that she was forced to throw at the men pursuing her through the alley. "From now on, my carriage will be sent for you every Wednesday night. You will limit your library time to that evening and are restricted to the inside of the building."

The simple way he spoke left no room for argument. Nola wanted to ask a hundred more questions, but he was too formal and proper to approach. Mindful of her place in the household, she retook the chair across from him and Dottie.

"Can you stay a little longer?" Dottie asked, reaching out to pat Gavin's hand once more.

"No." He shook his head and smiled under his rough beard. "Though, your invitation to my home is always open when you are ready."

"I will," Dottie agreed. "As you have stated, Nola still needs me."

"Will you visit the library with her soon?" he asked, coming to his feet.

"Of course," Dottie agreed kindly.

"Delightful," He held out his hand to Davey once more. "Mr. Ellis, I am entrusting this woman to your care." He eyed Dottie as a child sees his mother. "And you can expect that paperwork soon."

"Thank you," Davey answered, realizing for the first time that he had just been handed a small fortune.

"Good day, Miss Valerian." He opened the door to see Luke stepping up onto the porch. "Mr. Ellis," Gavin offered his handshake. "Congratulations on your archaeology degree. I understand you will start your position at the museum in a week or two."

Luke looked up at him in total confusion of Gavin's impressive knowledge of their family details. "Yes, thank you, Lord Graelohr."

"I am interested to see how your career carries out." Gavin switched places with Luke on the porch as he made his way to the carriage.

"As am I," Luke added. "Thank you for your visit. Please, do have a good day." His bewilderment was not hidden very well as Gavin's driver opened the carriage door and closed it behind the massive lord. "What in hell was he doing here?" Luke asked Davey as the carriage drove away.

Chapter Three

Seductive tension

"What did Mum say?" Luke asked, pacing around in the kitchen.

"Nothing, she just sat there staring up at him as if he were your father come back from the grave." Nola's retelling was as accurate as she could make it. "She had this look of complete adoration for Lord Graelohr. And he spoke as if they had known each other forever." Nola leaned her back against the wall. "None of it made sense to me, except him giving everything to Davey."

"By rights, he should have done it sooner." Luke pressed his knuckles against the table and stared off into the air before him. "Davey's made more than enough for this place since he turned sixteen." Picking up his hat off the table, Luke looked at the round brim. "What I don't get is why he's holding onto you."

"I don't know," Nola answered. "Also, he is insisting I go to college! Other girls began their attendance before they were close to twenty."

"Yes, but maybe that is his point," Luke folded his arms over his chest. "Maybe he wants you to go because you aren't married."

"What are you speculating? Could this be a punishment?"

"Not exactly, since you are adopted, he is legally responsible for you until you are married. Maybe he wants to broaden your education and introduce you to more eligible suitors?"

"And if I never marry?"

"Of course, you'll marry." Luke looked at her vacant expression and then at the strawberry tart under the glass cover. "Why aren't you married? Have you had any suitors since I've been gone?"

"None," she answered softly.

"You aren't fancy for other women, are you? I would never tell."

"No." She considered the thought carefully. "I've read of such things, but it does not entice me."

"Never mind," Luke dropped the subject. "Have any of Davey's friends caught your attention?"

"Stop." Nola placed her hand to her forehead. "I've already been given both the lecture and the talk by your mother. I don't need to hear it from you."

"Whoa, I wasn't going to get that much into detail. I just wanted to know if you had a beau."

"Well, I don't."

"Don't you think you should?"

"Shouldn't you have a significant acquaintance?" Nola squared her shoulders and faced his quirky smile.

"I will," Luke answered promisingly. "I've got the position at the museum. Now, I just need my own house." He sighed heavily and noted how the subject had changed. "Alright, I am just saying that maybe Lord Graelohr is obligated to care for you until a certain age or you get married."

"Fine, but what about everything else?"

"What is everything else?"

"The book," she stated quietly, pointing to the copy in front of Luke. "How did he get that and how does he know I go to the library every night?"

"Maybe he has the custodian spying on you. You did say that only the night man lets you in."

"Alright, then what about Dottie? Why has she agreed to go and stay with him whenever she is ready?" The question from her lips took the smile away from Luke.

"I don't know." Luke spun his hat on the table and then hit his fist on the wood. "Damn, I wish I had been here." Thinking further, he looked back at Nola. "Was he arrogant?"

"Not at all, why?"

"I'm not sure really. I just always figured he would be."

"He's been here before," Nola reminded him.

"Yes, but Davey and I were always sent outside while you were left to serve tea."

"He did say that we were not related." Her depression was easily heard.

"At least you got that out of him. It was never much of a concern since you are a horrible likeness."

"Do stop. I'm trying to be serious. He told me nothing else." Nola turned to face the door as Dottie's crutches could be heard at the top of the stairs. "I'm coming, Aunt Dottie." The call was sweet and gentle. "Are you going out?" she asked Luke before heading up to help Dottie get ready for bed.

"Yeah, me and the boys are heading to Charlie's place for cards." Realizing how her question sounded, Luke sighed as if he had made a huge mistake. "You are staying here, aren't you? I mean, Lord Graelohr does not seem like someone you want to upset."

"I'm staying in because your mother seems to be walking on cloud nine, and quite frankly that concerns me."

"Nola?" Dottie called from the top step.

"I'm on my way," she answered. "Put that down!" She watched Luke reach for another tart. "Those are for the morning."

"I know," he said as he popped the sweet in his mouth.

"You can be annoying, when you want to." Her irritated smile caused him to give an over-expressive grin. "Good night."

***

There were a few people in the alley, but none noticed Nola.

Keeping her head down and her eyes up, she listened as her heels clicked on the pavement. It was nothing more than disobedient. There was no need for or interest in going to the library that night. Had Lord Graelohr granted permission to go at any time, she might have stayed home for the rest of her life.

Her skirts were perfect for the long walk. Just barely reaching the top of her shoes, she had no worries of tripping if she did need to take off in a hurry. Still, as she crossed Falkenstein Avenue and headed toward the final two cross alleys she felt a sigh of relief.

A glass bottle broke in an alley behind her and for a moment she considered running. Keeping herself calm, Nola held her steady pace maintaining her cool exterior. Just before her, a tall man stood against a doorway glancing in her direction. There was something peculiar about him.

"You look lost," he stated loudly. Nola attempted to ignore him. "Or out for sport?" As she continued passed, he jingled some keys in his pockets. "I mean you no harm."

"Then, you won't mind if I continue on my way." Nola barely glanced over her shoulder at the man. To speak with an unknown man in a dark alley in the middle of the night, it was just ignorant.

"How do I know you?" He stepped away from the door and rose to full height. For a second, he did seem familiar to her. Nola knew better than to stop but did take a second glance.

"You are mistaken. Do not think for one moment that I am to be taken for a fool." Chivalry was losing hold on the world and men had become less virtuous than generations past. Knowing several lectures from Dottie, Nola gently hastened her clicking heels.

"You are no fool, indeed." Polite and friendly, his conversation seemed strange, similar to dialogue one would read in old books. The man, keeping some distance, slowly took up his long strides behind her. "We have to know each other through some line."

"Line?" Nola halted for a moment at the strange comparison but began walking swiftly before her thoughts verbalized. "I have no idea what you mean, and I have somewhere to be." Stepping into the last of the dark roads she could see the streetlamp on Halweg Boulevard.

"I seem threatening to you," he announced. "It's not my intention." Nola continued, hurrying to the lamp-lit road. "Just give me ten seconds of your time." He maintained a safe distance behind her. "You walk to the first streetlight there," he pointed in front of her, "and I'll stay here in the alley. No harm will come to either of us." Finally, reaching the brightly lit Avenue, Nola turned to face the stranger.

She was curiously confused and asked, "Why are you following me?"

"That should be obvious. Why do you fear me?" Taking in her first real look at him, Nola noticed his light blue eyes and blond almost reddish hair. He seemed of some fortune for the clothes he was wearing. However, he was slightly unshaven and a little rough around the edges. "Are you a recluse?"

"I am trying to be," she answered. Strangely, he was correct. There was something inside her that felt a very real sense of danger. The sensation of that emotion was completely new to her. "Would you mind allowing me to proceed ...unaccompanied?"

"My name is Jarron." He remained where he was as Nola stood with the light post between them. "Who are you?"

"No one of concern," she answered quietly.

"I don't mean to trespass if this is your territory. I'm merely new to the area." He was intriguing. Something about the man did seem recognizable. She could not tell if it were his face, voice, or everything in general. She was curious. However, smart enough to stay at a safe distance.

"I must be going," Nola whispered looking at the library steps down the street.

"To the library? May I join you?"

"No," she took a step back as he moved out of the alley. Seeing her retreat, Jarron backed away. "You are quite timid." His expression froze for a moment as if deep in thought.

"You are far too persistent." Nola turned to the library once more.

"Why is he following you?" Jarron turned back down the alley and looked behind him.

"Who?" Nola looked behind the stranger but did not see anyone.

"Never mind." Jarron's interest changed as he ducked back into the alley. "We have a more important guest." Holding his gaze on Nola, he waited.

"I find you very strange, Sir. I would prefer it if you were to be on your way." Nola moved to take a step toward the library, but it was then that the sensation ...the pure knowledge of Gavin Graelohr's presence came over her. Without turning around, she could feel him moving closer.

"Is there a problem?" Lord Graelohr crossed the street and came to Nola's side.

"I do not know this man," Nola admitted quickly. Impossible to ignore, Gavin's shirt was unbuttoned at the top without a tie. Why she noticed the thickness of his neck became perplexing. Clearing her throat, she dropped her gaze to the cobblestone.

"Of course not. This is the reason I requested you use our carriage." Gavin stepped closer. "I am Lord Graelohr." Raising his hand to the stranger, he waited for an introduction.

"Yes, Lord Graelohr." He accepted the handshake. "Jarron Tempest, on my way to Clariotte." His explanation was given quickly. "Your charge is very timid." He motioned to Nola. "I hope I did not offend."

"She suffers emotional trauma," Gavin stood directly behind Nola. Somehow, his nearness indicated to her to be silent. "We take no offence to your passing through."

"I see." His light hair brushed against his face as the wind blew. "Well, Mistress of Graelohr, I hope you are well in time..." The title did not sit well with Nola.

"My name is ..." Nola was unable to finish her statement. At the mention of her name, the slight pressure of Gavin's fingertips on the back of her neck erased all thoughts of speaking. Frozen expressionless, she found herself lost from the conversation.

Abruptly, an intense warmth ran over her body as if she were standing naked by an open fire. Her skin tingled and shivered. An exquisite desire took over, leaving her body craving and aching for more of his touch. Her eyes glossed over, and her skin flushed. She wanted to lean back; she wanted him to move his hand all over her neck. No, more than her neck. Reaching up to press her fingers to his wrist, she gently closed her eyes. It was rapture, pure and simple. In that single moment, Nola experienced her first uninhibited sensual desire. The fact that she was fawning backward against his chest went completely unnoticed under the trance.

"Be on your way, Mr. Tempest." Gavin removed his gentle touch from the back of her neck, releasing Nola from the strange splendor.

"Of course," Jarron smiled at the expressive features on Nola's face. "I see I was wasting my time."

Completely numb from his release, Nola watched silently as Gavin stepped around her to place himself between her and Jarron. The stranger nodded his head politely to them both and walked back into the alley. Not long after Gavin turned to face her, but Nola had still not fully recovered from his enchanting touch.

"I am sorry for touching you without permission," he whispered. "There was no alternative." As he spoke, Gavin replaced the gloves he had been wearing. Nola's eyes were still glowing from his touch. It was obvious that she was struggling with the event.

Unable to understand any of it, she averted her gaze and tried to walk past him.

Slowly the realization of how she leaned against him, and even reached for his hand overtook her senses. Sopping for a moment, Nola put her hand to her chest. She did not feel any of the emotions she did before, hardly even embarrassment for her own actions. In all reality, the gravity of the experience was inconceivable.

"Nola do not fear me. I had no intention of making you uncomfortable." Gavin stood before her and placed his fingertips to the base of her chin. She inhaled suddenly, waiting for the stir of emotions to return, but none followed. "There is much for you to learn." Nola stepped away from his touch, not knowing if or when the embarrassing emotion he drew from her would return. "You are beginning to attract attention," Gavin stated, turning to look down the alley.

A strange pressure began to build in her ears, and for a moment she felt ill. Trying to hide her discomfort she rubbed the side of her neck. It was then that the humming sound inside her head was realized. Nola looked up at Gavin to see if he could hear it, but he was still peering down the alley.

Instantly, her vision shifted from her eyesight to a golden haze. No longer could she see Gavin at all. She could see down the alley nearly all the way to Baggerty Bridge. The colored tinge made everything self-illuminate. She could see people passing by Falkenstein Avenue. She could see Luke as he hurried down the way, muttering to himself insults toward Nola, but it was the vision of Jarron that held focus. He seemed twice as detailed as the others. His features did not hold the same golden tint. He was brighter, with more of a white illumination around him. Then, as the vision began to confuse her more and the ringing became intense, Nola lost her balance, utilizing a nearby lamp post, she leaned heavily.

"Nola?" Gavin called.

"Don't touch me!" She warned, coming out of the vision.

"No, of course not." He agreed, keeping his distance. "Are you alright?" With her sight fully returned as quickly as it left, she looked down the dark alley.

"Luke?" She called quietly, hoping he would hear her.

"Are you ill?" Gavin asked again.

"Luke?" She called again. Gavin looked behind him, but Luke was still too far away. "Luke?" she called, peering past Gavin.

Finally, hearing her call, Luke hurried through the narrow street. "Nola!" He could see her standing just behind Lord Graelohr.

"Wait." Gavin held up his hand to the intruder. "Stay your distance," he spoke firmly to Luke. "Nola, what did you see?"

"Nothing," she answered, not realizing that she was as wide eyed as an owl.

"You saw him coming, didn't you?" Gavin's voice was almost silent. "You saw him in the alley."

"Of course," she answered.

"From that distance... with no light?" When the words left his mouth, Nola realized how impossible it sounded.

"Take me home," she called to Luke. Ignoring Lord Graelohr from that moment on, Luke hurried to her side.

"I've got you," he stated, wrapping both arms around her waist. Gavin stood well over a foot taller, but Luke glared at him as if he were no more than a rat. "Let's go." Nola wrapped her arm around his and leaned on him slightly as she walked. Exhausted, confused, and distraught, she leaned her head on his arm. Without hesitation, Luke reached around her shoulder and held her to him as they moved on. "That's it," he warned. "From now on, you go nowhere without me!"

"Agreed, Luke." She nodded gently under his chin. "Just take me home."

***

"I work from sunup to sundown. If you want her to be picked up after she is done at the school, you are going to have to do it." Davey used his swollen hand to pour the pot of coffee. It was obvious that he was fighting the night before.

"Good morning," Nola stepped into the kitchen after getting ready for the schoolhouse. "Aren't you going to eat?" she asked Luke.

"Why are you dressed like that?" Luke eyed the handsome dark purple gown. "And why is your hair all curled?"

"I don't know," Nola answered innocently. "Is it inappropriate?"

"Tell me you are going to pick her up." Luke returned his attention to Davey. "I've got an interview with a man that has a two-bedroom apartment for lease two blocks away from the museum. If I miss this appointment, I lose the lot." Luke shook his head and placed the bowl of cold slimy oats in the sink. "That was revolting," he remarked on the breakfast.

"Well, you been home long enough now. The hot meals in the morning have gone as quickly as Mum's attendance downstairs." Tipping his cup, Davey sniffled a little.

"I do my best with the meals." Nola wrapped her scarf around her neck and began to button her coat. "I don't need either of you to walk me home. I simply need a ride there because it is my turn to bring in firewood."

"If this is your best cooking, we'll be better off if you stop all together," Davey argued. "And I'm not picking you up."

"I'm not missing out on this apartment," Luke warned.

"For heaven's sake, no one is asking you to." Placing her hat on her head, Nola sighed. "I've walked home for the past two years, Luke." Davey chuckled and went to reach for the pot again.

"Davey..." Luke reached over and grabbed Davey's forearm. "Promise me you'll see her home." The elder brother looked at his arm and followed it up to Luke. "Look at her," Luke whispered.

Davey had noticed the slight change in Nola, but on that morning the difference was even more apparent. Ever since Luke brought her home ill a few nights before, Nola had been wearing gowns with more color. Her hair had been worn differently every day, and she was taking much more time with her appearance. Not that she was ever inattentive to fashion, but Nola was glowing.

"Fine," Davey agreed. "But you better get this apartment. Your job starts tomorrow and I'm not carting your ass across the city and back."

"With the money I'll be making I will have my own horse and carriage in half a month," Luke stated.

"I'm leaving," Nola threw up her hands and left the kitchen. "Aunt Dottie, do you need anything before I come home?"

"I'm fine, dear." The elderly woman answered from her room upstairs.

"Alright, the butcher's son will be making a delivery in about an hour." Nola fixed her gloves as Davey came to the parlor and picked up her stack of wood. "Will you be down by then?"

"I'll be fine," Dottie called.

Checking her reflection quickly in the mirror, Nola turned on her heels and picked up her stack of textbooks. Once Davey had opened the door, she nodded to Luke.

"Good luck," she offered.

"I know you will get the place."

"I'm sure of it," he answered.

"Come on," Davey called. "I'm already late."

"You are not late, just dramatic." Nola gave the sly remark.

"Get in the carriage," he warned.

"Fine, I have to have the stove going before Miss Peetz gets there anyway." Climbing up into the open rig, she pulled her burgundy dress with cream-colored accents behind her.

"Why are you dressed like that?" Davey asked as he climbed in the buggy with her.

"Should I change?" The constant attention on her wardrobe was making her very self-conscious.

"You look nice." He wrapped the leather reins around his gloves.

"Then why shouldn't I wear it?" Nola straightened her shoulders as the horse began to pull the buggy.

"You look like you are trying to impress someone." Davey turned the horse out of the yard and started toward Darlington Avenue. "Is this all for your trip to the library tonight?"

"I'm not sure," Nola answered honestly. "Is that wrong?"

"Yes," he answered quickly. "The whole idea of you going there is wrong. You've got no business traipsing around the city at night in some rich man's carriage." Davey looked at her affronted expression. "You look nice, Nola. I just think there is something wrong with all of this. Everything about Lord Graelohr and his relationship with Mum has me on edge."

"They are strange together," she admitted.

"He is strange on his own," Davey added, driving the horse past Baggerty Bridge.

The comment led Nola to recall how Gavin suddenly appeared behind her near the alley, and how his touch affected her body with such strange force. She could envision his face completely and hear his voice clearly in her mind. Again, the warm feeling of curiosity raced through her blood. Forcing the memory away, she realized the schoolhouse was just up ahead.

"I'll pick you up here right after the bell," Davey stated, slowing the rig to a crawl. "If I am late, wait right here for Luke!"

"I will," she sighed, "though this is all unnecessary."

"I'm pretty sure Luke knows what he is talking about this time." Davey nodded at Nola's curvy and sharp- looking dress.

Chapter Four

Intimate History

The snow fell in large clusters like the seeds of a dandelion in spring. Nola's black boots left delicate tracks in the fluff as Luke squished the tiny prints with each step. "I have an idea," he offered with a precious smile. "Why don't I go with you tonight... and after you study whatever it is you're studying... we can go celebrate." With his hands on her shoulders, he stopped her from getting into the carriage.

"I'm very happy that you got the apartment, but I will be fine." Nola placed her hands in her muff and watched a few crystalline flakes fall from the sky. "Besides, the first time Davey caught me in a pub he would cart me off over his shoulder and lock me in my bedroom."

"We can go anywhere you want." Luke stayed right in her line of sight, trying to sway her mind from the fabulous carriage there to transport Nola to the library.

"I have to go." Nola insisted as the young carriage driver holding the door open for her cleared his throat. "This will be much safer than my walking."

"I know," Luke agreed, releasing his hold on her. Running his hand along the side of his neck, he tried to think of something else to dissuade her from leaving so late. "Let me come with you. I have a degree. I could help with your studies."

"You don't even know what I am studying." Nola smiled and climbed up into the velvet-lined carriage.

"Then show me," he added, noting how brilliant she looked inside the luxurious cab.

"Stop worrying," she stated as the driver closed the door. "I'll be home soon."

Standing there cold and restless, Luke watched as the team of horses pulled the extravagant carriage out of the yard. Shaking the snow out of his hair, he returned to the steps of the porch. There, he watched until the glass windowed carriage turned at the start of Baggerty Bridge.

Nola could not believe the luxury of such a contraption. Velvet covered everything inside. There were four lanterns on the outside, illuminating every angle of the street around her. However, the curtains were gently drawn to conceal passengers inside.

She half-expected Lord Graelohr to be inside the carriage, the fact that he was not, left her with a twinge of disappointment. As

45

of late, her thoughts had been little more than memories of the instantaneous desire he awakened.

She had never even grown curious of a man's touch before. If anything, the few times she did catch Davey or Luke kissing a girl left her annoyed or jealous that she had never felt such attraction.

However, Jarron, the man she saw in the alley, slightly gained her attention. Still, it was the simple touch of Gavin's fingertips that made her mind whirl and her body weak. It was exhilarating, and she desperately wanted to feel it once more.

Pulling the loose pieces of fur out of her hand muff, Nola waited as the gilded chariot trotted down the dark streets toward the library. It had been so long since she had reached the steps of the establishment that she wondered if the staff had thought her dead. Finally, seeing the lights of Halweg Boulevard, she waited for the carriage to bring her to the front of the building. Once stopped, she reached for the door just as the driver opened it.

"Is there anything else, Miss?"

"No, thank you," she answered hurrying to the marble stairs of the grand building.

"We will wait here then," the driver called from behind.

Nola glanced over her shoulder to him for a moment and then quickly hurried up the twenty-two steps to the immense double doors. With the slightest effort, the door opened, releasing the scent of century-old books and hundreds of floral arrangements that were replaced every week.

"I thought for sure that cousin of yours had you under lock and key." A kind elderly man approached from the side of the great room. "Welcome back, Miss Valerian."

"Mr. Gillian, how have you faired these past days?" Nola listened as the door to the library was closed and locked behind her.

"Well enough," he answered. "I am glad you made your way back."

"It has been a busy season."

"And your aunt, how is she?"

"Well," Nola removed her long coat and pulled the strap of her muff over her head. "She has been better, now since her youngest son returned from school."

"Good," Mr. Gillian answered. "I am sure you have a lot of work to look into," he began pleasantly. "Lord Graelohr has taken an interest in your studies I see."

"Excuse me?"

"Lord Graelohr... he came by early this week and ensured that we would have a private room ready for you." The elderly man took her coat from her and motioned toward a hallway near the back of the library. "I assumed you would know."

"I did not," she answered with a heavy sigh.

"Well, as far as I was told, you are welcome to stay as long as you like. The library is closed to everyone else." His bright blue eyes and brilliant smile eased Nola quite a bit. "I will even leave you in peace and take up my own reading out here. If you follow that hall straight ahead, you are in the last room on the right."

"Thank you," Nola whispered before heading down the silent hallway.

The library was enormous. Most of the tables, desks, and chairs were in the center of the main floor with shelves of books surrounding the outside walls. At the four corners of the main room, oak stairways led to the open second balcony lined with more books and slightly less chairs. There were two grand fireplaces, one at each end, and then another two smaller fireplaces on the second floor. At the back of the library, Nola followed the single hallway as she had been instructed, but to a room she had never been in before.

Opening the last door on the right, she found a toasty room similar in size to her aunt's parlor. There was just enough space in it for the fireplace, a hutch with shelves, and a large rosewood table.

The wallpaper was darker than the rest of the décor in the library, but it was still quite extravagant. Gold diamonds shaped the wall design, and the chandelier was adorned with a few gold ornaments. It was all very tasteful but different from the rest of the building.

Setting her coat on the back of a chair, Nola returned to the main room of the library. With no one around, she was free to indulge in delights that Dottie and the boys would find inappropriate. Taking the small open staircase to the balcony, Nola ventured across the creaking floor. Along the center of the outside wall was a large glass case filled with books. All of them were locked safely away because of their priceless age, but when Nola came Mr. Gillian would leave the case open.

Sliding the glass aside, Nola removed the single book that held her interest for the past few months. Translated into English in the late sixteen-hundreds, the book was a recollection of every religion-based trial and punishment from the fifteenth century on. Within the leather binding were tales of witchcraft, heinous murderers, demonic possession, and use of dark magic.

Hoisting the heavy log into her arms, Nola closed the glass and began to walk back to the small well-lit room. However, once she stepped in front of the window, a familiar sensation fell over her.

Slowing her steps, she glanced out the window. Lord Graelohr's mansion was just across the street. Even being so far away could produce an exquisite calm in her emotions.

In her mind, there had to be some kind of connection between the two of them. Either she was born with some sort of magic within her, something that could sense his nearness and take vision through his eyes, or he was able to project the sensations onto her. The experience a few nights before was leading her to the latter conclusion. Either way, she needed an answer.

Carrying the book back down the stairs, Nola returned to the small room. It was then that she recalled the dictionary for the more extravagant words that were no longer commonly used.

With a heavy sigh, Nola felt a deep familiar lull, but did not want to lose her focus. With heightened awareness she continued to the private study room. All focus disappeared completely as Gavin stood before her.

Her eyes followed the lines of his dark tailored suit until her head nearly rested on her shoulders. The dark red silk vest and black necktie brought her attention to the shape of his thick jaw, full lips, and deep dark eyes. Even his raven hair seemed to follow order with the impressiveness of his suit. Taking a step back, she thought of the book behind her and hoped he would not show interest.

"Lord Graelohr," she bobbed politely. "I was somehow expecting you."

"Were you?" he asked, taking note of how attractive she dressed. "I am sorry for the intrusion, but I think it is time you and I spoke... alone." Remaining in the doorway, he stood as expressionless as she.

There was nothing to fear, he was her legal guardian and had never spent more than a year from her view. She wanted to throw a million questions at him. She also wanted to lift the collar of her dress, certain that her skin could not again be touched.

"Yes, Sir." Her hands folded together before her waist.

"You have been wanting to talk to me for some months now, am I correct?" Nola knew he meant her many nights waiting on the bench outside.

"I have," she answered him honestly. "Though, I was hoping for a less private setting." Glancing down the hallway, she wondered if Mr. Gillian was aware of Gavin's presence.

"Privacy is imperative. No one except your aunt will know that I am here, not even Mr. Gillian," he promised. "But it will be easier to keep it that way if he does not see me standing in the hallway."

Stepping back into the room, Nola watched how suddenly the small space seemed completely occupied by his large form. Gavin was unconditionally the best specimen of man she had ever encountered, and it quickly led to a brief memory of his touch.

"What are you reading?" He asked glancing over the leather binding.

"I have a weakness for distorted history," she answered flipping the book upside down. "Please ignore it." His smile was the only answer she needed. Returning to her chair, she waited for him to remove his long coat before they sat down at opposite sides of the table. "Will you answer a question?"

"I am willing to answer more than one, but not everything at this time." His honesty was clear in his dark eyes. "First, I want to know how far back your memories go." When she looked slightly confused, he restated the question. "Do you remember your parents?"

"No," she answered plainly. "Quite honestly, the day they placed my brother in my arms at the orphanage is my first memory."

"Who told you that he was your brother?" Gavin asked, glancing at the book once more.

"The head mistress," she answered, "but I already knew. I could feel it."

"I believe you." Gavin breathed heavily. "Do you remember Dottie and Arthur coming to find you?"

"Yes, Arthur came alone at first." She nodded her head, then realized she was staring at him. "We were called into Sister Catherine's office to meet a man, he asked if we were cold, both of us answered no, and he left."

"It was January tenth," Gavin looked down at the carpenter's woodwork on the furniture and continued, "You were presented to him barefoot in your nightdresses in a room with no fire."

"Yes," Nola answered, wondering how he could not understand such facts. "The next day, we washed, dressed, and stood outside the front door to wait for him and Dottie."

"Were you happy to leave?"

"Yes," Nola answered. "Neither my brother nor I were comfortable with the other children at the orphanage."

"No, I suppose you weren't."

"Do you know who my parents are? Are they dead?" Nola asked the burning question as she stared at her hands.

"I have been looking for your parents for nearly ten years." Gavin leaned slightly over the table, drawing her attention. "I will find out who they are."

"Why?" Nola asked. "Why does it matter to you?"

"That you will learn another time," he answered flatly, leaving no room for argument.

"Who was that man the other night?" She could feel her ears start to hum, but she concentrated on tuning out the sound. "Excuse me," she whispered placing her hand to the base of her ear. "A slight headache."

"It is not a headache." Gavin stood up and walked around the table to her. Nola would have argued if the humming had not become nearly intolerable. Gently moving her long dark hair aside, Gavin tenderly touched her shoulder. "Do you experience this often?" With a deep breath, Nola felt the pressure release in her head and the humming subsided. The simple touch felt like a magic tonic. Nola sat still, wondering how the moment could vanish so quickly when she could never stop it before. It was then that she realized Gavin was aware of her affliction. "What you suffer is a gift. Proof of it cannot be found anywhere inside that book or any other."

"How can you know what I suffer?" Nola tried to look up at him. Taking the chair next to her, Gavin sat down.

"You see through the eyes of others," he whispered.

"No," Nola turned in her chair to face him. The depth of his dark eyes provoked the truth. "Not others ...just yours."

"Mine?" Gavin looked confused. He leaned back for several seconds, staring into her rich dark eyes. "Can you control it?"

"Not at all." It was a relief to tell part of her deepest secrets.

The way Gavin appeared convinced Nola that he believed her completely, seeming both amazed and concerned.

"Is this something new or have you been dealing with it for some time?" Strangely, Gavin smiled again. It was an expression she had not gotten used to.

"It happened for the first time the night Esteban was murdered." She looked away from his eyes. "It isn't often, but most of the time you are very near when it occurs."

"How do you know if I am close or not?"

"I just know." Her answer was vague, but so was the truth. "Does this happen to you?"

"No," he answered quickly. "I have never had the experience."

"How do I make it stop?" She was almost desperate for an answer.

"Believe me, if I knew I would tell you." He almost chuckled. "The thought of you seeing through my eyes is, quite frankly, disturbing." Nola realized then how awkward her admission must have been for him. Still, the subtle humor lightened the atmosphere.

"I'm sorry, I never thought of it..." She didn't know how to continue. "I'm sorry."

"It's alright." His perfect smile eased her considerably. "I'll just be sure to keep my distance if I am to do anything you should not see."

"Will it ever go away?"

"No, but you will learn to control it."

"I can't." She shook her head with the statement. "I've tried for months."

"Is that why you sit outside my home until the lamplighter comes? Are you trying to use this gift?"

His question drew a hint of embarrassment. It was then that Nola realized how many different and complete emotions she felt since Gavin had entered the room. She was relieved when he appeared at the door, excited when he smiled in her direction, and tranquil when he came to sit next to her. Strangely, she felt alive and uninhibited for the first time. However, just as quickly, Nola realized how angry Luke was going to be when he learned of Gavin's visit.

"What is it?" he asked, seeing her draw back in her seat. For the past few minutes, she had been leaning forward, eyes fixed and eager for every second of conversation. "Are you alright?"

"I should be going," she whispered.

"I didn't mean to embarrass you." Maintaining a debonair exterior, he spoke innocently. "To be honest, I became a little worried when I did not see you outside my home for those few days." He was so much more than any man she had ever met before. There was no doubt that she was attracted to him. Every feature of his face was alluring, and the sound of his voice drew her closer. Nola analyzed every inch of Gavin's face before her moralistic upbringing raised its ugly head once more.

"Forgive me," she whispered coming to her feet. "Aunt Dottie will send the boys looking for me before long."

"She has raised you well."

"I am difficult for her." Nola picked up her coat, but Gavin came to his feet instantly to hold it for her. "She feels much more emotion for me than I for her."

"If that were true you wouldn't show her so much respect." He slid the coat over her arms and watched as she pulled her thick curls out of the collar.

"Am I showing respect, or avoiding arguments?"

"You will grieve for her as much as her sons when her time comes." Releasing her coat, he replaced her chair under the table. Nola considered his words and found agreement with the idea. "I have a book for you to study." Reaching inside his own coat pocket, Gavin withdrew a medium-sized leather-bound book. "It is old, and irreplaceable. I am only entrusting it to you for a week or two while I am out of the country."

"This is French," Nola whispered as she glanced at the cover. "My French is horrible."

"It will be worth the effort," he stated as she reached for the book. Nola was careful not to touch his fingers as she pulled the leather away from him. The pages were twice as thick as modern paper, and the fibers were visible in a crisscross manner.

"I will do my best."

"Good," Gavin answered. "Will you need to visit the library while I am gone?" Motioning toward the book on the table, he sighed heavily. "The answers you seek are not written anywhere inside this building. Though, you may find a few inside this book."

"Am I forbidden to explore the library's options?"

"I will not forbid you from anything," he answered lightly with a generous grin. "I was going to let my driver know whether or not to continue picking you up."

"Is this book enough to last me for two weeks?"

"You did say your French was horrible," he smiled. Nola lowered her gaze and tried not to appear quite so agreeable to his sense of humor. When she raised her head, he was gazing at her. "Send for my carriage at any time. I will leave instructions for you to have it."

"Thank you," she whispered.

"Good night, Miss Valerian," Gavin stated, nodding his head and leaving the room without a second glance.

It took Nola a few more moments to move. So much of Gavin took up her concentration the book almost slipped out of her hand.

Distant and almost gliding as if she were in a dream, she left the small room and closed the door.

***

It seemed like only days before the world was alive with color.

The trees were green, the grass was full, and there were berries and flowers everywhere. Now it was a vast snow-covered wasteland, bitter and dirty with ash, coal, and mud.

"Wait here," Davey said as he pulled the carriage down a side street and hopped out of the seat.

"Where are you going?" Nola asked as he waited for a few people to pass by the sidewalk. When the coast was clear, he climbed the steps to a small residence and rang the bell. Even with the canvas top pulled up over the carriage, snow was still falling on her muff.

With little else to do, Nola flicked each individual flake off the fox fur.

The door to the residence opened and a young lady seemed happily surprised to see Davey. She was quite attractive, light blonde hair and a becoming smile. Nola watched her face become radiant as Davey handed her a brown paper package. The woman wrapped her arms around Davey in a spontaneous embrace. It almost looked like he was going to break her ribs with his strength but in a moment it was over. She politely released him, and Davey turned to head back to the carriage. With a smile and kind wave, the woman nodded to Nola before re-entering the house.

"Who was that?" Nola asked as Davey took the reins once more.

"Claudette Stephens," he answered.

"What did you give her?" Even as the carriage turned around on the road, Nola looked back at the little house.

"A present." Releasing the brake, he waited before tapping the horse's reins. "It's her birthday."

"Are you courting her?"

"Courting her?" Davey asked. "I was courting her last spring." The irritated tone of his voice turned softer. "It's a little more than that now."

"Why haven't you brought her by the house?"

"To meet Mum? How do you think that would go?" Davey made a snickering sound as the horse drove past the bridge and made its way toward the schoolhouse. "By noon she would be in a fit wondering if I was going to leave her or if she had to make room for another woman in the house."

"She would be happy for you." Although Nola was not one to imagine, she could see how Davey's theory could be correct. "Wait, you've been seeing her since spring? That is a long time... when are you going to tell your mother?"

"I don't know," he whispered before glancing over at her. "I was wondering if you could say something. Maybe you could give her an inkling?"

"Why?"

"I don't know, to give her time to think about it." Davey pulled the carriage up alongside the school. "Hey," he grabbed her arm gently before she could get out. "Just make sure Mum knows I'm not going anywhere?" He sighed and let his blue eyes span over the fresh snow. "I don't want her thinking that I'm going to leave her alone... especially now that Luke is moving across town."

"Does Claudette know how much you like her?"

"I'm going to marry her," Davey admitted, staring at his boots. "I just haven't figured out how."

"What do you mean?"

"Just mention her to Mum some way, will you?" He looked concerned.

"Alright," Nola agreed as she stepped out of the carriage. "She will be happy for you both."

"We'll see," he stated.

***

If she understood three words out of a sentence she was doing well. Nola sighed heavily with the book in her hands, knowing that she was not going to get too far. Luke would have been able to finish the book in a matter of days. However, she did not know if Gavin would mind, or if Luke would make a connection between Nola and the book's secrets. Without his help, she was not going to find out what those secrets were.

Nola had pressed her nose to the pages for over two whole days. All she could get out of the book was that it was written by a monk named Louis Dubois and he was a record keeper in a monastery. Her understanding of numbers meant that the book had been written in the twelfth century, something that could not possibly be true. No one was going to hand out a six-hundred-year-old book. However, it could very well have been a copy from the twelfth century. The fibers were easily visible, and the ink faded like an old scar.

Returning to the writings of the monk, Nola had deciphered that Louis was a prior from a Benedictine monastery. It seemed that the author spent nearly a lifetime in a scriptorium penning word for word the pages of the scriptures. He was also responsible for the day- to-day log of everything that happened inside the monastery, which didn't seem to be much. Still, there were pages of information that Nola was unable to read.

"Can I come in?" The question was obviously rhetorical as Luke opened her bedroom door.

"I thought you were going out." Nola closed the book and set it beside her on the bed.

"I was, but my luck ran out and I figured on staying out of trouble for once."

"You lost all your money playing cards," Nola assumed.

"Yea," he agreed and closed the door behind him. "That's about the way of it." Walking over to the window he drew the thick green curtain. "I saw you were still up and figured I'd see if you got any further in that French book of yours."

"How did you know it was French?" she asked, sliding her legs off the bed and onto the floor.

"I stole a peek at it this morning when you were frying the eggs."

"You have no business going through my things." Nola scolded Luke as he drew an apple out of his pocket.

"I know," he spoke flatly. "But what is the point of being family if you can't intrude on one another's privacy?" His unending smile made it impossible to be mad at him. Nola handed him the book with another sigh. "Wow, this is ancient." He bit into the apple and looked at the pages.

"Hold it with both hands. Yes, it is old."

"Fine." He moved the apple into his palm and held the book with his fingers. "Old isn't the word for this book. The language is ancient. You know the difference between our English and that spoken during Shakespeare's time." Turning the book upside down to keep both hands on it, Luke took another bite of apple over expressing his talent. "You're never going to understand this."

"I know," she sighed.

"Is it important?" he asked, flipping through the pages.

"I have no idea." She answered honestly. "Lord Graelohr asked me to read it for some reason."

"Scoot over," Luke huffed, pulling another apple out of his pocket, and tossing it to her. "I'll get you through some of it."

Taking the apple, Nola returned to the bed, sitting up on the pillows. Situating the lamp closer on the bedside table, Luke leaned against the headboard and opened the stiff pages. Strangely, just as they were as children, the two were inseparable.

"How far did you get?" he asked, drawing his feet up onto the bed.

"There," she leaned over and pointed to the gibberish that dotted the pages.

"Alright," Luke sighed and turned the book into the light. "This is not going to be easy." Nola settled in beside him and leaned closer as he opened the book. "Are you sure you're alright with this?"

"I welcome the help."

"That is not what I mean." Luke looked down at Nola as she pulled her quilt up over them.

"You used to read to me every night," she whispered. His expression was strange. He didn't have his normal quirky smile and he seemed worried about something.

"That was a few years ago." Luke looked down at the book and then back to Nola. He waited for her to catch his meaning. When she lifted the apple and took a large bite, he realized that their proximity and her well-developed age was only an issue to him.

"Are we not supposed to read?" She urged him on without a clue as to his strange behavior.

"Alright," he whispered, running his finger over the thick page. When he found the first passage, he slowly translated to modern English. "More come to our doors to seek refuge. Sin and indecent law have torn at the country..." Luke looked at the page tilting his head. "I don't know what it says here, but I think he means more men are seeking shelter within the monastery's walls. Normally, that is not allowed."

"Go on." Nola took another bite of her apple.

"This is an account of the names of men that came to find sanctuary after some malevolent tragedy." He ran his hand over the names placed in a column in the center. "Do you want me to read them?"

"No, skip on."

"Here, this is several days later. He says, 'Much of the village was destroyed or damaged by the soldiers. Many of the peasants have escaped or been murdered during the last raid. Three children were brought this morning to hide within our walls. They join the two that came yesterday and welcomed the four that were brought before sunset.' Luke followed his finger down the list of names. "Do I need to read these?"

"Move on," she instructed, chewing steadily on her apple.

"That is sounding right under my ear, you know." The deep rasp of his voice hummed below her head.

"Sorry," she mumbled before reaching over his chest to put the apple on the table.

Instead of returning to her upright position, Nola curled up on his shoulder as she had done throughout her childhood when he would read to her. Luke moved her hair under his chin and rested his arm on her shoulder. There had always been comfort with him. Davey always tried to be nice, but Luke really took Nola and Esteban under his wing.

He read on, slowly describing the young ages of the children and what they were expected to do while they waited for the family to claim them. She listened carefully, but her ear was just above Luke's steadily beating heart. She could hear every thump, every breath, and the reverberation of his voice in her ears. It was strangely soothing.

Nola would have been the first to admit that she was not fond of physical contact with Aunt Dottie or Davey. Even a hug on a holiday felt as comfortable as a corset. However, everything with Luke flowed like a gentle river. She never had to lie, she never had to withhold her opinions, and she could touch him without feeling inappropriate. He was by far her favorite companion and always had been.

"This is all a list of scriptures and duties that the scribe performs daily. It looks like he spent every daylight hour outside writing and returned to the cellarium as soon as the candles were lit." Luke explained. "That's another of his duties. He was teaching the children over five how to make candles." Turning the page, he glanced down at Nola. "This is going to be a long dull book."

"Keep reading," she whispered revealing her tired voice.

"Are you falling asleep?" He pulled her hair back and looked at her heavy eyes. "I thought this was some sort of study."

"I'm listening..."

"You're using me as a pillow, that's what you are doing."

"You're too skinny to be a pillow," she reached her arm over his stomach and pushed the book up again. "Read please."

"I'm not skinny," he argued. "I'd look a lot bigger if Davey wasn't my brother. He makes everyone look scrawny." Nola yawned instead of joining his argument.

"Are you going to read?" she asked, turning her head just enough to look up into his eyes.

The dim light dilated her eyes and made them appear as large as saucers. Her brunette hair streamed down her face, covering her shoulder, and brushing over his arm. Her features had always been gentle and alluring, but her position within his arms illuminated her in a way that he was not prepared for.

"Maybe tomorrow." Luke closed the book and handed it back to her. "It's not very interesting and it is putting me to sleep."

"Just a few more pages? There isn't much time left before you move away." Her tone clearly noted that she was not aware of why he had to leave her.

"I know," he agreed. "I promise, I'll read more tomorrow." Reaching for the door, he paused to look back at her. "Good night."

Chapter Five

Visitors and Demons

"Do you think he is with her?" Dottie put down her knitting and gazed up at Nola attentively. "When he goes out so late at night?"

"No," Nola answered with complete faith. "Absolutely not... she is far too proper for that. No, when Davey goes out, he is either drinking or fighting. Claudette Stephens would not be seen in that circle." Realizing how ill she had spoken of Davey, Nola tried to retract her comment. "I did not mean to insult Davey."

"I've become used to your straight forwardness," Dottie replied. "There is no need to apologize."

"Good."

"Now, use your conversation skills to tell me why Davey did not mention that he was in love." Picking up her needles, she returned to her diligent task.

"He does not want you to think that he is leaving you. I was specifically instructed to tell you that he isn't going anywhere."

"Well of course he is not going anywhere. This is his house now. When he marries, his wife will come here."

"I'm certain, he is worried about that as well," she admitted setting her book down on the table next to the fire. "With him considering a permanent relationship with Claudette, I'm certain he is worried that you may feel troubled."

"A mother is not troubled when her son finds love," she declared. Nola heard the catch in her voice and the sigh that followed. "Alright, I may feel a little less important. Still, I want others to love my children as I do. None of you should wander through these erratic desolate days alone." Dottie glanced at Nola and put down her knitting once more. "You still feel no fancy for anyone... do you?" As she considered her own words, Dottie watched Nola's curious expression. "Except Lord Graelohr..."

"I try not to put a great deal of consideration on it. Honestly, he, Davey, and Luke are the only three men I have ever known. Lord Graelohr interests me because I know nothing about him."

Picking up her feet, she placed her thick wool socks on the seat of the chair where Dottie's other leg would have been. Dottie welcomed the closeness and covered Nola's legs with the other end of the blanket. As the two faced each other next to the fire Nola picked up a second set of needles and took another skein of yarn to work on the opposite end with her.

"What are you two doing?" Luke asked as he entered from the back of the house. Dropping his leather case near the door he eyed their seating arrangement.

"We've finished five blankets like this over the last two winters." Dottie smiled at Nola. "Quite a team, we are," she added.

"Well, make room for one more. I've just spent an hour just trying to get across town."

"How was your first day?" Dottie asked, as Luke leaned down and kissed her cheek.

"Invigorating, as sarcastically as that can be said." His expression agreed. "Four years' worth of study led me to this day. The day that I could put on a clean suit; take a cab across the bridge to the city square, where I could hold my head high... as I catalogued every file alphabetically."

"You spent the day filing?" Nola asked.

"Absolutely," he answered with an irritated grin. "I am to study under the current curator for at least two years before the museum puts any faith in me. Unfortunately, the curator left for an expedition currently taking place in Uganda. Until he returns, I file papers." His distress was as visible as the ink on his fingers. "He should be back in a few weeks."

"Don't fret," Dottie reached up and patted his hand. "You'll have a splendid career. Give it time." As always, her smile and quick comforting did the trick.

"I feel fortunate. It just wasn't a splendid day." He looked at the tightly knitted blanket and felt the soft yarn. "I did manage to get an invite to the museum's Egyptian re-open. They have had four more mummies and quite a lot of artifacts donated. When they remodel the Egyptology room there will be a large social event including wine, dancing, and exquisite tastes from all over the world."

"That sounds lovely." Dottie offered a dreamy stare as if she could almost see the finery.

"I hope so." He glanced at Nola. "I was instructed to bring guests."

"All those people, gussied up and gossiping, who in their right mind would want to attend something so arduous?" Nola flipped the yarn over the end of her needle as Luke leaned a little closer.

"I'll buy you a new dress..."

"No," she answered flatly. "I would never consider it. How could you even ask?"

"You know her better than that, Luke." Dottie sighed. "What would make you ask?"

"Common sense, Mum. I am unattached. She is unattached, and this is a perfect opportunity for us both to meet new acquaintances on the other side of the city."

"No." Nola stated again.

"You have to at least think about it," he argued. "If I go alone, it will make me look desperate or awkward."

"If you take your cousin... you will look pathetic," Nola added with a smile.

"Taking a sister looks pathetic."

"I am not your sister."

"You are not my cousin either," he added softly.

"Stop," Dottie demanded. "You are stressing my nerves."

"Fine," Luke laughed. "Then I'm getting you all a ticket."

"Go and get changed." Dottie looked at the immaculate gray suit. "I'm not washing soot off of that because you sat too close to the fire."

"Alright," he agreed as he stood up.

"Then you can come down and read some of this book for us," Nola added.

"That book is boring!" He yelled, making his way up the stairs.

"He may be right, you know." Dottie snipped off the end of her yarn, tied it in place and picked up another color. "It may be a good chance for you to meet eligible men."

"I don't think so." Nola shook her head.

"You are not getting your heart set on Gavin Graelohr, are you?"

"He is intriguing, but I have my heart set on no one. I swear, Aunt Dottie, I have no intention to consider anyone at this point." Her tone was solid and simple.

"You should," Dottie warned.

"I know," she agreed.

"Alright," Luke returned in his dark trousers and gray sweater. "Where is that horrible book?"

"Here," Nola handed it up without taking her eyes off the blanket. "We have finished the second entry."

"Fantastic," he scoffed, opening the musty pages. Before Luke could read a word there was a knock at the front door.

"At this hour?" Dottie whispered.

"It isn't that late, Mum." Luke stood up and handed the book to Nola. "It is just getting darker sooner." Nola placed the book under the blanket and took her feet off Dottie's chair. When Luke opened the door, he stood silent for a few seconds. "Can I help you?" Luke asked.

"Good evening. My name is Jarron Tempest. I'm looking for Nola," the man spoke in a familiar voice. By the time she had placed the familiar sound Luke stepped aside. Mr. Tempest stood waiting, just outside the door.

"Mr. Tempest?" Nola came to her feet and walked toward him. "Why are you here?" Her question sounded rude to the man that spent several minutes following her down a dark alley.

"Nola, who is this man?" Dottie nearly came out of her chair at Nola's tone.

"It is not my intention to alarm you." He remained cool and gave a warm smile to Luke and Dottie. "Nola and I met a few nights ago and I believe we may have gotten off on the wrong foot." Presenting a handful of lilies, he waited for her to except the gift.

"Where would you find lilies at this time of year?" Dottie asked. The narrowing of her brow made it clear that she was skeptical of the visitor.

"A new hothouse was just opened on Halweg Boulevard," he answered from the porch. "They have everything from carnations to birds of paradise."

"Well, aren't they beautiful?" She gazed at the delicate flowers. "Nola, either invite the man in or take your conversation outside. I do not wish to heat the neighborhood." Dottie held a darling smile, trying to ease her harsh words.

"Alright," she agreed. "Wait here." Closing the door to the visitor, she turned back into the room.

"That was a little rude," Luke whispered. "Invite him in."

"Not entirely uncalled for," Dottie piped up. "What kind of man comes to call on a lady at this time of night?" Disapproval was evident in her glossy eyes.

"He's just passing through town," Nola answered as she reached for her boots in the closet. "I suspect he is looking to be sure that he hasn't offended Lord Graelohr.

"Child... what are you going on about?" Dottie asked. "Who is that man?"

"Someone I ran into, and we spoke for a few minutes. Lord Graelohr saw us talking and sent Mr. Tempest on his way." Nola almost tripped as she pulled her boot on. Tucking the laces inside, she reached for her shawl.

"Were you instructed not to speak with him?" Dottie held a grave tone.

"No," she answered with a shake of her head. "Nothing like that." Pulling the thick wool around her arms, she reached for the door.

"I'm staying right here," Luke warned from the side of the door.

"Suit yourself." Nola opened the door and stepped out into the winter.

"I've caused quite a stir," Jarron admitted.

"It's not the first time but will it be the last?" she asked, folding the wool over her chest.

"You're not cold, are you?" He asked.

"Are you?" Nola eyed the fashionable jacket that was not meant for the chilling evening. Shaking his head, Jarron moved in a half-circle around her.

"No, I'm not cold." His hair was the color of straw, and his eyes were as bright as Arion blue. Kind in features, there was something worrisome about him. "It is polite of you to ask, since you did not invite me in."

"I did not invite you at all."

"Touché." He smiled again. Jarron was intriguing but not nearly similar to the state of her addiction to Gavin. "I should have sent a card."

"What do you want?" Nola asked boldly. He looked at her cautiously, as if trying to evaluate the consequence of his words.

"You are not one for gifts or flattery, are you?"

"I am not sociable," she admitted easily.

"Yes, you've made that quite clear." He leaned against the banister unaffected by the snow on his hands. "Then I will get right to the point. My mentor is aware that Lord Graelohr has had a ward for some time now. He is requesting an introduction."

"I'm sorry?" Nola shook her head gently. "I do not wish to meet anyone."

"Mr. Percy will contact Lord Graelohr on the matter, soon. I would expect a visit to be scheduled before the end of the week." Jarron tilted his head and gave a genuine smile. "My reason for interrupting you, was due to being unable to reach Lord Graelohr. I was hoping you would convey the message." He stood away from the banister without shaking the snow off his hand. Nola watched him for signs of discomfort, but he seemed quite unaffected by the frozen particles. "Your pet is annoying."

"My pet?" Nola glanced over her shoulder to see Luke's shadow pressed up against the window.

"I have to leave but I hope to be present when you visit." He began to walk down the front steps. "You will relay the message for me?"

"I am unable to," she answered honestly. "Lord Graelohr is traveling. There is no set date when he will return."

"Fascinating..." Jarron continued off the porch and onto the walkway. "Well, perhaps we will see you before he gets the message." Nodding his head politely, Jarron touched his fingers to his hat. "Good evening."

"Good evening," she answered quietly. Unscathed by the meeting, Nola turned to place her hand on the door, but Luke yanked it open first.

"Are you daft? Do you have any common sense?" Luke began badgering her the moment the door closed. "Nola? Where are you going?" he asked as she immediately headed up the stairs.

"To my room."

"We are going to talk about this!"

"I will think about it for a while and try to make head or tails of it first," she answered blatantly. "This was confusing, and I have no intentions of dissecting it through your yelling."

"Mum," Luke turned to Dottie. "Aren't you going to stop her?"

"Why would I? I wish I would know enough to maul over a situation before words fell out of my mouth." Dottie refused to look at either. She simply focused on her knitting.

***

There was no time to wait. "Wake up," Luke closed the door behind him and went to the side of her bed. "Nola, wake up!"

"What is it?" Clinging the blankets to her chest, she hid her eyes from the light of the lantern. "Is it Dottie?"

"No, she's fine. Listen to this!" Shoving her legs over on the bed he sat down next to her and put the light on the table. "On this day, the second month of the year one-thousand one-hundred and seventy-two... two female prisoners were brought to the cathedral, charged with iniquity and the foulest of murders."

"What are you talking about?" Nola had barely reached the deepest of sleep when he pulled her awake.

"The priest... in the book that Graelohr gave you," Turning to her with complete annoyance he lifted the lantern directly into her eyes. "Wake up! This is purely bizarre!"

"Alright," she shoved his arm away and he replaced the lantern. "Tell me."

"This is more than a few entries past where we left off, but this ... his ...the writing changed dramatically here. Like he was moving the quill faster without any care for the appearance of the words. That is what drove my attention to it when I flipped through the pages."

"What does it say?" Nola was finally intrigued.

"That is what I am trying to tell you." He read it once more. "On this day... two female prisoners were brought to the monastery, charged with iniquity and the foulest of murders. Having killed six Knights during their capture, they brought the demons to our church for examination. Soulless creatures of heinous nightmares, the beasts were chained in the cellarium with four men set on guard." Luke touched the page with his index finger as Nola leaned over his shoulder. "I must admit my uncertainty with the beasts underfoot.

Consequently, we have all been warned to extinguish our fears. Father Briar has expressed that our trepidation will only give them strength.

"Demons?" Nola looked at the strange word. "What does he mean?"

"Here," Luke skipped ahead a little and continued reading. "They exhibit great strength for females and exhume no remorse for their horrible crimes. I have yet to lay eyes on them but understand them to be desirable female beasts with pristine saber teeth and eyes that relinquish one's free will. As a precaution, we have all abandoned the church and monastery to dwell in the small huts within the perimeter of the walls. I myself have taken up residence in the abbey with the orphans for the time being. Our faith is our shield, and we are all heavily armored."

"What does that mean?" Nola could barely make sense of the scribbles.

"Whatever was brought to them, this priest, Louis Dubois, was definitely afraid." Luke showed her the book as if it would help. "They were all afraid." He pointed to the small scribbles of crucifixes that were drawn on the page.

"Keep reading!" she instructed.

"That is the maddening thing. At this point, Louis Dubois stops writing as documentation and begins to write the details as a letter to his brother." Luke pointed at the words that Nola could understand easily as 'Dear Brother'. "He goes on to say," Luke took a large breath. "Waiting for morning light to rid the world of such demons, the congregation took vigil in the church. Alas, in the dead of night the alarm was sounded, and the monsters escaped their chains.

To our horror, Dear Brother, the wretched creatures found our abbey and drained the blood of all nine sons and daughters. The demons left all infants barely alive, waiting to die. Before dawns light could rid of us the damned, both creatures fled into the early shadows with a speed that could not be followed."

"How horrible?" Nola held her hand to her lips.

"Why would Lord Graelohr give this to you?" Luke closed the book and held it in front of Nola. Remaining silent she tried to imagine an answer. "Obviously, he has no idea that you have a hard time sleeping to begin with." Nola took the book and wished she could read more of it.

"Have you gotten any further?"

"No, but I am not staying up all night to read about those things coming back to the monastery and finishing off the rest of the people until tomorrow."

"You don't know if that happened," Nola wanted him to continue but the clock tower outside quietly chimed the second hour of the new day.

"Well, I am not going to bother to find out until tomorrow. I just thought you should hear this without Mum knitting near your feet."

"Wise choice," Nola agreed, swiping her bedridden hair aside. "And you better not let her get wind of any of this either," he warned. "We will have to read anything more tomorrow after she has gone to bed."

"She is accompanying me to the library tomorrow night."

"Then we will look at it after you get home." He stood up and walked back to the door. "And the next time you see Lord Graelohr... ask him why he would give you such a book."

"This cannot be what he meant for me to study," Nola whispered, staring at the book.

"Well, Louis Dubois, does not continue for too much longer. I have glanced at the pages ahead to see that another prior takes up the daily log."

"Do you know why?"

"No, I honestly know nothing more, yet. Since I must work in five hours, I figure it will wait for another time."

"I understand," she agreed. "Thank you for telling me."

"I'm not sure that you should have this book, Nola." Opening the door and waiting for Dottie's peaceful snoring, Luke left the room.

***

"The day was grueling with Davey hounding her for answers about Mr. Tempest visiting the night before. He even began to sound like his father telling Dottie that neither of them was going to the library that night without him tagging along. When Dottie stomped her crutches and said that they were being met by Lord Graelohr that Nola showed interest.

She helped Dottie get dressed in her best gown and fix her silver hair in the latest fashion. However, her aunt was not about to answer any of the questions she tried to ask. In the end, Nola remained silent. The carriage ride seemed eternal except when Dottie got a glimpse of Tucksten Bridge. Then, the rest of the journey was simple praise for modern engineering and Davey's backbone.

Despite the boorish conversation, Nola could feel Gavin's presence as they drew nearer.

Even as the carriage pulled up to the library, Nola could barely contain her excitement. She had not spoken with Gavin in a week, and word of his hasty return left her in anticipation. So fierce was her desire to see him that she nearly forgot her aunt in a hurry to get inside. Once she returned to her duty, Dottie was quick to pat her hand and forgive her.

"I am sure that you are more anxious than I am, but I cannot climb down these stairs alone," Dottie whispered.

Just then, the double doors of the library opened quietly as Gavin Graelohr stepped into the night and walked to the carriage. He offered a nod of his head to Nola while reaching up to Dottie. "Permit me to assist?"

"Oh, aren't you a dear?" she asked, reaching out for his hand. "Grant me the liberty?" he asked, holding out both hands to her. "Carrying you would be much easier."

"Of course," she answered looking at the incredible flight of stairs that led to the open doors. "I do have a fear of slipping on this snow."

"I can take care of that," Gavin answered sweetly.

He smiled at Nola briefly before wrapping his arms around Dottie and cradling her like a child. Effortlessly, Gavin carried her step by step up to the library. At no point could Nola see an ounce of distress from the task. The man seemed to emit perfection with his incredible stamina, wavy hair, and sensual shoulders. His height towered over the driver and even Mr. Gillian by more than a head as he reached the top of the stairs. All of the factors together forced Nola to recall the one moment his fingers touched the back of her neck and the way she could have melted against his hand. Suddenly, Gavin turned to her with a strange smile.

"Mind your thoughts," he spoke in a warning tone with the same slight grin. Instantly, Nola ignored the beauty of his face and turned her mind into his meaning. Without shame, Nola lowered her gaze. There was so much she needed to learn about him.

"You can't carry me for the rest of my life," Dottie giggled as they stood inside the great room. She looked as love struck as a puppy and Gavin showed expressive care to her at every second. When at last Mr. Gillian closed and locked the door Gavin set her down.

"Your room is ready, Sir." Gillian bowed politely to the lord. "Thank you," Gavin answered, giving Dottie's crutches back to her. "We will not be needing your assistance tonight."

"Very good," Mr. Gillian answered.

The glances and smiles that transpired between Dottie and Gavin were surreal. Nola wanted to know what was so binding between them, but she was not brave enough to ask. All she could imagine was the same feeling of bliss Gavin gave Nola. Her aunt was quite aware of his abilities. Several moments later, Dottie was assisted into the same room Nola had visited last time and seated at the large table.

"How was your journey?" Nola asked as she removed her coat. A warm fire was burning with a single lit candle on the table.

"Disrupted ahead of schedule," Gavin answered. "Jarron Tempest was not given leave to return through Thedford. His second visit to my city was very bold and unwelcomed."

"How did you know that he was here?" Nola looked at Dottie as Gavin draped his coat over the back of a chair. Immediately after, he walked behind her chair for her to sit.

"You have your talents, I have mine." Glancing at Dottie, he gave her a small courteous nod.

"Nola," Dottie folded her hands in front of her and leaned forward. "Lord Graelohr and I should not be the ones to tell you what you are about to hear." The sincerity in her voice was both worrisome and consoling.

"I'm not here to study, am I?"

"Yes, actually you will learn more tonight than you can ever imagine," Gavin answered, taking the seat at the end of the table between them.

"But you will learn it in an unconventional way," Dottie added.

"What does that mean?" Nola stared into her aunt's glimmering eyes.

"Your parents should have come for you years ago. You should have been made ready for the changes taking place in your life. However, Gavin has not been able to find them." Dottie's skin looked slightly pale as she spoke.

"My parents?" She beamed with curiosity.

"You were not unwanted, Nola." Gavin began quietly. "Your parents were unable to raise you for many reasons, but we were hoping they would return before you had to leave the Ellis's home."

"Am I to leave you?" She looked at Dottie.

"Soon, but only you will know when." Her aunt spoke gently. "You have exhibited many of the characteristics that we have been watching for, but there are still many more severe changes yet to come."

"I don't understand." Nola leaned forward. "What changes?"

"Did you read the book I gave you?" Lord Graelohr asked.

"There wasn't time. My French is poor, and Luke read as much as he could..."

"You let Luke read it?" Dottie asked.

"It's alright," Gavin explained. "My main interest was that she was given the information somehow, and I was unavoidably detained." Patting Dottie's hand he spoke very kindly. "I am glad she had help."

"What does the book have to do with me?" The question was directed to Gavin.

"Did you read the passages by Louis Dubois?"

"Not all of them. The last we read, two demons were brought to the monastery and murdered all of the children before they escaped," she answered.

"You were one page shy of the miracle." He smirked strangely.

"Miracle?" Nola was shocked by the term. "What of those horrid creatures was a miracle?"

"Not the creatures, Nola... the children." Gavin held his hand out in expectation of her handing over the book.

"The children?" Nola felt the weight of the thick pages.

Taking the leather-bound book from her hand, Gavin turned to the page just before Luke finished reading.

"Permit me," Gavin whispered. There, he began to read aloud. "Four sons and five daughters have been left to the church." Nola instinctively pushed the candle closer to him, letting more light hit the page. Gavin glanced up with a strange grin before skimming over some less important details. "By name of sons: Fuller, Gwain, Reynard, and Donte. By name of daughters: Colette, Ysabelle, Clarice, Ava, and Cecily." Looking up to Nola, he tapped his finger on the page. "These names must be engraved in your memory. You will need to know them every day for the rest of your existence."

"Why is that?" Nola asked.

"Because..." Gavin sighed heavily and held her stare. "You are a part of their legacy, their bloodline."

"No, it was six hundred years ago, and I am an orphan with no family to speak of."

"That is not true," Dottie argued. Recalling that she was part of Dottie's family, she nodded and waited for Gavin's explanation. "We are your family."

"Try to listen without formed decision." Gavin returned to the book. "Allow me to carry on..." He did not wait for her to agree. "Louis Dubois continues his letter to say, 'Filled with grief and faith, the congregation took up prayer in the abbey for the lives of the doomed children. Father Briar went so far as to perform funeral rights on them all. By some divine act and much to our delight, dear brother, when dawn arose all but two survived the demonic attack. Their pain was immeasurable, but the ritual tests for possession were performed when they regained their strength. Sunlight was welcomed, food was tolerated, and our blessed water ran over their skin without scarring.

Our prayers have been answered, brother. None of the seven children demonstrate any signs of the creature's damnation."

Placing the ribbon between the pages, Gavin closed the book. He waited for the information to seep into her mind. However, Nola looked very unaffected by the information.

"Somehow I am descendant to one of these seven infants?" she asked, still confused.

"They are known as the Seven Keys and yes, you must be of their bloodline. Though I do not know which ancestor is yours," Gavin answered coming to his feet.

"Impossible... How could I ...?"

"I am a descendant of the Seven Keys." Gavin came around the table and took the chair next to her. "We are all intertwined in a

70

very tangled web of senses that allows us to feel a very powerful connection with other descendants." Reaching out to take Nola's hand he moved his finger over her glove. As soon as she felt pressure from his fingers, she was aware of his influence. Then, as he slid his bare hand over her glove, the tip barely touched the skin of her wrist. "I can feel you just as readily as you feel me," he whispered. Nola inhaled at the instant gratification of free-flowing emotion. Bliss, enticement, and peace rushed into her like waves rolling under her skin. It was powerful and addictive, causing her to move her hand closer. "What you are experiencing right now can only be felt by our kind." Removing his touch, he stood up and gave Nola a moment to recover from the instant depression that came from his release. "You have no control over it, but it will become somewhat less distracting with time." Knowing the intense phenomenon, he was impressed, Gavin stood up. When he walked to the other side of the room Dottie reached over the table and tried to take Nola's hands. Without thinking, Nola recoiled from her aunt. She did not know if she wanted to feel it over and over, or never again. "I have been told that others feel these emotions regularly but are still extremely susceptible to our touch."

"What about you?" With his touch released, Nola was able to ignore the confusion. Returning to the information given, she glanced up at her aunt. "Are you part of this line of descendants?"

"Sadly no," Dottie answered. "My family has no blood connection to you. This is the single reason why you have never been able to love us with the same fervor." When Nola shook her head, Dottie continued. "You simply lack ability." Trying to ease Nola's obvious argument of shared love, the old woman quickly whispered, "oh child, you are imbedded in our hearts just as we are in your heart. We simply succumb to our emotions easier than your kind. Gavin is much more experienced, darling. You lack the ability to love those unlike yourself."

"He can?" Nola glanced from one to another, noting the pure adoration they shared. "You have mothered me for nearly thirteen years, yet he clearly displays more emotion than I feel."

"You mustn't blame yourself, Nola. I know you love me!" Dottie was noticeably clear. "Lord Graelohr and I have been close, since long before I met Arthur." She reached out to Nola, once more ignored. "You are simply in limbo right now. Since you were a child, you had to ignore these differences inside of you. You have been raised to conform to our lifestyle, tolerating our mood swings and accepting our ignorance... not only in childhood but womanhood as well. Now, just when you have made peace with yourself you face the most dramatic change of all."

"What change?" Nola held her hands up in exasperation. Glancing at Gavin in the corner of the room, she waited for an answer. "What is becoming so different about me?"

"You are beginning to emanate," Gavin explained. "Excuse me?"

"How do you think Jarron Tempest found you?" Behind Dottie, he held the back of her chair.

"I would not know."

"The same way you feel when I am near," he answered calmly. "He could sense your presence just as strongly as I. It is called ... emanation. It is one of our signature transformations."

"Emanation, signature transformations? You make it sound as if I am not human." Full of fear, she waited for an explanation.

"Humanity is not in question. Though, our adapted bloodline and the changes you will experience make you stronger. Most of these will go unnoticed to all but you," Gavin sighed as he spoke. "However, some traits will resonate without your control." Looking for a way to reach her understanding, he began pacing behind Dottie's chair. Coming closer to the fire, he wiped a bit of condensation off the pitcher on the mantle. "Resistance to cold and lack of emotion are present from birth. However, your emanation is the most expressive trait. There is nothing you can do to stop it, but you can conceal it. Which, may be a good idea from here on out." He spoke very quietly.

"Why would I want to do that?" Nola quickly considered everything she was learning and began to fold the information together. "Is this because of Mr. Tempest?"

"This is complicated, Nola, but yes... you must stay clear of Mr. Tempest." Even though he was stern, he was not forceful.

"You will not tell me why?"

"I can only say that he is not safe just yet." Gavin looked over to Dottie and saw the worry in her eyes.

"Is he a danger to my family?"

"Yes," Gavin answered, keeping a sound stare on her. "Very much."

"No," Dottie argued. "Gavin, do not make her fear for us."

"Alright," he agreed taking the chair at the head of the table once more. "Your family is safe under my protection. You live within my field of emanation, approximately a twenty-mile radius around my permanent home in Thedford City. It is considered my territory, and our kind does not enter another's territory without permission."

Gavin reached out and took Dottie's hand. "Your family is protected. Should Mr. Tempest enter my domain again without his benefactor, I will end his curiosity." Nola looked truly bothered by the statement, but even more so by the way Dottie held his hand.

"End him... why? Why would anyone be a danger to us? You tell me of changes, but nothing has changed." Nola smiled and shook her head. "A man met me on the street, learned where I lived and came to see me. Nothing about this is strange except your reaction to it." Reaching the end of her patience, she placed her hand to her forehead. "Even if I am a descendant of the children in this book, what does it matter? All you are telling me is that I will eventually feel the emotions that have been lost to me since Esteban died."

"Esteban was murdered because of what we are... because of what is in this book." The stone-cold menacing tone of Gavin's voice silenced her immediately. Nola did not expect his reaction, especially since she had not raised her voice. "It is not just your emotions that will be changing, Nola. It is the very essence of your life that will transform." Gavin stood up and walked over to the fireplace. Taking the large water pitcher off the mantel, he doused the flames. "You will become more powerful than the creatures that created our tremendous bloodline." The hiss and crackle of wood surrounded the room. Nola struggled for her eyes to adjust to the sudden darkness, relying on the simple candle. When Gavin turned, his eyes had changed, filled with a silvery glow. "You will be feared." Pinching his fingers over the wick, he extinguished the flame, filling Nola with a panic she had never imagined. With all the appearance of a terrifying animal in the night, he stood inches away from her... silently staring. His eyes were nothing more than mirrors, trapping all sources of light and glowing with their own source.

"What are you?" Nola could feel the intricate carving of the chair digging into her shoulders as she tried to back away.

"You should keep in mind, we are the same, you and I." Gavin whispered.

"Gavin please..." Dottie pleaded, reaching out to him in the darkness. "You're frightening me."

Instantly, the illuminant silver disappeared, and Nola could hear him moving away. The sound of his clothing shuffled for a moment, but she did not dare to move. It was not until she heard the strike of a match that she realized she had stopped breathing.

Lighting the candle once more, Gavin held her stare as his eyes slowly lost nearly all their luminance. Inhaling slowly, he walked away from the fireplace, drawing his hand along Dottie's shoulders as he made his way to the door.

"Beyond being called one of seven keys, we are known as an Absolute." His voice seemed to echo slightly without the fire to light the room. "And you are becoming one of us."

"I beg your pardon?" Nola leaned forward; certain she had heard him wrong.

"Yes, I think this is enough for one night." Dottie pushed her chair back and tried to get to her feet.

"My apologies," Gavin whispered to her, helping her to stand. "I'm just not used to it anymore," Dottie admitted. "It has been years since I've seen your shining eyes. It is unsettling in my old age," the woman admitted. "I need a warning when you are going to do that sort of thing." Gently, she patted his hand.

"I'll keep that in mind." Gavin lightened his tone considerably. "Let me help you to the carriage and let you get safely home." Without looking back at Nola, he lifted Dottie into his arms and carried her out of the room toward the carriage.

It took several seconds before Nola could bring herself to her feet. Her mind tried to rationalize what she had seen. Light and shadow could have been playing tricks. However, she knew in her soul that she had seen something unnatural. Gavin was something more than human and whatever it was, scared the hell out of her.

Throwing her coat over her arms, she left the room in a hurry. By the time she made it outside, Dottie was waiting in the carriage, and Lord Graelohr was nowhere to be seen.

"Come child," Dottie called from inside the velvet cab. "It is late, and I am weary."

Chapter Six

Uncomfortable Knowledge

Davey was stomping around the kitchen, fit to be tied. No matter how many times Dottie sighed, he would continue to lecture, "Well, did you know that she quit her job?" Davey dropped the plucked duck in the sink and turned around to watch Dottie peel the potatoes. His cheeks were rosy, and his hands looked beet-red when he took off his gloves.

"She didn't," Dottie whispered with little surprise.

"Miss Peetz stopped me on my way home, asking if I could talk her into reconsidering. Looks like they don't have anyone with a teaching license this side of the bridge... said they needed her for at least another few weeks if we could persuade her." Crossing one boot over the other and leaning against the counter, he glared at his mother. "She was a handful before, but now this ...Lord Graelohr business

...has turned her into a buffoon." Davey folded his arms over his chest. His hair was dark with grease and ashes, making his blue eyes seem even brighter. "If she isn't going to be teaching, she had better be doing more around the house... like pealing those potatoes!"

"She has much on her mind right now, son. Give her time." Dottie maintained her gentle tone, continuing her task.

Davey stood straight. He squared his shoulders and looked down at his mother, "What the hell is that supposed to mean, anyway? Give her time. Why do women think time is an object we can hand out?" He shook his head and poured water over the duck. Dottie was curious how the subject changed but remained quiet at his ranting. "I have just as much time in my day as you do in yours."

"Davey, I'm not so sure that Nola is why you are so upset." Dottie wondered openly.

"Mum, the girl has got to do something with her life. What will she do when she can't help you anymore? You won't be here forever." He opened the door to the ice box and pulled out the jar of milk. It was the third night in a row that dinner was not ready when he got home, and Davey was losing his patience.

"You are simply hungry," Dottie swayed his attention. "Thank you for stopping at the market. I'll call Nola down and by the time you are all cleaned up dinner will be on the table."

"Not tonight," drinking straight from the jar, he placed it back in the ice box. "I've got plans."

"Before you eat?" She took another potato and cored out one of the brown spots.

"I'll go eat with some friends." His short answer tweaked her curiosity further.

"Isn't it a little early for your boys to be out on the town?"

"I'll be home early." Leaning over and kissing the top of her hair, Davey left the kitchen. Dottie had become used to the smell of his hard work, but it was still hard to tolerate.

"Why don't you show your affection after you've changed your clothes," she whispered sweetly. "I'll be more attentive when you smell better."

"As soon as I'm cleaned up, I have to leave." He stopped short of the door and looked back. "Will you talk to Nola about going back to work?"

"I'm not sure if that is a good idea." Dottie went back to her task. "But I will ask her about it."

***

The crackle of the fire was just as loud as the wind that howled at the windows. Dottie had retired hours ago, Davey came home early and went right to bed, but Nola rejected rest. She wanted every ounce of information she could get out of the leather-bound book, but she was learning nothing with it resting gently on Luke's lap.

He had fallen asleep just a few minutes before reading passage after passage of endless nothing. After Louis Dubois's final entry, a young friar took over the journal, penning the routine details of monastery life. Though, he was under instruction to care for and document the activities of the seven miracle children. The last of what Luke had read was of their duties to the gardens. In the dead center of a sentence, his words slurred, his head leaned back against the chair, and he fell instantly asleep.

Nola had been hounding him every second he was in the house to read to her. They skimmed over everything that was unimportant and only read the passages about the children. Still, the book was thick, the language was ancient, and Luke's new job had him stressed enough. As the fire crackled on, she watched him sleep.

Gently pulling the book out of his grasp, Nola flipped through the pages. All she could understand was that the children were considered healthy. They were well-behaved and revered as the sacred survivors of true evil. Everyone in the monastery cared for them deeply. Luke found nothing in the book that seemed even remotely similar to Nola.

Nola was very private about her strange traits. She had always been clearly unemotional, but what she had learned from Lord Graelohr made her silent. Turning to yet another page of foreign code she sighed heavily, wishing she could wake Luke.

He had asked her at least twenty times about Lord Graelohr. He asked how Dottie was acquainted. He asked why there was a sudden interest, and he asked what they had talked about. At one point he even asked if Nola knew anything about the new electric lighting in Lord Graelohr's mansion. All questions went unanswered, yet he still studied and read with her as often as he could. Nola glanced at the barely noticeable cleft in his chin, his wild thick hair, and kind features. She had always thought he would be married long before Davey. As it turned out, the only woman he ever loved left him broken enough to run away from home for over four years.

"Luke," Nola whispered. "Luke... you've fallen asleep."

"Hmm..." he opened his eyes wide and looked around the room. "Right..." Groaning, he came out of the chair. "Just mark the page and we'll pick up some other time." Waving carelessly toward the book he steadied himself to climb the stairs. "I have to go to bed."

"Good night," she whispered, grabbing the railing, and watching him begin the long journey.

Instantly, Nola realized that the room behind her was completely empty. It was easy to hear Luke at the top of the stairs, walking across the upper floorboards to get to his room, but there was something different about the space around her. The air felt barren, as if a wave had slowly rolled onto the beach and pulled everything back out to sea with it.

Coming to her feet, Nola walked to the front window and peered at the clock tower in the distance. All summer long, the branches and leaves of the trees kept the magnificent monument hidden. Once winter came, there was nothing to block her view. Still, it was too far away to read the hands, tell the time, and barely hear the bells, but it was comforting to see.

The emptiness around Nola slowly brought her mind to Gavin.

The vacant sentiment that fell around her was easily identified. Somehow, Gavin Graelohr had moved far enough away for her not to feel his presence. It was a strange and miserable realization.

Leaving the window, she picked up the book and turned to the front entries by Louis Dubois and the first written account of the demons in the monastery. Using all her concentration, Nola studied the words. One passage that Luke had apparently skimmed over caught her attention. One of the words used was 'Revenant'. The only thing she could think of were stories that Davey would tell around

All-Hollows-Eve. He told tales about how the dead would wear disguises and return to the living for one night. One story mentioned how an undead creature called a Revenant would rise from its grave to feed on the flesh of the living. According to Davey, the creature stalked his family for sixteen years. It was half-decayed, bound to the night, and unable to die until certain rituals were performed.

Nola was never one to believe the tales but reading the book before her and recalling the hallowed glow of Lord Graelohr's eyes gave her much to think about. Still, Davey described the creature as ghoulish and disgusting, while Gavin was nothing less than perfect.

The fire had dimmed, crackling slightly in the night, and darkening the room. On the wall beside the coat hooks, Nola investigated the mirror. She did not want to be something she could not understand. Stepping closer and gazing into her reflection she concentrated on her eyes. Like her hair, her eyes had always been a deep rich brown. Her facial features were highly more symmetrical than most women, leaving her certain that she was attractive. There had never been a lack of smiles toward her, but she considered it more of a nuisance than flattery. Continuing to look in the mirror, she stepped closer. Nola concentrated on her eyes, she wanted to know if there was any possibility that she was indeed like Gavin. Yet, no matter how long she stood there, her eyes did not take on the strange appearance that Gavin's had. Reassuring that she was not a strange creature of ancient bloodline.

With a sigh that mimicked her annoyance, Nola dropped the book on the table. It was simply another night of more questions than answers. The only thing she knew for certain was that her eyes were constantly brown and only reflected slight light from her pupils, quite unlike Gavin Graelohr.

Succumbing to the late hour, Nola checked the gate in front of the fire and climbed the stairs to her room. She would know nothing more before meeting Lord Graelohr at the library the following night and she was very apprehensive about going alone.

Her feet were light, but the floorboards still creaked slightly. At the top of the stairs, she rounded the railing to pass Luke's door, but he was wide awake, leaning against the frame.

"I thought you were sleeping," she whispered.

"I'm getting there," he answered, pushing the thick wool of his sweater up further on his forearms. "Nola... you know I'm leaving tomorrow... right?"

"Yes, of course I do," she spoke quietly, careful not to wake Dottie. "Why do you ask?"

"It just seems like every time I see you, I'm always getting ready to leave again." His shoulders drooped slightly, and he glanced more at her hair than at her eyes.

"You've been gone far more than you've been here."

"Right, but this time I'm not coming back." His voice sounded grave. "This time it's for real."

"You're moving three miles away." She placed her hand on his shoulder.

At that exact moment, she could feel the room lighten, the air cleared, and everything seemed so much more relaxed. She could tell in those few seconds that Gavin had come close enough for her to feel. Welcoming the familiar comfort, she grinned up at Luke.

"Three miles is a long way when I am working all the time," he added. "What if you and Davey keep arguing like you do?"

"We don't argue, and I can walk the distance, if necessary. Aren't you eager for this?" She squeezed his arm lightly and then let go.

"I'm not ready to leave you." The admission was steady and undoubted. Nola could read his expression easily. Luke meant every word.

"It's three miles." Again, she restated the truth.

"You're right," he agreed. Reaching out, Luke pulled her into a tender embrace. "You'll be fine without me."

"I won't be without you. I'll see you more than you think." She squeezed him for a moment and then almost let go. Then, Luke placed his hand on her hair and kissed the top of her head. "Why are you so bothered by this?"

"I'm not bothered," he chuckled. The quick light-hearted tone was one he used often when he lied.

"I know you too well." She shook her head, feeling the scratchy material of the wool in her hands. "Tell me why you are so concerned."

"Can't you tell... even a little?"

"Tell what?"

"Nola," he sighed heavily, lifting her chin even though she was staring right at him. "Ever since my second year at the university, I haven't been coming home to see Mum and Davey."

"Of course, you have." Suddenly, Nola was very aware of her surroundings. There seemed to be a slight sense of urgency building. Luke seemed strained, like trying to break glass in his hands without being cut. However, there was something else. Something more urgent, something directly tied to the yearning look in his eyes.

"No, I haven't." Luke declared carefully. Nola knew she was in an awkward predicament but still wanted to hear every word he had to say. "Do you still see me as your cousin?" Luke pleaded with her. Nola knew he did not want her to answer. "We are in no way related." Her surprised expression should have been enough to stop Luke from any further admission. He appeared so forlorn that she stood silent, unable to find the words that would appease him.

Meanwhile, she noticed his gaze toward her lips.

She had kissed him every holiday since she was twelve, and she had kissed him every time he came and left for school. However, the way he looked at her then was quite different, and she knew his kiss would be different as well. Standing perfectly still, and allowing him liberty, Nola waited for his lips to brush against hers. The closer he came, the more curious she became. Then, just before their lips met, Luke leaned slightly to the side and let his lips fall gently on her cheek. His kiss lasted for only a moment before he backed away.

"Good night," he whispered, placing his hand on the door. "Good night," Nola answered, aware of the odd tension.

On occasion Luke was needlessly distracted by his sentiments. However, this time, Nola was completely aware of how precious the moment between them felt. She wanted nothing more than to make him feel better, to make herself feel less of a loss. She did not want him to close the door and she reached out to stop it.

"Nola?" Dottie called from her bedroom.

"It's me, Aunt Dottie," she whispered stepping away from Luke. "Sorry to wake you. I am just going to bed." Before she could whisper another word, Luke had closed his door.

***

The thin golden veils were before her once more, but this time the room was lit by glorious daylight. Nola turned toward the window and saw how the rays pierced the slight shadows and lit up the tiny flecks of dust in the air. Following the light, she turned her view around the room to face the bed.

There he slept with sheets of white linen covering half his body. Lying on his side, Gavin's dark hair stood in contrast to his pillow. There was no fire in the room, yet he looked as comfortable as if it were late spring. Carefully, Nola drew even closer.

His chest rose and fell but there was not even so much as a twitch in his muscles. The serenity was luring and as a result, she brought herself even closer. The striking masculinity of his face, the fullness of his lips, and the temptation of his bare skin was too much to resist.

There was no feeling in her body at all. In fact, once she was aware that it was a vision, Nola began trying to control it. Focus was difficult. It was not one steady view but a series of views, each from a different proximity. Getting the vision to remain steady took a lot of concentration.

His face moved slightly against the pillow. The surprise almost caused her to lose focus. Then, a sound began to grow. It was like a low growl but more serrated like deep grumbling. Nola steadied her view and searched for the sound's origin. Just as she saw the slight vibration coming from Gavin's neck, his eyes opened.

Baring incredible keen white teeth, he shot up from the pillow toward her view.

Nola shrieked. A thud and searing pain woke her instantly.

Having no idea what had happened, she placed her hand on the top of her head. The pain was minimal, but her vision did not hold the dreamlike haze. Realizing that most would have been in severe pain, she glanced behind her. The fright from her vision was so fierce that she threw her head into the edge of the nightstand as she woke up.

"Nola?" Dottie called. "Are you alright?"

She tried to answer. The warm liquid that spilled between her fingers kept her silent. Nola looked at her bed and saw the trickle of blood beneath her. Again, pain surged through her head to the point that she could not get up.

"Nola, answer me!" Dottie called from the bottom of the stairs. "If you don't answer me this second, I am sending for Davey!"

The warning was real, and Nola tried to call out, but the throbbing pain stopped her from doing anything more than gripping her head and sucking air in between her teeth. Seconds later, Nola heard Dottie open the front door and call one of the neighbors. Soon after that, her crutches could be heard slowly climbing stair after stair. Still, Nola could not rally herself out of the daze.

The blood continued to flow. Nola searched for something to press against her head. She was not afraid until she saw blood running down the length of her forearm. Finally, grabbing a hold of her robe, she applied pressure to the wound. Taking a better look at the end stand, she could see the dark liquid that coated a large portion of the corner.

"Please answer me!" Dottie cried with audible fear, still barely a quarter of the way up the stairs. "Are you alright?"

"I'm not sure," she answered honestly. "My head is cut, but I don't know how bad."

"Just hold still," Dottie called. "I'll be right there!"

Nola heard the crutches hitting the stairs a few times before landing on the floor. At first, she thought maybe her aunt had fallen, but a moment later she could hear the floorboards of the stairs creaking. Finally, with a feeling she could not explain, Nola watched as Dottie crawled into her bedroom on her hands and knee.

"I'm so sorry," Nola whispered seeing the crippled woman's fear and concern.

"Let me see." Dottie spoke as gently as she could, but Nola refused to remove the robe from her head. "Oh Lord," she looked at the amount of blood on the bed and climbed up beside her. "We have to sit you up." Pulling on Nola's arm, the woman braced herself against the headboard for leverage. "You've got to slow the bleeding." It took some maneuvering, but the two of them managed to bring Nola upright. "What happened?"

"I don't know. I must have gotten turned around in my bed." Nola looked at the table once more. "I awoke with a fright and hit the corner."

"It must have been one incredible fright." The edge of the table was covered in so much blood that Dottie was instantly worried. "I need to know how deep this goes." Nola allowed her to remove the cloth for a moment. "Oh dear, how on earth did you manage this?"

"Mum, Nola?" Davey called as soon as the front door opened. "Upstairs!" Dottie called down. "Nola struck her head. We need a large chunk of ice from the icebox and a clean cloth!"

"Do I need to have it stitched?" The apprehension in her voice was unavoidable. "Will you send for a doctor?"

"No," Dottie hushed her softly. "There is no need for that."

"What are these doing down here?" Davey called from the bottom of the stairs. Both were aware that he was talking about the crutches.

"Please, Davey... just leave them and bring the ice."

"Alright..." They could hear him running through the house and then making his way up the stairs. It gave Nola a warm feeling that Dottie crawled up a flight of stairs at nearly sixty years old. It also made her curious as to why Davey would run so fast. She knew the words they would use. 'We are family' But now, it all seemed a little different. They were not family. Yet, Davey ran as fast as if it been Dottie injured.

"The pain is easing." Nola released her hold on the robe as Dottie took over applying pressure. Dottie did not need to know that the pain was almost nothing. "I still can't seem to see straight."

"Well, that's not a surprise. This is an impressive blow from a simple dream. Not an exceptionally good way to wake up, in my opinion." Dottie admitted, noticing the bloodstains.

Nola chose not to discuss the nightmare further. Her reaction was involuntary, but the consequences were obvious. Hearing Davey enter the room; she tried to lift her head to look at him. A quick glimpse was all she could manage before a slight throbbing started.

"Hey," Davey instantly knelt in front of her. "Nola, what happened?" He could see blood splattered all over the sheets, but there was no panic or tears.

"A nightmare caused her to smack her head on the table," Dottie explained.

"Come here," Davey pulled her closer, "I'm going to take a quick look at it, alright?"

"It's still bleeding," she warned him.

"I'm sure I've seen worse," he whispered, careful not to belittle the situation. Standing up, he leaned over her head and lifted the towel slightly. "Well, there is a lot of blood, but no brain." He placed the cloth back over the wound. "So, that isn't damaged."

"This is not a time to be foolish," Dottie warned.

"I'm sorry," he apologized without a grin. "It's pretty deep." He nodded his head. "You should probably see a doctor."

"No," Dottie refused softly. "Let's give it some more time and see if we can get the bleeding to slow."

"This could be serious," Davey quietly argued with his mother.

"You'll scare her," Dottie whispered back.

"I'm not scared." Nola turned just enough to look up at them. "It hurts, but my vision is improving, and it is significantly better."

"Can you stand?" Davey asked. "If you can stand without help, I'll forgo the physician."

"We can't afford one anyway," Nola pointed out.

"I gave my word that I would take care of you. If you cannot stand, then we will have someone look at it." Davey spoke as gently as Dottie and there was no doubt that he was sincere.

"Fine," Nola agreed, holding tight to her head, and coming slowly to her feet. "There," she stated. "It is no more than a simple cut."

"Here," Davey handed her the ice wrapped in cloth. "I'll stay home for a while but if I see one stumble or one mumbled word comes out of your mouth, you are going to hospital."

"I'll be fine," Nola assured him as he stepped back to the door. Suddenly, Dottie was in front of her with a gentle smile.

"You'll be alright," the older lady whispered. "It will heal."

"I'm going to get some towels and water to clean this up." Davey nodded toward the bloody mess before returning to the staircase. "Just stay there."

"Well, now he'll be in a tizzy all day." Dottie huffed. "You shouldn't have called him."

"I didn't know what had happened." Letting Nola return to sit on the bed Dottie gently pressed a clean cloth to the wound. "It will heal," she whispered.

"I know," Nola agreed.

"No," Dottie shook her head and stared deeply into her eyes. "In a day or so you will have no evidence of this."

"It may take a bit longer than that."

"Not for you." Dottie removed the cloth to see that the bleeding had nearly stopped. Nola glanced up at her curiously. "You will heal completely before the week's end, no stitches, no scars." Returning to the stairs, Davey's boots sounded loudly on the steps.

"How is that possible?" Nola whispered.

"Because of how special you are," Dottie hushed her voice. Letting the conversation drop, she welcomed Davey back into the room.

***

Never, at any other time, would she have wanted to go back home. Fear and uncertainty were not emotions that she was used to. However, as Nola looked at the road, she sat uneasy. It was a surprise when Dottie refused to join her at the library that evening. It was even more surprising when she insisted that Nola went despite her injury. Again, she considered having the driver turn around and take her home.

Dottie had placed a bandage over her wound and hidden it with a scarf and a hat, but it wasn't her appearance that bothered her. It was the constant humming in her head and the idea of seeing Gavin. She was frightened the last time she saw him and his strange glowing eyes. The book revealed nothing in her last week of study, and she was not entirely sure the dream that woke her that morning was not a real vision. The very thought of meeting him under the circumstances was almost ...what some would consider ...embarrassing. It simply would have been easier to manage with Dottie by her side.

Nola jolted forward as the carriage came to a halt a few blocks away from the library. She wouldn't have been alarmed if not for the warning tone of the driver. Male voices were heard, but she could not make them out. Unsure how to lower the window, she pulled back the velvet material and glanced out into the night. The humming became much more vivid, but there was little pain from her injury. Despite the oddity, she peered into the night.

"You there, move out of the way!" The driver called loudly. A large carriage, dark polished lacquer with black iron trim, sat just at the corner of Falkenstein Avenue. Nola pressed her head to the window to see what was ahead just as the feeling of being watched fell over her.

"A word with Lord Graelohr, please," an unknown man's voice called up to the driver.

"You are but half a mile from his house. Make your way there." The driver answered coldly.

"Is Lord Graelohr not in the carriage?" The man called again. Strangely, the feeling of being watched began to pass and Nola was able to see the back end of the horse that blocked the path. "It seems he is a hard man to get a hold of." Coming down from the horse, the man stepped closer to the front of the carriage. When the lamp light cast over his face, Nola became concerned. "Would it be possible to speak with the lady then?" Jarron Tempest asked, glancing at Nola. "It will only take a moment."

"Stand away from this carriage," the driver warned. "Good evening, Nola. My apologies for the interruption,"

Jarron began stepping toward the door.

Nola could feel Gavin's approach before she could see him.

From the shadows, she heard a loud thud, like two large boots landing from a fall of good height. Still, she could see nothing. Then, the steady click of wooden heals on cobblestone drew her attention to a nearby alley. Glancing up to the beautiful carriage, she watched as Gavin stepped out of the shadows and into the street.

With a menacing stare and eyes black as night, her benefactor came toward the carriage. Nola's heart nearly stopped at the sight of him. His menacing stare, the calm collected sway of his form as he came near, and the way he focused on Jarron made her fear their confrontation.

"Your allowance in my territory is revoked," Gavin stated as calm as could be. Stepping between the carriage and Mr. Tempest, he glanced back toward Nola for a second. "I have no more leniencies." Gavin waved his attention toward the expensive dark carriage. Nola followed his gaze and caught a glimpse of the passenger inside. In a split second, she caught a pair of slightly reflective eyes. "I will not issue an invitation to Mr. Percy or anyone else for the time being." Maintaining a serious tone, Gavin turned back to Jarron. "You have half an hour to remove your horses before I claim them and anything else you leave behind." Casting another glance at the carriage, Gavin opened the door of his own coach. Nola was very quick to slide out of his way.

"...our apologies for intruding," Jarron smiled brilliantly at Nola, bowing as Gavin entered the coach and closed the door. A whistle called out and the carriage began to roll once again leaving Jarron and the luxurious coach behind.

"Sit back," Gavin whispered as Nola tried to inspect the carriage as they passed. "To the manor, Marcus." Gavin called to the young driver.

"What does he want from me?" she asked, feigning brave. "Curiosity," Gavin answered calmly. "There is no need for concern."

"He just stopped your carriage in the middle of the road. My curiosity is inevitable." Nola turned around but could not see anything on the road behind her. "I thought you were not going to let him come back?"

"I couldn't tell he was here." He situated his jacket, careful not to touch her. "Could you?" The question was gentle.

"No," she whispered.

"Mr. Percy was in the carriage." Gavin looked out the window as they turned on to Halweg Boulevard. "His emanation suppressed any sense of Mr. Tempest."

"Who is Mr. Percy?" Nola watched out the window as they drove right by the library. "Where are we going?"

"Well, with Mr. Percy so adamant on meeting you, we had best prepare you for the occasion." Just then the carriage stopped as the gates to Graelohr mansion were opened. "Our kind is exceedingly rare. It will not be long before he returns to meet the new peer for the party. However, I will not explain anything about him until you are ready to make his acquaintance. For the rest of the night, I want you to focus on learning the brunt of what I can teach you."

After weeks of waiting, sitting on the bench across the street attempting any kind of vision, Nola was looking out the carriage window beside Graelohr mansion. Three stories tall, the gray stone building stood immaculate against the newly fallen snow. Perfectly trimmed shrubs grew upwards along the walls, lining the windows and decorating the crystal landscape. Once inside, the large iron gates swung shut and were locked with a loud click.

"My aunt will not approve of this." Realizing how many rules of etiquette were being broken, Nola turned to Gavin.

"The present circumstances call for it." The door was opened as the carriage rounded the driveway and came to rest at the front door. "Please," he held out his hand. "I will see you home as soon as it is safe."

Not even Davey could have stopped her from going inside the magnificent building. Just a glimpse would have been worth a month's worth of lectures. Accepting his hand, Nola gathered her mauve skirts to climb out of the carriage. As she placed her boots in the snow, Gavin waved two men from the side of the house forward. As soon as they were close, he leaned into one man's ear and whispered something before turning to Nola.

"I believe I left my hat," Gavin motioned past Nola into the carriage.

"I can get that for you," she offered, leaning back to retrieve the black pin striped bowler from the cab.

Turning back to him in less than a moment, Nola realized both men had gone like a blur from her vision. Out of the corner of her eye she caught movement by the black gate. With barely enough time to turn her head, Nola watched both men jump at the stone columns beside the gate and scale the sheer fifteen-foot-high walls with only their hands and feet. With more stealth than a cat and nimble as a shadow, they jumped extreme heights and clawed their way up, only to leap from view.

"Thank you," taking his hat, Gavin spoke loudly, unable to pull her attention away from the men that bolted off the sidewalk and dipped into the woods at a speed too fast to see. "Would you like to come inside?"

"I don't think so." Nola had not pulled her attention away from the woods. Whatever she had witnessed was just as impossible as what Gavin could do with his eyes. "Maybe we would be better going to the library."

"They will be sure Mr. Tempest follows my instruction in a timely manner." Gavin reached out and took Nola's gloved hand. She was frozen and wide eyed at what she had just witnessed. "Would you like me to send for your aunt?"

"How did they do that?" Her gaze would not change.

"That is enough for now, Marcus," Gavin called up to the driver. Nola watched as the carriage driver tipped his hat. With a couple clicks from his cheek, the carriage pressed on toward the back of the house. "Come inside, Nola." Gavin pleaded soothingly. "You are perfectly safe here. Gents, would you return to the Capstan District and invite Mrs. Ellis to join us."

"Please don't," Nola whispered. "It is late and cold. It would not be good for her to come out in this weather. She will have to understand." Afraid of what she just saw, Nola was not about to bring Dottie anywhere near the mansion.

"Good," Gavin pulled her hand and led the way to the large front door. "Did you bring the book?"

"Yes," she answered as Gavin opened the arched door and entered a small foyer. "How did those men move that fast?" she asked again.

"I have given you everything you need to find that out for yourself. Maybe it is just time to be blunt." Gavin closed the door behind her.

Nola had a complete vision of how vast Gavin's wealth was.

The stone beneath her feet was white with thin gray lines in the marble. The walls were enormous in height, lifting to a light gray ceiling. A golden chandelier the size of a wagon wheel lit the room directly above with an array of strange glowing glass. In the center below it, a round table with a mass of exotic flowers filled the room. The foyer itself was larger than their parlor at home. Gavin walked on ahead, pulling his jacket off his arms nearing a table. However, Nola only stared at the strangely lit ceiling.

"It's an enigma to the people around here." He explained, watching her gaze at the light. "It is created by a heated current that flows through a small filament inside. It is popular in Central America, and I indulged myself having it incorporated throughout my home. A building out back houses the power. I prefer lamplight but appreciate having the technology." Finishing the explanation, Gavin turned back. "Come on," he called. "There is much to go over." Nola stood still with her hand on the door.

"I want to know how those men jumped over that wall." Nola spoke with determination and no fear. Her stubbornness was irritatingly understandable. Even though Gavin was annoyed with Mr. Percy and furious with Mr. Tempest, he understood Nola's defiance.

"If I tell you while you are standing at that door, you will run." Pulling his sleeves back up over his thick arms he returned to stand before her.

"Then I certainly don't want to be taken through a maze of hallways before given the answer, now do I?" Her hand gripped the handle as she waited for an answer.

"The word you know is Vampyre, two syllables, no harsh vowels," he whispered. "There are at least two more on the property and their hearing is excellent. So, keep all insults to a minimum and pronounce the word right if you are going to say it at all." His dark eyes seemed harsh as he towered over her during the lecture. "They kill and feed when necessary, and that little hop over the wall was not even a parlor trick compared to their capabilities." The depth of his voice seemed to increase as he spoke. Looking at the hand that gripped the door handle, he nodded. "Go ahead, run if you want. "None of them will harm you."

"Is that what you are?" Afraid of the night for the first time ever, Nola let go of the door. Gavin stood looming over her. His enormous stature felt comparable to an iron clad ship. Finally, when she reached for the door again, he turned and walked to the hallway that extended to the left.

"If you want to know... follow me," he stated. Less than five steps into the hallway the light from the chandelier began to fade.

Gavin walked on in the shadows, but Nola's steps were slow and unsteady in the dark. Just before the light faded completely, a room along the center of the hallway lit up with lamplight. "This way."

With a quicker pace, Nola ignored the extravagance of the carpeted hall and hurried to the dimly lit room. Inside the long narrow chamber, she could barely take in the grandeur. The powder blue walls and white ceiling went unnoticed as well as the gold stenciling on the columns and fireplace. The room could not gain her attention as Gavin untied his neck scarf and threw both the silk and the jacket over a wing-backed chair.

"I am not sociable just now. If you were anyone else, I would send you home." Unbuttoning the base of his collar, Gavin walked to a small rectangular table at the end of the room. "Since you are the purpose for Mr. Percy's unyielding curiosity, I suppose it would be best to tell you exactly why."

"Well then...," She stood by the chair nearest the wall to have a clear view of both the door and the windows. "...tell me."

"Vampyres are powerful. Mr. Tempest is the only one that you have made acquaintance with. That is why you were curious about him in the alley the night you met." Sitting down, he left his chair pushed out slightly as he waited for Nola to make herself comfortable across from him. "The book please?" He asked when she had finally sat down. "There are only eleven copies left in existence."

"Mr. Tempest is a...?" The book became slightly heavier after hearing its importance. Withdrawing it from her satchel, Nola slid it over the small gaming table toward him.

"Yes." Taking the book, he slid it aside.

"You called yourself an Absolute," Nola clarified, removing her hat and setting it beside her. "Are you like them?" Placing her hands on the table, she forced herself to stay calm.

"I can't answer that with one word." Gavin flipped up the cover on the book and let it fall.

"Then answer it the best way you can." Removing her hat, Nola checked to be sure that her silk scarf was in place covering her wound. The lamp illuminated the table and the chairs, but the room around them seemed dimmer as Gavin concentrated on the answer.

"Everything that separates you from average humans at this precise moment makes you an Absolute. Those exact same qualities also separate us from Vampyres." His words confused her for several moments until she broke down his meaning.

"My ability to know how far away you are separates me from humans," Nola answered.

"Alright, that is a bad example," Gavin admitted with a heavy sight. "Mr. Tempest can find you by using the same sense, but ours is extremely more precise." He held his fingertips together. "Seeing through my eyes and your visions are what I am talking about," he explained, "and... your ability to extend and receive emotion with me. Vampyres do not have the capability."

"I can barely feel emotion," she argued.

"You are infinitely wrong, but we will get to that another time." Gavin leaned against the back of the chair and stared at the lantern on the table. "Unlike Vampyres, we are born human. When our bodies mature to their physical peak we begin to reform." Gavin's voice became a deep lull. "Our talents... traits... come first, followed by a stronger perception of our senses. Soon, speed and

strength increase. Finally, our tolerance for human food dies."
Stunned into silence, Nola began to stare at the flame. Taking
advantage of her stillness, Gavin continued. "Vampyres are not as
fortunate as we are. They are not gradually changed from one form
to another. Theirs is harshly instantaneous and most never acquire
the abilities we are born with."

"Stop using the word *we*," Nola insisted. "I am not what you
say."

Gavin sighed heavily and ran his hand through his hair. He
could see the blood had drained from her face and her hands had
begun to shake slightly. He considered stopping, but there were
more pertinent details that had to be spoken. Sitting up slowly, he
reached for the lamp and turned up the flame.

"Humans vastly outnumber Vampyres. In a city like
Thedford, there are only between five and seven at a time. All of
which inhabit this home." He looked at the room around him. "Easy,
Nola," he whispered, completely sensing significant and instant fear.
"You and everyone you know are safe and always will be safe." He
expressed the words slowly with sincerity. "I am simply trying to
convey how rare you are." When her hands relaxed slightly, he sat
back again and continued. "Where there is one Vampyre for every
thousand humans, Vampyres outnumber us one hundred to one."
Even though Nola was practically in shock, he added the final detail.
"Of all Absolutes... females are the rarest." Nola's eyes shot up
quickly, realizing that the last fact was stated for good reason. "Most
don't survive ten years after they mature."

"Why?" It took every ounce of control she had to ask the
simple question.

"Childbirth," he stated gravely. "What is difficult for a human
is nearly impossible for our kind because of our body's ability to heal
itself." Sensing that she was reaching the end of her tolerance, Gavin
chose that moment to try and console her. "The wound on your
head... had I known it was you in my bedroom, I would not have
reacted the way I did." Slowly, her eyes shifted from the light to him.
Keeping his voice calm, he slowly stood up. "I felt someone watching
me, but with Elias Percy so close I assumed it was his meddling, not
your curiosity." He knew Nola was scared. Her arms were tense, and
her eyes were wide and glossy. Rounding the chair, Gavin placed a
hand on her shoulder. Less than a second later, Nola began to relax.
"Because Dottie and I are connected, I could feel her concern
enlightening me that it was you. Did she tell you that it will heal
completely in a day or two?"

"Yes," Nola answered. "Does my aunt know all of this?"

"And more," he admitted. "She was sworn not to tell you." The pressure of his hand increased for a moment. "Had she, I would have taken you away and had you raised by another family."

"Why would you do such a thing?"

"If you learned about this ten years ago, you would have run. I may not have been able to find you." Suddenly her frustration, fear, and anxiety began to wash away. It was drawn from her body by the touch of his hand. "It is cruel and unforgiving for an Absolute to go through these changes alone. That is why I have watched over you."

Free of the mind-numbing confusion, Nola breathed deeply as the thoughts slowed the whirlwind in her head. Suddenly, she realized that his touch had stabilized her fear. An unimaginable number of questions ransacked her mind, but she was able to sort them out carefully while he remained in contact. All at once, she realized the most agonizing truth. Turning gently, she leaned back to see his face.

"I don't want this," she whispered. "I don't want this knowledge."

"Neither did I." Gavin gave a half-smile. "But you have to have it to survive, Nola." He kept his gentle expression. "You have to know how dangerous you will become to people like Dottie, Davey, and Luke."

"Dangerous ... how?" she asked as he released her shoulder and walked back around to face her. Instantly, the feeling of worry and fear crept into her mind once more. The panic was intense enough to bring her to her feet. Still a good foot shorter than Gavin, she watched him cautiously.

"Inadvertently," he whispered, looking down at her sleeves. "You wouldn't mean to hurt them, but it is easy to break a bone when you do not know your own strength." Gently, her ebony hair fell over her shoulder, framing her high cheekbones as she swallowed hard.

"You have to know that I cannot believe you," she whispered. "I know I am different. I know there is something strange here... but it cannot be what you say." Desperate to escape the endless feeling of despair, she stepped in front of him and sought out his entrancing eyes. "Tell me this is a mistake. Tell me those men I saw weren't real, and that you are simply eccentric nobility teasing me for entertainment."

"Would I do that?" The depth of his dark blue eyes made them look brown.

"I hope so," she answered, tilting her head gently.

Gavin shook his head. A few perfect onyx waves moved in the process. "It is not in us to lie, Nola."

"Can you understand how fantastical this all sounds?" she asked carefully.

"Yes, and you now know that this connection," he reached out once more and touched her sleeve, "can make it much less painful." Directly from the base of his hand, the calming wave washed over her again. "I must warn you that there are consequences." Gavin trailed his index finger up the sleeve of her gown filling her with a gentle relief. "If I touch your skin... the sentiment can be different." His touch drew away from the lace cuff of her sleeve. "If I am not guarded, you will feel the same ...sentiment... you felt in the alley first meeting Mr. Tempest. Fortunately, clothing dulls the link."

Instead of answering, Nola nodded her head. She could not think of anything else other than how quickly he could soothe her rapid thoughts and constant concerns. The sense of peace was addicting, along with the underlying feeling of belonging.

"Esteban," Nola whispered, still comforted by Gavin's touch of her wrist. "He would wrap his arms around my shoulders as I carried him. It felt as if we were one person." She tilted her head, letting her hair slide lower on her arm. "It was stronger than this, more loving and complete."

"The bond between siblings is powerful." Gavin admitted. "Dottie had two loving children when she had you both." Careful to only touch the lock of hair, he brushed it back over her shoulder. "When he was gone, you were nothing more than a shell of girl." With a heavy sigh, he leaned closer to look in her eyes. "As an Absolute, you will feel a similar bond between any of our kind, even Vampyres."

"Vampyres? I doubt that." She argued quickly.

"Do you?" he asked, glancing down at the way she eagerly held her arm out to his touch. She began to pull away, and he grasped her wrist gently. "This is the single most cherished ability of our kind.

This connection..." Releasing her wrist he trailed his hand up her arm. "Without it, we are desolate." The feeling of comfort and familiarity rose in Nola's chest.

Until he spoke the words, she had never seen her life as desolate. However, standing in complete awareness of his presence and filled with new and raw emotion, she realized how true it was. Her life had been empty, haunted only by the memory of how much she had loved Esteban.

"I thought my brother took most of my heart with him when he was killed," she whispered. "I felt ...broken."

"No, have you noticed how much you have changed in the last weeks?" he asked, letting go of her arm. "There is much more to life for you. You just needed to know that you weren't alone." The release of his touch caused Nola to desire his nearness like never before.

Without fear of rejection, Nola walked straight up to Gavin and placed her forehead against his chest. At once, she felt the warm touch of his clothing and the intense comfort that came when his arms surrounded her. Even though she was completely wrapped in his embrace, Gavin kept his head raised high and his hands firmly on her back, careful not to touch her skin.

The worries of her family dissipated and the questions about her future faded away. Nola's only concern was how long she could hold on to him. As she raised her hands to hold against his sides, Gavin began to pull way.

"Alright," he stated, stepping away completely. "You should go." The instantaneous feeling of loss was almost unbearable for her. "You've learned enough for tonight." Somehow, Gavin's eyes had begun to change slightly, but not the frightening severity she had witnessed with Dottie. Gavin made a low growling sound as he moved back.

"What...?" Nola reached out and took his bare hand. "Wait...!"

It was a mistake, and Nola knew it immediately. The desire was instantaneous, visible in his eyes and the touch thrilled her. While their connection allowed her to sort through chaos and fear, Gavin had been fighting the raw sensual power she unknowingly evoked.

Overcome by the same desire he had silently resisted. Nola closed her eyes and lifted her head. A sound escaped Gavin's chest, much like the one she had heard him make in her vision.

Even though the growling continued, she wasn't afraid. His eyes were entrancing. His sheer mass was incredible. Nola wanted his touch, his kiss, his dominance. Gavin let his hand trail up her arm, over her face, and gently across the base of her neck. Nola's exhilaration was unbearable. With his fingers on the flesh of her neck she knew exactly what he wanted. She could feel his struggle between choosing to let her go and acting on her growing curiosity. Inhaling the scent of her hair, he bent down to her height. The nearness was too much for Nola. Desperately, she sought out his lips. Eager to please, Gavin kissed her with a controlled strength that only fueled her desire.

Complete clarity surrounded her. Nola could hear her own heartbeat, feel the blood rush through her veins, and sense the urgency between them. Brazenly, she accepted his kiss, reaching out for it time and time again. Nola's mind whirled at the sensation that coursed through her body. Every touch was felt as deep as her soul and each kiss brought a fallout of new knowledge and desire. The flame in the lantern fluttered gently across the table. Strangely, before he made any attempt to pull away, she could sense his withdrawal.

"You are years too young for this," he whispered as she stole another kiss. Every ounce of pressure was weighed carefully. There was something more than emotion and physical desire. Nola could sense what Gavin wanted. There was a purpose to her safety. His lips were hindered by her frailty and every time he touched her, he pulled back a little more. In the end, Gavin succumbed to his better judgment and backed away.

At that precise moment, before he released her completely, the sensation Nola acquired from Gavin began to clarify. A new knowledge formed between them. Much like the sense that told her Gavin was different from anyone else and how far away he was, Nola became aware of a factor hidden within Gavin's tender embrace.

Unsaid, yet crystal clear, Nola could feel his bold and degrading intention... his single desire to breed their bloodline.

Suddenly, Nola was just as aware of an oncoming intruder as Gavin. Separated by more than ten feet in a fraction of a second, Gavin turned toward the door and awaited the visitor. Nola, however, was still weak from their encounter.

"Come in," Gavin instructed.

"Excuse me, Lord Graelohr." One of the men from outside peered around the large door. "Everything is taken care of."

"Good," he answered softly. "Would you please escort Miss Valerian back home? We are finished for the evening."

"Of course," the man answered.

"Good night, Nola." Gavin's gentle expression barely revealed a smile. "I will continue to keep watch over you."

Silently, she picked up her hat and fastened it above her scarf.

The moments encounter would not leave her mind. The thought of being wanted for her ability to bear children left a sickening feeling in the pit of her stomach, even after how much she had just desired him.

Nola wondered if Dottie had known what Gavin seemed to expect from his young ward. The feeling of betrayal was seeded and grew steadily every moment. If their union were Gavin's eventual plan, it could have been set from the first moment Arthur came to see her and Esteban at the orphanage. It was quite possible that she had been secured with Dottie to be nothing more than a vessel for Gavin's children.

Chapter Seven

Run

Dottie had not yet ceased snoring as the front door closed behind Davey. Nola looked out at the morning sunrise and felt the intense exhaustion she felt each day in the early hours. It was not yet six in the morning, but most of the men from the Capstan District were either already gone or leaving their houses. Nola had been waiting for Davey to leave for what felt like hours. With no sleep she made her plans carefully. From what she learned the night before it was likely that Gavin would rest in the early hours of the morning, same as they weakened her.

Once Davey was no longer in sight, Nola picked up her small canvas bag and left her bedroom. Without a sound, her pace spanned over every floorboard that would creak or moan. She did not glance toward Dottie's room. She barely paused as she walked past the door where Luke once slept. Where most would have felt a complexity of emotions Nola only felt one, sadness.

Dottie Ellis had been serious at teaching Nola how other people behaved. Nola knew every emotion. Dottie would explain every teary eye at a funeral. She would point out moments that people would find irritating. Just as she explained that Nola was simply one of the special women. Out in the world there were special women who did not bow-down to such simple sentiments. Most of the special women were nuns.

Assuring Nola that convent life was not an option, Dottie taught her every quirky grin or ignorant eyebrow raise. Surprisingly, there was distress at leaving the home. Nola looked up at their doors once more and sighed. Sadness was there, but it was nothing like the simple aura of Gavin.

The stairs were easy to descend quietly. She knew where every creaky board was and how to avoid each one. Once she reached the parlor there was nothing to fear. The door was not nearly loud enough to wake her aunt and the falling temperatures would not affect her. Pulling on her boots and securing her hand muff around her collar, she left the house without bold determination.

The clock tower on Darlington Avenue rang out, signaling the last of the quiet hours before the shops would open, and the city became alive. With quick steps, she made her way to the road where all footprints blended into the new fallen snow.

Her dark tresses blew against her face with the wind. It was harsh, but not enough to deter her. Nola hastened her way to the busy streets of Thedford, thankful when the clock tower rose high above her. She needed to get out of the city before Dottie realized she was gone, or Gavin felt her distance.

There were only two directions to go. The river bent around the city, leaving her only three paths. Unfortunately, Jarron Tempest and Mr. Percy always seemed to head toward Clariotte. Going east she could follow the train tracks to Hambright, a city comparable in size to Thedford, or south to villages too small to mention. Hambright would have been the best option. Even if Gavin sought her out there would be plenty of places to hide, until she had a better plan.

Regrettably, the three-day walk-in snow would make her as easy to follow as a blood trail. Turning on her heels, Nola left Darlington Avenue and hurried south. With any luck, she could find a ride with any wagon headed out of the city.

***

Smack! The slap hit hard, and Gavin allowed his head to turn, out of respect.

"What did you do to her?" Dottie yelled! The red mark was becoming vibrant. Gavin felt his eyes darken but had no urge to retaliate. "Nola was injured when she came to see you last night. She practically begged me to come with her! She wanted to stay home.

Yet, I insisted she continued her lessons with you!" The elderly woman's voice carried through the mansion. Each pop of a crutch moved forward no matter how often he backed away. "Tell me what happened!"

Even with his pupils dilated and his eyes narrowed, Dottie Ellis never feared Gavin's animalistic nature. The trait had always impressed him. Gavin controlled the grumbling warning in his chest keeping it to a barely audible tone. Seeing Dottie's fury rage in such a weak frail body, he continued to step back.

"I will send men to both Hambright and Clariotte. We will find her." Finally, Gavin stopped backing away as Dottie held a thin dark spotted finger in his chest. Though he stood twice as tall, Gavin bowed to the old woman's will. "She will be alright," he tried to ease her mind.

"She obviously doesn't want to be found!" Dottie had not yet controlled her temper. "She left specifically when Davey nor I would have known. Whatever caused this, happened when she was with you last night. Now, what did you say to her?"

"She was confronted last night by Mr. Tempest. I thought it best to tell her everything for her own safety." Gavin answered only because of the tears that Dottie held back.

"And…" Dottie implored for the information.

"There was a complication… an unexpected moment… between us." Instantly, Dottie stepped back and stared at him wide-eyed. "She may have sensed something that I was trying to keep from her, but I cannot say for sure." Noticing the regression of Dottie's anger, he reached out to touch her hand. "Stay here. I will send word to Davey to come and get you. My men and I will start searching as soon as the sun sets." Before he could walk away Dottie grabbed the extravagant vase off the table in the foyer and smashed it onto the floor. Shattering into a thousand pieces the crash of the vase echoed through the enormous room.

"Davey is already out there as well as Luke! You will go now, Gavin!" She was beyond irate. "Your men cannot leave until dark, but you have no excuse!" Every heavy breath she took made her shoulders rise and fall. "You asked me to love her like my own and I do! You asked me to guard her with my life and I have! Now, get out there and find my daughter!"

"It is the end of my month, Dorothy. I am weak."

Dottie reached for another vase of flowers but did not pick them up. "Do not dare make excuses when you can take action!" Her hallowed eyes reflected their pain. "I want her found now!"

"You know what you are asking," Gavin whispered. "I can be twice as fast in daylight if I have sustenance." Softly, he tried to reason with her.

"Do you think your kind are the only evil in this world?" Dottie glared at him and raised her voice until it shook with fear and sadness. "Nola is young, she is beautiful, and she is frail." The words seethed between her teeth. "She could be twenty miles away by nightfall. You are the only person that can find her quickly."

"I need to rest and gain my strength." His rebuttal was quiet.

"Rest?" Her grave tone was as warning as could be. "I tell you this now, Gavin Graelohr." With a stern countenance, Dottie descended on him. Like a warrior in battle, she stood tall and spoke with the voice of a general. "If you do not find that child and bring her home, I will renounce any love I have ever felt for you and relinquish you from my home."

Feeling the passion in her threat, Gavin glanced down to the face he adored and the life that he had crippled. She had been his companion and advisor for over three decades, and her words weighed as heavy as stone.

"You would deny me what it takes to be strong enough to walk in daylight?"

"You have denied me much more." Dottie held back her single tear and held her chin high enough to face his extreme height. There was no mention of her deceased husband or her loss of limb. She knew there was no need for specifics. "Find her." Gavin looked out the window as the sun reached its highest point in the sky. "For whatever love once had, you will find her."

"I'll send for my horse," he answered.

***

After an hour of walking and a generous ride from a passing wagon, Nola could no longer feel Gavin's presence. It was both lonely and relieving. The watchful eye of her guardian was gone, but she no longer felt safe. Without her family and with little money she was left with limited decisions. Nightfall was fast approaching. She had seen how fast Vampyres could travel and if Gavin had sent them out after her there was not enough time to stop for the night.

The day was treacherous for the old man that drove her into town. The wind beat against his face forming ice in his beard and turning much of his exposed skin bright red. Fortunately, keeping her hood up and face down hid Nola's resilience to the unwavering cold.

The small village of Lockton had two things Nola had been searching for, food and a stagecoach. Thanking the old man kindly, Nola helped him unload his goods at the local market before making her way to the coach station. Luck was on her side as she bought a ticket for the last stage out. However, it tormented her to have to sit inside the station and wait for it to arrive.

Leaving the hood to her dark green cloak over her head, Nola walked to the bench across from the windows. The road outside was a mess of muddy tracks and the snow had begun to let up. Watching the road diligently, she waited for the lanterns of the stage to come into view.

"You may want to consider waiting until the morning," the ticket man stated from behind his booth. "We don't usually have a lot of Ladies traveling alone this late around here."

"I will be fine," she added keeping her head down. "Your concern is appreciated."

"You'll have Mr. Clement for a driver. He's a bit of a talker but has a good eye for the road. You should be in Shepton before morning. Do you have a plan after that?" Nola lifted her head with curiosity. The way he asked the question made her wonder if there was a reason for it. "They don't run their stage on a Sunday."

"That is fine," she whispered. "Thank you for your concern." Returning her attention to the window, she ignored his obvious pause for her to engage in conversation.

"Not much for talking?" he asked after a few silent moments. Refusing to answer, she continued to stare out the window.

The idea of being stranded in a strange town for a day did not bother her too much. It was the night hours that scared her. Thankfully, she would be on a coach for most of the evening, far out of Gavin's emanation. Though she had learned exactly what he had been preparing her for, he was not her greatest fear. The Vampyres that scurried across a vast field, scaled incredible stone walls, and disappeared into the shadows were the source of terror.

Just the knowledge that creatures like Vampyres existed sent a chill up her spine. Though she tried to ignore them at the mansion, she did know that they were hardly different from any human in physical features, despite their perfect symmetry and pleasing features. She had not seen the legendary fangs or hallowed eyes and pale-thin skin that she would have expected. The two men she briefly saw looked as normal as Jarron Tempest. Fortunately, her encounters with him did teach her that she could sense a difference between Vampyres and humans, even if it was slight and eerie. With any luck, that difference would keep her away from them.

Removing a small envelope from her pocket, Nola read the address once again, wondering if it was the right time to mail the letter to Luke. She knew he would worry. She knew he would be out looking for her, trying to ease Dottie's grief. Still, she was not far enough away. Replacing it in her pocket she stared out the window once more, hoping she could find some way to see him again. Finally in the distance, the lanterns of the stagecoach came into view.

**

"You can't expect Luke to go out of the city right now. He just started his job. One mess up this early and Luke's sure to lose that nice apartment he just moved into." Davey pulled a couple of shirts out of his drawer and tossed them into his travel bag. "I was all over Thedford yesterday. She isn't here."

"I know she is not here. This is why I need your brother to go to the villages while you're in Hambright," Dottie argued. "His employer is sure to understand!"

101

"No, Mum. He is not. Luke has already talked to him. There must be a crisis at the museum because it sounds like the whole thing will fall down if Luke isn't filing papers." Tossing a pair of pants into the case he faced his mother. "You've got Lord Graelohr and his men looking all over for her." He sighed heavily. "We will find her."

"I may be old. I may be slow, but I am still sharp in my wits, Davey. That girl hasn't been in the city for at least twenty-four hours."

"That's why I'm going to Hambright."

"Why won't you listen to me?" Dottie placed a gentle hand on Davey's thick forearm. "She's not in any city."

"Then where is she?" Davey slammed the lid of his trunk closed.

"Somewhere there are not a lot of people. Think about it!" She let go of his arm and tried to persuade him. "Nola goes to great lengths to avoid crowds. Why would she trade one city for another?"

"Graelohr has already searched the villages. If she were there, he would have found her." Clutching the handle, Davey belted the bag closed. "I'll send a letter if it takes me more than a few days. Luke is going to come and stay with you after work."

"I don't need a nursemaid," she scoffed. "He can do better by finding Nola!"

"Try to sleep in the parlor as much as possible for now. Stay off the steps," he whispered. "I'll have Mrs. Laghterly come and check up on you now and again."

"Just go," she grumbled. "Just go and bring her home."

***

There was someone near, close but still invisible. Nola barely opened her eyes to see the room lit by multicolored glass. The stained windows let in plenty of sunlight and a few candles at the altar had been lit, but there was no one else in the church. Still, she felt as if she were being stared at. The church had been a terrible place to rest, but a good place to hide.

Uncertainty began to build as the sleep wore off. She had no idea what time it was or how long she had been there, but Nola felt certain that she was seen. Grabbing her satchel from the pew, she came to her feet and looked around. Still, there was no one in the room.

"Nola..." a strange voice called on the breeze.

Ragged and shallow, her breathing slowed considerably. Her name was called, but in such a way that she could not be sure she heard it with her ears or with her mind. Nola looked at every crevasse of the tiny church to no avail. She was alone and apparently going mad from lack of sleep.

Pulling the strap of her bag over her head, Nola hooked it over her shoulder and took one last look around the church. Her mind was set to keep moving, traveling by night and sleeping in the day despite the increasingly bad weather. There were no other options. When Gavin's kiss began to melt her very soul, she knew without a doubt, he planned for her to have his children. She could feel it. Everything from the strength of his concern for her to his better judgment about her age had such emotional power she could almost see his desire.

Nola shook the thought from her head. She was not a cow. It was not the middle-ages and there was no way in hell she would become a simple breeding possession.

She did not have a destination or a plan. Having been, quite literally, in Gavin's shadow for ten years she had to get away. There had been so many changes, so much information and nothing she could do about any of it. Her only choice was to run until something made sense.

Her thoughts distracted her from the deep bass hum around her. The thin rug beneath her feet cushioned her steps and kept them silent, but she still heard the shuffling of her shoes over the buzzing that seemed to be growing louder with every moment. It wasn't until she pulled the door of the church open and saw the exquisite dark wood carriage sitting in the snow that she fully took note of the overbearing sound.

"Don't be frightened." A male voice, identical to the one that called her name inside the church, stopped her dead in her tracks. "I wouldn't dream of causing you any harm." Nola turned around instantly to see a man leaning up against the building. He was as breathtaking as Gavin, tall, strong, and striking. Nola looked back at the carriage to be sure that she recognized it from the alley, but it was the sensation of familiarity that sealed her impression.

"You must be Mr. Percy," she whispered clutching her bag and stepping away.

"I'm not chasing you." Pushing off away from the building, he checked the timepiece in his hand. "I have a meeting with a local lawyer in a few minutes." He looked at her from head to toe and back again. "This meeting is purely coincidental." His slight smirk eased her tension. "It's alright. You can relax if you want to. Gavin is at least twenty miles away and I have only a moment before prior engagements."

"What do you want?" Nola was very blunt with her words. His honey brown eyes drew her attention slightly more than his perfectly playful smile. Still, she was very wary of him.

"I simply wanted to meet you." He came closer to her and bent forward with a gentle laugh. Without a doubt, Nola was able to tell that Elias was more like Gavin than anyone else she had ever met. He was an Absolute. With that knowledge, she knew immediately that he would not harm her.

It was like staring at a painting. Elias was enormous, much like Gavin. He stood well over six feet tall and had the build of a Greek god. His eyes were amber, darker than her own, but entrancing none the less. His neck was thick and topped off by a face any women would swoon over. He seemed younger than Gavin, and a quite a bit cocky in comparison. It was not surprising Mr. Percy would employ someone like Mr. Tempest. Their personalities were noticeably confident.

"My name is Elias. I've waited a long time to meet another member of our gifted society." He held out his hand. When Nola didn't offer hers, he withdrew and stood up. "Are you always this serious?" His smile showed perfect teeth and added a playful change to his appearance.

"More-so as of late, I find," she answered honestly.

"I see," he whispered noting her dirty clothes and tired features. "Well, Miss Valerian," he stood still, staring at her silently for a few odd moments. Nola thought about asking him to continue, but his awkward silence was too distracting. "I don't even know what to say," he huffed out in a slight chuckle. "I always figured I would see you at Graelohr's with conversation prepared... and Gavin to annoy, but this is not the case." Looking at his pocket watch again, he sighed at the time. "And I really must be going."

Confused, Nola watched him walk to his carriage. His slate gray suit accentuated his incredible height as he glanced back over his shoulder. His ability to seem overconfident and insecure at the same time was bizarre to say the least. Still, she was surprised when he turned back with a card between his fingers.

"I am only about four miles out of town, should you need a place to rest." Nola made no move to take the card, and eventually Elias stepped forward and tucked it into her satchel. The humming became loud enough to feel the ground vibrate slightly beneath her boots. "My staff will welcome you, though you will not have much company until sunset... should you stay that long. Your safety would be my only intention. It is not in us to lie." Turning back to the carriage, he opened the door. The words she had often heard Gavin repeat held her attention. "It's entirely up to you," Elias added. "You could wash up, eat something solid, rest, and be on your way whenever you wanted." Her silent stare gave him no hint of her direction. "Alright then." He stepped inside the carriage. "I must apologize. This was a strange... and uncomfortable meeting." Elias offered another soft smile. "Have a nice day, Miss Valerian. It was my honor to have met you." Nodding to her slightly, he closed the door and tapped the window. A second later the driver snapped the reins gently and the carriage moved on. Glancing down and removing the card with his name on it, Nola looked from one end of the small town to the other. It was her lack of other options that led her to stare at the delicate typeset card. Slowly, and with heavy steps she left the stairs of the beautiful church.

Chapter Eight

Unexpected Answers

At least three more inches of snow had fallen before the two-story cottage came into view. The slated roof stood out against the thick snow but the house itself was hard to see. Thankfully, she only had to walk one last mile. The obliging driver that brought her that far was having too much trouble staying on the road. Consequently, Nola offered to walk the rest of the way, even though the toe of her boot had worn through.

Unlike Gavin's, Elias's house was much smaller and less majestic. It fit right in with the countryside as if it had been there for centuries. Lifting her feet through the snow, she found the tracks of the last carriage and followed them up to the door. Gently she rang the brass bell and waited. The snow fell heavy enough to almost re-cover the bell by the time the door was answered.

"Oh, you just come right in from that cold." A warm and friendly woman opened the large door. Nola's eyes had not adjusted to the change in lighting, and it took a few minutes for the woman's features to come into view. "Sorry it took so long to get down here. The house is bigger than it looks when you have to dust it." Out of the hallway the rather well-rounded lady with black tendrils and delicate skin stepped into the light. Her smile was glorious despite slightly crooked teeth.

"My name is Nola Valerian," she offered quickly, closing the door. "Mr. Percy invited me."

"I'm glad he did." The woman checked to see if there was anyone else out the window. "Did you walk here?" The lady looked at Nola's boots and skirts. "Good heaven's ... let's get you at least dry." Instantly wrapping her arm around Nola, the woman led her down the hallway. "Call me Madeline," she insisted. "Now what on earth brings you out in this weather?" As Nola took in the view of the simplistic country house, Madeline led her through the hallway very eager to meet her needs.

***

It was difficult to refuse the bed that was offered after washing and changing, but Nola was determined to be on her way. After a short rest, she awaited Elias to offer her thanks. It was not her intention to drift off to dream in the parlor chair. If it weren't for the light sound of footsteps in the hallway, she may have slept the rest of the evening. Despite the distraction, Nola found the golden haze beyond the field of reality. Somewhere far away, she could see the snow falling around the horse that Gavin was riding. He was surrounded by streets and strangers, searching for her, and asking questions to almost everyone.

"Were there any visitors this morning?" A male voice pulled her out of the dream.

"A woman named Nola came before noon." Madeline's voice was quiet.

"You were kind to her, I expect." Elias sounded pleasant drowning out the low resonating hum of his territory. The shuffling sound of boots on carpet let Nola know they were drawing near.

"Yes, it took a bit but once she had a bite to eat, she seemed rather polite."

"Good, if she had been ill-treated, we would be at war with Graelohr. I am sure of it."

"She has not complained," Madeline whispered.

"What do you mean?" The footsteps stopped just shy of the parlor room door. Sitting upright, Nola shook off the vision of Gavin and brushed the wrinkles out of her skirt. "Is she still here?"

"Well of course," the woman answered. "You can't expect me to have sent her back out in this weather." A moment later the door to the parlor opened and Nola quickly shot to her feet.

"I hope you don't mind my intrusion," she spoke quickly.

"Mind... I'm too surprised to mind." Elias dropped some papers on the side table and stood still. "... shocked actually."

"Thank you, for letting me stop by, but I should go now." Nola reached for her satchel next to the chair. "It is not my intention to intrude."

"Don't be silly," Elias stated. "You are welcome to do as you please," he offered quickly. "I can almost guarantee that we all ran at one time or another. However," he stepped into the center of the room, still ten feet away from her. "I would feel irresponsible to send you out in this weather."

"I am not your responsibility," she assured him.

"True, but I would definitely feel like an ass." He chuckled.

Nola looked to the floor in response to the foul language, but her smirk did not escape his notice. Holding his hands flat together in front of him, Elias smiled graciously. "Would you consider tolerating my company for an evening?" Looking out of the window he saw the grayness of the storm block out the daylight. Nola realized the same darkness and became concerned about running into Jarron Tempest. The last thing she was ready for was another Vampyre. In that moment, she realized Elias was as dangerous as Gavin. He had the same powers and the same advantages.

"Thank you, but I really must be going." Nola insisted with a polite smile and nervous nod.

"Madeline, please go make our guest something to eat for her journey." Elias turned to the buxom brunette. "She will need her strength."

"Give me just a few minutes." Madeline nodded in agreement to the idea. "I'll fix you right up."

"I appreciate your hospitality..."

"But you are afraid of my entourage," Elias stated calmly. "I saw how you reacted to Mr. Tempest the other night. His direct mannerism can be concerning." When she didn't argue, he took another step forward. "Still, he cannot harm you." Her look of disbelief pulled him closer. "You do know that don't you?"

"There is a difference between fearing someone and disliking them," she explained gently touching her neck.

"You don't know," he whispered staring at her in confused contemplation. "You are afraid that he can feed off of you."

Nola held her satchel with a clenched fist and lowered her head. There was so much that she did not understand. She had no idea how Elias knew her fears, if he could read her mind, sense her emotions, see her wild frantic thoughts. All she knew was that she was not going to get the answers from anyone except Gavin, Elias, or one of the creatures she was desperate to avoid. In a moment of panic, she walked straight past Elias and out the parlor room door.

"Nola," he called to her. "Your blood would be like poison to them." Still, she continued to the door. "Nola, wait!"

"Thank you for your hospitality, Mr. Percy. Lord Graelohr insisted I was not ready to make your acquaintance and I am certain now that he was right."

"Take my carriage," he nearly shouted to her. Nola stopped at the suggestion. "The horses are swift and smart. Take them as far as you need for as long as you want."

"Why would you offer such a thing?"

"Because as long as you are human you are in danger."

"Human?" She wondered at the description. Then, she wondered more about the warning. "Why?"

"Why?" He restated the question. "Nola, didn't Graelohr teach you anything?"

"Yes," she answered honestly, "...and no."

"Alright, hear my proposition and then make your own decision. Can you do that?" He walked down the hallway toward her. Nola nodded her head gently, noting how his eyes shined slightly in the lamp light. "Jarron and my other companions will rise within a few minutes." Shifting her feet, Nola looked at the floor beneath her and wondered where the Vampyres were. "It's alright," he smiled easily. "They are not in the house." Motioning to the window, he nodded toward a barn about fifty feet away from the house. "They find it uncomfortable to sleep any closer to my field of emanation. There is a deep humming sound."

"There is," she answered.

"Is it that uncomfortable?" he asked, honestly displaying a look of curiosity. "We can't tell these things about ourselves."

"It is low and deep, like wind through a hollowed log ... or the wings of a bumblebee." It was the best comparison she had, but it made Elias smile.

"That's embarrassing," he chuckled. "At least Graelohr's can feel like the static from a lightning storm, hence the implementation of electricity in his home. Mine is the buzz of a fat insect."

"No, it's deeper than that," she tried to retract the description, "...perhaps a bow against a cello?"

"It's all right. The worst it has been compared to ...was a deathly moan. I'll take the bumblebee, thank you." He brought her out of her thoughts with his smile. "Do you know what yours is like?"

"Mine?" She asked.

"Do you want to know?"

"Yes," she answered without a thought.

"Then stay, ask a few questions, get some rest in the morning, and head out when the weather is better." Holding his hands behind his back, Elias tilted his head in a submissive gesture. He was lighthearted and playful, so vastly different from Gavin. Nola found herself debating the idea despite Gavin's obvious distaste of him. "Madeline will warn the men not to enter the house or come anywhere near you."

"That would be rude." Nola pointed out.

"I've done worse," he nodded still maintaining his playful tone. "Come on," he called over his shoulder, heading back to the parlor. "Bring your waves with you."

"Waves?" She asked. Only when she followed did he continue talking.

"Your emanation," he spoke plainly, turning up the light in the deep green room. "It's an internal feeling... like the push and pull of tidal waves. It's gentle from a distance, barely even noticeable because of your age. However, up close is another matter." Nola faced him for a moment and then continued to the chair she had fallen asleep in. "Any emanation is distracting if not forced away."

"You can do that?"

"It's learned," he answered. "I would imagine you haven't got that figured out yet."

"No." Her honesty was quick.

"I can't teach it to you," he sighed depressingly. "I don't even know how I learned... it's been so long."

"Gavin said your kind was very similar to..."

"Vampyre?" As he spoke the word she seemed to shudder. "And what do you mean, your kind?"

"I'm not like you," she whispered. "Yes, you are." He almost snickered. "Why is this amusing?"

"Alright, from where I am sitting... Well, to Graelohr, Jarron, myself, and any other one of our kind... You come off as a lion trying to swear that you're a mouse."

"I'm not a lion, and I'm not a Vampyre either." Dropping her satchel to the floor she eased herself properly into the chair.

"We are called, Absolute." He said it with the same dense tone that Gavin spoke the word with. "If a Vampyre is a rowboat we are a steamship."

"This is all madness." Nola did not like the conversation already and the feeling of being trapped began to crawl upon her.

"Whoa," Elias whispered. "You're alright... no one is going to hurt you." He raised his hands in a calming manner. "Listen, I don't know what Graelohr told you or how long he has been preparing you for this, but it doesn't seem like you know a whole hell of a lot." Leaning closer he rested his elbows on his knees. "How about you ask me questions?" For the first time, Nola realized how far back in the chair she had pushed herself.

"Alright," she whispered, slowly moving forward. "Are Vampyres immortal?"

"Vampyres... I thought you would want to know about our kind?" He grinned slightly then shrugged his shoulder a little. "Alright, allow me to calm your fears. Nothing is immortal, nothing that I have ever heard of anyway. Sure, they will not die of age or disease and can heal most wounds, but they are bound to perish. It will just take something out of the ordinary." There was a heavy sigh as he sat back. "Sunlight, decapitation, piercing the heart, fire, and a few lesser-known rituals can end a Vampyres existence. Us, on the other hand, we are even more resilient to death. Only decapitation and heart removal are certain in our case."

"You can withstand fire?"

"I'm not going to prove it to you," he chuckled. "It hurts, it smells, and it takes weeks to heal."

"I wasn't asking, but it is good to know," Nola tried not to grin.

"You are quite literal." He rested his shoulders against the back of the chair. "Do you ever laugh?"

"Not really," she answered. "Luke makes me laugh once in a while, but not often."

"Is Luke your beau?" His amber eyes seemed to sparkle in the lamp light above his witty smile. Unwilling to bring Luke into the conversation, she averted her eyes.

"What do you live off of?" Nola braved the most difficult question.

"Are you asking me what we eat?" His expression could not be read. "Nola, how long have you known what you are?"

"I am not..." Beginning to argue, she thought better of her efforts. "Gavin has had me studying history for a few weeks, but it was only a few nights ago that he told me... that he explained..." Her words trailed off into silence.

"Alright," Elias looked at her directly for a moment before looking away. "Right..." Coming to his feet he walked toward the middle of the room. "Damn, I never thought I'd be the one to explain this to a changeling." Scratching his head, he looked back at her. "Nola, we survive the same way Vampyres do," he whispered. "We have to." Before she could suck in her breath, Elias held up his hand. "It's the quickest part of your change, but the most difficult to grasp... until your first time." Speaking swiftly, he paced around the room. "I heard one man waited eight months before his first feeding. Life was so precious to him, that even as unfeeling as we are to humans, he could not bring himself to eat until it was merciful. To this day, he only takes what he needs to survive."

"No," Nola shook her head feeling the tears well up in her eyes. Even with Elias, her emotions seemed to awaken. "See, I can't do that. I won't do that."

"Ask another question," he whispered. "Don't concern yourself with it now. It's not your time yet."

"I don't want it to be my time."

"Ask me something else," he whispered returning to the chair before her. "Ask me how old I am."

"No." Unable to suppress the thought of murdering innocent people, she shook her head.

"Ask me when I was born. Better yet, guess?" Leaning back in the chair he ignored the glistening tears in her eyes and the redness of her nose and cheeks. "I'll give you a hint. I was twenty-two the year Bach became the leader of his own orchestra."

"I don't want to know." Nola shook her head and closed her eyes to hide the tears.

"I was born the year of the witch trials," he continued. "But they were long over before I knew anything about them."

"I don't know." Nola tried to calm herself. "I can't even guess."

"I am one hundred and ninety-four," he whispered. "Absolutes tend to use decades to explain their age. I'm almost twenty for conversation purposes."

"How old is Gavin?" she asked, finally finding interest past the disgust.

"Old enough to have been attending Shakespeare's plays while he was still writing them," he smirked. "Even to an Absolute, age can still be made fun of. Graelohr was granted a Lordship by two different kings of the same country. Few ignore the title when they are speaking of him and even fewer call him Gavin." Though he reinvents himself or will have a female pose as his heir to keep the secrets. It has been several human lifetimes now."

"Is he revered for his age by others?" Nola asked, the disbelief of Elias's tales entranced her.

"Definitely," his sigh was heavy. "Though not as much as his sister. She is a full thirty years older."

"I wouldn't have guessed he had a sister."

"Would you have guessed him to be three hundred?" He did not allow her to answer. "Graelohr and Joslyn are one of eleven Absolutes to reach thirty decades. Most are either murdered or succumb to the loneliness." A slight huff escaped his chest. "I met a woman who caused me a bad day for fifteen years." Nola almost smiled at the admission.

To think of how little she knew of Gavin, she had to ask, "Have you met his sister?"

"A few times," he answered. "She and I get along much better than Graelohr and I, but that might have been the problem."

"Do you have fangs?" The question surprised them both as it lingered in the air. Elias twisted his head left and right, trying to relax his neck.

"Yes, four. Two each side beside my center teeth." His answer was quiet and serious, different from the rest of his conversation. "We contrast from Vampyre in that area as well. When we are threatened, we have two smaller fangs that protrude from the bottom jaw. They are shorter but serrated and extraordinarily strong."

"Why did your temperament change?" Nola's question sounded in a more serious tone than the rest of the evening.

"There are ethics that you will come to learn. Fangs are a private matter. Because they are not seen ...or used much, they tend to be a taboo conversation." Nola was obviously trying to hide her puzzlement. Elias continued, "Besides feeding and fighting, sexual desires bring them out as well. It can't be helped, but we still don't discuss them in front of company." The lightheartedness came back as Nola's face turned red. Embarrassment was still new to her and she reached up to her cheek. "I think we had best change the subject." He continued quickly. "My family lineage traces back to Gwain." He seemed eager to explain. "There are nine lines in my family. I have only met a few. Do you know your line?"

"No," she answered, hiding her embarrassment, yet still looking at the teeth showing through his slight smile. "Gavin is still searching."

"Sometimes it takes years to find one's lineage, one of the many drawbacks to being Absolute."

"And the others?"

"Well, one of the main drawbacks can be popularity. Trust the wrong person with the truth or let your lifestyle become public knowledge and you are as good as dead." He could see that she was contemplating his words. "We all have a few Vampyres that we trust... those that are sworn to us. However, because we are so much more powerful, most of them want us extinguished. This is easiest for them when you are human, showing the early signs of altering."

"Like I am now," she derived.

"Exactly." Raising his hand, he tilted his head slightly again. "I don't mean to scare you, but females are rare because they can bear children. It puts a higher price on your head. Gavin should have told you at least that."

"Of that much I am aware," she whispered. Instantly, Nola recalled Gavin and the way she felt rushed with desire when her hand took his, only to learn that he intended for her to give him children.

The feeling of betrayal came over her quickly.

"He has hurt you, hasn't he?" Elias kept his voice soft. Nola inhaled a ragged breath and tried to deny the accusation. "He has touched you."

"How do you know that?"

"Your eyes are very expressive, and your emanation is pushing me away. The sensation I feel from you is fear, like I am finding something not meant to be found. I'm just putting the two together. It is a strange feeling within your emanation wave."

"You have this ability to read my emotions." The assumption was well warranted. "All I can sense from you is the humming. Sometimes it can be felt physically."

"It will improve as you change. You will be able to sense deeper meaning eventually. Would you allow me to demonstrate?" He stood up and walked to the center of the room. "Don't be frightened. No harm will come to you."

Slowly, Elias put his hands together in front of him and closed his eyes. It took a few silent seconds, but eventually the hum that surrounded him began to grow. His hands pressed hard together, flexing the muscles in his arms. Unexpectedly, the sound became loud, fast. At first, she could only hear it. Then, as his shoulders tensed and his neck thickened, tightening his jaw, the sound transformed to a force that caused the entire floor to vibrate.

Deafening and intolerable, Nola covered her ears with her hands and pressed as hard as she could. She looked at the ground and almost picked up her feet, but before she could move the whole room began to shake. It was all centered-on Elias. In an instant, the pictures were rattling against the walls and the house felt like it was going to collapse.

"Please stop," she called out. Dust fell from the ceiling, and she considered running out of the room. "Please!" Then, just as quickly as it began, it faded back to its source. Elias opened his eyes and looked at the skewed pictures on the wall.

"I am stronger than that. Unfortunately, I haven't figured out how to eliminate my house from the consequences. You, you will be able to push people away with just a thought." Returning to his chair, he brushed the dust off his seat. "I didn't mean to scare you."

"You've done it again!" Madeline stormed into the room. "It will take me a week to get this all cleaned up, you know!" Bringing in a tray of grapes, cheese, and wine, she set it on a side table. "Well, now you can be sure that Jarron and the boys won't be bothering you for the rest of the evening. No one will come around tonight with you warning to drop the ceiling on them."

"Well, I had to get the message to them somehow," he answered as the woman stormed out of the room. "It was then that Nola understood the tense sensation of being unwelcomed as Elias pushed his emanation forth. It had not been meant for her, but for the others of his household.

Madeline called back, "I'm preparing a room for you, Miss Valerian, after the dust settles again. Then, I will retire for the night."

"Thank you, my darling," Elias called back to her.

"You can thank me by dusting and sweeping all this yourself," she hissed from down the hall.

"Is she your ...companion?" Nola asked.

"Yes, she loves me, and I care for her."

"However, she is not like us," she stated curiously.

"No, Madeline is human," Elias answered. When Nola looked confused, he smiled slyly. "She has been with me for many years, and I have offered to have her turned Vampyre, but she will not hear of it." A human and an Absolute, Nola considered how the world has suddenly changed.

"I don't understand." It slowly began to dawn on her that Vampyres were a product created by Absolutes.

"It irritates me that Graelohr didn't tell you these details. You should have been learning these things for the last year or two."

"But I haven't. He would not even let me see him," she replied. "Once in a while he would come to my aunt and instruct her on what I was to be studying or whether or not I should work to provide my income, but little more than that until a month ago." Stating the truth aloud brought forth her anger more than she anticipated. Noticing her

"You were sorely neglected," Elias spoke softly. His empathy was enough to remind Nola of her manners.

"I don't know." The snow still fell outside the window and Nola began to consider what all Gavin had done for Dottie. "He cared for my family, put my cousin through school and made sure we never went without."

"But you know nothing of your heritage, nothing that would prepare you for this time in your life," he whispered, "and he should never have touched you."

"It was my mistake. I reached out to him." Her admission was plagued with guilt.

"Before or after Jarron watched you meld to him on the street?" The tone of his voice lowered as well as his eyes. The question plagued her in many ways. "It was indecent of him to place that bond between you so soon." Unable to answer and angry that Elias knew of the moment, she looked at the food on the table.

"Would you mind?" she asked, eyeing the simple offer.

"Not at all." Elias immediately stood up and brought the plate to her, but all Nola could focus on was the fact that he would not eat with her. "Wine?" he asked, holding up the glass.

"Can you ingest anything other than...?"

"Yes," he answered with his humor returning. "I can consume any liquid I want but it has little taste, or effect, and I have no desire for it. Still, it comes in handy in human company." Pausing for a moment, he turned to her very seriously. "Please, don't mention that to Madeline. She believes wine is the only thing we have in common."

"Of course," she answered, taking the plate of food.

"I know I agreed to answer questions, but I would like to ask you a few, if you don't mind."

"Alright," Nola picked up a grape and popped it in her mouth. "Why are you running from Graelohr?" Elias smiled, showing

his perfectly normal teeth and cunningly handsome smile. Nola noted his height and muscular shape. She wanted to know if all Absolutes were tall and beautiful, but she was too concerned about the question at hand. For once, she considered lying.

"What did you do when you were told?" Swallowing the grape, she stared up at him.

He took the deflection as it was meant and indulged her curiosity, "I was thrilled," Elias answered. "I had just been reunited with my father and shown everything that he could do. Just the thought of being taken out of the coal mines was enough for me."

"I was cared for by my aunt and cousins, but they were sent by Gavin. I just found out many things that I cannot seem to cope with."

"Nola, where you go and what you do is your business, but you are not safe until you become Absolute. Lord Graelohr and I have a few vampyre's in our homes, most of them are outcasts from their own kind because of it. However, those that are not loyal do not want us alive because of our power. They will kill you."

"I don't want this," she whispered. "You will." He spoke assuredly. "Do you think I should return?"

"Yes," he answered quickly. "Lord Graelohr is intellectual, prosperous, and formidable. If you were seeking the preeminent mentor, he would be it."

"Is there anything I can do to stop this from happening to me?" Nola did not realize how quiet and helpless her question sounded.

"Short of getting yourself killed..." Elias shook his head. "...no."

"Then, there is no choice," she whispered. "I have to go back."

"For now, you should eat, rest, and ask me anything you wish," he answered. "My carriage will take you in the morning."

Chapter Nine

For the Love of Dottie

It was hard to believe how far she had traveled by herself, just days before. The light of dawn was still an hour away. The ground, blanketed in thick snow, let the sleigh skid across the road silently.

Having left nearly seven hours earlier, Nola did not expect to feel Gavin's presence so quickly. Barely past the first stagecoach station, she became aware of him storming toward her. A few minutes after that, Mr. Percy's sleigh came to a halt in the middle of the desolate road. Around her, the air felt alive with static. Any unpinned delicate strands of hair levitated because he was near. Suddenly, an intense electrical feeling in the air rose high, before dissipating to a low lull. Gavin had arrived.

"Miss, I believe this is your stop," the driver called.

Nola was not afraid to get out of the carriage. If anything, she was thankful to be headed home, but with much of the journey left she would be forced to explain herself to Gavin. By the charge in the air, she knew it was not going to be easy.

"Thank you," she stated after her door was opened. The snow- covered fields around her seemed as lifeless as she had felt since leaving the small cottage. However, without a choice, she raised her head to the man in the middle of the road.

"Come away, Nola." Gavin's voice carried over the frozen distance.

His suit was un-pressed, his hair was disarrayed, and the color of his skin looked slightly gray and yellowed. Until that moment, she had never seen him look more unsettled. Gavin stood in the middle of the road beside two horses and waited. Before she had decided to move, Elias's carriage had begun to turn around. It seemed as if even the horses could sense the tension between them.

Gavin stood calm and silent. His horse whinnied gently, bobbing its head up and down, but he still did not move. Looking at the desolate field around her, she knew there was no escape. She had to face him.

"Is Aunt Dottie alright?" The maddening silence forced her to ask.

"Yes," he answered. "I will take you to her." There was no emotion in his face, no smile no anger just grayish skin and hollowed eyes.

"Are you ill?" Finally, she forced her feet to move despite the snow soaking into her boot.

"I am weak." As he answered a small ray of sunlight penetrated the clouds and gently touched the field. The difference in light allowed Nola to see the nearly transparent flesh on his face. Gray lines crept through his features, veins as if stained by ink.

"What is wrong?" Hastening her pace, she came to stand before him. Gavin turned his head down to look in her eyes, letting her see they had turned completely black. Even the tiny vessels in the whites of his eyes had become gray.

"Get on the horse. We will stop and rest for the day. Then, I will get you home tonight." Nola felt her hair swipe past her face with a gust of wind as her feet left the ground. It was only as her bottom touched the saddle that she realized Gavin had lifted her onto the horse. Less than a moment later he was beside her on the second animal, leading her down the road.

The journey was made in silence. She wanted to ask why he was sick, to ask why he rode hunched over and winced when the sun managed to escape the thick clouds. She wanted to know how he had gotten to her so quickly when the journey had taken her two full days and nights, but he made no attempt to even look at her. Maintaining her silence, Nola repositioned herself on the horse and tried to learn how anyone could ride on the beasts.

***

The lines persisted in his skin, darkening with each hour that passed. Nola watched over Gavin silently, knowing that he was getting worse as the day went on. Making sure that the windows remained closed, and little sunlight entered the rented room, she sat back in the chair and watched him sleep.

Gavin had given her money for new clothes and boots and made no restrictions as he lay down in the dusty bed. The room at the Coach House was as clean as a cellar but she made no complaints, coming and going as she pleased. All the while, he slept barely drawing breath. The sun had begun to set in the afternoon sky as she returned to her vigil in the rocking chair.

Nola had given quite a bit of thought to what Elias had told her and to what she had learned from Gavin. To the best of her knowledge the only thing that could cause him to look so grave was lack of rest or deprivation of food. Even though she wanted him to be healed, she was not ready to see him feed. The chair creaked softly if she tilted it back too far. Therefore, she avoided too much motion on the contraption. Keeping the room as silent as possible she watched every person outside the window go about their daily lives, wondering which of them Gavin would kill and consume when he awoke.

Turning to look at her own wrists, she traced a finger down the light blue tint of her vein. It was puzzling how such a disturbing fluid could be the only requirement for his life. She also wondered how her blood could be seen as poison to the Vampyres that roamed the night. Again, looking toward the sun, she wondered if he would be strong enough to protect them both if he needed to. There was still a far way to travel back to Thedford and to be safe they needed to leave while it was still daylight.

Coming to her feet, Nola began pacing quietly in the room. The burgundy velvet dress swished gently as she turned, but barely audible to her ears. Running her fingers over her new silk gloves, she glanced out the window once more. It was obvious that Gavin's journey to find her had been the cause of his ailing state. If she had not gone so far, he would be well. Turning back into the room, she paced back over to the wall.

"Nola..." His voice was gruff as if he had been sleeping for days. Without thought, she hurried to the bedside and peered down at him. The black of his eyes had grown, leaving very little white color left around them. She was overcome with emotion, though she did not understand what she felt. "Rest," he whispered. "I would not have come for you if I could not protect you."

"I know what you need," she whispered as he turned onto his side to face her. "You have no strength."

"We will leave after sunset," he spoke through dry lips. "My eyes will be darker. It is best not to interact with anyone."

"I understand," she answered, still wishing he would return to his normal self without the need to take someone's life.

"You are safe. My men are here and will follow us back to Thedford. You have nothing to worry about." The blanket wrinkled up underneath his cheek and she reached forward to straighten it out.

"No," he warned quietly. "The reason we are here is because I was careless with your touch."

"I reached out to you." Nola withdrew her hand but knelt beside the bed.

"You shouldn't do that." Letting a small grin take over his pale lips, he closed his dark eyes again. Nola looked at the purple silk glove in her hand and slid the material over her fingers.

"You scared me." Gently, she knelt on the floor and leaned over the edge of his bed. With the back of her glove, Nola gently ran her fingers over the side of Gavin's face. "You scare me still." Lifting her fingers off his face she watched the dark ink-like lines fade for a moment. Seconds later, the stone-gray veins were visible once more. Again, she soothed them away with her hand only to watch them return.

"Why are you concerned with comforting me?" When he opened his eyes some of the white color had returned. The shock of his sudden change drew her back. "We all affect each other," he whispered closing his eyes once more. Nola considered moving away but remained on the floor beside the bed. "You would have the same effect on Mr. Percy if he were in this condition." For a moment, she stared at the lines in his skin, feeling more anguish than fear.

"He said that you were immortal," she whispered, touching another line to watch it fade.

"I would rather not teach you how our bodies rely on blood at this moment but believe me I am far from death."

"You don't look like it."

"I am of an incredibly old mind, Nola. It's right for my body to reflect it occasionally." Shifting his head on the pillow he made himself more comfortable.

"Mr. Percy had stated that you are three hundred years old."

"I am," he responded with a slight smile. "I became Absolute before I was twenty-three. Thankfully, my features continued to change until I was over thirty. It happens to the men of our kind. Women mature younger and tend to look younger. My sister, three decades older than, still looks in her twenties." He sighed and raised his dark eyes toward her. The color was fascinating, but still very disturbing.

"You should rest," she whispered wondering how she could feel so much for someone that still scared her.

"Please be still," he asked as she shifted her skirts beneath her. "In my current condition, the sound of your dress is as loud as thunder to me."

"Of course," she answered not having considered the idea.

Nola looked back to the window and looked at the falling sunlight. He had at least two more hours to rest and although she was not tired, she reached out to his hand and laid her head against the mattress.

Without a word, Gavin flexed his fingers around her glove.

***

121

"Marcus," Dottie yelled from the doorway. Having hobbled outside at the familiar sound of Gavin's carriage, she waited for word of Nola. "Did he find her?"

"Is she here?" Luke called, hurrying through the house. At the same time, Marcus nodded that Nola had been found.

"Finally, thank God she is safe," she exclaimed! "Now you stay there!" Dottie pointed to Luke boldly. "I will speak with her alone before she comes inside."

"It's freezing out, and you won't make it down the steps." Standing up from the chair, Luke reached for his coat.

"Mind me boy or I will put my crutch to you!" She raised her voice much more than necessary. "It's definitely her." Dottie watched as the carriage door opened and Nola stepped out. "Don't you come anywhere near this door, Luke. Marcus will aid me to her." Wrapping a shawl around her shoulders, Dottie let the driver, who had come to her aid, hold her arm as she made her way outside.

"She is fine," the man whispered, feeling Dottie rush to get to the girl.

"You are a dear man." Dottie leaned on him as she reached the walkway. "Thank you for going with Gavin."

"It was my pleasure," Marcus answered leaving her side as Gavin emerged from the carriage.

"Nola," Dottie held out her arms as the young woman was swept into her embrace.

"I did not mean to frighten you." Nola held the frail woman gently.

"You are safe. That is all that matters." Wiping a tear from her eye, Dottie finally looked up at Gavin. "What have you done?" she asked, letting go of Nola to reach up to his grave complexion. "Gavin, why have you done this?" Touching every line on his face and examining the visible veins in his hands, she began to well up with tears. "You fool," she whispered.

"Is there anything else you would ask of me, dearest?" His glossy black eyes and transparent skin stared down at Dottie.

There was no doubt Gavin was something otherworldly, even as the night obscured his features. Nola stepped to the side of the walkway and watched the strange reaction between them both. "Oh Gavin," Dottie held his face in her wrinkled fingers and ran her thumb over his lips. She pressed her lips together and sniffled quietly at his obvious painstaking distress. "I am so sorry. I did not mean for you to suffer." The tenderness in her voice was odd. It was neither the intimacy of a mother and son nor the affection of old friends. Nola wondered if Gavin had put Dottie under some illusion.

However, the illusion was spot on. Gavin took the frail hand and pressed his lips into the woman's palm.

"You questioned my love," Gavin whispered, holding her hand to his cheek. "Is this proof enough?"

"I just wanted her home. I thought you would feed during the night," the old woman whispered.

"Your request was my priority. You asked of me to return your child with haste." He sighed deeply, and grinned. Nola saw the sentiment in Dottie's eyes. Her affection for Lord Graelohr was not an illusion. From what Nola knew of emotions, they could overpower one's sense of strength, cold, and propriety. Whatever emotion Dottie felt, it was enough to keep her standing in the snow and utterly entranced. "For the past ten years I have been studying in the Orient. It is possible for me to survive twice as long on a single meal, but it needs to be particularly consistent." His eyes were as black as the tone of his voice. "A detail that will never outweigh my devotion to you."

"My words were hasty. I had no idea." A single crutch fell from under her arm as she reached high enough to stroke his wavy hair.

"If there is nothing else," Gavin pulled Dottie's hand away from his face and stepped back. "I will leave you to your reunion." Nola could not tell if it was his physical state or emotional state that caused him to look at Dottie in such a cruel way. His eyes were downcast, his lips were firm, and his brow seemed furled with disgust. "Nola, take her inside." He bent down to get her crutch and handed it to Nola. "I am still willing to teach you, but you will have to come to me."

"Gavin," Dottie called, placing the crutch back under her arm. "Enough," he called over his shoulder. "Nola, take her inside."

Without casting another glance, Gavin returned to the carriage and ordered Marcus to drive on.

Silently, Nola turned Dottie around and supported the closest crutch as they made their way up to the house. The walk was difficult with the snow, but they made it to the porch before Luke opened the door.

"Where the hell have you been?" Luke reached to take Dottie's arm, but she shrugged him off.

"You will not use that language in front of me." Dottie lifted her leg onto the step and then her crutches. "She is home, and she is safe. That is all there is to it!" Her eyes were wet with tears and her frail body was barely holding her upright.

"Like hell it is!" Luke yelled. "Where were you?" Grabbing Dottie's arm, he hauled her up carelessly.

"Be careful," Nola warned, lifting Dottie quickly to ease his jerking. "I ran away... realized I was wrong... and came home."

"Mum," Luke saw the tears streaming down Dottie's face. "See what you have caused?" He snarled at Nola before returning to Dottie. "Mum, are you alright?"

"Oh, I'm just so thankful to have her home again." Covering up the words she and Gavin just shared, she patted Luke's hand. "This worry has been exhausting. I think it might be best if we all retire for the evening and think of only important questions to ask in the morning."

"Where has she been is a fairly important question, I would say!" Luke was furious and not about to let Nola step any further into the room.

"Good," Dottie thrust her crutch in front of him and pushed him away. "You can ask her that one first as soon as we all wake up in the morning," she warned, still weeping from her encounter with Gavin. "Luke, go to bed or stay put here, but leave this be until the morning."

"I'll take you up to bed." Nola held onto her arm.

"That would be nice," Dottie agreed, "but no conversation tonight. We are all much too tired."

***

Nothing in the house had changed since Nola left, but as she walked down the stairs and through the parlor it was obvious that nothing would ever seem the same again. Every room seemed smaller, unfitting, as if she never belonged there. Sounds from the kitchen drew her near, but she was ready for the encounter.

"Is Davey gone?" Nola asked, as Luke dunked a biscuit into a pot of gravy on the stove.

"Good thing for you." Popping the gooey mess into his mouth, he poured a cup of coffee. It took him a few minutes to chew, and she pulled out a kitchen chair while she waited. "I wouldn't be in a hurry to see him if I were you. He's fitting to roast you on a spit."

"I don't doubt that." Nola sat down and looked up at him. "Luke, I didn't mean to scare anyone."

"Then you should have left a note, told someone, maybe not gone at all, but you sure as hell shouldn't have taken off by yourself for three days." He could barely take his eyes off her. Wide brown eyes stared at her, full of questions but obviously relieved to see her. "What happened?"

"I can't tell you that." Her answer was completely honest. "There is no point lying to you. I can't tell you the truth either. All I can say is I'm sorry and I will leave a note the next time."

"Next time?" He looked up to the ceiling and huffed. "You do this again and it will destroy Mum."

"She understands," Nola whispered.

"No, she doesn't bloody understand! What are you going on about, Nola?" He slammed his cup down on the table. "I haven't moved out but one week and you're disappearing into the countryside." Looking at the mess, he stood to grab a towel. "Davey says you've been getting more distant over the last few months, but I've seen it myself in a matter of days, and it all has something to do with Lord Graelohr!"

Both of them could hear the crutches on the steps. At first, Nola thought that Luke would stop lecturing to her since Dottie would soon be in the room. To the contrary, he wiped up the coffee, poured his cup full and got another one for his mother. "You had better start talking."

"We can talk about this later," Nola whispered, moving the jar of sugar closer to him.

We...?" He sat down and shoved three spoons of sweetener into the cup. "We are going to talk about this right now." Luke pointed his finger downward. "I want to know why this obsession of yours has you stalking that man all hours of the night. Then, when he does want to see you... you're running off like a timid rabbit."

"I cannot answer you," Nola stated clearly. Behind her, Dottie slowly made her way down the stairs. "I don't want to upset your mother anymore."

"Then you should have thought of that before traipsing all over the countryside for days at a time!" The fury in his expression pulled at Nola's sense of concern over anger.

"Luke," Dottie called from the hallway. "Aren't you missing work?"

"I've only been late the last two days. I don't think one more will really matter." He continued to stare at Nola. "It's only the career of my dreams! What is the worst they can do, sack me?"

"There is no need for sarcasm," Nola whispered scrapping her nail over some dry food left on the table. "I am not guilty for you not going to work." Her tone quieted as Dottie came into the kitchen.

"You are precisely guilty!" He raised his voice again. "How could you not be guilty? Did you think I would leave my mother here alone to mishap and circumstance while Davey was out scouring the countryside for your ass?"

"Enough!" Dottie set her crutches against the wall and sat down between them. "If you want to curse, you can do it outside. I won't have it in my house." Picking up the cup that Luke had poured for her, Dottie smelled the fresh brew. After taking a deep breath, she started her lecture. "Lord Graelohr explained to me what has been happening." Taking a small sip, she passed a small smile at Nola and then turned to Luke. "You have become reckless as of late." Keeping her voice serene, she turned directly to Nola. "I'm sure your life has been difficult without family... blood relation. Maybe knowing Luke has left home for good and Davey's found a lady companion has been hard for you to manage. As I understand it," Dottie lifted the mug to her lips and looked at Nola with a quick wink. "You are seeking your true family. Is that not, correct?"

"That is no excuse." Luke shook his head firmly.

"It might be." Dottie took a small spoon of sugar and poured it into her cup. "We don't know what it is like to walk in her footsteps, watching everyone leave her in this house with me."

"I'm not leaving her." Luke placed the tip of his finger to his chest before looking at Nola. "Is that what you think?"

"No," Nola answered quietly. She understood Dottie's fantastic story solution. Still, she did not want to lie.

"Is she right?" Luke leaned closer to her, searching her eyes for the truth. "Are you looking for your family?" Before she could open her mouth to deny the ridiculous accusation, Nola felt a sharp kick from Dottie's lone leg under the table. A quick glance was shared between the two women before Nola finally succumbed to the lie.

"Possibly," she whispered.

"Why didn't you come to me? I would have helped." Running his hand through his freshly cut hair, Luke leaned back in his chair. "Is that why you are so obsessed with Lord Graelohr? Is he helping you trace your family?"

"Yes," her answer was quick since it was partially the truth. "He knows some of my ancestry."

"You could have come to me." Reaching out to her, Luke gently took her hand. "I would have done something." Nola watched Dottie smile gently. The idea of a long-lost family instantly stopped Luke's unending lecture. As a result, she was quick to accept the half- truth. "Alright," he came to his feet and looked down at the table. "I guess, I don't know what I would do in your situation, but you cannot just up and leave! Just tell us before you go running off to the middle of nowhere." Pulling out his wallet, Luke looked down at the table. "I'm not going to do this. I'm not going to stand here and yell at you anymore. You're a grown woman." He set down a folded stack of money in front of her. "You can make your own choices."

"What's this?" She looked down at the money.

"It's money," he admitted. "Take Mum to the dress shop. You will both need new dresses for the Egyptian re-opening ceremony, tomorrow night."

"Luke..." Letting her forehead fall into her hand, Nola picked up the money.

"Yes," he leaned forward and spoke with the same rudeness she was showing. "Are you going to reject me after I told you about this a week ago?"

"I never said I would..." Again, a gentle kick from Dottie swayed the conversation. Nola shifted her legs away from her aunt's as she looked up to Luke. "What kind of dresses?"

"Something fancy," he answered. "And none of those stupid feathers I see all the time."

"Fine," Nola agreed, placing the bills in her apron. "Is Davey attending?"

"Am I not enough for you?" There was almost a hint of humor in his voice, but he was still angry. "Yes, and he will be just as nice as you, since these are my new employers." Folding the lapel of his jacket perfectly he stood tall. "I need to impress them as much as I can after these last few days. Bringing you along will keep my feet out of the fire as well." For a moment, his eyes strayed to the table. "If we aren't enough for you, I'm sure your Lord Graelohr will be in attendance." Returning his attention to her, he continued. "He is renowned as a generous supporter."

"You look very sharp, dear." Dottie smiled at her son. "Go on now. Leave Nola and I to our shopping. It is more tedious work than you would think for the two of us."

"I don't doubt that a bit. It will be easier if she doesn't go running off again." Crossing the room behind her chair, Luke stopped to kiss Dottie and then Nola on the head. His lips lingered on Nola's hair for a fraction of a second longer than expected. "I'll see you tomorrow then?" Almost silently, he drew the scent of her hair.

"We wouldn't miss it," Dottie grinned. "Would we, Nola?"

"Of course, not..." She forced a slight grin as he walked out of the house. As soon as he left, Nola turned directly to Dottie. "Why did you tell him that?"

"It's the truth," she answered, setting aside the concern for Luke's delicate kiss on Nola's head.

"No, I was not trying to find my family. You lied to him, and you've been lying to me for half of my life." Contempt began to surface as Nola faced the woman that had been paid to raise her. "I learned what exists out there." She held her stare firmly. "I learned what I am and why your precious Lord Graelohr has kept me underfoot."

"Yes," Dottie nodded and looked at the table for a moment. "I believe that my not telling you the truth is the same as lying." Looking up, she softly smiled. "However, it had to be done in order for you to have any sort of a normal childhood." Standing away from the table, Dottie took an apron out of a drawer and leaned against the furniture to get to the stove. "As for Lord Graelohr, I have no idea how your life would have been without him, but I am certain no good would have come of it."

"Do you know what he has kept me for?"

"Yes," Dottie answered, almost raising her voice. "He's kept you so you could live. You are an enigma. Nola, you will be an Absolute." Tying on the apron, she placed a frying pan on the stove and began to cook a few eggs.

"I don't see the nobility in his actions at all!" Nola glanced out the window to be sure Luke was too far away to hear. "Tell me you didn't know. Tell me you had no idea he has kept me underfoot to ... to...bear his offspring!" Nola came to her feet. Emotions were becoming extremely vivid with Gavin and even Elias. However, with Dottie, she was cold and callous.

"I'll not have that sort of talk in my kitchen." Pointing a greasy spatula at her, Dottie faced her boldly and spoke in a commanding tone. "You will not speak ill of that man in this house."

"Speak ill of him?" Nola stepped closer. "He may have given this family more than we could have asked for, but did it ever occur to you that I would be the one paying the price?" Remaining collected, she knew no reason to upset Dottie.

"Pay what price?" Dottie remained calm despite Nola's gentle verbal attack. "He's done nothing but nurture you in every way. He's seen you a whole of five times before this month to keep you away from his influence!" Scrambling the eggs, the spatula scraped quickly across the bottom of the pan. "I know that man better than you could ever realize. His only intention for you is to let you live!"

"You are wrong," she answered. "I have no idea how you know him so well, but I can feel what he wants from me. I could feel exactly what I was meant for the moment he kissed me!" Without warning, the spatula dropped onto the stove. Instantaneously, Dottie turned around placing the full force of her palm against Nola's cheek.

"Enough!" Dottie shouted.

Nola held her cheek and realized that of all the times Dottie slapped her, this was the angriest. Backing away from the woman, Nola carefully waited for her to start crying as she had all the time before. Yet, Dottie only appeared enraged. There were no tears, simply anger.

"Perhaps we should take this up later," Nola offered.

"Sit down!" Dottie yelled. Able to keep her fury disguised, Nola returned to her chair completely out of respect. "I'm sorry," Dottie took the pan from the heat and set it aside. "I knew this was possible, but I'm still not ready for it. You can't imagine how difficult it is for me to watch him grow attached to you." Still feeling the twinge of the strike, Nola remained silent. "If you want to know how I have come to understand Gavin Graelohr so well I will tell you, but the details are not to leave your lips for as long as you exist... swear this to me."

"I swear," Nola agreed, despite her steady anger and hurt.

Dottie took a deep breath and returned to the chair at the table.

"I was seventeen years old when I came to live with him," she began. "My mother had been gone for years and my father had just been killed at the harbor. Determined to stay independent I began searching for work." Fixing her skirts under the table, she continued, "I went to every agency I could think of, and then some that I just happened to find. At the end I was going door to door, offering housekeeping and childcare to anyone that would listen. On my worst day, I knocked on the door at Graelohr Manor." Her eyes softened and there was a slight smile, but Nola was still getting over the sting of the old lady's hand. "He was the most attractive and gentle man I had ever seen. He still is," she admitted. "He took me in, gave me a room of my own, and set out duties for me to perform with the rest of his staff. In less than a fortnight I was heart strung. No part of my life had ever been so comfortable, even as the little odd details began to pile up."

"Odd details?" Nola found herself engrossed in the tale.

Dottie leaned forward and began to explain. "The visitors that were escorted to the lower part of the house at night and no one saw ever again," she offered. "The strange men that seemed to appear and disappear out of thin air... all you could catch was a strange blur."

"I've seen that," Nola whispered.

Dottie reached for the bowl of apples and started peeling one with a small knife before whispering, "There was one woman that came to the house in a complete and utter depression. Both of her children died of illness, and she had sliced her wrists before she came to the house." Dottie's smile faded as her memories were set out on the table. "We worked together for several weeks, she and I. Gavin bought her gifts and tried to bring her out of the heartache, but in the end, she refused to live, attempting suicide thrice within the house. By this time, I was already deeply in love with my employer and sought to help him save this woman." Dottie shook her head for a moment. Gavin had taken a shine to me and at first it was simply mutual respect. Nola could not help lifting her fingers to her lips to silence the shock and surprise. "See, there were only two members of the staff allowed to go into the rooms below the manor. The housekeepers were clearly forbidden from entering the stairwell that led to the lower part. When I saw the poor woman wandering through the halls and toward the stairs... I knew something was wrong." Dottie lifted the hem of her apron in front of her and fiddled with the stitching. "It took me a moment to get my slippers and grab my housecoat, but by the time I returned to the hall she had descended the stairs." Nola was silent as Dottie inhaled deeply. "It was well lit down the staircase. I can still remember the white painted stone and black iron sconces on the walls. The cellar had a circular center room, surrounded by small stone walled cells with barred doors. In the middle was an extravagant parlor sofa. It was strange to see such a piece of furniture in a useless part of the house," Dottie spoke as if the vision were before her. "Still, my main concern was to bring the woman back up to her room before Gavin found us. I hadn't counted on him waiting for her behind the sofa."

"I don't think I want to hear this," Nola whispered.

"But you will," Dottie answered. "He called her to him very sweetly, touched her hair and held her in an embrace that I envied." Again, Dottie shook her head. "The woman began to cry and clung to him. Gavin asked her to stay for another week. He promised to send her to the theater and buy her new gowns, but she refused. All she wanted was the sweet bliss of death."

"Did he know you were there?"

"Yes," Dottie answered, raising her chin. "He looked directly at me more than once as I stood on the staircase, but the woman did not know. Her grief was too intense." Nola quieted her questions as Dottie sighed again. "He gave her every offer he could think of, but in the end, she simply wanted death. Before she could speak through another sob he squeezed her gently, kissed her forehead, and raised her chin." Her lips formed a smile, but the older woman was clearly upset. "I saw what he was that night. His eyes changed to white silver, his teeth lengthened into piercing daggers, and in less than a heartbeat he had sliced them into her neck." The thread in the apron held the material fast as she pulled at it. "I watched how easily and painlessly she was swept away from life. Her hands wrapped around his head but not to push him away, to pull him closer. It was the single most beautiful thing I had ever seen... a peaceful death."

"How could you stand there?"

"I was astonished and terrified," she admitted. "Never in all of my life had I dreamed that such creatures really existed. I stood there staring at him, wondering what his retribution against me would be."

"And..."

"Nothing," Dottie answered. "When she was gone, he carried her body to one of the small chambers and closed the door. I was too afraid to move, but he was not angry when he came to me. He simply explained that I did not belong down there and that my pay would be docked for disobedience. Then, he walked back up the stairs."

"How could you stay with him?"

"I admit, I was horrified at first, but where was I going to go?" Dottie stared into thin air, remembering. "I avoided him for days, maybe weeks, but nothing in the house changed. The linens still needed washing and there was always a hot meal ready for us employees." She inhaled slowly, fidgeting with her thumbnail. "I came upon him in his study by accident one evening. You can't imagine how strange it felt to be so afraid and so curious at the same time." Dottie kind of smiled as she explained. "He called me to him and stood up. I could barely make my feet cross the floor, so he came to me as if the wind had carried him. Before I could cry out, he touched my cheek. It was the purest emotion I had ever felt, and he swore to me then that he would never let any harm come to me."

"He killed a woman before your very eyes," Nola whispered very confused.

"And he offered her every chance to live," she admitted. "I'll be honest. It wasn't that way with everyone that came to the house.

Gavin does not always pick and choose. Some provoked him, some were political liabilities, and some were just in the wrong place at the wrong time, but all of them left this world quickly and almost all without pain." Dottie could see Nola's distress slowly grow. "Stay your judgment," she warned. "When is the last time you offered that much sympathy to your supper?"

"It's not the same thing."

"It is exactly the same thing! We are carnivores, Nola."

"How could you live with him like that?"

"It wasn't easy, but I loved him. To the point that I begged him to let me be turned, I loved him," she declared.

"What are you saying?"

"I'm saying that I did not want to live one day without him, and I certainly did not want to age in front of his beauty." Holding out a wrinkled hand, Dottie glanced at her spotted skin. "I wanted to be made Vampyre, as close to Absolute as I could get, to live every day with him." Sighing heavily, she lowered her hand below the table. "I was so young and naive."

"They could change you?"

"They could, but Gavin would not allow it. He did his best to be kind and understanding, but he couldn't feel what I felt. Had I been Vampyre... we would have at least had a chance." Dottie could tell that Nola was deeply disturbed. "My chest ached every time he left the manor. I watched myself grow into my late twenties and begin to lose my luster as he remained beautiful and strong. I was willing to do anything to be with him... but he would not let them turn me." She forced a smile. "He was right, and it was for the best. I don't know how he knew I would love Arthur when he was hired at the manor, or if he simply hoped for it. Either way, Gavin stayed in Europe for nearly a year until Arthur proposed. It was the only time in our friendship he did not send correspondence. He also stayed abroad until the marriage was complete. That was the year he had purchased this house for our family." Glancing at the room around her, Dottie smiled again. "He loved me enough to let me live a full life."

"And all he asked was that you raise me in return?"

"You were never a condition of what we already had," she clarified. "Arthur and I made a fantastic life together. Davey and Luke were half-grown by the time you were found. When Gavin asked, we were more than happy to take you and your brother in." She sat back in her chair and looked across the table. "It wasn't for your childbearing abilities that he protected you. Gavin already has a few children. He took you in because he knows what it is like to lose someone within the human years."

"He has children?"

"Yes, all three are older than me."

"Then why did I feel such an intense sensation? It was as if he had practically said the words." For the second time in less than a day her opinion of Gavin Graelohr had skewed.

"I can't tell you that. Although I know him better than anyone alive, I am not what you are." Dottie picked up Luke's money and straightened out the corners of the paper. "I'm not very hungry any longer," she whispered. "My son expects us to arrive in style." She handed Nola the money. "Perhaps we should just go shopping," she suggested. "Nola, I believe Luke cares for you with the same affection that I once felt for Gavin. Please, be careful with him." Taking her crutch from against the wall, Dottie came to her feet.

"Did you put something different in your eggs?" Nola asked as Dottie hobbled into the hallway.

"No, why do you ask?

"They smell... sweeter, like warm spices." The scent was faint, like fresh bread from the bakery carried on a strong wind. Still, the spices were apparent, along with a sense of heightened awareness. Nola looked aimlessly around the room.

"There could have been something left on the pan. I'm not sure." Dottie ordered as she made her way to the staircase. "We have more than a few stores to see. We should make haste."

Chapter Ten

Dangerous Cinnamon

If not for the Thedford Courthouse and Plaza Hotel, they would have had a clear image of Graelohr Manor. The museum was less than a mile from his house, but just out of sight. Nola could feel that he was close. In fact, she had no doubt that he was inside the museum somewhere and she was not ready to see him. The night he brought her back to Dottie he looked near death. Still, she could not ignore the feeling of being drawn to him. It was much stronger than when he was ill.

"I do hope Luke managed to find me a wheelchair," Dottie looked out the window at the people crowding into the tall and slender building. "These crutches will make the evening long and brutal."

A hum began in her ears, Nola blinked as the strange golden haze took over her sight. However, this time the vision was simple, an image of Luke's hands pushing a high-backed wheelchair toward the front door. Then, as quickly as it came it dissipated.

"He has one," Nola stated, careful not to share the new talent.

The occurrence of the odd vision had become clearer and more precise. However, it was still very unpredictable. "Just there." Nola nodded in Luke's direction.

"Where?" Dottie looked through the glass. Nola waited, but she could not see Luke with her own eyes.

"He's coming," she assured her aunt. Within the minute Luke arrived at the door pushing a rolling chair.

"Well, you were awfully sure about that," Dottie noted. She waited for the chair to be lowered by three men to the bottom stair.

"I suppose," Nola admitted, wondering why her vision was so short and direct. "Aunt Dottie, wait... don't get out yet."

"What is it?" she asked before Luke came to the carriage. "Smell this dress," Nola leaned forward slightly and lifted her chin.

"I told you before, all I can smell is your perfume... and it's quite lovely." Dottie patted her hand reassuringly.

"It's different... like cinnamon ... or warm flowers," Nola insisted.

"I can't smell anything of the sort," she admitted. "Now, do go before he starts lecturing us on being late."

"It's going to be unavoidable," Nola whispered as Luke brought the chair to them.

"You're late!" Luke began with a stern glare.

"Fashionably," Dottie answered calmly, lowering herself into the chair on the sidewalk. "Where is your brother?"

"Right here," Davey answered from behind with a lovely young lady on his arm. "Mother, I'd like you to meet Miss Claudette Stephens." In turn he held his hand out to Dottie. "Miss Stephens, this is my mother, Mrs. Dorothy Ellis."

"Oh," Dottie looked up at the gentle beauty. "Miss Stephens, it is lovely to meet you." Her smile and grace were unsurpassed as she raised her hand to touch the young ladies.

"I've heard much about you, Mrs. Ellis." Claudette seemed every bit the polite young lady.

"Wonderful! Introductions ...are done." Luke interrupted, grabbing Nola by the arm, and motioning for Davey to maneuver Dottie up the steps. "We're late and they have already opened the exhibit." Step by step, Davey lifted and manipulated the chair with ease until they were at last inside the lobby. "Mr. Pendleton," Luke called to the stout man greeting guest after guest. "This is my mother, Dorothy Ellis, my brother David Ellis, his friend Mrs. Stephen's, and my mother's companion Miss Valerian." At the mention of her name, Nola bowed politely to the thick curator that seemed covered in dark hair. He smiled, but it was obvious that he was barely tolerant.

"Welcome to the Wellsborogh Museum," Mr. Pendleton's Italian accent sounded annoyed rather than welcoming. "I am so pleased that you could make it, especially you Miss Valerian."

"Thank you," she nodded gently.

"Please, enjoy the evening and help yourself to the hors d'oeuvres. The champagne will find itself to you soon. The caterers will assist your every need." With his hands held behind his back Mr. Pendleton looked overly pompous.

"Thank you," Dottie whispered quietly. "I'm sure we are in for a splendid evening."

"Can I take your coat?" A man in a tuxedo came to Nola's side.

"Please," she sighed with relief. "It's quite warm in here." Both Dottie and Luke looked at her curiously as she handed over her cloak. Nola passed them a questioning glance, understanding her error as she looked around. They were still too close to the open doors and guests were clutching their coats to them until they were further into the lobby.

"Yes," Luke went along with her. "Thank you." Removing his jacket, he handed it to the man before glancing over Nola's attire. "Good heavens," he stopped suddenly and took in the full view.

The dress was a simple emerald color. Narrow at the neck and fitting at the bust, both the sleeves and skirts fanned outward on the way down. Black lace and appliqué beads decorated the center of the gown and along all hemlines. Against Nola's creamy skin and ebony hair, the ensemble was perfect.

"You look ... very nice," Davey said, in his stead. "Absolutely," Luke chimed in with his hands held out toward her. "I couldn't have said it better myself."

"Just darling," Mrs. Stephens agreed.

"Yes, Nola prides herself on classic elegance. Isn't that right, dear?" Dottie asked.

"Thank you," Nola nodded. The comment was not said impolitely, but she was terrible at pretending to be conversational. "Luke, what are we here to see?"

"Right, this way." Luke took up steering Dottie's wheelchair. "All of this has been here since the museum opened twenty-five years ago." He turned the chair down a large open hall and guided them all toward two towering Egyptian God statues, one of a jackal-headed human and the other with a falcon head. "However, Thoth and Anubis have just arrived."

"Where are the mummies?" Davey asked.

Luke ignored him. "Behind those extravagant statues we have added newly discovered relics, statues, pottery, and jewelry." He waited patiently behind a group of people as they wandered into the exhibit. "One of our own archeologists, Joslyn Jackson, has been working in the field for nearly five years under Pericles Newbury, the world's leading Egyptologist."

"Impressive," Dottie awed in sight of the twenty-foot statues. "What kind of people could believe in such creatures?" As the question was asked, she and Nola stared at the large figures of the jackal and crane headed human bodies.

"Where are the mummies?" Davey asked again.

"Ra was their sun God and Anubis, God that oversaw mummification and the journey to the afterlife," Luke added as he looked up at the jackal.

"So... where are the..." Davey began.

"On our left, is an entire room devoted to mummified remains." Luke was completely annoyed, but Davey just chuckled.

"Oh, I don't want to see that just yet," Dottie announced. "Go ahead and take Miss Stephens," Luke offered as he

looked at the incredible line of people waiting to get inside the room. "We will go on."

"Shall we?" Davey asked his companion. Without hesitation, the lady agreed and the two hurried to the end of the line.

"Thousands of years of history and all they want to see are dead bodies." Leaning on the back of the wheelchair, Luke sighed. "I choose not to indulge in morbid fascination."

"What is over there?" Dottie asked, unable to see hardly anything from her seated position.

"I'll get you there, Mum," Luke promised. "It's a display case filled with relics and charms. Thousands of years ago, small intricately detailed ornaments were tucked inside the wrappings of mummified bodies to protect the individual and bring them good fortune in the afterlife."

"How did Wellsborogh Museum come to acquire such a vast collection?" Nola asked as she glanced around the room of gold and stone antiques.

"See, the archeologist I was speaking of just happens to be very wealthy with family here in Thedford. It was a condition of her financial assistance that the display be sent here for a few months.

After which, most of this will be moved permanently to her home in Cairo when all is said and done."

"Fantastic," Nola admitted.

"Absolutely, it is one of the most extravagant displays in the world right now," Luke admitted.

"Not that," she whispered and shook her head. "The archeologist is a woman." Again, the curious, sweet smell of warm spices filled the surroundings. Nola lowered her head to her shoulder to smell her sleeve. The scent wasn't coming from her, but it was quickly becoming bothersome that no one else was affected. She also noticed the rooms seemed warmer as they toured the pottery and artwork.

"Oh, yes." Turning Dottie slightly to give her a better view of the ornamental cases against the walls, he continued to fight through the crowd. "I should have mentioned that. She is supposed to be here this evening. It would be nice to get a chance to meet her." Becoming a little wary of the strange aroma, Nola kept her distance from Luke as well as she could. "Are you alright?" he asked, noting the way she stepped aside.

"Of course," she answered quickly. "Though, it is a little warm in here." Just then, a familiar feeling of comfort and charged energy flowed into her somewhere unmistakably, the sensation of Gavin Graelohr filled her senses.

"Perhaps it is simply the size of the crowd," Dottie asked, keeping her shawl tightly around her shoulders to aid Nola's skewed perception. "There is still a chill."

"Perhaps," Nola agreed. Without looking around, she could feel the impending approach.

"I would like to get you over to the relics." Luke looked for a path through the herd of visitors. "Had you been here on time we would not have had this problem."

"What problem is that?" Lord Graelohr was suddenly beside Nola. The distraction of being warm had kept her from realizing how close he was. When she turned to face him, all evidence of any former malnourishment had been erased from his handsome features. His deep dark eyes regained their luster, and the pale gray shade was gone from his skin. He was brutally stunning, dressed in long tails and a starch white shirt, drawing attention from every woman around them.

"Lord Graelohr," Luke acknowledged him with a nervous glance.

"Quite a display you have here, Mr. Ellis. This is all very impressive." As he looked around them, Gavin grew aware of how limited Dottie's view was.

"I have had little to do with it, Lord Graelohr." Luke was unsure how to tolerate Gavin's presence. Lord Graelohr patted him on the back and for some reason, all confusion and curiosity left Luke's mind. None of the information had been forgotten. It was simply not important to the present situation. It never occurred to the young man that the loss of anger, fear, and inquisitiveness was due to the touch of Gavin's hand. "I will be sure to convey your compliments to the curator." Again, he tried to move Dottie closer to the exhibit.

"Allow me," Gavin stated, stepping in front of Dottie. "Excuse me," he called to the man directly in front of the wheelchair. "Would you step aside please?" Immediately, the man moved. Gavin called out to a few more people, but within a short period of time they were directly before the glass, dead center of the exhibit. "Did you get to work with any of these pieces?" Gavin asked Luke.

"None of it actually," Luke answered, grateful that Dottie had a clear view. "I will have to pay my dues like any new employee before I have any hands-on experience. Still, I have done my research on the exhibit and can answer any questions you may have."

A feminine voice, angelic enough to carry an entire church choir, sounded from behind Luke, "Excuse me, Sir, would you mind telling me why the small statue of Osiris, near Anubis is depicted with an ankh and flail in his grasp?" Turning to face the sweet sound, Luke could not help his stunned expression as he faced a brunette beauty.

She looked like a painting. Gowned in crimson and dripping with diamonds, the divine creature was clearly enamoring. Her figure was slender with entertaining curves, and the scarlet gown met those curves with perfection. Even Nola took a steady look at the bedazzling beauty. However, Nola sensed something very odd about the woman. The air around them held rich cinnamon and nutmeg. She had the instant knowledge that this woman was an Absolute. It was her presence that was responsible for the spiced scent and warm air.

"Yes," Luke cleared his throat and stared at the blue-eyed temptress. Dottie raised her hand to cover her smile at his reaction. "Actually," he began to explain with an unsteady voice. "That statue is incorrect." He swallowed hard after his voice cracked. "Osiris, God of the Underworld should have been holding a crook and a flail... not an ankh." Lowering his head, he tried to avoid her statuesque figure that was made to be adored. "Our reproduction department made the error too late to correct before the event. It was decided that most would not catch the imperfection."

"You are extraordinary with your Egyptology, Mr. Ellis." She nodded with a smile from full red lips.

"Thank you. To be honest, I've studied more history more than Egyptology," he offered boldly.

"Well, I will have to see if Mr. Pendleton really needs you as a curator. You might prove to be an asset in the field." With just as much interest, the lady took in his tailored suit and wild hair.

"My apologies, I am quite certain we have not been introduced." Luke remained polite as he held out his hand. "Though, you know who I am?"

"You, of all people should at least be an acquaintance," Gavin admitted to Luke. "This is my sister, Joslyn Jackson. This exhibit was largely acquired by her archeology team."

"You are Joslyn Jackson?" Luke asked in complete shock. His surprise was matched by Nola's. "We were speaking of you only a moment ago. I am honored."

"Wonderful." Her face lit up as she smiled. "I am glad to find our work is a success." Gavin held up his hand to introduce the group.

"I trust you remember Dorothy Falk, though her married name is Ellis." He spoke with a gentle tone.

"Dottie Falk?" Joslyn looked at the elderly woman in the wheelchair.

"It's me," she nodded, gently touching her white hair. "You look glorious as always, Joslyn. How have you been over the years?"

"Bored," she admitted as a tall dark-skinned man with rows of long braided hair came to wrap his arm around her. "I've been knee deep in sand without shade for what seems like thirty years," she giggled when she spoke making the timeframe sound like a joke. "I figured this collection rendered us a little due holiday." Accepting the generous attention from her tall dark companion, Joslyn turned back to Dottie. "This is your family?"

"Yes, my son Luke," Dottie introduced him eagerly, "and my niece, Nola."

"Nola Valerian?" The moment they made eye contact Nola was certain that the smell of incense and the localized warmth was generated by the stunning three-hundred-year-old Absolute before her. "You are quite faint... aren't you?" Unsure of what Joslyn meant, Nola looked to Gavin. "I've heard much about you," the temptress added.

"I wish I could say the same." Nola smiled weakly with slight hesitation.

"I'm sure Gavin would have mentioned more eventually. It is my own fault for staying away for so long." The man at her side was nearly as tall as Gavin and equally built-in stature. A trend was beginning to form in the male Absolutes she had met. However, his dark complexion and eyes gave him an air of mystery. "This is my husband, Leviathan."

"What an unusual name," Dottie mentioned. Instantly, Luke removed his steady gaze away from the married woman and returned his attention to the group. It was clear that a slight flush rose to Luke's cheeks when the man was introduced.

"It means, twisted one," Joslyn offered.

"It is a pleasure to meet you," he spoke with an exotic accent before placing all interest in his stunning wife. "Please, call me Levi."

"I had no idea you had taken up archeology," Dottie continued the conversation as Joslyn became entertained by Luke's embarrassment at their peculiar behavior.

"It has become more than a hobby." Joslyn glanced at Luke and gave him a very bold and flirtatious smile. "I'm sure Mr. Ellis would agree. These last years have seen more attraction to things both ancient ...and beautiful." Nola caught the Absolute's playful gaze and saw how Levi smirked at the subtle comment. Luke had no way of knowing that his appreciation for her appearance was being mocked. Still, it irritated Nola.

"I agree entirely." Luke nodded as he glanced back at the glass case. "The turnout for tonight is a tribute to that fact." Feeling protective under the circumstance, Nola reached out and wrapped her arm around Luke's. Both Gavin and Joslyn took note of her action, but not nearly as heavily as Luke. Pleasantly surprised, he wrapped his hand over hers.

"Well, forgive me for being rude, but I have a commitment to meet a few other guests. Still, this has been a pleasure." Grabbing a handful of red material, Joslyn smiled up at her brother. "They are fiercely entertaining," she whispered. "You must invite them to dinner. I would adore sinking my teeth into a little more conversation with Mr. Ellis." Nola barely held her temper as Gavin stepped forward and bowed to take Dottie's hand. "All in good fun of course, Dottie," Joslyn made sure to amend her behavior to the elderly woman. "Hopefully, we will see each other again." With a splendid smile, the immaculate beauty stepped away from the group, skirts swaying behind her.

"Excuse us," Gavin whispered. "I'm afraid my sister is tired from her journey and has quite a few people to meet yet this evening. Ignore her temperament." Though he spoke directly to Dottie, he glanced up at Nola twice.

"She has always been a handful. Did you know that she was coming?" Dottie's grace was unyielding. However, there was obvious concern in her tone.

"There was no message sent ahead but I had my suspicions. She arrived just before dawn yesterday and was unclear as to how long she is staying." Both he and Dottie glanced at Nola for a moment. "Perhaps another few days."

"I think she is quite charming," Luke offered blindly. Before he could comment further a guest pointed at one of the relics and veered his conversation back to the exhibit.

"Thank you, though she may need some female companionship while she is here." Gavin nodded with a blank stare. "Nola, would you accompany me for a few minutes?"

"I would, but this is Luke's evening," she replied coolly. "It's alright." Luke was quick to smile and shrug off the matter, still involved with the guest he was speaking to. "I have to find Davey and Miss Stephens anyway."

"Well then?" Gavin held out his arm to her. Nola looked at his sleeve but was wise enough not to touch him.

"I shall not be long." She reassured Dottie.

"My sister is very ...playful." Gavin began as they walked away from the exhibit.

"Playful, is not the word I would have chosen," Nola admitted. He motioned toward a tall white fountain at the side of the room and walked in the general direction. It was Nola who decided to stop and admire the array of seashells and mermaids in the stone basins.

"Well, keep the word to yourself. She can hear everything we are saying," he warned.

"She acted like a harlot in front of Luke and Aunt Dottie. That is the word I would have chosen." Nola showed no fear of Joslyn.

Gavin's face scrunched up a little at her boldness. "Alright, now that's enough." Keeping his eyes narrowed, he held her stare. "I sincerely hope that you two will get along."

"With my sincerest wishes, she can get along all the way back to Egypt, for all I care."

Quietly with his dark stare, he scolded her. "Not another word.

Joslyn's emanation can make you suffer from here. As soon as he stated the warning, Nola opened her mouth to beckon Joslyn forth. Before she could, however, Gavin placed his hand up to her mouth. Nola backed away before he could touch her. "She will not speak to your family again and she will put in a good word with Luke's employer. Is that fair?" The depth of his eyes was impossible to argue with.

"Tolerable," she answered. "Her emanation is heat, isn't it?"

"A sweet burning smell and the feeling of being trapped in a steam engine," he offered.

"Of course," Nola agreed, understanding the strange distraction throughout the day. Only then did she realize that she could heavily feel Gavin's influence for the first time. "Why could I sense her over you?"

"She is older and sharper. Joslyn is thirty years my senior, the oldest in the country, currently."

"That makes her much stronger than you?"

"I wouldn't say that." He defended himself readily. "She is vastly stronger than Levi and you will be barely noticeable next to her for many years. Her territory is larger than mine, but it is not always a benefit."

"What does that mean?"

"Had I known she was coming I would have spoken to you earlier. Having her here can be complicated." His eyes constantly scanned the room.

"Why is that?" Nola asked.

"It's difficult to explain and I will tell you more in a less public setting, but you may need to come and stay at the manor, until she leaves."

"No," Nola answered flatly. Her reply was loud enough to draw a few glances from the crowd around her. Suddenly becoming fascinated with a reproduction of an Egyptian crown, Nola avoided the unwanted attention. Gavin took up a place behind her and stared at the gold and blue coronet.

"It is more than a suggestion." Gavin watched her dark tresses slide back and forth as she shook her head. Leaning to her ear, he whispered softly, ignoring the curiosity of those around them. "Her emanation is so thick that it is difficult to detect another Absolute or Vampyre when she is near."

"Why should that affect me? The only other... Absolute," she whispered the word and glanced at him over her shoulder. "The only other is Mr. Percy. You said so yourself, and he has no mind to harm me."

"Yes, but Joslyn could have been followed by anyone, a pack of wild Vampyres for her entire journey and Levi would have no knowledge of it." Gavin slid his gray gloves off his hand and placed them in his pockets.

"But then Joslyn would know. I'm sure she would say something if they were in danger." Nola turned to face him directly, adamant that she was not going to change her mind.

"Not her," Gavin argued. "Her arrogance is warranted, but deadly. She will wait until she is cornered before defending herself. Not because she wants to avoid the situation but because she enjoys the rush of proving her strength."

"And you think I would be safer in a closer proximity?" Nola was dumbfounded at his reasoning.

"Joslyn and Levi can fend for themselves, but I cannot sense if someone comes near you."

"As far as I can tell, with the exception of my brother's death, I have never been close to danger. I am beginning to wonder if you are just trying to scare me." Nola's words were soft, but stern. Having quickly removed his glove, Gavin commanded Nola's attention.

Beneath the laced white glove, she felt his thumb slide under the cuff of her sleeve. It was far too fast for her to withdraw.

Once her voice was silenced, Gavin whispered, "You have been followed every night since you were fourteen years old. My men have saved you from four different vampyre's. We watched a trio of drunkards chase you in that alley, they were fortunate Davey was on hand, and most recently, I ended a chance encounter with Mr. Tempest." He spoke in her ear. Nola swallowed hard as she digested the new knowledge. "You are too far away from us for this added risk." His thumb drew over her bare skin letting his calm desire flow into her. "It is a rare opportunity for three Absolute's to be in one place at a time, it would be a grand event for there to be four of us."

Nola allowed the fantastic sensation of his hand to trail up her arm. It was so desirable and warm that she coiled her fingers around his forearm. There was no doubt Gavin was going to get what he wanted. Nola could not stand the thought of him letting her go.

Though it was far from the raw sensual desire that she had felt before, it was substantially erotic. She was purely content to stand there with him for the rest of the evening.

"You will have your own room, complete access to my library, and the advantage of learning from the three of us. How could you refuse such an opportunity?" His eyes bore into hers.

"There is propriety to consider," she whispered, letting Gavin know that she still retained a strong free will.

"Yes, and as your guardian it wouldn't be an issue." His voice seemed to lull her gently.

"My Aunt would disagree." The words sounded as if spoken by someone else. All she was aware of was his touch.

"For your safety, Dottie would let me take you to the orient if needed." There was a gentle hint to his devilish smile.

"It would hurt Luke." Even under the spell of Gavin's touch, Nola could not ignore the way Luke looked back through the crowd at her.

"So would your death... if I could not get to you in time." The fact was stated tenderly. "Just for a night or two, please?"

"Alright," Nola agreed, feeling little to no choice against his broad and unmistakable magnetism. "I will inform my aunt."

It felt like floating. The room was full of people, but Nola could hardly notice any of them. As Gavin drew her along the floor with her hand, she could feel his calming energy coursing through her. Her concern was evident, but greatly masked. He was larger than life, more breathtaking than any man alive, and she could feel how much he cared for her wellbeing. The maddening desires growing for him were not gone. They were subdued, hidden beneath a powerful intense need to sway her mind. Aware of what he was doing, Nola allowed him to lead.

"Mr. Ellis," Gavin waited for Davey to stop talking before he interrupted the family. "I have a situation and I am not sure whether to broach you or Mrs. Ellis on the subject."

"Why don't you tell both of us what you are up to," Dottie chuckled. She had been laughing when they approached and continued her merriment until she saw Gavin holding Nola's hand. Her attention on their hands almost lasted too long, but fortunately Davey did not notice. "What is it?"

"My sister has not been to visit for quite some time. She has taken a shine to Nola," Gavin spoke candidly. "I was hoping you would not mind her staying at Graelohr Manor for the next few days while Joslyn is visiting." Gavin squeezed Nola's hand gently as he felt her concern.

"I don't think that is such a good idea," Davey shook his head.

He took on a profoundly serious façade as Gavin held a smile. "It would be a treat for my sister. Rarely does she get the chance to visit with ladies of Nola's fine upbringing." He pressed on, glancing down at Dottie for assistance.

"Oh Davey, let the girl have a little fun," Dottie added.

"I thought she was having fun for half of the last week... on her own... running around the countryside." Davey kept his voice low, but his eyes warned Gavin not to press the issue.

"Are you Davey Ellis?" The sweet smell of spices filled the group as Joslyn's angelic voice appeared. "Are you the one working on the Tucksten Bridge?"

Without warning, Miss Stephens tightened her grip on Davey's arm as he took in his first view of Joslyn Jackson. His eyes scanned the red flowing chiffon and long beguiling hair. If he had been any less angry, he would have fallen for her beauty at first sight. As it was, he was impressed, but not deterred.

"Davey, this is my sister Mrs. Joslyn Jackson and her husband Levi." Gavin made the introduction knowing that the elder cousin's firm grasp on responsibility outweighed his interest in his sister.

"Yes, I am working on the bridge." Davey nodded to her with no more than a second glance.

"It's an amazing architectural feat. How long have you been on the project?" Joslyn took a glass of champagne from a waiter's tray and seemed deeply curious about the construction.

"Since it began five years ago," he answered quickly. "I understand you are visiting for a brief stay. I'm sure my cousin would be glad to entertain you tomorrow."

"Oh," Joslyn pouted. "See, it's still daylight where I am from, and I understood Nola to be... well... a night owl much like me."

"She's a night owl, but nothing like you, I bet." Luke offered the comment too quickly, embarrassing himself with the strangeness of the comment. "I would rather not nurture the quality. She has no need for it," Davey argued. He felt Dottie reach up and touch his wrist, but he paid her no attention. "I'm sure you can see my point of things."

"No, at this particular time, I don't." Gavin held his tone firm without anger. "I am making a simple request." The power struggle between Davey and Gavin continued. Then, a warm delicate breeze filled the air and Nola watched the view before her change. Joslyn seemed to shimmer like a view just above a smoldering surface. The image was only visible to Nola, as far as she could tell. Joslyn raised her hand to her ear, somehow sending a wave of miraged energy through Davey. His demeanor instantly became amiable.

"Gavin," Joslyn stepped forward with a brimming smile. "How thoughtless of us?" She patted Davey's arm that Claudette Stephens held with a death grip. "I should have had a more stable itinerary that included a visit with Nola. Another time, perhaps..."

"Davey," Claudette whispered. "Maybe it would be nice for Nola to visit with a woman of the world like Mrs. Jackson. She is bound for the university in a few months. You will not need to be so concerned for a few days' time."

"That is a riveting point," Dottie added with a smile. "It might do Nola some good to spend time with an educated lady like Mrs. Jackson."

Before Davey could object further, Joslyn leaned dangerously close in his ear and whispered something. Claudette was instantly on her guard and both Dottie and Luke looked curious, but Nola was still dependent on Gavin's calm emanation. If not for his collected composure, she would have been terrified.

"Perhaps a few nights away is just what she needs," Davey gave a sly smile as he replied.

"What?" Luke set his hands on his hips and looked from Davey to Dottie. "Are you serious?" His eyes widened and a small vein in his neck protruded. "Davey, what are you thinking?" When the elder brother nodded to Gavin, Luke ran his hand over his hair.

At the sound of Luke's objection, Nola pulled her hand free of Gavin's. Glancing at Joslyn, Nola forced a pleasant smile before facing Luke. "You still haven't shown me your apartment." Her voice was upbeat and cheerful. "As long as I am just down the road, I'm sure Mrs. Jackson would love to accompany me to visit you. It would be the perfect time to show us around."

"What a wonderful idea," Joslyn agreed, easily casting her spell on the bookworm. "I could tell you about all of our finds and the structure of the pyramids. I could even be persuaded to show you my private collection of charms and relics dug up over the years."

"Shouldn't they have been submitted and catalogued?" Luke playfully teased the temptress.

"Probably," Joslyn admitted. "Let us take Nola, please?" She begged with her arm around Gavin's. "I could really use some sophisticated company for a change."

"She is not prepared," Davey stated.

"Nonsense, I will see she is provided for, more than adequately." Gavin nodded his head toward Davey. It was a show of respect as well as a reminder of the Lord's superiority.

"Then my quarrel is invalid," Davey agreed, still grinning from whatever Joslyn had whispered in his ear. "Have a good visit." He nodded toward Nola.

"Will you be alright?" Nola asked Dottie.

"Of course," she answered. "Davey will be home as soon as he returns Miss Stephens, and Luke will be sure I am all settled in before he leaves for the night." The look of kindness in her eyes always amazed Nola. "Go and have some fun for a change. I'll see you soon enough."

***

"What did you say to Davey?" Nola asked, feeling the uncomfortable heat of Joslyn's nearness inside the carriage.

"I reminded him of how much time he would have with his fiancé. I reminded him you would be gone for the night once Dottie was asleep." Joslyn began to pull pins out of her hair and place them in her satchel. "And then, I put a little warm, slightly obnoxious, vision of him and his lady in his mind," she giggled. "Men are always easily swayed by seduction. Though, I am impressed at your cousin's intense protectiveness of you. It would be a shame for you to turn on him." She smiled as she removed more pins.

"Joslyn..." Gavin growled at her.

"Oh please, Gavin. Most turn on unsuspecting caregivers.

Why should Nola be any different?" Joslyn was blunt and crude. "We both know you made a promise to little Dottie, who by the way is not so little any longer, but do you think you could protect her from your little changeling?"

"Stop the carriage!" Nola demanded.

"Joslyn, that is enough." Gavin placed his hand on Nola's. The sensation pacified her for a moment, but her anger was too fierce to ignore.

"Right," she sighed heavily. "My courtesies are not what they should be," Joslyn admitted. "My age makes me ill-equipped to deal with humans very well."

"It's not age. It is poor mannerisms," Gavin corrected her.

Levi chuckled slightly until his wife cast him a stern glare.

"Please don't misunderstand. I feel for you at this junction in your existence." Returning to removing her pins, each wavy lock of hair cascaded into small curls on her shoulders. "Really, I do. However, sympathy is an emotion long buried in our sands of time."

"Has your decency been buried as well?" Nola asked as the carriage rolled over a bump in the road.

"Perhaps, but apparently, I have retained the sentiment of annoyance. Like it or not... you need me... and I ...have not known another female Absolute for quite some time."

"I understand the rarity," Nola glanced at Gavin for a moment and then turned out the window. Her thoughts strayed to their private moment in his study. "In fact, I preferred it."

"I don't think you do." Joslyn reached over and touched the back of Nola's hand. A numbing sensation flowed over her skin instantly.

Nola looked up at Joslyn and tried to pull her hand free of the tight grasp to no avail. The moment seemed strange at first, but soon a long drawn out feeling of seclusion and loneliness transferred from the beautiful Absolute. With the touch of her hand, everything became strange and dreamy. It was as if Nola could almost see the moments in Joslyn's life when she held all her pain because none of the males around her would have understood her suffering. She even felt the loss that came when Joslyn passed her daughter off to a human, knowing she would never see her again. Then, the pain of the child's death swayed into her. This was followed by the deaths of numerous loved ones and husbands killed over the centuries.

Eventually, the fear and terror of growing Vampyre attacks because of her age and abilities began to surface. If it weren't for Gavin's interference, Nola would have succumbed to the endless despair.

"Enough," Gavin called out. "You're making her upset."

"It was necessary," Joslyn whispered... slightly shaken from letting Nola get a glimpse of her softer side. "After thirty decades ... one forgets any other way of communication."

"Is that true?" Nola asked Gavin as the horses pulled up to the gate of Graelohr Manor.

"When it comes to important issues that are difficult to verbally convey... yes," he answered. The fact made perfect sense. All that Nola had learned of Joslyn in that one moment of contact would have taken hours to learn in conversation.

The large gates to the estate opened and the horses pulled them through the grounds. Unconsciously, Nola eyed the house and sought out anything that may have moved too fast or in an unnatural manner. Levi was the first to leave the carriage and he was quick to assist Joslyn, but Gavin made a point of having one of his staff help Nola out of the carriage. She knew then, he was worried about the last time they were so close at the manor.

"You have been told that the vampyre's that reside in our homes are family to us." Joslyn spoke in a questioning manner. "They would take a stake in our stead without being asked." As the door to the manor was opened, Nola saw the house in an entirely different light than before. The air seemed slightly orange or golden wherever the beauty stood. Joslyn led the way, forming a gentle wave of magnetic attraction. Appropriately, Nola followed the delicate gesture. "Gavin has a very large family. Some have moved out of the manor over hundreds of years ago and still come to visit." Looking back to Gavin, she watched as both he and Levi entered the doorway, their height nearly reaching the top of the door. "And the house still looks exactly the same," Joslyn giggled as she spun around in the great foyer. "This is pathetic," she announced with a giggle. "Though, I do like the new lighting."

"I like consistency," Gavin smiled as he answered.

"This is more consistent than death." Joslyn tilted her head in a teasing manner.

"It is yet to be as old as you." His response was quick. "Enough about your awful house." She shrugged off the insult.

"I will maintain my old rooms." Joslyn literally dropped her coat in the arms of the servant that came to assist them. She barked orders at him in the most gentile voice Nola had heard. "My husband and I need to rest before we begin." Levi took to her side when he was beckoned. Locating Nola's family bloodline and parents is bound to be difficult. However, tracking them will be hardly an effort for Levi."

"My parent's?" Nola asked with alarmed confusion. "My family?" Her curiosity and confusion brought the room a strange gravity shift. "What do you mean, track?" Nola removed her coat and handing it gently to the man. As her senses became more attuned to what she was thinking, the aura Joslyn created diminished. Soon, the whole of the mansion seemed less attractive.

"The reason my brother sent for us. The purpose of our visit." Joslyn smiled and waved her hand. "Levi is a renowned tracker," she stated with pride.

"I sent for you over a year ago," Gavin added quietly. Joslyn completely ignored the sly remark.

"My husband can find any Absolute or Vampyre in the world, without leaving the comforts of a parlor." Joslyn boasted.

Nola stood quietly before acknowledging the obvious, "I don't understand."

"You will after a while," Gavin explained before turning to his sister. "For now, we should get you two settled into a room and find Nola something to eat."

"See," Joslyn stepped up to Gavin. "This is why we asked you to take on the novice. Levi and I would have never thought of something as simple as feeding her." Nola did not appreciate the comment. For the first time, Joslyn and Levi were sensing Nola's wave of anger. The strength within the small fledgling was more than they expected. "I may have spoken out of turn," Joslyn whispered honestly. With caution, she smiled at Nola. "Forgive my ill behavior. I have much to remember about meeting new company." Trying to ease the air, Joslyn gave an enchanting smile. "Will you meet us in the parlor after we rest?" She asked.

Nola sighed with annoyance and walked away from them, moving closer to the lit hallway at the end of the foyer. There, Levi stood with his arms wrapped over a muscular chest.

Seeing the young woman would need some tempting, Levi raised his hand to Nola and spoke, "Before we rest, I would like to take a quick stroll around the house. Would you re-introduce me to the main floor, Miss Valerian? It has been decades since my eyes last beheld its ancient rooms."

"Yes, that would be kind of you," Gavin stated, nodding his head toward Nola.

Levi stepped across the room and distracted the woman from the elder's conversation. "Nola, Gavin mentioned you were a teacher. I, myself, have spent time in London as an educator." He purposely led her down the hallway with conversation about history and mathematics. When the two had departed completely, Gavin turned to his sister.

"Again, your loose tongue has made a mess for me to clean up," Gavin growled deep and quiet.

"Do you know that she is nearly fixed on you?" Joslyn asked. "When I took her hand all I could see were images of you. An almost disturbing amount, to be honest. She's been using you to practice her gift."

"She only knows one vampyre and Elias has the same sighted ability. Therefore, she can't use him. I am the only figure she uses just yet."

"Why aren't you teaching her? She could use her gift on any immortal in the vicinity. Gavin, she already cares for you. You cannot stop that. The only difference you can make is teaching her what she needs to know and letting your bond grow stronger."

"We are not her family." The depth of his consideration mirrored in his eyes.

"We are her kind." Joslyn maintained her gentle whisper.

"This is not my place," Gavin added. "I will not let her stay here."

"You will both suffer for it." Joslyn shook her head with a hollow stare. "I am quite serious, Gavin. She has already connected herself with you."

"She will find someone else," he stated in a firm whisper. "When she comes of age, you are taking her with you, or she will venture out on her own, but she cannot remain in my territory." Gavin stopped her short. He walked into the hallway just in front of Joslyn when Nola called from a distance.

"You are sending me away?" Nola asked, stepping out from the fourth door down the hallway. There, her jaw dropped open as the distance between them and Gavin was well out of ear's range. They were easily half the house away. Nola hesitated, wondering how she had correctly heard. For the clarity in which she heard their voices, she believed them to be just outside the doorway. Yet, there she stood, twenty feet away from them hearing their every whisper. The sound became intensified as she turned her ears to listen. All could see her astonishment. Acute hearing was one of two traits that an Absolute gained almost immediately. The second came with discomfort in the final days of adolescence.

"Say something," she whispered needing the recreation to affirm the truth. Gavin leaned to his sister's ear and followed her instruction.

"Give us some time alone. I will send for you when we are ready." Gavin nodded to Nola when he had finished. Joslyn turned to see Nola place her hands to her mouth in surprise. She had heard the private whisper and was both amazed and scared by the ability.

Without another word, the elder Absolute took Levi's hand and led him away from the foyer toward the second floor. In a flash, they were both nowhere to be seen. It took a moment for Nola to realize what had happened to the couple. Strangely, she could still hear their voices in a quiet hum.

Nola stood frozen solid. Fully aware of her impeccable hearing. There had been a low static sound, a background whisper or hint of music that just always seemed to be there. However now, it was clear as a bell. The wind, the trees, and the footsteps of the servants above. A all were in her ears and mind. The world seemed so incredibly vast at that moment. Noises that were not meant to be heard began to categorize themselves in her mind. Still, her heart could not ignore what Gavin had told Joslyn. She was to leave his territory.

"You are going to send me away?" Nola lowered her hands and tried to deal with one issue at a time.

"What did you expect me to do?" He closed the gap between them. "Four days ago, you left everything you knew because you believed I was trying to trap you. Now, you are upset to learn that I'll not let you stay?"

"Yes!" Nola exclaimed, raising her voice louder than she had ever done. "Yes! I am very upset! Did you think I would gracefully accept being scared out of my wits, only to be returned here, and then ...abandoned for the second time in my life?" Her eyes were wide and brimming with tears she refused to acknowledge. "What about my family? What about Aunt Dottie, Luke, and Davey? Will they have to travel for days on end to come and visit me? Why?" Her hands began to tremble. "And why, in bloody hell, am I so constantly irrational as of late?"

"Listen to me." Intending to reach forward, his hand withdrew immediately due to the force of her emotions. "Can you please try and calm down?" He asked again before reaching out. Wanting the subtle touch, she swallowed hard and tried to lessen her anger, but it was useless. It was gentle but thick, like wading through water. Gavin drew back and looked at the room behind her. "Come in here," he called. "Please, if you would. We could use a little privacy."

"Is there such a thing?" she asked as he led her into the mahogany room with a large desk. "I can hear everything. How can they not hear us?"

"Please, close the door," he whispered. Once the door was closed nearly all the sounds around her disappeared. "Like many others in this house this room has very thick glass and solid walls. When that door is closed, every word spoken is concealed. All rooms are equipped in this way and have been since my father's father built it. We thrive through privacy." While his words filled the air, all else had disappeared. The static and distractions had vanished the moment the door closed. It was as if Nola had returned to normal. However, when the light from the hallway was extinguished the silvery glow to Gavin's eyes returned.

"Why would you send me away?" She lowered her voice despite the silence. "How could you tell me half of what I need to know, follow me for days when I try to get away from you, and then say that you are going to kick me out of your territory the minute I become what you are ...we are?" The entire time she spoke her eyes focused on the strange refraction in his eyes.

"Your hearing is just another step. You have much to experience yet." He stayed his distance. "We can't be in the same city as we are now. Look at what it does to us." It was not meant to sound sensual when he whispered. "We are constantly drawn together." He walked through the room taking a box of matches out of a drawer and lit a candle on the desk. "And you still don't know if you can trust me or not."

"I'm here, aren't I?"

"Yes, because I held your hand and touched your skin."

"No." Nola followed him over beside the desk and took the matches out of his hand. The single candle allowed vision in the room, but it also left Gavin's eyes slightly affected. "You do not control me... everything I feel from you is more than powerful suggestion." Nola closed the matches in the drawer and looked up to his masculine, beautiful face. "This," she reached out to him and took his hand. "This feeling of contentment is the only part of any transformation I would welcome. Everything else is tormenting. If I know that I must go through this only to lose the one connection I have with another person, then it isn't worth it." Gavin looked down at her hand before pulling away.

"There are hundreds of us, Nola. Four of us are under one roof right now. Several cities around the world house as many as six Absolutes simultaneously. I am not the only one you will ever know."

"You will throw me out into the world with nothing?" She cast out her hand before rubbing her brow with it.

"Fine," he gave in at last. "Stay. This is what you know, and you can learn everything you need to in the safety of the city you grew up in. I will leave."

"Where will you go?" The desperation was a new feeling for her to experience.

"I have houses all over the world. Think about it, Nola. We don't age. It's hard to stay in the same place for too long." Gavin lowered his voice as a lock of her hair fell from one of her pins when she looked down. "We come back to our ancestral homes every forty years or so as our own child. People tell us how much we look like our father, and the circle continues."

"Either way, you will make me go on without you."

"If you have trust in me, trust that this is best for you." Gavin reached up and tucked the wayward curl behind her ear. "You will meet others."

"I've met others," Nola whispered as she took a step closer to him. "I've met Elias, Joslyn, and Levi. Not one of them affected me in such a way." She looked up with a lost expression. "I sat with Elias for hours. I felt Joslyn's hand. You said that I would feel a bond of belonging... but I have no such regard with them." Gavin narrowed his gaze and seemed confused by her words. "I feel less for them than I do for Dottie and Luke. The only person I have any attachment to... is you."

"Maybe you need to wait until you have changed more?"

"I don't believe that." She reached up and touched her palm to his cheek. Slowly, Gavin closed his eyes and let her influence seep into him. Nola was very aware of her own fear and despair, but she was unsure of how much he could feel. "Why is it that you need to send me away?"

"There are two ways to survive this existence," he took her wrist, "either bound to someone like Joslyn and Levi, or alone."

"And you chose alone?"

"I had no choice." He stepped back. "I told you that childbirth was difficult for our kind. To be honest, it is nearly impossible." Letting go of her hand, he placed his in his pockets. "I watched my wife struggle through three children before the fourth killed her. What she endured was something no human could ever understand, and it is not just the labor process that is difficult. Our bodies constantly want to heal themselves. For a woman, it means that their own physical being is trying to eliminate the growth of the child. The child, being Absolute, repairs any damage the mother's

154

body can do. For months, there is nothing but pain, and that is before the labor process." Gavin began to shake his head gently. "A female Absolute can count on more suffering and loss than any other creature on earth."

"I understand," she whispered, fearing the new knowledge. "Gavin, I'm not even sure that I want... I'm not certain what sort of... bond," an exasperated sigh escaped her chest. "I am simply saying that I don't want to be without you."

"Right," he nodded his head and then returned to stand before her. "It is imperative to be fair to you," whispering softly, he held her stare as he removed his hand from his pocket and reached out to touch her chin. "It would appear as if I caged you. You would learn nothing of the world, Nola." As if he had instantly started a fire, Gavin's desire ran deep.

Nola took his hand in hers and felt the blood course through her veins. There was no force in the world strong enough to resist him. Quietly, the deep growling sound came from his chest, and she knew it was animal behavior. Nola exhaled gently, needing him to be closer.

Closing the gap between them, she came into his arms. His eyes were beautiful, his lips were full, and the sensation of being with him thickened her pulse. Unable to control her own curiosity, she reached up to his face. Gavin hesitated, but once she pulled on his neck, he eagerly captured her lips.

Clenched hands would not let him escape. Willingly she kissed him time and time again, needing more with every touch. The thrill was fantastic, and the desire immeasurable. Her hands slid inside his coat and wrapped around his thick arms. His chest felt as solid as rock, yet his skin was warm and exciting. She felt her breathing grow shallow and her heart begin to pound. Every tantalizing kiss drove her on to explore every part of his body. She could feel that he was proving a point. He somehow conveyed that she needed to stop, and she knew that she would... eventually. Nola reached her hands around his sides and felt the strong muscles of his back. She wanted to feel his skin beneath her hands, to touch each part of him slowly and gently, to know where the erotic desire would take them. However, Gavin placed his hands on her shoulders and began to pull away.

"Wait," she whispered, not wanting to stop. Nola lowered her head to his chest and wrapped her arms around him.

"Where do you think these moments will lead," he asked in a husky whisper. "How long do you think I would be able to keep myself away from you?"

"You seem to be very good at it," she whispered.

"I won't always," he answered, lifting her chin to his gaze. "The more we meet like this, privately; I know I will test my own limits." As he spoke, Nola trailed her fingers down the center of his back. He reacted by arching slightly. "You need to stop."

"I'm stopping," she closed her eyes and brought her hand along his side and up his chest once more. "I promise, I'll stop." Reaching around his neck she stood on her toes to bring her lips to one more kiss. Gavin growled again and granted her liberty. This time, however, Nola went too far. Her kiss deepened and she allowed him to part her lips, savoring more of her than he had before. She pressed against his body. Strong hands wrapped around her torso. Gavin's breathing grew deeper, his embrace became tighter, and his kiss lowered to her neck.

Nola closed her eyes and let him slide his lips along her skin.

Never had she felt such intense pleasure. He seemed to be everywhere. His hands roamed freely, and she pulled him as close as she could, letting her lips brush against his ear. The bliss was beginning to overwhelm her.

In that moment, the two sharp points of his teeth grazed the side of her neck. Like being shot from a rifle, she found herself across the room holding her neck. There was no blood on her hand. There was no pain. Still, he stood next to the desk with long white fangs protruding below his upper lip. Letting his thumb and forefinger trace the sharp teeth, he rotated his head. The fangs then extended, fully.

"It's a reaction," he whispered. "Everything tends to expand at the same time," he chuckled, hoping she would find some humor in his candor. Taking off the jacket, he laid it on the desk. "Come here," he called lifting his hand and curling his finger twice. "You may as well get used to them. Before long you will have your own."

"I can't," she answered.

"It's alright, I'd never hurt you."

"No... I can't seem to move." The depth of her fear was clear.

Visibly frozen to the spot, she waited as Gavin walked over to her. The entire distance, her eyes stayed on the razor-sharp teeth.

Taking her wrist, Gavin lifted her hand to his face and covered his mouth with the inside of her hand. Slowly raising his chin, he drew the sharp fangs against her skin, trailing to the tips of her fingers. The daggers extended halfway down her tiny finger, sending a chill up her spine. She watched them draw upward, back into the upper jaw. Gavin licked his teeth once they were gone, and Nola saw a trickle of blood on tip of his tongue.

"Does it hurt?"

"In a good way," he answered. "I can't explain it any better than that." Sensing something Nola was not aware of; Gavin grabbed his jacket and threw it over his shoulders. The urgency made no sense to her. "Stay still," he warned. Pulling the door open forcefully, he watched as Joslyn arrived at the doorway in a blur of her red dress.

"There's trouble," she said, taking her hand and pressing it against Gavin's chest. Closing his eyes, he grew rigid and tense.

"They're at the house!" Gavin growled a sudden yell.

Instantly, Levi was in the room.

"There's two of them," Levi added, curtains and papers lifted from the breeze of the instant motion.

"Dottie," Gavin whispered. He pointed to Nola and commanded his sister. "Bring her!" Then, just as fast as Joslyn and Levi arrived, Gavin disappeared.

"What's going on?" Nola asked as Levi left with such speed that her eyes could not catch his movement. "Joslyn?"

"I'm going to take you to Dottie," Joslyn answered. "But I need to you to trust me and remain calm." Nola looked to the door and felt the urge to run to the house. "Nola, trust me." With her arms wrapped around her, Joslyn held her head to her shoulder. "Keep your eyes closed."

"I have to go!"

"Shh," Joslyn warned. Instantly, a wind swirled around them without either of them moving. "Keep your eyes closed." Dust seemed to come from everywhere and Nola could feel tiny sand-like particles brushing against her skin, through her hair and past her skirts. Everything was silent for a moment. She could feel Joslyn's arms around her tightly but had no idea of what was happening. Then, in an instant it all ended. Around them, the room had changed.

Once the wind slowed down, Nola opened her eyes to look at the swirl of ash around them. Embers would ignite but no heat was transferred. It was an effect of movement so fast; it was as if time, in a solid form, had been burned. Before Nola could ask where they were, a familiar voice called out.

"Nola," Dottie called. Opening her eyes, Nola realized that she was in her own parlor. The room had been ransacked and Dottie, covered in blood, propped up against the wall. "Come here child," Dottie called, wrapping her arms around Nola. Blood trickled from her mouth, and she could not move her right arm. Immediately, Nola went to her side in horror.

"They've gone." Gavin looked back at Levi. "Track them!" He ordered. Joslyn turned toward the door, but Gavin held her shoulder. "I need you to stay." Joslyn nodded her head before he returned to Dottie's side.

"They came for your book," Dottie could barely hold her eyes open, but as long as Gavin was touching her there was less pain. "Luke…" she cried as much as her body would allow. "They took my son."

"Did you see them?" Gavin tried to ease Nola away from Dottie's grasp. "Dorothy, I need to know if you saw their faces."

"No," she answered. "They came in through the window and the door. Luke was aiding me to the stairs when they hit him. They asked twice for the book, but I never saw them…" In a breath, she tried to remain conscious. "A force pulled me across the room and threw me against this wall."

"I saw two of them." Joslyn piped up. "They came from the west.

"Get Luke back," Dottie tried to raise her broken arm to Gavin. "You have to find him!"

"I will," he answered, supporting the break in her bone. "Levi is hunting, right now. I need to take care of you first."

"Aunt Dottie," Nola called, wiping the blood from her face. To her horror, a single cough brought more blood to her aged lips. "You're going to be alright," Nola cried gently.

"I'm broken, my dear." Dottie forced a smile, though her eyes could barely stay open. "This body has served me well enough. I'd like to be free of it," she whispered. "It is time to let go," she muttered in a strained voice.

"No," Nola began to cry for the only mother she ever knew. "We'll get you to a hospital. Gavin can get the carriage ready. They can help." The older woman ignored the plea.

"Gavin," Dottie reached for him. "You made me a promise. It is time to keep your word." There was debilitating sadness in his dark eyes. Without a sound, Gavin brought her hand to his lips and kissed it gently. Turning to look at Joslyn, he came to his feet.

"I'll take her to the manor," Joslyn took control of the situation. Seeing Gavin distraught, and Nola in shock, Joslyn acted quickly. "Get a horse and meet me there." Barking orders, she picked Dottie up as if she weighed no more than a leaf. "There is bleeding inside the body." A hint of silver glow shown in the Absolute's eyes. "She has little time left." Gently cradling Dottie against her, Joslyn closed her eyes. "Dorothy, I can only travel with you," Joslyn whispered. The old woman nodded her head and mumbled an answer of some sort. With a nod of her head, the wind picked up again and a dust filled smoke overtook the room. Gavin grabbed onto Nola and pulled her out of the vicinity. She could not actually see Joslyn or Dottie leave, just a whirlwind of ash.

It was the last night she was ever going to get to see her aunt.

The tears came immediately, an emotion she had never felt before. Sadness overwhelmed her and Nola could barely understand that Gavin was readying the horse as she stood stone solid in the small stable.

"Come on," he pulled her hand and lifted her up into the saddle.

The horse sounded like thunder as it bolted down the road. Neither Gavin nor Nola wore coats in the winter wind, but the cold never pierced their skin. It was a long and painful journey.

Nola's mind swirled with confusion and questions, wondering where Luke was and if Gavin would keep his word to find him. She could feel fury within Gavin, through the jolting of the horse. Nola knew he did not want her to know his torment. Fortunately, her grief was too intense. Dottie would never lecture her again, would never help pick out dresses and would never offer those tiny bits of information that reminded her to be a better person. A small sob escaped her lips as she pressed her head against Gavin's back.

Nola still needed Dottie. She needed that gentle and understanding person in her life and was not ready to face the world alone. An unrestrained sob escaped, and Nola realized how much she was crying. Just past Baggerty bridge Gavin pulled the horse to a stop. Turning around as much as he could, he wrapped an arm around her waist. Before Nola could wipe her tears, he hauled her around him and cradled her in his arms.

"I'm sorry," he whispered, stroking her hair, and tucking her head below his chin. "I'm so sorry."

"We have to go," Nola lifted her tear-stained face to his view. "She can't die alone."

"She won't, but you will not see her again." Gavin answered, again leading the horse on. "I made her a promise, and I intend to keep it." The horse continued slowly at first, then faster and faster.

"I want to be there." Nola felt a sudden panic. "I need to see her."

"No, Nola. Dottie and I have an agreement." He continued to hold her off the saddle as the horse blazed through the city. "She will not be alone."

Chapter Eleven

Short Sighted

Behind the thick emerald curtain, the clouds were full and heavy. Still, not nearly as heavy as Nola's heart. It was truly a day for mourning. Glancing out the window she could see the hotel rise four stories in the distance. Gavin sent someone to clean Dottie's house, but Davey still could not stay there.

Trying to keep Davey at ease, Gavin gave him a room at the hotel until he was ready to move back home. Nola wanted to accompany him, but Davey found comfort with Miss Stephens and didn't seem to know how to handle Nola with Luke missing. Gavin's offer to watch over his charge was easily accepted. To their surprise, Davey blamed himself for the attack. He believed it had something to do with his late-night fighting. A full investigation by the police was being carried out, but Nola knew that they would not find anything useful.

Dottie's body was found in the house, at the bottom of the stairs. It was as if she had simply stumbled and fallen. Gavin mentioned that the coroner reported a heart attack as cause of death, and the body was removed without examination. Nola knew it must have cost him a great fortune for the secrecy, but she was grateful.

Just that morning, covered by the thick and heavy fog, Dottie Ellis was laid to rest in a winter grave. Numb straight to the core, Nola stared out the window. Her mind rolled over and over her last memories of Dottie, and how devastating it was when Gavin carried her to the vault below the house.

Nola was not allowed to follow Gavin the night he carried Dottie to the lower part of the manor. Yet, Joslyn was there.

Somehow guiding Nola's vision, the oldest Absolute lent her eyesight. It was all as Dottie once retold of the unhappy maid that met her end by Gavin's hand instead of suicide. Joslyn remained near the base of the stairway. Carefully leaving Gavin space to whisper with his old friend. Dottie held strong arms and leaned against his chest.

The walls were white, and there was a small sofa in the center of the round room. Gavin stroked Dottie's hair, told her how much she was loved in this life and reminded her of those that waited for her in the next.

In the unsettling, gilded view, Gavin held her on the sofa and rocked back and forth with her in a tight embrace. Then, with incredible speed, he barred his teeth and sunk them into her neck. It

160

was over before Dottie could draw another breath. However, Joslyn forced her vision to remain on Gavin until his shoulders shook and he wept over the old woman's body. Gavin's despair was unbearable.

Nola could not stand the vision after that. Nor could she tolerate the lasting memory. It was fortunate that Joslyn's shoe heels clicked on the marble floor outside the large personal room.

"Nola," Joslyn entered the room, accompanied by Levi. "We need to talk."

"Yes," Nola asked. She regained composure and stood without emotion.

"You see," Joslyn began, stepping into the room in a deep gold dress and sitting on the edge of her bed. "It will be dark in a few hours."

"Go on," Nola insisted softly.

"We think we may have found someone that could take us to Luke."

"Where?" Letting the heavy emerald curtain fall back before the window, she turned to face them. "Where is he?"

"We need you to tell us," Joslyn explained. "See, we haven't physically found him." Joslyn tilted her head to the side and spoke as gently as she could. "We just know that he has been in the area."

"My ability is tracking." Levi came to sit next to Joslyn. Their manners were that of family or familiarity. Both of which Nola had come to find strangely comfortable. "With my thoughts and concentration, I can feel and hear any Vampyre or Absolute from nearly anywhere in the world. In my mind's eye, I see their faces for a moment and can hear a few words of what they are saying. It is possible for me to focus on the individual for minutes at a time, but I only see them and get an idea of where they are. From there I can track them down quite easily."

"A particular Vampyre traveling east has been repeating the word Graelohr and talking about the book," Joslyn added. "Levi can take us to him physically, but the Vampyre is sure to sense us coming, alerting whoever has Luke. You, on the other hand, can give us a little disguise. Use Levi's sight to see if the Vampyre is with Luke. With the information you give us we can reach him quickly and get out safely."

"I don't know how to choose a person to see through," Nola answered, shaking her head. "I'm not even sure how I do it at all."

"Do you feel up to trying something?" Joslyn came to her feet and crossed the room to the window. "Can you try seeing through Levi?"

Nola glanced back at the darkened window and touched the green curtain once more. Her sorrow was deep, and when Joslyn held out her hands, she didn't want to take them. She did not want the pain of Dottie's loss to feel dissipated. She wanted to wallow in grief and just let it hurt. Still, time was imperative to find Luke. In turn, Nola held out her hands and nodded.

Surprisingly, grief was not subdued. If anything, she could feel Joslyn's sadness for Gavin and what he felt. It was a brief passing of emotion before Joslyn guided Nola to focus. It was odd to have a simple touch from Joslyn impress so much intention. Thus, Nola concentrated on Levi as instructed. She imagined where he was sitting, his thick black coiled braids, and the deep gray suit that he wore. Her concentration lingered on his dark masculine features and deep eyes. Still, she did not know how to use his sight.

"Relax," Joslyn said, letting go of her hands and trailing her touch around to stand behind her shoulders. "Perhaps if you stopped trying to see him and focused on seeing us." Nola took the idea and sincerely gave it her best effort.

"I'm not sure how," Nola answered after several moments of trying.

"Alright," Joslyn let go of her and stepped to the center of the room. "Would you like to try it with Levi to find my sight? It may be easier since we are friends." There was a question-like tone to her voice.

"Alright," Nola agreed, still suffering the grief of Dottie and loss of Luke. "I'll try." Coming to his feet, Levi stepped over to take her hands.

"She's close, and she is looking right at us," Levi spoke gently with his calming island accent. What do you look like through her eyes?" He squeezed Nola's hands gently letting a subtle and creeping hint of emotion flow through him. He was very faint compared to Joslyn and Gavin. Still, Nola let him calm her down and helped her focus on the task at hand.

"All I can feel is devotion to you and his love of music." Letting go of his hands, Nola turned to Joslyn.

"I was afraid of that. Levi is a very young Absolute; his sixty years is not enough to generate much help." Twirling a lock of hair between her fingers, Joslyn set her fascinating blue eyes on her husband. "At least in this circumstance," she teased him quietly. "So," she sighed and returned to the bed. "In all this time, you have only been able to use Gavin's sight, never Mr. Percy or any other Vampyre?"

"No," Nola shook her head. "Just Gavin... and you the one time."

"No," Joslyn sighed as she answered. "I forced your gift on you through me. It is very difficult to do, and I'm not sure I could do it again. We need you to choose the host." The disappointment in her voice was hidden carefully. "Well, all right, we know that you have the gift. Let's just try to find something to trigger it." She looked around the room and glanced at Levi on the bed. "For starters, you've been in this room far too long and we have completely invaded your privacy." She held out her hand to Levi. "Let's go down into the parlor and try to think of ideas. If we can't use you, maybe Levi can come up with something else that will help us."

"That is a good idea," Levi admitted.

"Alright," Nola agreed, looking back at the dark emerald curtain, knowing that the light behind it was fading.

Her head was heavy, and her chest still ached with tension.

The sadness was still nearly unbearable, but Nola had split her emotions between grief for Dottie and fear for Luke. It had been a full two days since he had been missing and the only clue was a small bit of hope from Levi. Trying to focus on helping, Nola raised her chin gently and followed the pair down the hall. However, a curtain from one of the rooms grabbed her attention.

Thin curtains of vanilla silk surrounded a large thick bed inside the private room. Intrigued by familiarity, Nola paused to peer inside the door. An ancient wooden dresser with a large oval mirror stood against the wall and she knew she had been there before. The same soft white candles stood on two pedestals inside the gray room. She had seen it before from a different point of view.

"What is it?" Joslyn asked as Nola entered the large bedroom and looked at the wide-open space.

"I've seen this room before," she whispered. Nola walked to the side of the room where the same curtain that surrounded the bed trailed down the wall as decoration. "I've been here."

"You mean, you have seen this through Gavin?" Joslyn stepped into the room.

"No, I saw him. I saw him stand right there." Her hand motioned to the dresser. "It was like a dream. He looked at his reflection and then..." Nola stopped speaking until the memory was perfectly clear. "He looked in the mirror as if he had seen me. I was seeing it from over here." Glancing up at the silk, Nola reached out to touch the fabric. "This is Gavin's bedroom." Her eyes trailed to the bed. "I've seen him sleep there." Joslyn looked at Nola strangely and then back to Levi. It was obvious that Nola had said something that affected her, but she could not tell if it was good or bad.

"Come on," Joslyn beckoned. "Are you up to facing Gavin yet?"

"I have seen him." Nola left the room and followed down the hallway to the stairs.

"No, you've ignored him. Even at the funeral." Joslyn kept up her pace. "You haven't cast one glance toward him, nor have you been within a fifteen-foot radius." Her yellow gold skirts slid across the floor as they descended the stairs.

"I don't really remember," she answered, barely able to recall him standing across the cemetery from her.

Nola followed them to a large parlor with blue carpet and gold decorative wallpaper. A large piano sat near the corner with three bay windows at the side of the room. Just in front of the roaring fire, Gavin sat with some papers in his hand. When they entered, he set them down on the table.

His eyes were hollow, his expression dreary, and brow furled when their eyes met. The ache he felt showed in his face. Even Nola could not deny it. Yet, it was not just his sorrow that surprised her, it was a flash of guilt. The way his eyes quickly cast down to the floor gave proof of how accountable he felt.

"This may be too soon," Gavin warned Joslyn as Nola turned away from him.

Something in the sound of his voice turned her back. She did not want him to feel so much pain. Unlike any passion she had ever felt, Nola wanted nothing more than the comfort that only they could give each other. The knowledge that all the confusion and suffering she felt could be lessened by the touch of his skin pulled Nola inside the room. Fixatedly, she crossed the floor and came face to face with his surprised reserve.

"Is everything alright?" Gavin came to his feet and towered before Nola. His head bent with concern in his dark eyes. Nola knew that her forgiveness was all he needed and not a second went by before she rushed into his arms. Finally, for Nola the world disappeared. Her arms wrapped around Gavin, barely able to get them to reach around his broad shoulders. Her head was buried in his chest, and he held her as tight as he could. His shock, shared equally by both Joslyn and Levi, wore off quickly.

"Are you alright?" he asked, gently pushing her hair aside and kissing her brow.

The words would not come to her. Within his arms, Nola could not only feel her depression and heartache, but she became aware of Gavin's as well. Filled with pain and suffering, he was overcome with responsibility for the attack on Dottie's home, Luke's absence, and regret for having to take Dottie's life. His passion was so overwhelming that Nola could barely speak. Gavin continued to stand and speak as if the emotions were easily kept in check.

"We'll wait outside," Levi suggested as he took Joslyn's hand.

The woman was so surprised by the tender moment that she simply stared at the two of them. "Joslyn..." Levi called.

"No," Nola sniffled once, wiped her eyes with her sleeve, and backed away from Gavin. "We need to find Luke." Having kept hold of her hand, Gavin squeezed her fingers. "Can you teach me how to see through someone?" She asked him.

"Did you find something?" Gavin looked at Levi.

"A glimpse," Levi answered. "There is a man. His face is not clear, and he doesn't belong in this area. Yet, he's been here looking for the book and has mentioned your name several times." Removing a silk handkerchief from his pocket he offered it to Nola. "We could use her help."

"Alright," Gavin agreed. "How often have you been able to use my sight?" he asked, leading Nola toward one of the sofas.

"Not often," she answered, holding his hand. "I'm not sure how I even do it. It happens when I least expect it."

"Let's start with consistencies," Joslyn proposed. "Where were you the last time it happened?"

"Without you, it was when Mr. Tempest saw me in the alleyway near the library."

"About what time of day was it?"

"Late, maybe ten at night," Nola answered.

"Before that?" Joslyn proceeded with the inquisition. "Most of the time I was either staring out the window, or

staring at the pages of a book, but I was not focusing on anything in particular." Feeling guilty for the deep intrusion on Gavin's privacy, she tried to defend herself. "Something would provoke a memory and it was like a daydream, but not mine. The view becomes tinted. I saw either these hallways, the large bedroom at the top of the stares, or sometimes strange things... like the horse beneath him or him walking through the snow."

"All of the visions occurred at night?" Levi sat at one of the chairs and tried to put the puzzle together.

"Yes, very few were in the morning and those were in the early hours when I was exhausted."

"You were awake all day when you had the visions at night?" Joslyn was still standing next to Levi, but she seemed to have an idea.

"Yes, I worked at the school and helped Dottie in the evening."

"Maybe fatigue helps?" She questioned. "At this point, with your difficulty sleeping... maybe being completely exhausted lets the vision flow without consciousness muddling it up?"

"It is plausible," Levi offered.

"Then it would have worked upstairs," Nola whispered. "There is no denying that I am tired. All we need now is for me to know how to instigate the ability."

"I have an idea." Gavin stood up and walked over to the closest side table, taking an old novel out of the drawer. "Why don't you try to focus on this for a while? It's about England's politics and poverty." He handed the book to Nola. "While you are doing that, the three of us will separate and leave our minds open to you."

"Can't you just stay here?" Nola asked, not wanting him to leave.

"You are safe. I'll be back soon," he promised. "Just give yourself time to try this."

"Alright," she agreed half-heartedly. "But what do we do if I can't make the vision happen?"

"Then we will find him without it," Gavin promised.

Levi added carefully, "Luke has been missing for almost forty-eight hours. We have to find him soon."

"I understand." Nola agreed and opened the book. With a heavy sigh, Gavin left the room followed by Joslyn and Levi.

"Whoever had him knew that Dottie would not survive and that we would not make a move until the funeral was over. We should have retaliated the night he was taken," Joslyn whispered in the hallway.

"She can hear you perfectly," Gavin reminded her. After a short, worried gaze between brother and sister, the three of them separated.

Nola shook off the comment from the hallway and stared at the old, yellow-tinged pages of the book. She was able to scan over the words. Still, in the back of her mind she knew Joslyn was right. She knew that Luke had been gone too long, but they had no idea where to start looking.

Guilt plagued her mind as she thought of leaving him at the museum. He wanted her to stay. She should have stayed, but the events of the night would not have changed Dottie's fate. Letting the book fall to her lap, Nola let her arm fall to the side of the chair.

There was too much stress for her to concentrate. She couldn't stop her mind from wondering over Luke's fate. Giving up completely, she stood up and set the book on the table.

The house seemed enormous without Gavin in the room. It was full of his presence, but she wanted him closer. The way that he soothed her was incomparable. Stepping toward the door, she glanced at the clock. He hadn't been gone for ten minutes and she was ready to seek him out.

Nola stopped beside the door and leaned her head against the frame. It was ridiculous to go to him. She remembered the feeling of his lips and the passion that consumed her each time she was in his arms. He was far too sensual for her to refuse. Even if she did find him in the gigantic manor, there was no way she could keep her wits about her. Grief would place her in his arms and passion would take her to his bed.

Sighing heavily, Nola turned back around and returned to the room. She needed to focus on Luke. Closing the door behind her, she walked over to the window. Thick blue curtains hung to the floor in front of gray lace. The secondary curtain was thin and easy to see through. The sun was gone but the moon had not fully risen.

The city seemed alight from the manor. The hotel windows were filled with a yellow glow, and she could see the streetlights lit in front of the library. Focused on one of the lights, she let her mind stray. Unimportant thoughts filled her head, the color of the library carpet, the old books she used to borrow, and the journey from the library to home. Somehow, staring through that window, a tinted yellow view of her gown came to her mind.

It was definitely her gown though it seemed greener in sight. The turquoise shade was brightened by the golden haze. After a moment, the view began to widen, and she realized it was her own form she was seeing from behind. Long dark locks of hair trailed down her back with shimmering combs holding it in place. It was when Nola turned around that she became frightened. In the darkness, her eyes had a definite silver glow. However, it wasn't her image that frightened her. It was a fact that she could not see who was walking directly in front of her. She could only see their view.

"Stop," she held up her hand, but the vision descended on her faster. "Stop!" she screamed, backing into the window fully aware of how wide-eyed and scared she looked. Nola could see herself blinking her eyes and shaking her head long before the sight grew dark.

"Nola, it's me!" Gavin grabbed her arms, feeling her thrash against him. "What is it?" He asked.

Her loud sigh was instantaneous. Nola placed her hands to her eyes and rubbed them to be sure that she could see clearly.

"I have no control over it," she whispered. "I could see my own face, but I could not tell it was from you!"

"You were using my sight?" He asked to be sure.

"You scared the hell out of me!" Pushing him away, she held her palms to her eyes for another moment. "It was like I was blind from my own body!"

"Are you alright?" Joslyn asked from the door with Levi right behind her.

"I'm fine," she answered, noting how quickly they came from the door to stand beside her.

"I scared her," Gavin admitted keeping his distance.

"She scared us all," Joslyn offered quickly. "What happened?" As she asked the question, Gavin stood behind Nola waiting to comfort her. Nola held one arm across her chest with her hand to her forehead as she nodded.

"Nothing," Gavin stated quite calmly.

"I'm fine. Thank you." Nola sighed and held her chest.

"Alright," Joslyn agreed. "Then we are just going to head back upstairs." Her voice trailed off softly. "Levi and I have some things to finish up..." Levi took her hand and began to pull her out of the room. "If you should need us..."

"I'll be alright," Nola offered as the door was closed behind them. Once they were alone again, she turned to face Gavin. "Were you trying to scare the life out of me?"

"I'm sorry." His voice was deep and grating. "I am not entirely certain if you are using your gift. Joslyn is overbearing to one's senses. The only thing I can recognize is your transcending." When she looked bewildered, he clarified. "When you saw me in my bedroom and hit your head... that was transcending. I can sense that, but I did not know you were using my sight, just now."

"I can't even begin to tell you how terrifying that was." Nola moved to the nearest chair and sat down.

"When you were facing me, even as you yelled, you were seeing through my eyes?"

"Yes," she admitted.

"What were you doing before that?"

"I'm not sure... staring out the window, I think." She looked up at him, tilting her head all the way back.

"Were you thinking about me?"

"No." the defensive tone to her voice was undeniable. "I mean, I was... before I went to the window, but when I had the vision, I was thinking of unimportant details. Little things about the library... I think."

"If I stay right here in the room with you, would you try it again?"

"Gavin, I couldn't see for a few seconds. My person was someone else, for a moment. Do you have any idea how terrifying that was?" She rubbed her forehead once again.

"I could see your face. You were distraught, but it wouldn't happen like that again. I'm right here, and I will look out the window with you or at whatever you want to look at. You know you can do it."

"What good does it do to see through your eyes?"

"You need to learn how to use it. With any luck you're going to learn how to see through the Vampyre that took Luke." He reminded her. Before she could shake her head, Gavin had pulled her up out of the chair. "Think about Luke." His voice was very deep and brooding. "He was beaten enough to leave a fair amount of blood at the house, and he was the only other human to read the pages of that ancient book. Whoever has him will do whatever is necessary to get the information they are looking for." Nola stared up at him, feeling urgency with the touch of his hands. "Right now, I am assuming that they have not sent a note or offered a trade because they feel Luke can give them the information they need. As long as he keeps quiet... they will keep him alive."

"No," she shook her head. "They are just holding him." The hysterical sound of her voice was barely hidden. "Luke doesn't know what that book was about. He only read bits and pieces with me! He doesn't know the full details of what we are or how you came to be!"

"I'm going to find him," Gavin stated clearly with his hands on her shoulders. "I need to know if you can help me." Nola nodded her head to the question. "You just had a vision moments ago. Let's try to bring it back through someone closer to Luke."

Nola let go of his hands and walked back over to the window. Her mind was filled with horrifying thoughts and the stress of trying to conjure up something she couldn't control. Still, she placed her fingers on the gray lace and peered out toward the city.

"Would you stand behind me please?" She asked. "If it works, and I see through your eyes instead it will upset me less if I am not staring at myself again."

Gavin didn't answer; he simply crossed the floor to stand behind her. It took a moment, but he had to remind himself not to stare at her hair. When Nola sighed, he reached down and placed a steady hand against her side, offering her whatever comfort he could.

"Just think of him, the same way you thought of the library before your mind began to travel," he whispered.

Nola knew Gavin had no idea what he was suggesting, but she used the idea all the same. Letting images of Luke flow into her mind, the only thing she could think of was how close she had grown to him over the past few weeks. Nola remembered them staying up late eating apples and making fun of Davey, his unruly wayward hair and eyes that seemed to smile without using his lips. He had become such an important part of her life that when she found out what she was; it was only because of Luke that she denied it.

It was impossible to hold him in her mind for another moment. Gavin unintentionally changed the tightness of his hand on her waist and drew her back to the present. Nola sighed and looked out at the city before her. It was strange how narrow her field of vision became when she was remembering something compared to when she was looking for something. Just as her mind began to scatter and she considered how much snow had fallen that year, Nola could see the thin yellow veil fall in front of her eyes.

"I'm right here," Gavin whispered as her breathing went shallow and her body rigid.

Nola was still looking at the city, but the tinted color was undeniably there. Making the conscious decision to fall into the golden haze, the city disappeared around her. Instead, she was offered a strange view from behind a dark covering of some sort. There was a hole in the cloth over her eyes and she could see wood planking beneath her feet. The feet below her were moving, thick brown boots with dark trousers above them. One of the boots kicked a rock on the planking and she could see through the bottom of the cloth where it slid into the water. Staying with the vision, she watched each step on the planking until she was sure that she was seeing water between the boards at her feet. Suddenly, the feet changed direction unsteadily, as if being guided by someone else, up a flat board with the water directly below. When the change was made, the hole in the cloth shifted revealing a sliver of the moon in the sky above. The color faded quickly, revealing Thedford City once more.

"They are taking Luke onto a ship!"

"How do you know?" Gavin resisted turning her around to face him. "Are you still seeing him?"

"No," Nola answered as she turned to face Gavin directly. "Through him..."

"That isn't likely," he spoke quickly. "Tell me what you saw."

"There is something over his head, like a hood or a loose bag. He can see his feet and where he is stepping ... and there is one tiny hole in the cloth just above his right eye. At his feet, there are wood planks of a boat dock and in the sky, he can see a small sliver of the moon fairly high in the sky." Grabbing onto his forearm, she held Gavin firmly. "It's Luke!"

"Nola," he whispered. "Absolutes can't use humans as hosts."

"Yes, I can!" She nodded her head. "I completely forgot." The look of wonder on her face was unending. "It happened the night of the museum event. I watched him wheel a chair out of the door to Dottie." Desperate to convince him, Nola took his hands. "I know he is being led onto a ship right now," she pleaded with him. "You have to believe me."

"I believe you, but it shouldn't be possible."

"What do we do?" she asked, completely excited about what she had seen.

"If the moon was high above him, then Luke is several hours east of here, seven at the least. We'll send Levi to track them. His emanation is weak, so they won't sense him coming. Joslyn and I will follow.

"Alright," she agreed, turning to walk toward the door. "Nola," he called as she reached for the handle. The glass

bulbs in the lanterns grew slightly brighter. However, his eyes held the same reflective glow. "Back away from the door." His hands remained just barely away from his sides as a continuous charge of static energy began to flow through the room. Nola stood where she was with her hand near the doorknob. When she defied him and reached closer, the metal ignited a blue spark and zapped out to her finger. Nola jumped back, grabbing her hand, and staring at Gavin. "Sorry," he whispered. "That was unintentional."

"What are you doing?" Nola asked as the hair on her neck began to stand on end.

"Getting someone's attention," he answered. "Don't touch anything made of metal for a few seconds." When there was a knock on the door, he glanced at the handle before answering. "Come in."

Suddenly, she could feel them. Two people were close to the other side of the room. Nola was aware of their vicinity in a way that became very helpful. A realization came into focus as she stared at the door. Feeling as if a large part of her mind had suddenly switched on, Nola knew what was happening in the house. She could sense two Vampyre men, one taller than the other, coming down the hall. When the door opened the two men that scaled the stone column the first night Nola came to the manor walked into the room. Expecting to fear them, she welcomed the hollow feeling that resided.

"It's early. Is there something wrong?" One of them asked. "Miss Valerian," he bowed to her.

"I think it's time you met." Gavin motioned to the first man.

He was average in stature, tall for a human but short compared to Gavin. He had wavy light hair and bright blue eyes. Nola recognized him immediately and bobbed politely, stepping slightly closer to Gavin. "This is Mack Banit. He has been traveling with me for as long as I can remember."

"It's a pleasure to finally meet you, Miss Valerian. My apologies for startling you the first we met." Mack nodded gently, showing a very slight glow to his eyes. When Nola responded silently, Gavin moved to the other gentlemen.

"And this is Hugh Pattlow. He is the genius behind electricity.

He recently spent over a year in northern America studying the engineering behind the power and its uses." As Gavin made the introduction, Nola tried to see the men as something more than vicious creatures.

"Miss," Hugh bowed politely. His gentle green eyes and full lips were not as hideous as she imagined. "Gavin is one of the leading investors in the scientific field."

"I can imagine," Nola added.

"Come in." Gavin called through the open door as Levi came into view.

Standing beside the two Vampyres, Levi was the comparison of Goliath. Instinctively the two smaller men made room for the Absolute. Only then did Nola realize how much she had become used to their incredible height and size. The only time she had paid much attention to the difference was when Gavin and Levi were at the museum event. As they stood in the room, Vampyre beside Absolute, the physical distinction was definite. However, the Absolutes did not scare her in the least. The Vampyres on the other hand, Nola could not ignore the way they felt edgy, unnatural.

"Luke Ellis is being held east of the harbor. We still don't know who is responsible." Gavin spoke clearly and directly to the three men. "Right now, Luke Ellis is being loaded on a ship, likely headed north." Gavin explained as Joslyn came into the room rubbing her hand.

"You saw them?" Joslyn asked.

"No," Nola answered. "But I saw enough to know where they were."

"Alright," she reached out to Levi and took his hand. "We will wait here. Send for me when you find something."

"I will," Levi answered, lifting his jacket slightly and checking the concealed dagger sheath at his side. Nola glanced toward Hugh and Mack, seeing that they too had knives at their side. The show of weapons made her very nervous and without realizing it, she reached out to take Gavin's arm.

"There is no need to conceal ourselves from Nola any longer, but everything we do in front of Luke has to be as human as possible." Gavin gave the order despite the confused audience. "We can't have him questioning our methods in a week or two."

"Gavin, whoever has him has already shown themselves," Joslyn spoke quietly. "How are you going to handle that?"

"Let's find him first and deal with the complications later." Gavin sighed heavily, knowing Nola was going to dislike what he said next. "Feed on the way. You'll need your strength." Hugh and Mack managed to hide their gratitude, but Levi smiled outright before leaving the room.

"Levi," Joslyn called quickly. He turned in the doorway and saw the heartfelt expression on her delicate face.

"Is that concern you hide behind those sapphire eyes?" His exotic accent filled the room. "Do you not know how fierce I am?"

"I trained you well." Joslyn tried to smile as she reached for her husband. "Don't disappoint me."

"Do I ever?" he asked before slowly capturing her lips in a warm and tender kiss. Before Joslyn opened her eyes he was gone, having sped through the hallway quickly passing Mack and Hugh. When she turned back to Gavin, there was a very real sadness in her expression. She thought about speaking and parted her lips for a moment but changed her mind and left the room.

"What is wrong with her?" Nola asked, knowing Joslyn could hear the question.

"Do you remember how empty you felt all those times I left the city?" he asked, walking over, and closing the door.

"There was a difference," Nola admitted sheepishly.

"For Joslyn, when Levi leaves her territory, it is painful and frightening. For her, if something happens to him, it won't hurt her for months or a year as it would a human. That kind of pain and suffering will last many lifetimes." Gavin remained on the opposite side of the room. "There will be someone coming to the house very soon. You may want to ready yourself."

"Who is coming?" Too many things were happening at once, and Nola could barely think straight.

"A friend of yours," his heavy sigh sounded irritated. "Elias Percy." Confused and too worried about Gavin's changing temper to ask why, Nola went to the center of the room and sat down. "Nola," his voice growled like a wild animal. "I want you to look nice for him."

"I don't understand," she whispered, coming to her feet. "Why is he coming?"

"He is the only other Absolute in the country that can teach you how to use your sight."

"Did you send for him?" she asked, slowly becoming annoyed with Gavin's hinted intention.

"Yes. It will take him a few hours to get here. Joslyn should have something you could wear."

"Another time perhaps," Nola stated plainly. "Today, I buried the only mother I have ever known and watched Luke be bound and carried onto a ship. You will have to pass me off to Mr. Percy some other day."

Remaining silent, Gavin looked down at her dress and then tilted his head to the side. There was time for her to be alone. Pressing his lips firmly together he reached for the handle of the door and left Nola to herself. It was only after he was gone that Nola looked down at her dress and realized that although the turquoise color looked nice on her, the dirty snow from the cemetery had soiled the hem and her sleeves were still stuffed with handkerchiefs.

***

The scent of smoke and ash filled her senses enough to make breathing difficult. She had been asked twice to relax, but Joslyn was in quite a state over Mr. Percy's approaching visit. She had helped Nola change and dress her hair, but all of it was done with a jaded temperament.

"Don't mind me," Joslyn waved a burgundy laced fan toward Nola to keep her cool. "I simply feel like you are the main course, and I am fattening you up for Mr. Percy's next meal." She spat out her words as she eyed the deep wine color that draped perfectly over Nola's figure.

"Joslyn," Nola whispered, trying not to feel the intense burning under her skin. "I appreciate the dress, but I'm not comfortable with your choice of analogies."

"I'm so sorry," she whispered, remembering Nola's human disadvantage. "Good Lord that was poor form on my part." Unable to help herself, Joslyn began to chuckle. "I didn't mean that."

"I know what you meant," Nola allowed herself to smile slightly.

"Oh, food..." Standing up from her bed, Joslyn dropped the fan on the vanity. "Nola, when is the last time you've eaten?" Placing her hand to her forehead, Joslyn tried to remember for her.

"I'm not hungry," she answered.

"No, you don't understand... grief can make you lose your appetite. You've probably never felt this much sorrow before." Taking her hands, Joslyn pulled her up from the chair.

"I don't know what I feel." Letting the admission flow freely, Nola shrugged her shoulders. "Whatever it is, it's potent enough to be physical. My chest hurts, my head feels heavy, and every step through this day has been difficult. However, hunger is the last thing I feel."

"That is grief." Joslyn placed her palm against Nola's cheek. "Gavin can take some of that from you. I'm not sure why he hasn't."

"He has his own sadness right now." Nola kindly removed Joslyn's hand from her face, trying to remind Joslyn of the heat she was creating.

"Regardless, we are feeding you anyway," she stated pulling Nola out of the room.

Pain seared through her flesh. "Stop!" Nola was forced to shake off her hand. Her skin turned red and rose slightly where Joslyn had touched. She recoiled and looked at the Absolute with a slight amount of fear. The effect, though painful, was fading quickly.

"I've been married to Levi for over a decade now and Elias Percy still makes my blood boil," Joslyn shook her head as she spoke. "That was not my intention." She glanced down at her hand. "I did not realize how intensely I am acting, right now."

"Please, just don't touch me." Nola tried to sound understanding.

"We are usually very cautious of such things. I'm sorry." Joslyn continued down the hall to the stairwell. "I just don't know why out of all of the traits you could have inherited from your parents, you had to get sighted."

"I can't answer that," Nola whispered.

"I know you can't, but when we find out whom your parents are I am going to ring their neck for making me tolerate a night with Elias Percy!" As she reached the bottom of the stairs, they rounded the corner to face Gavin. "When is the last time you fed her?"

"I'm not sure," Gavin answered, holding out his hand to Joslyn. Annoyed and furious at the offer, Joslyn looked down at his hand. Reluctantly, she allowed him to touch the base of her neck. For a moment Nola could feel the heat rise again, but all at once the intense burning sensation stopped completely.

"I'm fine..." Joslyn inhaled slowly, fully in control of emanation after Gavin pulled away. "Where do you keep your food?" Even before she made a sound Nola could feel the relieving difference.

"Chained in the cellar," Gavin answered flatly.

"I do not appreciate you humor." Holding up her hands, Nola looked away from them. "And you both have poor taste of it."

"My apologies," Gavin agreed. "I'll have the staff make you something. Go ahead into the dining room. I'll join you there." With a wink of his dark eye, he left them in the hallway.

"I honestly don't know which one of us hates this idea more, me or him."

"What do you mean?" Nola asked.

"Well, Gavin may live in another country most of the time, but there has been constant affection between us for over three hundred years. Absolute siblings are almost impossible to separate for long."

I believe you." Taking a moment to remember Esteban, Nola nodded her head.

"I imagine you do." Joslyn sighed, knowing of the small boy's death. "Gavin was with me when Elias chose a Vampyre companion ...in my stead. We were not together long, but it was long enough for me to need nearly a decade to recover."

"When we met, Mr. Percy spoke of you fondly. I assumed you were still friends."

"I'd have it no other way." Smiling a little more, Joslyn opened the door to the dining room and turned on the electric light. "As far as he knew I was content with his decision and didn't care at all." Her eyes took on a devious glare as she rounded the chairs at the table. "Which is why, when his little harlot got herself decapitated and he came crawling back to me, I dangled Levi in front of him like a brand-new toy in an orphanage." Even despite the cruel image, Nola allowed herself to chuckle. "I know how uncomfortable this evening will be for me. I just wonder how well my brother will make it through."

"Why is that?" Nola asked.

"Oh, you just wait." The wicked tone of her voice rang through the room. "Once Elias turns on his devilish charm, Gavin's detachment from you will not last long." Casting a knowing grin from ear to ear, Joslyn nearly laughed. "I'll be surprised if he doesn't claim you while you are still human." Nola's mouth fell open slightly at the bold admission. "Don't look so surprised. You know you've thought of him," she spoke honestly.

"Joslyn!" Gavin called sternly from way down the hall. "What?" she asked, completely annoyed, lifting her head in

his direction. "Don't use that tone with me! You wanted her distracted from the remains of the day. I can't think of a better subject that would dissuade one's mind!" Before he came into view, she leaned down into Nola's ear. "The human and Absolute coupling is not a big deal," she whispered. "It's like a nun with a tattoo... fun to talk about, but in the end nobody really cares."

"Why would a nun have a tattoo?" Taken back, Nola tried to hold her expression.

"You are completely missing my point!"

"Enough!" Gavin finally appeared with a plate of fried chicken and potatoes. In his other hand he held three glasses with a bottle of wine tucked in his arm. "You are in luck," he stated as he placed the food in front of her. "It turns out my steward just returned from a trip and was heating up some for himself."

"I'm not taking his, am I?"

"Not at all, there was plenty." Setting down a glass beside her, he uncorked the bottle of wine.

"Can I skip the pleasantry?" Joslyn asked, looking at the other glasses in his hand.

"No... Nola is a guest and all conversation from this point on will be appropriate for a guest." The formal tone of his hidden command made Joslyn roll her eyes. However, she took the glass and gave a brilliantly overdramatized smile.

"I disagree," she argued as Nola slowly began to eat the potatoes. "I've only been here a few days and I'm already bored with your brooding and denial of affection. I can't imagine what her last couple of months has been like."

"Joslyn!"

"Seriously, Gavin!" Raising her voice, she nearly came out of her chair. "There is more tension between you two, than the cables holding up all of Tucksten Bridge! Are you too proud to admit that you care for a twenty-one-year-old human?"

"Twenty-five," Nola interrupted between bites. "What did you say?" Joslyn asked.

"Nola... don't!" Gavin warned as if she were about to jump off a building.

"How old did you say you were?" The intense curiosity in Joslyn's voice was alarming. Gavin sighed heavily and ran his hand through his hair.

"I'm nearly twenty-five," Nola answered warily.

"There must be some mistake." Wide eyed and turning pale, Joslyn sat back in her chair. "She can't be more than twenty-two. It isn't possible."

"What is it?" Nola asked, setting down the fork and barely swallowing her food. "What did I say?"

"No," Joslyn whispered. "There must have been a mistake at the orphanage. She can't be more than twenty-two at the most." Her tone was still grave and unsettling.

"I know how old I am." Confused, Nola looked from Joslyn to Gavin. "Tell me what is wrong!"

"You should have turned fully at least two years ago," Gavin whispered.

"What difference does it make?" she asked, still unsure of what it all meant.

"But she is Absolute in nearly every way." Still captivated, Joslyn held the arms of her chair. "I can sense her, I can smell her, I can see it in her eyes."

"I know," Gavin leaned forward at the table and held his sister's stare. "Not even Levi can know about this," Gavin warned.

"I'm not sure I can keep something like this from him." The sincere shock in her voice was impossible to ignore. "This is unprecedented."

"What is?" Nola asked. At that very moment, the doorbell rang through the hall.

"No one can know, especially Elias Percy." Gavin stood up and unbuttoned the neck of his shirt.

"You were going to let Elias in here without telling me this?" Joslyn was still in awe. "Do you know what he will do to her?"

"He doesn't know," Gavin declared.

"Is there something wrong with me?" Nola could not help but feel the uncertainty.

"No Absolute ever went a day past twenty-two, and you are telling me that she is nearly three years older than that? What else aren't you telling me?"

"Ignore it for the moment!" Gavin called to the butler as the man made his way toward the front door. "Joslyn, this isn't the right time for this."

"What else?" She yelled. "She already let it slip that she can transcend... a talent only a hundred-year-old Absolute could ever possess!" Gavin stared at the table and let his fist hit the top lightly for a few seconds. "Tell me, so I know what we are dealing with!"

"The vision she had... in the parlor," Gavin whispered. "She says it was through Luke's eyes."

"Have they turned him?" Joslyn questioned. "No," He shook his head.

"He is human!" The older sister exclaimed.

"Lower your voice!" Gavin warned, thankful for the solid walls. "Nola, no matter what you and Elias talk about, do not admit your age." He came to his feet and stepped beside her.

"I don't understand," she whispered as he pulled back her chair.

"Just..." Gavin took her hand and kissed the back of her wrist, imprinting how much he needed her to keep the secret. "Please keep this between us for now."

"What about being able to see through Luke?"

"That is fine. Tell him. Maybe, he knows more about that than we do." Gavin turned toward the hallway to address the steward. "Let him in," he called to the butler. "You are fine. Just don't bring up your age." The large door at the end of the main hall opened, but Nola was led into an adjourning parlor room before walking through to the main part of the house.

"Alright," she agreed. Again, the touch of his hand diluted her confusion over the conversation and emotion of the day. Within a few seconds, she was able to stand tall and enter another room to see Elias standing near the window. Only then did Gavin release her hand.

His smile was enough to lighten the entire room. Although she was desperately attached to Gavin, Elias was a handsome breath of fresh air in a house overflowing with stress. Dressed to the nines in a dark suit and black silk tie, he looked as if he had been in a box seat at an opera. Every piece of hair was perfectly in place and his honey brown eyes were entrancing from ten feet away.

"Lord Graelohr, I wasn't expecting such a sudden invitation." He spoke, taking in the sight of Nola and Joslyn. "Is everything alright?"

"Well, if it isn't Elias Percy..." Joslyn crossed the room as if she were floating on air. "Aren't you a sight?"

"There's my girl," Elias smiled and welcomed her into his very quick embrace. "Are you still with the islander?" he asked playfully, scanning over her attire.

"Blissfully," she answered with a sly smile.

"I assumed as much." Elias released his embrace much quicker than Joslyn expected him too. "He is taking very good care of you." Again, he smiled over her stunning features. "Miss Valerian, I hope you've been well."

"There's been some tragedy in Nola's family recently," Gavin answered. "Her aunt has been murdered and a member of her family has been taken."

"Dorothy Ellis?" Elias held a firm somber stare. "My sincerest apologies to both of you." He nodded toward Gavin. His compassion was evident and honest. "There must be some way I can help."

Accepting the honest comment, the two shook hands, "Yes, there is," Gavin admitted. "Nola is unable to control her talent." There was noticeable hesitation as he enlightened Elias. I was hoping you would take an interest in training her how to use her sight."

"I would be glad to." Returning his hands behind his back, Elias took on a formal stance. "Permit me to pry. This seems more urgent than the general request," Elias noted.

"Those responsible for Dottie," Gavin nodded his head as he humored the request. "They also took her youngest son, Luke. Nola has seen that he is alive, but her gift is limited, leaving his location vague."

"I can look for him, if it would help." Elias offered quickly, making sure to hold Nola's stare. "Teaching Nola to control her sight would take... a considerable time. I could do it in less than a few hours."

"Nola has already made a solid connection. She just needs to learn how to reuse it."

"I understand. Once that communication is open it is very simple to maintain it," Elias agreed. "What did you see?" He asked Nola, stepping to the front of the sofa.

"It's complicated," she answered as she looked toward Gavin unsteadily.

"How was it complicated?" There was a definite curiosity in his gaze. "Was it a blocked vision, hazy and covered by thick fog?"

"No," Nola glanced at Joslyn and Gavin briefly before answering. "It was very clear, but there was a cloth or sack in front of his eyes."

"Alright, then the Vampyre you are using must be being punished for something," he sighed heavily. "It would be easier to find another host."

"This particular host is imperative," Gavin spoke with a finalizing tone.

"I see..." Elias wanted to question the reason but knew better. "How do you know the man you are looking for is with him?"

"I know," Nola admitted. "I could see them leading him across a pier and onto a ship."

"Did Luke look alright?" Elias asked.

"I'm not sure," Nola answered. "I could not see him."

"Nola's endowment is not what we expected." Gavin whispered. "She is not seeing through a Vampyre."

"An Absolute?" Elias guessed.

"The human, Luke." Gavin answered, slowly bringing the room to silence.

At first, it was clear that Elias didn't believe her. He looked down at the sofa and then back to Gavin. Unwilling to insult the idea, Elias remained speechless. His expressions were easily understood, and Nola felt the need to defend her ability. Finally breaking the silence, Joslyn reached out to touch Nola's shoulder.

"Elias is very careful about judgments. His lack of conversation can be unnerving but know that he does not doubt you." Her sincerity was calming for Nola.

"Not at all," Elias clarified. "I am stunned, but I believe you." He stopped, making sure he had her full attention. "It is not in you to lie."

"No," Nola agreed. "It isn't."

"You are aware that humans are not cerebral enough to use as
hosts."

"I have been told," she answered. "Yet, there is no mistaking what I saw."

"It will take weeks to contact the only other sighted Absolute I am familiar with," Gavin spoke, taking control of the conversation. "Any assistance you can offer would be appreciated." He looked at the sofa behind Elias but still did not offer his guest a seat.

"I am not sure how much I can help." Elias looked back at the chair and sat down comfortably without an invitation. "Teaching her how to extend her sight to a Vampyre is simple, to an Absolute is challenging, but to a human..." he shook his head. "I wouldn't know where to begin." Adjusting his jacket, Elias focused on Nola. "Can you control your gift through your mentor?" Boldly he motioned toward Gavin.

"No." There was despair in Nola's answer. "I've spent months trying to no avail."

"At least that I can rectify," Elias admitted, warily approaching Gavin and Joslyn. "Would you permit a few intrusions on your privacy?"

"Would you permit me to inflict my ability on you?" Joslyn held a warning tone.

"Your talents were inflicted on me for many years without complaint," Elias taunted her with a raised eyebrow.

"As obliging as I have been for you," Joslyn spoke to Nola. "I must decline my assistance." Walking to the door, she pulled her golden skirt behind her. "I will leave you to your tutor, though you should mind his wicked ways." There was a playful smile on her face as she left the room. Once she left, however, Gavin reclaimed their attention.

"There are two of my men in the house," he offered. "Any of us should suit, except Joslyn." His clarification was given flatly. "I still have some documents to review upstairs." He turned away. "The moment we have clarification from Levi... we will have to leave."

"It shouldn't take too long." The taunting tone in his voice was completely absent with Joslyn not in the room. He behaved quite civil and proper in her absence.

"Good," Gavin stated clearly before leaving the room and closing the door behind him.

"I always wondered if those doors would drown out sound." He sat forward and motioned to the chair across from him.

"They do," Nola admitted before thinking better of the truth. "Though I am sure they have their limits."

"Everything with Lord Graelohr has a limit."

"What does that mean?" she asked, taking the seat across from
him.

"It means that I am being watched like a hawk from both the Vampyre outside the window behind me, seventy feet into the woods, and read like a book by Joslyn's curiosity. Though, I'm sure she will dissipate now that I have mentioned it." The moment he said the words a strange weight, barely noticed by Nola before, lifted slightly in the room. There was no visible change, but there was an increased feeling of privacy. "Alright," he sat back on the sofa and adjusted his jacket for a second time. "Joslyn is making herself known." The humor in his voice was unmistakable. "Shall we get started?"

"Will the attention interfere?" Nola asked, aware of the same strange warmth.

"Only if I make Joslyn angry." His playful smile never ceased.

Fully understanding that his personal temperature was not going to change he smiled, sat up, and gently removed his coat.

"She holds much venom for you."

"Venom?" Elias chuckled at the choice of words. "No, she enjoys my taunting, even if it is inappropriate since her marriage. None-the-less, I understand we are short on time."

"We are," Nola agreed, looking around the room and realizing that only with concentration could she sense Gavin's closeness and Joslyn's sweet smell.

"Then let's get started," he offered. "How do we do that?" Nola asked.

"First, you have to understand that your gift is more like the music than the instrument." He raised a single eyebrow as he spoke. "Instead of trying to make it play, you have to learn how to listen." Still sitting forward, he glanced at the color of Nola's dress. Against the light blue in the room, Nola's deep burgundy dress was distracting.

"Please, go on?" At the edge of her seat, she reminded herself that finding Luke depended on her quick ability to learn.

"First of all, you need to stay calm." He looked at her desperate desire and offered a charming smile. "You were handed a gift, not a curse." His soothing voice persuaded her to sit back slightly. Unlike your other traits... speed, agility, strength... this one you can't force. You have to fall into the vision, somewhat like sleep."

"I don't sleep easily," she admitted.

"Hmm..." Coming to his feet, Elias moved to the window and closed the curtain. His long-tailored trousers led up to a starched white shirt that clung to thick shoulders. "Neither do I."

"Then how am I supposed to fall into it?" Her eyes strayed until she realized what she was doing. Once she caught herself, Nola shook off her subtle curiosity.

"Ironically it is a forced relaxation, for as possible as that is." His brilliant smile and pearly white teeth beckoned her to come to her feet. "Think of it as something you want to enjoy as opposed to something you have to do, much like a daydream that you can control."

"But I can't control it." The carpet sank below her slippers as she crossed the room.

"And that is where the problem is the same as the solution."

"Well... where do I start?" Nola walked over to the darkened window. "Gavin had me looking out the window last time." She thought about opening the drapes, but he was directly in the way. "I know that I have to concentrate on the person I want to use and then let my mind wander after that... but I still have no control over starting the vision."

"That is because you don't control the beginning, only the end," he spoke cynically.

"You're not making any sense." Her annoyance was evident.

"Alright," he whispered with a chuckle. "Think of it this way." Turning to her, he held out his hand too far away to be an offer of contact. "You spend half of your day trying not to doze off... trying to stay awake through the monotonous hours of human companionship. Without knowing it, you are constantly seeking out those that are like you. Your mind, your body... it longs to be connected to other education. All you have to do is stop fighting it with your false sense of reality." Knowing that he was within inches of her, Elias moved inconspicuously out of her reach. "Fall into the boredom."

"I don't feel bored," she answered honestly. "I'm filled with sorrow, concern, and fear, but I haven't felt boredom in weeks."

"Not literally..." Elias changed his tone. "For a moment I had forgotten how candid you are." If it weren't for his continuous smile and appealing eyes, Nola would have been offended. "What I am trying to say is... think about anything else but the vision and it will come to you."

"Anything else?"

"Anything, as long as it is not stressful, hurtful, or too in depth to slide away from," he whispered as he took a step closer. "You have to relax completely... mind and body. When you have seen what you've wanted, you simply choose not to see any more."

"You make it sound so easy." Listening to the deep mellow hum of his voice, she found herself staring at the silk tie around his thick neck. Small dark brown hairs barely pierced his skin along his jaw line, increasing the masculine features of Elias's face. His amber brown eyes held the dim light with flecks of gold and again she had to look away.

"For me it is," he answered, standing tall and squaring his shoulders. In ten years, I have not faced half of the distress you have seen in these few days." Leaning closer, he persuaded her to look at him. "If you are going to do this, you will have to get past these moments of sorrow."

"Alright," she agreed, holding up her hands to him. "Do I focus on Gavin or the man outside?" Elias looked down at her uplifted palms with curiosity.

"You don't need me." He shook his head, holding his hands back.

"Both Joslyn and Levi said that it would help me focus."

"Try," he encouraged her, stepping backward. "Think of Gavin, since you and he are obviously connected. Focus on finding him inside the house for a few moments and then let your mind wander as if it were traveling through the hallways."

"Alright," Nola agreed. Inhaling deeply, she closed her eyes and pictured Gavin's dark features, wide eyes, perfect lips, and incredible height. She remembered the way he looked as he slept in his bed, and she focused on that image. It was accidental when she compared his smile to Elias's. Nola did not mean to shift from Gavin's stunning perfection to Elias's cunning wit and devilish demeanor. The comparison between their two opposite temperaments was purely accidental. Barely evident, the golden haze began to appear along with the usual slight humming sound. Unfortunately, her growing curiosity about Elias kept the vision at bay "No," she whispered. "It is like a haze that clouds over my mind, but I can't seem to fall into it."

"Where is your mind taking you?"

"I'd rather not say."

"Can you give me an idea?" he asked.

"I was completely focused on Gavin for quite a while."

"And then?" He lowered his gaze to her dress once more.

"Then it wandered to various thoughts." Her vague answer began to frustrate him.

"Did the vision at least begin?" he asked.

"There was a different color and a hint of something more, but I couldn't reach it." She glanced up at him with a hopeless sigh. "This day has been very trying. The last time I was able to have a vision Gavin was helping to keep me composed." Slowly, Elias placed his hands in his pockets.

"Your stress is considerable. Still, I think you should try it again." Even as he spoke Nola found herself staring into his golden-brown eyes. His jaw was very square and every inch of him was toned and perfectly curved. It was strange that up until that point Joslyn, Levi, and Gavin all seemed to welcome the idea of physical contact when Elias was obviously avoiding it.

"Alright," Nola agreed. Walking over to the window she lifted the drapery and gazed out at the city. A small lantern light hung in some of the windows, but it wasn't the same as the strange glow that surrounded her. With her mind trying to focus on Gavin, all she could think was Elias didn't want to touch her. Gavin's dark hair and deep eyes stayed in her mind for a few moments. However, when she remembered the first time, she reached out to him in the library and the result was a thrilling attack of his affection. No matter how far away Elias stood from Nola, she still wondered what his touch would be like. Several moments had passed before she realized how in depth she was concentrating on Elias.

"This isn't working," she whispered.

"You're not relaxed," he answered coming closer to the window. "There is too much out there." Turning her attention away from the window he shook his head. "Keep your mind free of distraction. Try not to feel emotion, any emotion. Let your mind escape."

"I'm sorry," Nola shrugged her shoulders slightly. "All I can feel today is emotion, loss of my aunt, loss of Luke, and the inability to change anything about the last few months."

"Alright," Coming across the room Elias withdrew his hands from his pockets and held them out to her. "We will try it again."

"Joslyn pulled me into a vision once," Nola whispered as he came close enough to reach. "Can you do that?" For some reason, she hesitated to take his hands.

"Joslyn does not actually have the gift of sight. She is powerful enough to force you to use yours, even against your will, but no, I cannot do that." Slowly, Nola took his hands with concern for the possible rush. "I can help keep you calm but the sight is for you to find."

Nola closed her eyes and waited but the air felt completely empty around her. There was nothing from Elias except a calm quiet sedation. With Gavin, Joslyn, and even Levi she was able to receive something. However, Elias was vacant of every single emotion.

Instantly, Nola felt as if her heart had been placed in a box and locked away. She felt numb. There was no sensation of his hands, no temperature of Joslyn, and no influence of Gavin. She could not feel the loss of Dottie or scared for Luke. It felt as if she were standing in a cell. Completely secluded from every living being. It was terrifying and lonely. Instantly, the fear of complete isolation took over. The emptiness was vast. Her eyesight was unchanged, she could see Elias, but felt utterly and painfully alone. In quick response, she began to repeat Luke's name in her mind. It started out slowly, then became a mindful chant.

"You are concentrating too hard," Elias whispered. "Try to find Gavin, it should be easier."

Using the complete emotional clarity that he emanated, Nola tried desperately to think of Gavin. She tried to imagine him in the library or the parlor but was too distracted. Without control of her mind, she began to wonder why Elias was not affecting her. She almost wanted a slight bit of desire, the rush of him wanting her.

Inadvertently, she began to imagine what his arms felt like, what his kiss would do to her, and if she would crave him like she did Gavin. Pulling away instantly, Nola stepped back and turned away from Elias. She could feel the flush of her cheeks and the strange rapid heartbeat in her chest.

"What is it?" Elias asked completely confused. "What's wrong?"

"Nothing," Nola tried to answer. "I'm just unable to do this."

"What are you thinking of?" The slight chuckle to his voice caused her to glance at him for a moment. "Nothing," she declared.

"You are as red as a beet, Nola." Again, his voice was playful.

When she looked back, he had moved closer with his evil grin. "I'm not exactly focused."

"You are focused on something," he chuckled. Her warning glare did not bother him at all. "What is it? If I know what it is, I might be able to help."

"Everyone else relayed a feeling when they touch me. Joslyn and Levi conveyed much of themselves and Gavin... I can't even explain how he made me feel." Shyly she looked down at the floor. "I just expected something different from you."

"Something different?" He lowered his voice and eyed her peculiarly. "How much different? I am a male Absolute, Nola." He moved forward slowly. "You are an intelligent, strong willed and vibrant woman that any man would desire. I could easily impress with everything that Gavin gave you." A single eyebrow rose gently. "Maybe even more..." His daring smile was impossible to question. "But this is a most inappropriate time." The sincerity in his voice was clear. "Right now, I need to keep all of my personal ...sentiments as distant from you as I can. You have enough for both of us." He smiled again, lifting her chin with the tip of his finger. "I have the ability to keep my desires and thoughts to myself when I touch you. It is part of my gift. With it, let me clear away your emotions, while you focus on finding your friend."

"Alright," Nola agreed. Elias took hold of her hand. "Remember, fall into it without fear. This is just another part of you," he whispered as she closed her eyes. "Picture Luke as clearly as you can see him, remember a conversation or a moment between you two. When you are focused on him entirely, open your eyes and find something to lull your conscious thought and physical sight."

Automatically, Nola recalled staring at Luke's face in the upstairs hallway. He so carefully approached the conversation about their relationship that Nola wasn't exactly sure what he meant.

However now, so far away from the moment, everything was much clearer. Nola opened her eyes but remembered every detail of Luke's face. With Elias holding her hand, she turned toward the window to peer at the city in the distance.

Elias whispered, "allow your thoughts to wander and they will return to the last image that caused the most concentration." So quietly were his words, Nola wasn't sure he used his mouth.

She remembered the first time she met Elias and how he seemed to call her name, right next to her, when he was standing outside the church. Looking out over the lit streets, she compared that church to the large buildings of Thedford City. It was when she found herself staring at a single lantern that the golden haze began to creep into her mind.

"That's it," Elias whispered holding her hand tighter. "Don't fear it. It cannot hurt you."

Very little came to her mind. It felt like she was blind for several seconds before a small bit of light shone through the hole in the sack. Luke was still bound, but he was most definitely closer to the ground. Through the fiber lined hole in the mask, she could see straw cast out over a wooden floor. Rope hung on the walls and barrels lined the small room, but there was no one with him that she could see. Fortunately, Luke continued to change his view, searching for his own surroundings. There were stairs far across from him with much lighter above. It looked like he was in a cellar or a stockroom.

"He is in a room below something," she relayed. "They still have him tied up, and the cover is still on his face, but he can see ropes and barrels."

"Can you stay with the vision?"

"No." Nola opened her eyes and turned back to Elias. "It's gone."

"Alright," he whispered gently patting her shoulder. "At least we know that you are incredibly gifted for your age." The mention of her age forced her to recoil from his touch, afraid that she would somehow convey the one thing Gavin warned her to keep secret. "I say this should be enough to appease your guardian for one night."

"Yes, thank you," Nola agreed.

"Most of what you have to learn no one can teach you. This is your talent and I have little advice to offer, except that you are not emotionally stable enough to handle these visions, right now." Moving closer to the sofa, Elias picked up his coat and began to push his arms through the sleeves. "You will need to let Gavin or Joslyn help you for at least a while." Lifting the back of his coat he checked his neck scarf and collar.

"Thank you," Nola offered as the door to the study slowly opened with Gavin standing in the hall.

"I'm sorry to interrupt, but we must be leaving." Gavin did not seem to mind the fact that Elias looked ready to leave.

"What?" Nola wrapped her arms over her stomach. "Where are we going?"

"We will be taking the carriage toward the bay," Gavin explained. "Just heading in the direction of your vision will help us, for the moment. Joslyn will catch up to us when she learns something more."

"I would like to help." Elias stepped in front of Gavin. "I have no doubt that you would, but no." Gavin refused instantly with steel in his voice. "There will be three of us and a half- ling in jeopardy as is. We do not need to put you at risk." His tone was cold, his words were calm, but his sincerity was crystal clear.

"Three Absolutes could take on an army. There is no risk." Without a hint of exaggeration in his voice, Elias stated the fact. Nola turned to face them both, keenly aware of her complete discomfort.

"This is not your affair," Gavin warned him. "Unless you can guarantee that you can teach Nola to use her sight, there is no room for you."

"There is no guarantee. Much of what she has to learn cannot be taught, but she has a good hold on the basic idea."

"Then there really is no use for you, is there?" Gavin's eyes rolled over toward the door as he hinted blatantly for Elias to leave.

"No," Elias agreed feeling the heat of the mansion steadily rise. "I suppose not," Elias answered before bowing to Nola. "It has been a delight, Miss Valerian. Take care and stay close to your guardian. You are not safe on your own."

"Good night," she whispered. Elias stayed clear of Gavin as he made his way to the door.

"Lord Graelohr," he whispered politely, walking out of the room. Both Gavin and Nola watched him leave, letting the awkward silence grow menacingly in his absence. After several seconds, the large door at the end of the hall closed, signaling their privacy.

"Was he able to help you?"

"Yes, in fact I saw him again... well, through him I guess." Nola was still unsure of how to word her meaning.

"And?"

"He is in a small room. There is still something covering his face, but I can see rope hanging and barrels on the floor." She tried to remember the images as Gavin came closer.

"Go on," he urged.

"It looks like there are some short stairs with an opening above them. Wherever he is, there is more daylight above."

"That would make perfect sense if he were on a ship or in a warehouse," Gavin agreed.

"What should we do?" The thought of running to the carriage and leaving at that moment came into her mind.

"Get your coat," Gavin answered. "We need to get on the road."

Chapter Twelve
Road Weary

There was a listless sleep brought on by the sway of the carriage and the waning grief. Gavin had kept a steady hand on her sleeve, certain not to touch her skin. Nola rested her head back against the velvet bench, but the random bumps in the road would wake her often. Each time she opened her eyes, Gavin stared out the window as if looking for something.

"What is it?" Nola asked, noticing his constant gaze. "Marcus," Gavin nodded his head toward the front of the carriage, "my driver. We need to stop."

"Why would we stop? We've been traveling barely an hour."

"You still have much to learn. Marcus is a young Vampyre. His strength will not last if he does not feed nightly."

"Feed?" She could barely continue the words that were in her head. "You mean he has to kill someone... now?"

"No." The answer was slow and steady. "He is well-disciplined. Marcus knows how much he can take from a human and still spare them death, should he choose." Seeing glowing lamplight from a small town ahead, Gavin tapped on the ceiling. Shortly after, Marcus turned the horses onto a second road and headed toward the town. "There are some out there that keep humans as servants, or even lovers to feed their appetite without drawing attention from the outside world."

"You don't have to kill people?" The way her voice lit up revealed her hope.

"Marcus doesn't, neither does Mr. Banit or Mr. Pattlow. I'm afraid Jarron Tempest, on the other hand, has no qualms about taking human life." Gavin never turned his gaze from the window. "He is by far the eldest and most advanced. In some cases, older than many Absolutes. Your concern is understandable."

"I asked about you," Nola stated withdrawing her hand from his. She could see from his stern expression and averted gaze that he did not want to answer. "Do you have to kill?"

"Every time," he answered, turning his soft glowing eyes towards her. "No one survives an Absolute."

"Why not?" The carriage slowed down as they entered the small rural village. No more than a handful of shops lined the single road, and less than twenty houses could be seen from her window. "Why is it a Vampyre can spare a life, and you can't?" The carriage came to a halt and Gavin opened the door quickly stepping out of the cab. "You won't answer me?" She stayed where she was as Marcus climbed down to the road and headed toward the tavern.

"I'll meet you inside." Gavin spoke briefly to Marcus before turning back to Nola.

"You are going with him?"

"Beware of questions you don't want answered," he warned. "If you ask again, I will tell you."

"Then, I'm asking." Staying inside the cab, she faced him completely. The burgundy dress looked black in the dead of night and almost faded into the lush velvet seat beneath her. "Are you going to...?"

"We are vicious, Nola." His eyes shimmered in the light as he pulled out a pair of glasses with bright red colored lenses. Placing them over his eyes hid the tell-tale glow. "We are more powerful and require more sustenance. It is common for more than one human to be sacrificed to our hunger, and the longer we wait to feed... the more it takes to sate our appetite." The glasses made him appear more mysterious than ever before. She had seen colored lenses worn by aristocrats in the daylight but on Gavin they looked precariously distracting. "Everything we are and everything we do is absolute. There is no vacillating."

"I can't be a part of this," she warned. Shaking her head, she glanced at the tavern across the way.

"Stay here." His command was quick.

"You don't need to do this, now. Do you? I heard what you told Dottie." She maintained her petition. "I heard that you could go a full month. You were as gray as a storm a few days ago. You can't tell me you're not strong!"

"And maybe if I hadn't starved myself to prove my devotion, I could have saved her. Perhaps, if I took what I needed instead of just enough to look human, all of this may have been avoided. However, I do not exist in past decisions or apprehension of the future. I exist in this moment with my current set of requirements. At this moment, I require nourishment."

"No," moving to the opposite door, she reached for the handle and pushed it open. "I can't do this. I can't let you do this."

"Where are you going to go?" Gavin asked, suddenly before her with his hand on the door. She didn't know if he had gone around the carriage or over it, but either way she was not going to escape him. His eyes were black, and his lips protruded, barely covering his pearly white fangs.

"Get out of my way!" She insisted, trying to push past him, and fighting her own fear of his ferocity.

"Fine," Gavin raised his hands and let her exit the carriage. "I'll stay, but there is nothing I can do about Marcus. He has to go." Glancing between the carriage and the horses Gavin could see the driver getting well acquainted with a barmaid. "He's a fast talker, so it won't take him long."

"What do you mean?" She followed his gaze through the window.

"All of them are easy prey in there." He nodded to the patrons. "Each one of them is lonely, sad, and some riddled with addiction. All he has to do is act like he cares or that he finds them as fascinating as they find themselves." Listening carefully, they could both hear the slight chatter coming from the closed windows. "The women are easier to get to than the men." The sound of his voice was strangely enticing as he leaned closer to her ear. "Free of illness or deformities Vampyres are always viewed as more attractive than humans. Marcus will tell a woman everything she wants to hear, even if it is just the promise of a few coins and have her entranced and drained in less than a half hour."

"If she's left alive, won't she call the authorities? Won't they come after him?" Nola wasn't sure if she was worried about the woman or the Vampyre.

"She won't even know what happened. She will be exhausted for a few days but recover completely."

"How could she not know?" She was very much aware of how close he stood and how his breath passed over her skin. "Will the wounds just disappear?"

"There are places on one's body that are difficult to see..." He whispered in a gruff tone. "If you do notice a wound down there... Who are you going to show?" Nola turned to glare at him through the red lenses and caught him glancing over her figure. In an instant, Gavin put more than a foot of space between them.

"Don't speak to me about such things." Caught off guard by the sudden rush that coursed through her, Nola thought it best to seem insulted. "I thought you were above vulgarity." Turning away from his crude remark Nola walked back to the carriage door.

"So far you've been wrong about everything that refers to me." Keeping his attention equally divided between Nola and Marcus, he stayed where he was. "What kind of man were you expecting?"

"I had questions, not presumption." Placing her back to the carriage door, she let the muscles of her legs straighten after the ride.

"As surprising as it may be, everyone can be a little vulgar at times." There was a slight curl to his lips as he spoke.

"No, not everyone," she sighed heavily. Nola looked down to the toe of her boot and kicked a nearby pebble.

"You're right." Gavin came before her. "Dottie would have never said such a thing and she would have scolded me, had she heard it." Placing his hands in his pockets he peered through the window of the carriage to the tavern. Marcus was standing near the door getting ready to leave with an auburn-haired woman.

"Did you love her?" Nola asked Gavin quietly. The question caught him off guard and Gavin took a step back for a silent moment.

"Yes," he answered. "I loved her as much as you love Luke." Before she could comment, Gavin held up his hand. "I've seen you with him. He makes you smile, and I've sensed how you've wanted him to hold you." Again, Nola opened her mouth to deny the accusations, but Gavin shook his head. "I loved her, but only because of how much she loved me."

Across the street, the door to the tavern opened and Marcus appeared with his arm around the redhead's shoulders. Whispering sweet lies in her ear he led her through the small gap between the bar and a barber shop. The woman's careless giggles annoyed Nola's sensitive hearing.

"Luke is the only person that makes me feel safe. That does not mean that I love him."

"You seem to forget. I can read everything about you." He stepped away slowly. "Just my speaking his name makes you uncomfortable." Again, he backed up but offered her a smile. "Your emanation is pushing against me."

"Is it?"

"You would be surprised how strong, when you called me vulgar." He chuckled for a second, letting her hear the unfamiliar lighthearted tone. Looking past the horses, Gavin saw the shadow of a man walking from the tavern past the front of the barber shop. "You should get back in the carriage."

"Are we leaving?"

"Soon enough," he instructed opening the door.

"What is that?" Nola turned to look through the window as the woman's slight cries could be heard.

"It's not what you think," Gavin explained with a grin. "Don't worry, just get in." Before Nola could place her hand on the door, the air around her became charged with static. Gavin stood straight up for a moment before disappearing, leaving only the words, "Stay here," carried on the wind.

"Gavin?" Nola called.

He was gone, having moved so fast that she could not see anything. There was no blur, no trace, and no tracks. All she knew was that he had likely gone to Marcus. Panic set in immediately. Nola lifted the hem of her dress and ran across the road, unsure of what she was looking for. The sound and muffled voices led her down the alley.

When a piercing female scream echoed through the night air, she bolted forward between the two buildings. Through the darkness she ran, sliding between the crates of garbage and keeping her footing through the mud. Before she was halfway through all sound ceased and it was far more eerie than anything before.

Coming to the end of the path, Nola saw them. The woman's dress was half undone as Marcus lay on the ground with a knife wound gaping from his neck. Next to them, a pimp protecting his feminine investment stood above. The whoremaster's bloodied hand gripped the knife in Marcus's neck.

The response was savage. Unhinged, Gavin lifted the armed aggressor with a single hand. All four of his razor-sharp fangs sunk into the victim's neck as a deep growl sounded from his chest. Warm blood was devoured so fast that not a drop fell. The once-plump body plunged against Gavin's monstrosity, cringing into a form of dry gray flesh. The air in the man's lungs rushed from the rapid shrinking of his tissue. The sound was a deathly hollowed gasp, lasting as Gavin held him suspended.

The woman held her dress together, frozen with fear by the glowing eyes of the Absolute. There was no time for her to scream and she couldn't run. Before the large man's body hit the ground, Gavin grabbed the woman by the back of her hair. She could control no reaction to the fear. Just the vision of Gavin's four fangs wrought sheer terror in the woman. There was no compassion as Gavin lifted her to his teeth. He was more of a monster than any Vampyre.

Suddenly, Nola felt a violent wind and a vigorous pull, but not before she saw Gavin sink his teeth into the woman's neck, twisting her head to snap the bones. With incredible strength an unseen man lifted Nola, hauling her away from the alley. She knew she was fighting a Vampyre. Nola kicked, squirmed, and tried to scream, but the unknown assailant seemed to be everywhere. His hand covered her mouth as his arm completely wrapped her body against his. She could see nothing until the inside of the carriage surrounded her.

"You're alright," the man swore. "It's me, ... Mack Banit." Suddenly the blur of motion ceased enough for her to recognize him. "I'm not going to hurt you. I would never hurt you."

"Let me out," she stated feigning brave. His eyes were a bright blue and there were small smears of blood on his collar.

"That is the last thing I am going to do," he warned. "Stay in here."

Again, she felt the rush of wind as he left her. Then, the carriage sagged with sudden weight in the driver's seat. Nola sat on the edge of the bench as the horses pulled them forward. Just past the narrow alley she could see the glow of firelight behind the buildings. It didn't take long to figure out that the flames were set purposely to hide the mangled bodies. Yet, there was hardly any time to look back as the carriage sped down the road.

A sharp turn nearly capsized the carriage. Both of her hands pressed against the walls of the cab to keep braced during the incredible speed. Mack snapped the reins loud and fast, hurling the horses through the night until nothing but heavy wood surrounded them.

"Open the door!" Mack called above the beating hooves and shaking metal springs.

She heard him clearly but could not take her hands off the carriage walls. Between the rushing trees around her, the sway of the high-speed carriage, and the vision of two brutal murders Nola could not move. All at once, the carriage tilted on its side heavier than before.

"Nola, open the door!" Gavin appeared hanging standing on the step outside the door with Marcus hunched over his shoulder.

Instinctively, she slid to the opposite side of the cab, looking at the door and judging the speed if she were to jump out. "Open it!" He ordered, watching every tree on the road, making sure Marcus would not get injured.

Nola could see the blood that stained Gavin's sleeves, shirt, and chin. His eyes reflected through the red glasses, making him more terrifying than anything she could fear as a child. His fangs gleamed against the bloodstains, and he lifted his top lip above them ferociously.

"Stop!" She screamed. Mack's speed was so incredible that before she had finished her plea, he had left the driver's seat, opened the side door for Gavin, and returned to steer the racing carriage.

Gavin's immense form slid inside behind Marcus, laying the injured Vampyre on the seat across from Nola. The door was closed, her dress was ripped, and the wound in his neck was covered before Nola had time to crawl back into the corner.

"You have heightened hearing for a reason." Gavin's hollowed tone was directed at Marcus. "He could have taken your head."

"I had it under control," Marcus growled, holding the torn material from Nola's dress to his wound.

"Stop at the river!" Gavin called to Mack.

"Keep going," Marcus argued, spewing some blood from his lips. "I'm fine."

"No, you're not." Turning to glance at Nola's petrified pale face, he sighed heavily. "That wound was nearly fatal. It will not heal immediately. You're staying behind."

"It's one knife wound!" He took offense instantly. Like a child eager to earn respect, Marcus sat up ignoring the pain. "We've all faced fire, swords, and gunfire. You're going to take me out of this over a knife?"

"Out of what? We don't even know what we are getting into." Gavin clarified, watching the blood seep into the dress material.

Marcus would have to feed again before sunrise to counter the depth of the wound. "That will keep you under for at least two days. Once we stop, you are heading back to the manor." Fiercely angry, Gavin faced Marcus, teeth still bared. "What did you expect? You know better than to feed out in the open!"

"She was in more of a hurry than I was." Pulling the soaked material away from the wound, he could see that the bleeding had slowed. The gash remained open, but somehow it turned black as if the flesh inside was rotting. As a result, a foul odor quickly seeped from it. "I don't know if that fat bloke was a jealous lover or a whore's keeper, but he came out of nowhere." His words were hard to make out the more he spoke.

"Stop talking, let your body heal," Gavin furiously lectured. "You've got to learn to listen no matter how hungry you are. This could have ended you!" Around him, the carriage felt eerie, as if a storm were brewing in a small space. The hair on Nola's head stood on end, and Marcus began to cower away. The energy in the carriage was so intense that a spark ignited between Gavin's hand and the metal knob of the door. It was only one thin strand of light, but it traveled over two inches to reach his hand. Finally aware of how enraged he was, Gavin rolled back his shoulders, drew in his teeth, and took a slow calming breath. "Are you alright?" he asked, turning to Nola. His neck was thicker than normal, his body seemed pumped with energy and every muscle flexed. Though his teeth and eyes were normal, he was still very on edge.

For the first time, Nola wished she had the speed and strength of a Vampyre. Being inside the cab, human and frail, she had no defense against any of them. Even the air around her was unsafe.

What she had seen was the most horrific thing in her life, and she was trapped next to the monstrosity responsible.

"Where did Mack come from? What was he doing there?" Marcus asked, fully aware that Nola was incapable of speaking.

"The same thing you were, only he did it right." Gavin answered. "Nola," he turned to her again. "Are you hurt?" Glancing over her arms, hands, and fingers he looked to see if Mack had accidentally injured her in any way. "Let me see," he slowly reached over to raise her chin.

The scent from Marcus's wound hung on his skin. Her mind was unsettled by the death dealer before her. Nola jerked her head away. Seeing the cold reality, Gavin removed his hand. "I told you to stay in the carriage," he reminded her. Turning to the window, he pushed two tiny springs sliding the glass open. "Head towards the water." The directions were shouted up to Mack. "Get as far off the road as possible."

"There is a gap up ahead," Mack called back. "It looks rough so hold on."

Nola braced herself with one hand on the seat and one by the door. Still, she was tossed around mercilessly. Once the carriage was off the road it slowed down considerably. The terrain, however, was even worse. One large bump nearly sent her flying out of her seat, but Gavin held her down with a hand covered in blackish blood. As if it burned through her, Nola shoved it away.

It seemed to take forever for the carriage to come to a stop. When it did, Nola was the first to escape the cab, hurrying to a distant tree to empty the contents of her stomach. Every part of her body shook from the rocking of the carriage and her head whirled from the ride, but her belly had been churning since she saw Gavin in the alley.

"I don't miss that," Marcus commented as he walked to the water. "And she thinks we are disgusting."

"Clean yourself up and stay away from her," Gavin ordered.

By the time Nola lifted her head Mack Banit was walking toward her dragging a large shrub in his hand. She glanced toward the horses and back before she realized he was covering their tracks.

With the speed at which they moved, no human would ever be able to find them, but the horses were another matter.

"Are you alright?" Mack asked. "I didn't hurt you, did I?"

His face would have looked kind and concerned. The blood had been wiped from his mouth but left its trace on his sleeve. No matter how innocent his blue eyes appeared, there was still a Vampyre before her. Unable to speak, she gently shook her head.

"Hugh went on ahead with Levi." As he spoke, Mack walked to the riverbank where Gavin and Marcus knelt to wash. "They figure they are close to Luke Ellis, but they still don't have a fixed location." Throwing the shrub into the woods, he leaned over and wet his sleeve where the bloodstain remained. "I was just going to follow them when I noticed you were in town."

"Good, I need you to stay with us. We will send Marcus back to Thedford." Gavin stood up and began to take off his shirt.

"What happened?" Mack asked, staring at the hole in Marcus's neck.

"Jealous lover or something," Marcus answered, looking at the gaping wound. The bleeding stopped completely, but the flesh was still cut wide open showing his gnarly insides.

"A neck wound like that doesn't heal right away, not even on an old Vampyre. I'll have to close it to stop the odor and quicken your recovery." Mack shook his head. "Did you withdraw your fangs in time?" Mack retrieved a small sewing pouch out of the carriage and began to stitch the skin together.

"No," Marcus whispered.

"No, he didn't." Standing upright, towering over them both, Gavin threw his shirt at Marcus. "He stood right up and faced the man showing himself to anyone that would see!" Marcus caught the shirt and lowered his head. "You're a damn fool and you're going to get yourself killed! You're not fast enough for two people out in the open!" His rage was slowly increasing as well as the static in the air. "Your cocky, Marcus. It's going to make you a target someday.

Change your shirt and cover it up. You're not going back to Thedford wearing that."

Nola kept her distance as the three of them argued. When Gavin began to walk back to the carriage she stepped behind the nearest tree. She had seen him without a shirt before, but this time was different. Every muscle in his body flexed. His veins were so thick they pushed up under his skin. The only reason Nola could imagine for the change in his physique was the fact he had just ingested the blood of two people.

From a small trunk tied to the back of the carriage Gavin pulled out a clean shirt. He checked to make sure Marcus was changing before turning his attention to Nola. His eyes cast down toward his chest as he pulled the clean shirt over his shoulders. While fastening the buttons he walked toward her. Nola looked for an escape, but even if there had been somewhere she could go, she would never be fast enough.

"Are you hurt?" Again, the question was asked. Unable to answer, she just looked up at him. "Are you crying because of what you saw, or are you in pain?" Until then, Nola didn't know her face was streaked with tears. He paused and waited for her answer, but none came.

"She's in shock," Mack answered. "She doesn't even know if anything is broken."

"Can you get back in the rig?" Gavin asked, aware of the intense push and pull that resonated from the small woman. Nola shook her head instantly. The idea of the cramped space with him inside turned her stomach again. Luckily, she was able to control it. "Mack, can you come take a look at her? Make sure she's all right."

"She doesn't want me anywhere near her." Standing up, he shook his arm so fast that the material was completely dry when he stopped. "I cannot get three feet from her and she's pushing me away."

"It's not just you," Gavin admitted to the old vampyre.

"Yeah, well I can barely get near her like she is now. Calm her down first, and I will." It was stated as if it were more of an order than a request.

"Nola," Gavin faced her from about five feet away. His voice was low and calming and replaced his glasses to hide the silver in his eyes. "Alright," he began noticing how she continued to back away. "Nobody needs to look at you. Nobody needs to touch you, but we do have to get back in the carriage if we are going to get to Luke. At this rate, if Levi thinks he is close to finding him, we may be able to get there by daybreak."

She could not get the image of the murder out of her head. Mercilessly and with godlike strength Gavin killed a man and woman right before her eyes and not three days before he had done the same to her aunt. Whether or not he was there to find Luke, Nola did not want him anywhere near her. As Gavin tried to take a step forward, she noticed his hesitation. After an extended moment she realized that it wasn't only hesitation that stopped him. It was almost like he was fighting against something.

"Don't look at me like that," he whispered. The hatred in her eyes was unforgiving. "I will not hurt you." Again, he tried to take a step forward, but set his foot back down. "Alright, do you want to find Luke?" Staying the distance, he waited for her to nod her head. "We can't do that unless you get in the carriage. I don't want to touch you. I don't want to pick you up and carry you back there, but we either must go now, or you have to head back to Thedford with Marcus. Either way, you have to get in the carriage."

The choice wasn't easy. With Gavin at a distance, she was able to consider the idea of heading back to the hotel to stay with Davey. Without her they could get to Luke faster, but she had no way of knowing if he would be safe with them or not. Davey would know nothing of the events of the last few days and simply coddle her as if she were only in mourning over Dottie. Weighing the details, Nola didn't realize that Gavin had taken two steps closer.

"Stay where you are," she insisted, holding up her hand.

Before she realized her error, Gavin took hold of it. "Please, let go." Even as she asked, she could feel the sweet sincerity in his touch. Her eyes closed, the last of her tears fell, and she lowered her head in submission. His protective nature melded into her, revealing how he had been caring for Marcus for years and how defensive his actions became when the man in the alley plunged his knife to Marcus.

Forced to feel his emotions, Nola's clear judgment was clouded. With her guard fully down, Gavin was able to step forward.

"You're alright," he whispered, letting his fingers touch every inch of exposed skin. From her hands to her neck, and finally her face, passing his emotions into her. "I'm sorry for you saw. I'm sorry Mack had to pull you back, and I'm sorry you don't want me near right now." He seemed enormous, wrapping her in his arms and erasing her confusion. "Nola, I need you to decide. If you want to go back, Marcus will take you straight to Davey." Like smooth silk, the words slipped from his lips and into her hair. "We can go on without you."

"I don't want to go anywhere with you," she answered honestly. She did not except his embrace, standing still as he held her.

"Marcus," he called loudly over her head. "You're taking Miss Valerian back to Thedford. Keep to the main roads and make sure she gets to Davey Ellis."

"I'm not going with him." Shaking her head, she looked into Gavin's reflective eyes.

"Then what do you want?"

"I want you to take your hands off me. I'm not riding in that carriage with you or anyone else except Luke." Nola held his gaze as he let go of her. "Once Luke is safe, I am going with him. I would rather die, than to be what you are." Reaching up, she removed the red glasses. "There is no point in hiding anything now, is there?" Shoving the glasses into his hand, she turned to hear rustling in the woods behind her. All of them stood silent, watching the darkness. A twig snapped, an owl called out, and the sound of the wind had somehow changed.

"It's Joslyn." Gavin broke the silence a second before Nola could smell the sweet burning spices in the air. Both Mack and Marcus stood up straight, waiting for her appearance. Off in the distance, a pink flash of light slowed to a stunning dress and curly locks of red hair. Only when she slowed to a human pace could they see her perfectly pale features amplified by dark makeup around her eyes and bright red lips.

"What in blue blazes happened back there?" Joslyn approached with a wild look of annoyance. "That town is bustling with a sudden fire that has 'Ignorant Vampyre' written all over it." Like a Queen entering her throne room, Joslyn walked over to Marcus. "Get out of here. I could smell that wound a mile away." Waving her hand at her nose she turned and looked at Mack and assessed the horses. "Levi is close to Luke Ellis. We need to get moving. These horses will be well tired by daybreak with the way you've been running them. Turn them around and slow down." Stepping over to Nola she looked at Gavin. "What is it?" she asked, noticing the stiff air between them.

"I have fed," Gavin whispered still watching Nola. "Anyone could tell that." Joslyn glanced over his massive form.

"Nola didn't like what she saw," he added as he turned back toward the carriage.

"Why were you even there?" Joslyn asked her directly. Nola was not about to answer her and began to walk to the carriage. "Did you take her with you?" She asked her brother.

"No." Gavin closed the trunk in the back of the rig and secured it once more. "She followed me." Bewildered, Joslyn watched as Mack and Gavin checked the carriage over.

"As much as I'd like to ease your conscience, it's a relatively common occurrence for us to feed." With truly little sensitivity, Joslyn took up the subject.

"It will never be common for me." Nola felt better with her there, but she could not shake her ill feeling.

"Everyone uses those words, Nola. We all saw our human lives as the only reality possible." Wrapping her arm around Nola's, Joslyn led her to the carriage.

"Not all of us," Mack added as Marcus helped him get the horses to face the road.

"That's true," Joslyn agreed. "You and Marcus were forced into your existence overnight. The hunger you faced overtook your humanity."

"I am not saying that it is any easier," Mack added, climbing up into the driver's seat. "But we didn't have to think about it."

"What is the biggest problem?" Joslyn turned to face Nola. "Are you upset that you will have to live like this, or are you upset that Gavin does?"

Looking down at her hand, she could see that Joslyn had gently placed a single finger on her wrist. With the slightest unknown touch, it was probable that she was reading Nola's emotions. Stopping suddenly, Gavin turned around and looked directly at Nola. His expression was gentle and filled with concern, but Nola could not answer. With the question asked, all she could do was consider that Joslyn was right.

"Let's go," Gavin called, climbing up into the driver's seat.

Mack opened the door and waited for the women.

"What do you think you are doing?" Joslyn asked Gavin. "I'm driving." He answered.

"Like hell you are! You are three hundred years old. You are a Lord twice over. You are not driving this rig over a little tiff with a fledgling." Placing her hand on her hip, Joslyn cocked her head to the side. "Either you both ride in the carriage or she can drive the damn thing!"

"Do not forget yourself, Joslyn." Gavin warned.

"No," Nola interrupted, feeling the tension as fire and static filled the air. "She's right." Unable to maintain eye contact with him looking so fierce, she hurried to the carriage. "It is your carriage, and I wouldn't presume to know how to drive it."

"Good, it's settled then." With a brilliant smile, Joslyn stepped up behind her. "If we don't get this thing moving quickly, I am liable to head off before you. My Levi and Mr. Ellis are not that far away."

Chapter Thirteen

Bad Ideas

Joslyn sat on pins and needles, eyeing the town below through the small glass window. The carriage came to a stop at the summit of a steep hill. With a click of the latch Gavin opened the door and stepped onto the quiet road. Stretching his legs, he walked toward Mack.

"Are we there?" Nola asked, lifting her head off Joslyn's shoulder.

"We are in Port Chatsworth." Fixing the sleeve of her dress, Joslyn sat upright while Nola straightened out her neck. "This is where Levi is," Joslyn explained.

The sky held a deep regal shade of purple. It was more than an hour until dawn, and the stars were losing their luster. Strangely, Nola remembered nothing of the entire trip. She recalled getting into the carriage, but Joslyn's constant conversation lulled her into a deep sleep.

"Why are we stopping here?" Nola asked, listening to Mack and Gavin's quiet conversation.

"Mack can't stay with us much longer. He needs to find shelter before dawn." As Joslyn explained, Nola looked out over the horizon to see a vast darkness in the distance.

"What is that sound?" Nola asked, leaning toward the window. "The ocean," Joslyn answered. "And it isn't nearly far enough

away," she added.

"I've never seen the ocean." Nola continued to gaze in the dark distance.

"It's highly overrated." Nodding her head towards the dimly lit windows of the town, Joslyn motioned for Nola to look closely. "At the bottom of this hill is a small fishing village. Right now, Gavin is pointing out the local churches and high-ground cemeteries to Mack."

"Whatever for?" Nola turned to ask with blatant confusion.

After a silent moment of thought, she lowered her head. "Does Mack have to sleep in a coffin?"

"No," Joslyn giggled slightly. "They are not as primitive as legend would have you believe." Fixing a wayward curl, she sighed heavily. "Vampyres can sleep anywhere that sunlight does not reach them. They can sleep in hotels, houses, tents, or anywhere else they choose. The benefit to sleeping in a crypt ... it is very unlikely someone will disturb you." If needing to heal or hide – one has months of privacy and silence.

"Oddly enough, that makes a lot of sense." Nola admitted, wiping a strand of hair from her face.

"We try to keep it simple." Joslyn smirked as Gavin returned to the door.

"Alright, Mack is taking us into town." When his massive form climbed into the carriage Nola instinctively drew away from him. Gavin's horrid acts of murder could not escape her vision and again he took that form. "It looks like they only have one hotel, and it might be stretching your standards a little." Ignoring Nola's timid actions, he retook his seat on the bench. "We will get a couple of rooms there and find out what we can when day breaks." Instantly the carriage took up its wayward sway again.

"Levi will know something," Joslyn answered. "With any luck, we could be heading home with your Mr. Ellis before nightfall."

"Speaking of that," Gavin whispered, directly facing Nola. "There is a chance that he doesn't know about Dottie." Even though he was as large as an ox, he still managed to sound gentle. "You will have to find a way of keeping everything about us secret, while telling him what happened."

"He will already know about the Vampyres." Nola shook her head and shrugged her shoulders.

"Not entirely," Joslyn answered. "If he was unconscious when they took him, he may not know anything."

"We will also need to know what he has told them about the book," Gavin added.

"If he has said anything," Nola defended Luke quickly. "He is not as feeble as you think."

"He's human, Nola. You cannot get any weaker than that," Joslyn argued.

"You found him fascinating." There was a temper in Nola's voice, aimed directly toward Joslyn.

"For an after-dinner snack, maybe..." Joslyn huffed.

"That's enough," Gavin warned his sister. "I wasn't serious," Joslyn snuffed at him.

"We were just making conversation." Coming to her defense, Nola also sneered at Gavin.

"One more word out of either of you and you're both walking," he warned without a shred of humor.

***

"The manager wasn't very happy at first, but the extra coin seemed to lighten him up a bit." Handing Gavin back his money, Mack continued to explain. "I got the three rooms you asked for, but it wasn't cheap."

"Are they next to each other?" Gavin asked, looking up at the lightening sky.

"Nearly." Mack handed two trunks to Gavin. "There are a few rooms between them, but they are all on the second floor."

"Good," Gavin answered taking the keys. "I've got the trunks. You go on. Feed, then find us after sunset."

"There's a bakery and a small tavern just at the backside of that alley." Mack pointed across from the hotel. "The man said it was the best food in town... just in case the lady gets hungry." Nodding slightly to Nola, Mack began to walk away.

"Thank you," Nola whispered. For a Vampyre, Mack was overly concerned for her well-being. It was a comforting thought. "Well," Joslyn looked up at the shabby establishment with half a smile. "At least we are on the second floor."

"If you can find something, better get me a room too," Gavin added as he led the way.

"I think it's lovely." Nola eyed the quaint white awnings and the big blue shutters. It was much smaller than any hotel in Thedford City, but it was still tasteful in its own country way.

"Come to my home in Egypt. I will show you lovely." Joslyn swayed past the oak door and into the hollow foyer.

Gavin did not look around. He simply walked straight to the stairs with both cases in hand, but once they reached the second floor he slowed down. Standing near the end of the hallway a large, shadowed form held his attention.

"Levi!" Joslyn swept past her brother and hurried as fast as the situation would allow. "With Gavin's annoying static I could barely tell you were here."

"You are very slow." Wrapping his arms around his wife he lifted her off the floor. "I expected you hours ago."

"I keep telling you to teach horses how to fly." Through her brilliant smile, Joslyn teased her husband. His only reply was to capture her lips.

"Here," Gavin tossed Levi a key. "Take it inside."

"Wait!" Nola hurried to the tall islander. "Where is Luke?"

"He's alright," Levi answered. "As far as I know he is fairly unharmed."

"Is he being guarded?" Gavin asked.

"By many," Levi answered. "There is nothing we can do for several hours."

"I can think of something we can do," Joslyn whispered into his ear with a giggle.

"Where are they keeping him?" Nola asked, desperate for them to feel the same urgency she did.

"He is on a ship," his answer seemed more final than it should have. "It will not return until the sun has fallen."

"Nola," Gavin reached for her arm, but stopped as she pulled away. "Get at least an hour of rest. We can go out later to see if we can learn something more."

"The tavern is a good place," Levi offered as Joslyn wrapped her snow-white hands around his arm. "Talk to a man named Tucker. He is informative if you keep buying his food and drink." Even as he tried to be informative, Joslyn could not help the urge to lead him toward the door. Her time away from him could not have ended soon enough. With a playful smile, Levi gave her the key and followed her down the hallway.

"We will put you between our two rooms." Gavin looked at the five doors at the top of the hall and saw that Nola's was closer to his. After trying the wrong key first, the door finally opened. "This isn't so bad," he whispered as he entered.

"It is fine, thank you." Nola had to wait for him to enter the room completely before she could get around his immense form.

"I'm going to ask that you stay in here." Watching her cower away from him, Gavin returned to the door. "If you have to go somewhere, come and get me or Joslyn."

"I will," she replied.

"Nola," he whispered as he stepped into the room again. Instantly, she slid away from the door. No matter how simple his expression was or how gentle he spoke, she could not ignore the image burned into her head. She had seen Gavin's fangs before, but the slaughter of two people was an atrocious act. Nola had watched him tear into the woman's neck like a lion ripping flesh from its prey.

"Please don't come in," she whispered, unable to find strength in her voice. He disobeyed instantly.

"I've kept you safe all these years... and you think I would hurt you now?" Closing the door, he remained where he was. "I'm no different now than I was a week ago. Joslyn, Levi, Elias, all of us feed. How we survive was never our choice."

"How long will you look like that?" she asked, motioning toward him without pointing out a particular feature. Gavin looked down at his chest and let his gaze span over his arm. Though he had not actually grown any larger, he did look as if he had been chopping wood all day.

"About a day or two," he answered. Aware of her scrutiny he offered more detail. "My senses are heightened. From here, I can listen to your heartbeat. I can even hear the fabric of your dress constrict as you inhale." Slowly, he reached over and lit the lantern on the table. As the room filled with light the slight glow in his eyes diminished. "There are more gold flecks in the amber of your eyes, and there is a stitch missing in your collar."

It was pointless to look down. Nola had no doubt that he could see everything he had described. His slow and patient tone seemed as reassuring as ever and again she felt the strange security he offered.

Though the vision of the night before had not diminished, it was impossible to ignore the safety she felt with him.

"Should I say good night, or good morning?" she asked, recalling the benefits of silence.

Without answering, Gavin nodded his head and stepped out of the room. Slowly the door closed, and the latch caught with a click.

Nola waited for a moment to hear his footsteps in the hallway, but he was silent. Still, she could tell that he was no longer as nearby.

Inhaling slowly, she stepped over to the side of the bed and sat down.

***

The door opened a crack as she waited, peering into the hallway. Dawn had come and gone waning into the more decent hours of the morning. Normally when everyone else was waking up, Nola found it impossible not to fall asleep. However, having slept for most of the carriage ride, she couldn't help but be awake.

She knew that if she had tried to sneak down the hallway Gavin or Joslyn would have instantly caught on to her mischief. However, after months of sneaking out of Dottie's house, Nola had a few clever ideas on how not to get caught. A slow creaking door and tiptoed footsteps down the hall were sure to set off Gavin's senses. He was no doubt keeping a keen ear on her. On the other hand, walking with another parting guest was bound to sound less obvious.

With her breathing even and shallow, Nola waited for a mother and daughter to hurry with their packages down the hall. Thankfully, the young girl had a habit of dragging her feet, letting the heel of her shoes slide across the carpet. Using her sensitive hearing, Nola was able to match her footsteps to the little girls as she exited the room and hurried in step behind the pair. Carefully holding her breath past Gavin's door, Nola escaped the second-floor hallway and hurried down the stairs. Though it seemed impossible an hour before, Nola stepped out of the hotel and took in the foggy morning of Port Chatsworth.

It was the most western part of England that she had ever been to, but she could not see the ocean through the fog. It was almost impossible to see the opposite side of the road in the thick misty haze. Port Chatsworth was a series of paint chipped stores and even less impressive houses. The chandlery was the largest shop on the street, twice the size of the merchant shop. As late as the morning was, the baker and produce stand were not doing that much business. One by one the ladies scurried from their homes to run their errands, but as quick as a flash they all retreated to their houses. Seeing the tavern at the end of the road, Nola headed for the only source of information she knew of.

Squinting her eyes, Nola tried to make out the words on the sign above the door. She could easily see the painted fish with fist-like fins, but the name Tall-Tale Tavern was almost impossible to read. Inside the thick glass windows, she could see a few men inside, hunched over the tables. Taking a deep breath, Nola opened the door.

"G-morning Ma'am." The man behind the counter stopped wiping long enough to address her. As he continued to finish cleaning the bar top, Nola took the chance to gaze quickly at the patrons. All of them were deep in whispers when she came in, but the room fell silent. As if changing the subject, due to the only female in the building, a few smiles passed her way and all individual conversations flopped to simple talk of the weather and the fishing.

"Good morning, I was wondering if I could bother you for a cup of tea?"

"The coffee is fresher," he offered with a smile. "It's still a bit brisk out there and it'll warm you better, but I can heat up some tea if you'd like."

"Please, don't trouble yourself," Nola replied as she continued to the bar top. "Coffee will suit me just fine, thank you."

"Would you care for a table?"

Nola looked around the establishment and considered his offer. There was one table near a window, but it beheld a foggy view of the silent town.

"Would you mind if I stood here. I've been traveling all night," she asked with a shy smile.

"Be my guest." With an understanding nod he returned to the coffee.

Reaching into her purse, Nola pulled out a coin to set it on the table. Just as she did, her intense hearing picked up a conversation far across the room. Pausing to keep her ear turned toward the men, she listened intently.

"There was no blood?" One of the men asked.

"Well, there had been. There were stains on his clothes and rips in his wrists and shoulder, but the wound was dry." The tap of his fork on the table landed as loud as a hammer to Nola's ears.

"What are you saying?" Another man asked.

"I don't have a clue," the familiar voice answered. "I just know what the family told me. The mortician has had all four bodies found the same way."

"Here you are." The tender sat Nola's cup of coffee down in front of her. The saucer hit the table with a clink so loud to her ears that she almost jumped. "I didn't mean to surprise you." Taking a look at the groups of diners behind her, he drew her attention away from overhearing. "Are you staying in Chatsworth long?"

"No, just passing through I'm afraid. It seems like a very quaint small town." Her hearing strained for anything in the distance but concentrating on the other end of the room only made things closer to her sound louder. She could hear her own lips touch the rim of the cup as she took her first sip. Deciding not to torture herself, she eased her concentration and looked up at the man before her. "Are you the owner?"

"On a good day, I am." He smiled again. "On the bad days, I say it belongs to my wife." The extra weight around his belly and cheeks gave him a gentle appearance. With a balding head and deep-set blue eyes over his thick beard, he looked very much like Santa Claus.

"Ah, I see." Nola chuckled slightly and took a drink from her cup. "I'm sure she appreciates it."

"Are you hungry? We had a nice lot of fish come in this morning. We also have hotcakes, though they are more like runny dumplings, and some petrified biscuits with lumpy gravy."

"It sounds appetizing," she clenched her teeth and imagined the food.

"My wife has been at home these last few weeks with the little ones. My brother, the magician in the kitchen, has been helping out lately."

"It sounds like a profitable arrangement." Nola could smell the combination of fish and hotcakes and decided not to order anything. "Are you eager for your wife to return?" Trying not to sound like she was prying, Nola kept her tone light.

"Not at all," instantly his tone turned serious. Realizing that he had given away something he did not intend on, he grabbed the pot of coffee and filled up her cup.

"Tucker," one of the guests held up his cup. "I'll take some more of that."

"I'll be right back, miss." Gripping the pot firmly, he left the tall counter and began to walk between the tables. The use of his name proved that Nola had found the source of information that Levi was talking about, but she was still unsure of what to ask him.

Waiting until he came back, her mind whirled for information on Luke.

"There doesn't seem to be many women and children outside today. Everyone is in such a hurry to get back in their houses." Nola knew she was testing rough waters by the way the man diverted his eyes. "Is there something to be concerned about?" Keeping his eyes cast downward, the once charming man took on a grave decorum. "Mr. Tucker, is it?"

"Yes, my name is Tucker," he answered softly. "Miss, I don't want to put worry on you, but this isn't the safest town to be passing through just now."

"May I ask why?" Lowering her tone to the same whisper he offered, Nola leaned forward.

"There's been some strange goings on around here." Lifting a pudgy finger, he pointed around the room. "These boys in here are all workers from the coal mine just outside of town. They are just getting ready to go home from a long night of patrolling the streets." Taking a rag and wiping out a large mug, he nodded his head toward the kitchen. "They will all go back out tonight until we find out who is behind the chaos."

"Chaos?" Nola asked, urging him gently to continue. "Chatsworth is becoming a dangerous place." Setting the towel down, Tucker shook his head. "On top of four people gone missing, there has been two killings." He glanced at the men sitting at the far table. "One of them was a mate of theirs. They thought he was a casualty from one of the explosions they do out there, till they realized that there was something not right about the body."

"What wasn't right?" Nola asked.

"That I'd rather not tell you about, with you being a proper lady and all. Now, I don't want to scare you, Miss, but I do want you to keep indoors once the sun sets and I wouldn't go wandering around alone."

"Yes, of course," she stated eagerly leaning forward. "Tell me, Mr. Tucker. Do you know anything more?" Before he could refuse her question, Nola glanced around and then placed her hand gently in front of his. "I didn't know of the disappearances before I came here, but we may have something in common. My friend has gone missing just this last week, and I'm not sure that the disappearances in this town are that much different than his."

"Is that why you came here?" Mr. Tucker asked cautiously. "My guardian and I heard that he may have been brought this way and were hoping to find anything that would help." Trying to show the desperation she felt, Nola wiped her eye as if she were fighting back tears.

"Where are you from?"

"Thedford City," she answered. As soon as she answered, Mr. Tucker looked around the room and sighed, maintaining his averted gaze. "We've been driving all night seeking anything, a clue, or some hope..."

"I don't know where your friend is, Miss, but I can say that I think you are closer now than you were yesterday." Running his hand along his beard, he leaned on his elbows across the bar top from her. "One of the men came across a business card from the Thedford City Museum just yesterday." Carefully, he glanced behind Nola to be sure no one else was listening.

"Where?" Nola asked a little loudly. The conversations stopped behind her for a few moments, but when Mr. Tucker looked to his patrons, they all went back to their private conversations. "Where is the card?" She asked quieter.

"Easy now," he held up his hand. "The constable has the card, but it was found in one of the warehouses down by the dock. They were looking for a missing woman but all they found was some rope, one fancy cufflink, and the museum card." Moving even closer to her, he maintained the private conversation. "Have you seen the constable yet? If you came all the way from Thedford City and there is any kind of connection, the local authority needs to know."

"I just may have to do that, especially if they have a cufflink. They may let me see it." Pushing the cup of coffee forward, Nola set an extra coin on the table. "Will you tell me where the warehouse was that they found the things in?"

"We don't need young ladies poking their nose where it doesn't belong." Speaking firmly for the first time, Mr. Tucker caused her to stop short. "I'm not trying to be rude, Miss. It's just that you seem like a nice decent young lady, and I would hate to be responsible for anything happening to you."

"I assure you; I wouldn't dream of going anywhere alone after what all I have just heard."

"Alright then, take Bassett Street down to Harbor. Then, cross to the left. Behind the old chandlery there is the abandoned warehouse."

"Thank you," Nola stated leaving the extra coin on the table. "You've been very helpful."

"You won't go alone, will you?" Gentle concern showed through his bright eyes.

"You have my word, Mr. Tucker." she stated clearly before turning to walk out of the door. "Thank you."

Outside the Tall-Tale Tavern, dense cold fog began to roll into the port. The Inn was only a few blocks away, but completely impossible to see. An elderly couple passed by, and Nola stepped back to allow them more room on the walkway, but when she lifted her head a familiar form in the distance caught her attention. There, a little more than a street ahead of her stood a tall man with reddish blonde hair.

Nola stared intently into the fog as the couple slowly walked along. The stranger in the distance turned slightly and she could see his profile perfectly. The moment she recognized Jarron Tempest he lifted his face toward her and held her puzzled stare.

"Oh, excuse me," the old woman moaned as she side-stepped, bumping accidently into Nola. "I'm so clumsy these days." Her hand landed on Nola's arm but instead of retracting it immediately she held on for a moment.

"No, excuse me," Nola stated gently. Casting her eyes up quickly to make sure she had seen Jarron, Nola stared into the empty fog once more. "Are you alright?"

"Oh yes," the lady answered. Her fuzzy gray hair poked out of her kerchief. "Don't mind me. I'm just not as sure footed as I once was."

"Come along, Ethel. Let the lady be on her way." Her husband offered a nod of appreciation. Nola held her attention on the distance, barely aware that the woman still held her wrist.

"You are such a beautiful young girl," the old woman stared at Nola's hand where she held it.

"Thank you." Again, glancing down both streets, Nola searched for the man she knew she had seen. "Did you just see someone standing there?" she asked, pointing to the shop she had seen Jarron. It was awkward that the woman would not release Nola's arm and she began to wonder if the old woman was mentally stable.

"Where is that, Dear?" The woman asked.

"There," Nola pointed directly. "A tall man with amber hair? He was standing just there," she declared.

"No," the woman answered. "Are you missing someone?"

"No." Realizing that she could not offer or ask anything with Jarron and his precise hearing so close, Nola removed her hand from the woman. "I must have been mistaken." She tried to ease herself away from the woman.

"Can we help you?" The lady tried to reach out to Nola again. "There must be something we can do for you." Never had Nola experienced a person feeling such a desire to hold her hand. It reminded her of the strange phenomenon that Aunt Dottie had shared with Gavin.

"Thank you." Nola looked back at the woman and saw a deep serene expression on her aged face. There was no doubt that Nola must have affected the woman in the same way Absolutes affected humans. "I'm quite alright," Nola added. Something caught her attention and she instantly looked to her left and down another few streets. There, just between two shops, Jarron stood staring directly at her. "You should be going," Nola gently took the lady's elbow and moved her along the walkway.

"Yes," the lady mumbled with a deliriously happy smile on her face. "You are so kind. Isn't she just the sweetest thing?"

"If you say so," the man gazed at his bewitched wife. "What's gotten into you?"

"Whatever do you mean?" The woman asked. "Come on then," she grasped his arm very firmly. "If this young Missy thinks we need to get home, then we had best do as she says."

Distracted by the couple for only a moment longer, Nola took her eyes off Jarron. In that split second, he was gone. The elderly couple left the walkway and hurried across the road, but Nola was frozen. She had never considered that Vampyres could move around in the daytime if the sun was completely blocked by fog. More of her curiosity dove into the reasons why Jarron would be there in the first place, and if he had anything to do with Luke. Either way, she was alone and wandering around an unfamiliar town with at least one Vampyre stalking the streets.

It didn't take long for her to panic. Nola considered everything Mr. Tucker had said, the disappearances and murders the last few days certainly made it sound like at least one Vampyre was in the area, and since they did not have to kill to feed, there could be plenty more.

Stepping backward, she glanced at the elderly couple, making sure they were still on their way down the street. Panic began to rise in her chest as she looked back where Jarron was to find him gone again. Nola couldn't even move. He was the one Vampyre that scared her the most and she could feel his eyes on her. Completely frozen, she looked back toward the Inn once more. To get to Gavin, she would have to walk right past where Jarron had just been. However, he had made no qualms about approaching her in previous meetings.

Her feet moved two steps forward, but she couldn't even enter the street. Nola's mind recalled how Jarron stood there with his eyes directly on her. He was still watching her; she could feel it. She began to contemplate her options.

"What should I do?" Nola whispered to herself. Glancing at the tavern behind her, she considered going back inside. It was unlikely that Jarron would follow her, but she wasn't sure of anything. All she knew was that she wanted Gavin there at that moment.

"I find your fear of me both insulting and entertaining." His voice was in her ear as she turned away from the tavern. In that split second, Jarron had come to stand a foot before her.

"What are you doing here?" Instantly, her hand went to her chest.

"Hmm... that is an interesting question." His smile was unnerving. "A more interesting question is what are you doing out here without your guardian? You know, this has become a very dangerous town lately."

"I've heard," she whispered. "I can't help wondering if you have something to do with that."

"Most definitely," he answered directly. "Where is Luke Ellis?" Nola glared at him.

"Now, what makes you think I would know?" He stepped to her side and gazed down both streets. It would not have taken a genius to see that he obviously knew something. Jarron's eyes held a playful stare.

"What other business would you have here?" Nola asked. "I would not expect your presence here to be a mere coincidence. Is Luke alive?"

"As far as I know, he is. I haven't heard of anyone killing him yet."

"Did Mr. Percy come with you?" Glancing around the small town, Nola looked for Elias and stood quietly for a moment to see if she could hear any sort of humming sound.

"You would not be able to tell if he were due to Joslyn's emanation. However, I will admit that the last time I saw Elias, he was summoned to Graelohr Manor."

"Tell me where I can find Luke," Nola stepped back the second Jarron took a step forward.

"You really are jumpy," he stated, completely amused by her fear. "What is it you think I am going to do to you? It's far too early in the morning for a beheading." Nola instinctively placed her hand to her neck and tried to shake the image of her little brother being sliced by a blade. "Oh, that's right... You are still human. It wouldn't take more than a good bump on the head." He made a tisking sound with his teeth. "You really should be careful."

"I'm not entirely alone," Nola offered. "We both know I'm still close enough to Gavin to be protected."

"Oh, I know. Graelohr and his troublesome sister are here. Their territory creates an annoying racket in one's ears." He tucked his hands in his pockets. "What you don't know ...is how many of us there are."

"Us?" Nola glanced around quickly. "How many are there?"

"You must understand... I'm not going to hand over ...my acquaintances, simply because I have a personal understanding with Elias Percy." Lowering his voice, Jarron added, "That being said, it has come to my attention that your friend has read a very interesting book. You would be surprised how many Vampyres happened to be interested in deciphering that information. He could be held here for quite some time."

She could hear her tone becoming stronger as she stated, "I want Luke back home."

"Home to what, exactly? His dead mother?"

"If you had anything to do with it," A rage came over Nola that replaced all fear, "Gavin will tear you to pieces." She stared into the blue of his eyes and could actually see his body sway backward as her anger rose.

"He would have known, if I had." Jarron somehow maintained his ground. "The way he kept tabs on that old woman was repulsive, even with the understanding that she raised you to be his mate," he sneered.

The insult was enough to fuel Nola's intent to escape. She knew she was in danger. Heading across the street, she hurried to the other side. Stepping up onto the raised walkway, she concentrated on containing her emotions. However, Jarron was in front of her the moment she stepped onto the next block. "Why are you running away from me, when I am the closest you have ever been to your darling cousin?"

"Where is Luke?" Nola almost yelled, exasperated by his company.

"If I know my friends, and I'm pretty confident that I do, he's probably on a ship just out of the harbor."

"Where are they taking him?"

"Nowhere, it's simply a very convenient storage location for food." Shrugging his shoulders, he answered flatly.

Nola's mouth fell open and her eyes closed at the gruesome thought. She could barely tolerate the fact that Luke had been taken, bound, and beaten but to learn of him being fed off by monsters was too much. "Which ship?" Her tone was neither warning nor cruel. You obviously have some stake in this."

With a polite nod, Jarron replied, "Your calm demeanor is admirable. However, it is not my place to speak of the situation."

"I'm going to get Gavin." She warned.

"Do you have any idea how many of us there are?" Jarron maintained a sinister sneer.

"Do you have any idea how menacing Lord Graelohr is?" At the boldness of the comment, Nola took a step back and rethought her temper. "He is aware that Luke is being held by your kind. Is Mr. Percy?"

"Your concern is poorly guided," he warned. "If Gavin goes anywhere near that den, you will be responsible for the annihilation of a three-hundred-year-old Absolute. One small ambush would end his existence." Walking over to the nearest building, he leaned his back against it. "Do you want that hanging over your head?"

"He won't be alone, and he will have a plan."

"Will he?" Removing a cigarette from his vest pocket, Jarron lit the end with a match. "I see him as the type to jump in the water and swim to the nearest boat to please you. I mean, you're not likely to give heirs to a man that let your brother, your aunt, ...and your cousin die. You wouldn't want to be responsible for that, would you?" Taking a large puff of his cigarette, he sniffled and stared at her. "I'll tell you what... I will take you to Luke."

"Alone... so they can kill me," she whispered.

"They wouldn't kill you." He inhaled another puff after he spoke. "Even Vampyres have politics. It's been decided that you may be different than the others. I think you have realized that by now," he held an intense gaze. "Your blood is poisonous and killing you would bring more trouble than letting you live," Jarron stepped away from the wall and walked closer to her. "Especially since you are surrounded by a trio of Absolutes and an acquaintance to my own employer." He made a complete circle around her and then stopped directly in front. "I might be able to arrange the release of your friend, if you are willing to undergo a little inquisition."

"You would let him go for the answers to a few questions?"

"Ah, no. You misunderstand me. I am not holding the man you seek. I simply have a good idea of where he is, and enough influence to suggest his release ...if you were to donate some information."

"Like what, exactly?" Her throat felt swollen, and she looked to the Inn again, but Gavin was too far away and sound asleep. "How do I know that you aren't lying? Do you expect me to trust your word? You could have no idea where Luke was taken. You have no evidence of anything."

"I wish I could offer you better proof, but all I have is a single cufflink." Removing a black onyx silver link from the same vest pocket that held the cigarette, he tossed it to Nola. Her catch wasn't graceful due to her surprise, but she managed to grab the trinket. "I'm sure there is more of him to be found if you care to look with me.

However, feel free to wait and incorporate Lord Graelohr. I'm sure he would love to cross the open waters and brave a ship full of Vampyres."

She was still close to Gavin. Every boat in the harbor was within his range of sensation. Plus, Joslyn and Levi could track her and carry her to safety if need be. Nola looked at the small cufflink and considered the danger Luke was facing.

"Alright," she stated seeing Luke's valuable in her hand.

Staring at the silver and black cufflink, Nola faced a harsh realization. She would trade her uncertain future for Luke's safety. "Take me to him."

"Noble of you," Jarron whispered. "For once, you surprise me." Looking down toward the fog covered harbor, he held out his hand for her to walk ahead. "Well, Miss Valerian, allow me to escort you to the harbor."

Chapter Fourteen
Truth Bound

The smell slightly burned her nose. Great waves crashed against the shore. Every foamy crest broke against the rocks of the harbor. At once, Nola turned to the small ship that would take them clear out into the vast sea and reconsidered her decision. In the distance, the masts of a ship could be seen furled and anchored just on the edge of the horizon. Knowing that it was Luke's prison was the only thing that kept her from turning and running away from the water.

"Are you afraid of a little water?" Jarron asked.

"Is Luke out there?" She ignored his question by asking her own.

"Come across," Jarron instructed as he pointed to the plank between the dock and the small skiff that would transport them the immense distance. "Hold this," he stated handing her a wooden pole. "I think it's best if we don't touch... wouldn't you agree?"

"Nothing would please me more." Nola took hold of the stick, lifted her blue and beige dress, and stepped onto the plank. The entire event caused a rise in panic. She had never been in a boat before and certainly not one over rough water. The sound of the ocean was overwhelming, and her fear of Jarron was not helping her stay calm. "I can't." Nola jumped off the plank and returned to the safety of the dock. The rolling pitch of the rowboat was terrifying.

"Luke is not going to get any closer to you," Jarron reminded her as he shoved the stick at her again. "Grab hold and step in. I'll not wait much longer."

"Alright!" Nola took hold of the stick and stepped onto the plank. However, as her hands wrapped around the end, Jarron hauled her into the boat. With her footing lost, she tumbled to the wooden planks between the narrow benches.

"There," he stated as he lifted a large piece of canvas. "That wasn't so bad, was it?" Nola grabbed her shoulder where it struck the bench and stared up at him, finally realizing how much danger she was in. "You're going to need this." He tossed her a canvas. "Cover up any exposed skin. You don't want to get wet."

"Let me off," Nola scurried to get upright, but by the time she had, Jarron had used the oars to shove them well off the dock. "Let me off!" she yelled, scurrying over to the side of the boat.

"I wouldn't do that if I were you." He could see her plan to jump. "Didn't your precious Lord Graelohr ever warn you about salt water?"

Just as he asked the question, Nola grabbed the edge of the rowboat and the water that had lapped up around the wood. A fast-burning sensation leapt into her hands. Pulling her fingers back, she watched as the pain intensified and her skin turned red and blistered. Fighting the urge to scream she watched as the dock grew further and further away from her.

"What is this?" she asked, horrified by the painful sting where each drop of water had touched.

"Proof that you have the possibility of becoming Absolute," Jarron answered. "Consider yourself lucky. If you were a fully-fledged Absolute, your skin would have shriveled to the bone.

Imagine how enjoyable that will be for your Lord Graelohr, should he choose to reclaim you."

"I knew I couldn't trust you." Nola stared at her hands as they shook from the pain.

"It's not that bad, really. I tried to protect you. Maybe now …you will listen to me and use the canvas." Sitting down on the furthest bench, Jarron began to row far out into the large waves. "I'd hurry up if I were you. It will take a bit of strength and speed to get us out of the surf. My eyes will be on the water, not you." With a single hand, he tossed the edge of the canvas up, letting it flop over her head.

Clutching her hands to her chest, Nola's fear began to build. He was indeed the cruel and vicious beast she had always suspected of him, and at his mercy. The water splashed around the boat, pitching over every wave. Some water pooled at the bottom of the craft, and she lifted her skirts to avoid any saturation. Terrified, she closed her eyes and thought of Gavin and how foolish she was to leave him.

She wanted to scream, to cry, and to take the stick Jarron had used to haul her into the boat and beat him with it. Amidst the roaring water and the spray that pelted the canvas, all she could do was close her eyes and hope the water never touched her again.

She needed Gavin, but there was no way he could get to her now. Still, she prayed for her ability to see him. Calling out to him in her mind, she relied on every memory she had and tried to force her gift. If she could just see if he was awake, to see if he had realized that she was gone, it would be enough to give her hope.

Surrounded by the rushing waves, all hope of escape failed. "There," Jarron grabbed the bottom of the canvas and hauled it off her. "That's better." Sprinkles of saltwater hit her skin, burning blotches on her neck and wrists. Thankfully she had her face covered when the canvas flung free. "The worst is behind us.

Well, behind me anyway," he chuckled menacingly. The fog lifted some as they journeyed further away from shore. "I daresay that was probably just the beginning for you." Nola checked the floor of the boat for any pooling water and scurried away from it as much as she could.

However, as she realized how it was clearly past dawn despite thick clouds, she glanced up at the Ancient Vampyre before her.

"You are immune." She whispered watching as the rays of light did nothing to his skin. In the near distance, the tall ship loomed on the water.

"Like you, I have a lesser reaction." He was impossible to see, though she could feel each movement in the boat. As she avoided the water as much as possible, he began to explain. "Where the saltwater would drain another Absolute of all their bodily fluids, much like salt on a slug, it merely blisters you. Comparatively, I am uncomfortable under such cloud cover."

"How is this possible?" Emotion was fortunately at bay. Her senses heightened, but it was awareness and not fear.

"We have much in common." Jarron's answer was flat as the boat turned toward the side of the larger ship.

Each wave brought increased terror for Nola. Silently, she watched as a man at the rail sent over ropes to attach to the side of the skiff. Jarron was quick to fasten the vessel and within minutes they were hoisted into the air and over to the deck of the ship. Above them, the man eyed Nola as a cat would a mouse. However, she could tell that he was human.

"Who is he?" Nola asked, seeing countless sets of bite marks on the terrifyingly pale man's arms and neck.

"I have no idea. Still, he seems like a useful young chap," Jarron added, standing up and climbing down onto the deck.

"Mr. Tempest, they are waiting for you below, Sir." The light and weakened sailor presented himself to Jarron dutifully. "No!" Nola tried to fight the young man that reached for her arm. "I'm not moving until I see Luke!"

With a heavy sigh, Jarron commanded the pale sailor, "Get her out of there," he ordered.

"Come along," the man ordered as he reached into the boat.

Grabbing Nola by the sleeve, he hauled her over the edge of the dinghy and caught her just before she hit the ship's deck. With more force than necessary, the man hauled her to her feet and held her, a little too firm.

"Ow ...unhand me!" Nola yelled. Before realizing what happened, Jarron hauled back his fist and sent it flying into the man's face. His feet left the deck, and long hair flew by her view as he shot backward. The railing behind him made a snapping sound at the sudden impact. Intense fear shot through Nola at the Vampyre's speed and strength.

"You harm one hair on her head and mine will be the last face you see!" Jarron maintained his stern voice without raising the volume. "Miss Valerian, please follow me below. There is someone down there you would like to see."

"Take me to him," Nola whispered, horrified at what she had seen and praying that Luke had not faced the same brutality.

Bending down over a hatch, Jarron knocked on the wood three times before lifting the cover and letting the sunlight bleed into the hull of the vessel. Motioning for her to lead the way, he maintained his distance. Taking one terrified step at a time, Nola descended the steep stairs. The sunlight created a blinding effect in the pitch-black hull, but once Jarron's form created a shadow above her, she could see small flickers of oil lamps from the large space below.

"Take a left," Jarron directed, "Through the next doorway and down the steps."

In front of her, a woman chained to a pillar scurried away from them. Her dress was filthy, and her eyes were stained with tears. The marks on her neck proved that she was a captive, but Nola found it easier to look away than to stare, knowing she could not help.

Ahead of her, the strange smell of fresh dirt hung in the air. It was thick, like a garden after heavy rain. Descending the small set of steps through a narrow doorway, she came to a deck where only the center path was cleared. The rest of the room was divided into large mounds of earth, each large enough to cover a human body. Silently, Jarron lifted his hand and motioned to the light at the end of the deck. There, she could hear the slight rattle of a chain.

"He's there," Jarron stated. In her mind, she noted the nearly twenty separate mounds of dirt, but her focus was on finding Luke. Her feet hurried past the dirt covered floor and she nearly ran to the back of the darkened room.

At last, as she rounded the last narrow doorway, she could see his form kneeling on a straw covered floor. His once handsome tuxedo was tattered and torn. The starch white shirt was ripped completely with blood splattered down the front of his thin undershirt. He looked dirty and thin with a filthy sack over his head, but he was alive and twisting the iron shackles around his wrists.

"Luke?" Nola ran to him and fell to the floor before him.

"Nola..." his voice was weak as he lifted his head. Nola instantly grabbed the sack and pulled it carefully off him. His eyes, dark and glossy, slowly opened to her. He was bruised with a swollen lip, but she could not see any bite marks on his skin or major defects that would mark him forever. "What are you doing here?"

"I'm going to get you out of this," she whispered, reaching to the wrist cuffs. "Are you alright?" She asked, moving her skirts so she could get closer to him. A wave of relief like no other swept through her as she wrapped her arms around him. His skin was pale, and the full weight of his head fell on her shoulder.

"I want him released!" she commanded, turning to face Jarron. His dark trousers and brown shirt made him almost invisible despite the single dim lantern.

"Well, you were right." Jarron spoke with his eyes directly on Luke. "She is enthusiastic about you." Ignoring everything he said, Nola raised her hands to Luke's face. Bringing her forehead to his, tears welled up in her eyes.

"Let him go," she pleaded again. "I don't care the cost!"

"I'm not the one with the keys." Jarron nodded to another passage leading further into the hull. "Perhaps it's time to negotiate with those who do?"

Nola could not remove her eyes from Luke, whispering, "I'm so sorry for getting you involved in this." Turning back to Luke, she caressed his face and ran her hands through his hair. "I will get you out of here."

"Nola, no..." he tried to argue, but his voice was too weak.

"He needs water." Nola turned back to Jarron. Irritation rang through his sigh as he motioned for a woman to bring a ladle of water to Luke.

"You have three seconds," Jarron warned her. When the woman returned, Nola quickly placed the water to Luke's lips.

"I'm going to help you, I promise." Nola kissed Luke's forehead before standing up. She moved toward the passage, glancing back at Luke as his head fell forward. "If I don't come back, hope is not lost. Lord Graelohr is coming for you," Turning to glare at Jarron she added, "... with others."

"Through there," Jarron motioned to the passageway. He obviously concerned himself little with Luke or the threat of Gavin.

Without options, she obeyed. Through the doorway, Nola ducked her head and let her eyes adjust to the dimmer light. It was nearly pitch black, except for one candle dripping from a wall sconce. The sound of shuffling across the floor led her to look in the corner beside her. There she could see the long flowing tresses of a woman as she hid her face in a man's neck. When Nola's boot stepped directly onto the hard wood she turned around, revealing her fangs and the trail of blood that poured from the man's shoulder. Smiling with bloodied fangs, the vixen's eyes sparkled in the candlelight as she turned back to continue feeding. The man was too weak to try and fight the creature.

More sounds filled her ears and instinctively she tuned into her newfound perception. Above her, a Vampyre hovered in the cramped space between the ceiling and the braces. He was staring at her silently, fangs protruding from his upper lip. In the back of the room another sat with a long narrow file sharpening the outer edges of his oddly long canines. The sound was grating. Nola tuned in her hearing as much as she could to avoid it.

"Welcome to hell, Love." A woman's voice called from a chair behind some crates. Dressed in a poor and tattered dress, her obvious profession spoke for itself as the woman draped her bosom eagerly in front of a male Vampyre. "Be nice, and they will be nicer," she giggled, caressing the man's head as he sank his teeth into her neck. The scene was too much. Nola averted her eyes from the grotesque image.

"It's quite enjoyable for them, really." Jarron whispered. "We have the decency to offer pleasure in return for their sacrifice ...instead of sucking them down to their bones and burning what's left of their remains."

Terrified and desperate to escape, Nola hurried through the next passage following the increasing light. In moments, the brighter room was around her. Darting her eyes back and forth, she was surprised to find the space empty of Vampyres or human captives.

The room was much larger with tables along the walls and a single high-back chair centered near the far end. With a plush red velvet seat and intricately carved mahogany, the chair gave it all the appearance of a makeshift thrown room.

She asked, glancing back at Jarron, "What is this place?"

"Hello Nola," a familiar voice called. Elias Percy stood near a set of thick black curtains at the far end of the room. It was then she realized the tossing of the waves and the creaking of the ship's ropes had kept her from realizing the unnatural low hum around her.

224

"They all implied, you couldn't be trusted. What do you want?" Nola moved to the center of the deck and stopped when she saw the details of the large chair. It was not made of wood but deep brown stained bone, several bones, melded together to create a hideous depiction. Fingers and forearms stretched out of the back, reaching as if trying to escape their prison. Holding her hand to her throat she turned away from the monstrous chair.

"You are earlier than I expected," Elias stood near the far end, toying with the dark material that blocked the ships windows. "Sneaking out of Lord Graelohr's reach must have been easier than I assumed."

"They were right about you," she whispered. "You weren't to be trusted."

"The past is always clearer than the present." Elias offered, moving to one of the tables and pouring a large glass of wine. The thud of his boots held her attention as he crossed the floor with the glass. Stepping back, she refused to take it. However, his speed forced the cup in her hand and held it firm as she tried to throw it.

"You killed the only mother I have ever known," she hissed as Elias stood firm, maintaining the glass within her fingers.

"The unfortunate circumstance has been resolved." He maintained his proximity, allowing Nola to feel his controlled power. "I was not the one that killed her. The particular assistant has already met the sun. Dottie's wounds were in error, but it was your precious Lord Graelohr that took her life."

"Unhand me," she hissed. Despite feeling the truth through his touch.

Elias was slow to release her hand, but Nola was quick to throw the wine. With the reflexes of a snake, Elias grabbed the glass from her fingers and twirled it in the air before her, catching every single ruby drop of wine before it fell. In her stunned silence, Elias replaced the vessel in her fingers and held out his hand, waiting to see if she would throw it again.

"What is it that you want?" Nola held terrified fascination in a silent glare.

"I want what is best for all Absolutes," Elias kept his amber eyes on the glass.

"And that is...?"

"To protect our women and children." Behind her, Nola could hear Jarron begin to leave the room.

"Wait," she called to him, boldly. "I want Luke released."

"We have no further use for him," Elias agreed without argument. "However, him making it off the ship alive is very unlikely. Perhaps, you should remind him he would be safer where he is ...but remove the chains." Raising his hand to the narrow passageway he allowed Jarron to leave the room. When the Vampyre was gone, Elias returned his attention to Nola. "Your ...cousin has seen what we are and how we exist. If he does make it to the water, he is unlikely to make it to the shore. There is also the very fact that if he says one word about our existence, the authorities will lock him in the first asylum that has room. They will shock his brain with electric probes., just to try and help the poor sod."

"Let him leave with me," she pleaded. "You have my word that I will keep him from telling anyone."

"Nola, there's been a misunderstanding." Elias shook his head and reached out to touch her chin. "You will not be leaving."

The touch of his hand was terrifying. All at once, Nola could feel his desire for complete control of her. She was to belong to him always, to live as his wife. Her arm strained as she tried to pull away, but Elias held her firm, making her understand every detail of his intentions. The information came all too fast in waves of emotion and images. Elias would try to make her complaint, but he would lock her away if he had to. There would be no escape unless she could no longer give him the heirs he deserved. Unable to fight her way free, Nola forced her mind to convey only thoughts of Gavin. Her memory re-captured every detail of his face and how honestly, she believed he would kill Elias for touching her. Pain shot through Nola's neck as his fingers gripped like a vice. Elias hauled her to within a few inches of his face and stared down at her with ice cold eyes.

"I don't think you understand. Only two Absolutes have the power to get to this ship. One will arrive any moment, and the other is Joslyn." His stone-cold voice scared Nola as much as the pressure on her neck. "She would never be so ignorant as to jump blindly across salt water to a ship that could contain any number of Vampyres." Nola pulled at his wrist, but the attempt was almost laughable until he felt her intense fear. "No," he answered the question, although she had never asked. "I will not hurt you." Suddenly, he looked around the room as if he were hearing something in the distance. At about the same time, Nola strained her ears to focus on the eerie sound of wind and sand. Elias grabbed onto the back of Nola's head, pulling her protectively to him. She would have fought the attempt, had safety not been crucial.

"Close your eyes or be blinded," Elias warned. Through his skin she could sense his honesty and did as he commanded. However, the feeling that surrounded her made it almost impossible not to look. A combination of thick white sand and mist began to whirl around the cabin, smacking against the wood walls and falling like pebbles onto the floor. Within seconds, the terrifying phenomenon was so severe that the room was engulfed in a strange storm. The dust pelted her face, forcing her to shut her eyes. Then, it came to an abrupt stop.

"I understood that you would wait until I called for you," Elias stated as he released his hold on Nola.

Scared yet curious, Nola listened to the sound of tiny beads of sand hitting the floor as she opened her eyes. Throughout the room, black dust fell from ceiling to floor. Whatever tiny specks landed near her feet sought out the cracks in the wood to dissipate into nothing.

Behind Elias stood a vision of true beauty, a tall thin woman with white, blonde hair and crystalline blue eyes. From the creases in her pink satin dress, black specks of dust fell and disappeared into the flooring. Nola looked down at her own clothes to see some of the same dust falling from her skirts. Before her, the mystical beauty stood with a gentle smile. Her hair, blonde to the presence of gold hung down in long curls. She looked not more than a day over twenty years. Eyes of cobalt and lips of pink rose were set perfectly within pearl skin.

"Do you have my book?" The light skinned beauty asked in a voice as soft as silk.

"No, Mistress." he answered. "Gavin's house is heavily guarded. We did manage to detain a human that has read the book." Elias bowed his head. "He is here. He is a scholar, and his memory is keen."

"That was resourceful of you," she stated plainly with her eyes directly on Nola. "Are you Novallia Valerian?"

"She has been raised with the name Nola." Elias stepped backward, allowing the small woman a better look at Nola.

"Pity," the woman whispered. "Her birth name was so much more elegant. Novallia was my favorite sixteenth-century poet." Reaching forward, the woman lifted a lock of Nola's dark hair. "Nola sounds very common. Still, you have grown beautifully." There was a grace and power from her that Nola could not only feel, but she could see. Strangely, a very slight glow of pink and orange color surrounded the woman, a subtle and slight aura that appeared and disappeared sporadically. "Where is Graelohr?"

"I thought perhaps you may want to talk to Nola alone ...first? She is still unaware of her change in situation." Though

Elias's words were soft, their impact struck Nola with the weight of a falling brick.

"How thoughtful of you," the magnificent goddess whispered. Reaching down to Nola's hands, the woman waited. Without thought, Nola recoiled. The strange power she could see was not one she wanted to feel. "Nothing will transpire between us," the gentle woman whispered. "You've been lost to me for a very long time, my dear."

"I don't understand," she whispered stepping as far away from them as she could. "Who are you?"

"Please, do not fear me. My name is Ysabelle." Slowly swaying her skirts across the floor toward Nola, she reached out her hands. "My grandson has taken very good care of you."

"I have been lured here by trickery and the ill treatment of someone close to me. I do not consider Mr. Percy's actions honorable in any way," Nola answered honestly.

"No dear, the man I was referring to is Gavin Graelohr." Seeing that Nola was not going to raise her hands, the woman reached to take them. Though Nola was expecting to feel a rush of emotion from the woman, there was nothing but a slight sense of empathy. "Who did this to your hands?" she asked, looking at the blisters.

"A Vampyre named Jarron Tempest," Nola answered blatantly.

"Jarron did this?" The question was directed at Elias. "I want him brought to me." The sound of her voice was angelic as she looked over the blisters and touched them gently. The pain had subsided since Nola reached the ship, but the wounds had not begun to heal.

Elias cleared his throat as a warning and both women turned to the distraction. Once the room was silent, he held out his hand about waist high. Pressing down quickly and pulling up his fingers, as if he had hit something invisible, a wave of sound and vibration soared through the ship. It was as if something large had fallen and landed directly where Elias stood. Moments after the resonance, Jarron Tempest walked back into the room.

"There you are..." Ysabelle smiled and extended her arms. "...my child." Jarron walked to her and eagerly accepted her embrace. "Would you like to explain why you would do such a thing to your sister?" Ysabelle asked.

"Sister?" Nola could barely hold her shock. "That is quite impossible. My brother died as a child."

"You and Jarron are not born of the same woman, nor the same man." Ysabelle explained. "But both of you are my creations." Making her way back to Nola, Ysabelle took her hands once more. "You, my daughter, are the first of miracles. Love Jarron as I do, he and the others were not fortunate enough to survive the gift put into them. Jarron, for example, died immediately to rise as he is ...an altered Vampyre. He has aged like an Absolute, able to stand sunlight, and exists on less feedings. However, he and the others are not among the living." Placing her hand against Nola's shoulder, she smiled perfectly. "Your human heart never once stopped beating and your emanation was present the morning after I made you."

"Made me..." Nola let go of the woman's hands and stepped away.

"Yes, the same way I myself was created." Seeing Nola's revulsion, Ysabelle slowly explained. "I know you have read our book, which I would like returned to me. Elias tells me your French is lacking, but at least my name should have stood out."

"Ysabelle..." Nola whispered the word. Her memory carried her back to the pages of the old text. "You are one of the Seven Keys."

"I am," she answered. "By name of sons: Fuller, Gwain, Reynard, and Donte. By name of daughters: Colette, Ysabelle, Clarice, Ava, and Cecily." Reciting the lines of the book, she watched Nola's puzzled expression. "I am the last surviving female. Among my children I am the mother of Graelohr, who is father to Gavin and Joslyn." Once our number of female Absolutes began to dwindle, childbirth led many desperate females to seek out their own death. A decision was made to attempt new creations." Entranced by the strange way Ysabelle's voice traveled through the room, Nola remained still. "Using the ancient book and legends, we were able to recreate the process. You, my darling, are the first female to survive. It was my own grandson who stumbled upon you and the other of my youngest sun risen-children."

"Esteban?" Nola whispered. "My brother?"

"Created a year after you, Esteban was the only of the males to emit an emanation. Like yours, his emanation was present immediately." A slight sigh escaped her chest. "Gavin was able to find both of you only because I had left you and Esteban together.

Once he had his overprotective hands on you both, Joslyn and Leviathan were the only Absolutes allowed to enter his territory." The confounded sadness Nola felt was overwhelming. Caressing the side of her pale cheek, Ysabelle tried to speak as gently as she could. "You are a new generation, Nola. You can continue this extraordinary race."

"You fed on us?" The sway of the ship seemed to increase. Balance became harder to control. "Why would you do such a thing?" Her mind whirled fast, darting from one concept to the next until nothing made sense. "I had a mother?"

"No dear, you were found in an orphanage, same as Elias, same as I." Ysabelle answered.

"No, I'm not the same." Shaking her head, she looked directly at Elias. "I have not turned."

"You will," he reassured her. "You have all the traits of an Absolute."

"And how many more years do you think that will take?" Boldly, she balled her fists and raised her chin. "I will soon pass my twenty-fifth year and have nothing more than exceptional hearing and an annoying sense of emotion."

"That is impossible. You are only twenty and one years of age." The definitive tone of her voice nearly ended the conversation. "You have yet to reach maturity."

"False," Nola stated firmly without fear. "I do not assume to know my true date of birth, but to mistake four years?"

"You were the younger of the three girls." Ysabelle folded her hands together in front of her pastel dress. "The elders were lost to Vampyres in Romania."

"Forgive me, Mistress, but the girls in Romania did appear many years this woman's junior." Jarron spoke up from the back of the room.

"If you are so sure that I am mistaken... taste her." Ysabelle made the offer as if Nola were no more than a piece of cake. "It takes very little to determine one's age."

"As gifted as I am, Mistress..." Jarron bowed his head gracefully, keeping his stunning blue eyes on Ysabelle, "... the blood of an Absolute is still poisonous to me."

"Alright then." She turned to Elias, completely ignoring the look of horror on Nola's face. "You have served me diligently these last years for her hand. Tell me how old she is."

"I am young yet to expect that kind of control," Elias glanced at Nola before speaking quietly to Ysabelle.

"If you take more than you need, I assure you," The woman never changed her enchantingly simple expression. "You will die before her."

"No," Nola began to back away. "I am telling you. I was born in the spring of Eighteen Sixty-one!" Elias looked as large as a lion as he crossed the floorboards in front of her. "No!" She screamed.

"Nola!" Luke's voice could be heard through the belly of the ship as Elias wrapped his hand around her thin wrist.

"Please!" She pleaded as his fangs pierced through his gums, causing a trickle of blood to race down the tips as they grew. His tongue licked them slightly once they reached their full length. "Elias don't, please!" The grip of his hand forced him to feel her terror, but when she felt his own fear Elias retracted his fangs. For a single moment they were both aware of how difficult it would be for him to follow Ysabelle's order.

"Alright," he whispered, gently holding the sides of her face, and kissing her forehead, Elias used kindness and seduction to calm her. "Shh..." When he touched her the second time, his doubt was vacant. All intentions transpired through touch, and she felt his power. "I do not mean to scare you." All his energy focused on taking away her fear. With a finger to her chin, he brought her gaze to his stare. "I don't scare you," he hummed, kissing the top of her hair. It was truly manipulation at its finest. "You trust me not to hurt you," he whispered with the low humming sound escaping his chest. Nola, barely aware of any concern and fear, was unable to avoid placing her hands on his chest. She had no idea the honey-colored gaze with slight silver reflection was an extension of his power. "Lift your head for me," Elias instructed. All hope of free-will was contorted and Nola obediently leaned upward to grant him access.

The dull hum in the room was ignorable, but the gentle feel of his lips was not. He was not Gavin, and she conveyed it to him endlessly. Still, Elias caressed her cheek and gently brought his lips to hers twice. With her commonsense fading, Nola willingly reached out to him a third time. His hand roamed over her shoulder and brushed her hair behind her back. It was then that his kiss deepened. There was more desire in his touch as he pulled her close. The gentle hum surrounded the room as he lifted her chin. His eyes were entrancing. In a single moment, she was unaware of where she was or what was happening.

When his hand tilted her head to the side, Nola felt an irrepressible twinge of fear. Not even Elias could take it away. In turn, he kissed her neck gently letting the tip of his nose run along the side of her ear. Her skin seemed to grow warm where he touched, and her fear lessened slightly when his lips caressed her neck time after time.

Piercing pain seized through her entire body as Elias sank his fangs into her flesh. Nola's breath stopped completely, her eyes shot wide open, and the room began to spin. Deep within her neck muscles she could feel his teeth, thick and immobilizing. Her heart began to pound, blood coursing from everywhere in her body, all of it drawing up to her neck. Tiny specks of light began to float before her eyes as the intrusion was finally ended. Elias ripped his head upward pulling the massive fangs from her neck, letting her blood trickle down his lip and drip onto her shoulder.

"Nola," he called through his fangs. With the back of his sleeve, he wiped his mouth, withdrew his canines, and licked his lips. "Easy now..." Ripping a piece of cloth from her dress, he held it to the wound in her neck. She was completely aware of his fear that he had taken too much. Behind him, Nola could see Ysabelle holding her hand up to him with the strange aura surrounding her fingers. It was so slight that Nola was not certain that she had seen it at all. "You're alright," Elias whispered, sending her the message that he needed her to be strong. "You just need to rest."

"Well?" Ysabelle returned to stand by Jarron's side as Elias supported Nola's weight under his arm.

"She is telling the truth. Not only is she twenty-five... she is still human." Elias answered, nearly breathless from the event.

"That is almost convenient," Ysabelle stated as she looked over Nola. Drawing her hand over the wounds, she touched the center of each. The blood ceased to flow out of Nola's body, but her weakness remained. "Raise her hand," Ysabelle ordered.

"What are your intentions?" The depth of his voice revealed his surge of power from her blood.

"You have never had a wife." She carefully turned Nola around so that her back was supported against Elias's chest. "I suggest a trial of marriage."

"Marriage?" He repeated.

"Yes, you have a taste for humans." There was a hint of sarcasm in her tone. "I will give you one year with her. If you cannot produce an heir or win her affection, the bond will be broken." Ysabelle stopped speaking momentarily and looked off into the distance. A thought could almost be seen in her expression. "If truth be told, she may be more useful to us in human form. Since she does not risk the complications of a full Absolute, she can raise her children herself. It would be an extraordinary venture for the two of you." Closing her eyes, Ysabelle took both his wrist and hers, holding them firmly in her hands. "Unless you eat them," she sighed heavily.

"No," Nola pleaded with what strength she had left. With a gentle hand, Ysabelle touched Nola's lips and took hold of her wrists.

"Do you accept my offer?" She asked Elias with no concern for Nola.

"Graelohr will be a problem."

"A fact that is not my problem," Ysabelle reminded him. "Do you accept the binding?"

"Yes," he answered, feeling Nola slide down against his chest. "You need to hurry. She will not be conscious long."

"Very well," she answered.

Holding one of Nola's hands and one from Elias, Ysabelle closed her eyes. Slowly, Nola began to feel Elias's concern for her. She assumed it was because they were still physically connected, but the more Ysabelle held her wrist and his, the more persistent the feeling became.

The ship around them dissipated into a hazy view of sunlit rays of light with specks of silvery dust. Nola felt the original Absolute place their hands in a clasped hold before lifting her chin. As if calling upon an ethereal power unseen and unknown to Nola, the world seemed to stop. Within a moment, Ysabelle released her hold on the couple's hands.

Instantly, a wave of vibration passed through them. Elias's life became part of her own. Nola could somehow understand his entire existence. He hated the smell of seafood. He hated living near water but loved snow. He had not chosen Nola and was not prepared for the commitment he was making. However, he was dutiful and willing to be her mate.

Elias would remain insatiable. He wanted more than one woman all the time but would kill and die for Nola from that point forward. She understood how she could call him from a distance. She could ask him for anything, and he would provide. It was full and clear why he had not let her touch him previously, Elias was a different Absolute than Gavin. He was not comparable to a charge of electricity. Elias Percy was dark. Younger and twice as wild, he had no remorse for taking her as his mate.

The commotion he caused in his home was merely a hint of the depth he could make one feel. Nola was lost in every moment with him. Never had she felt so complete and vulnerable. She could not look away from his eyes. Every breath he took appeared golden in her mind's sight.

A dangerous, controlling, and unimaginable sense of love swept through Nola. Then, it hit her all at once, Nola understood what had happened. She and Elias had been permanently connected to each other by Ysabelle. The feeling of his touch coursed through her skin. Struggling to become separate, Nola pushed him away and stumbled to the nearest column in the room. Still, she could feel everything that had passed between them.

"What have you done?" She shook her head despite the burning wounds in her neck. Silenced by Nola's intensely overbearing emotions, Elias swallowed hard and remained still. It took several minutes for him to stop staring at the source.

"Quite the commitment, isn't it?" Ysabelle asked him. "I imagine that her extremely troubled emotions will take you some time to disregard." Turning to Nola, Ysabelle observed the obvious suffering. "Still, this is what we planned all along. Perhaps ... we intended a different timeframe." She stared up into his wide amber eyes. "If you hurt her, you will feel it. If you deceive her, she will know." Just as the truth was seeping into Elias's mind, Ysabelle dealt the final blow. "If she dies, you will mourn her loss for centuries."

"I understand." The stern countenance of Elias's answer was sufficient for Ysabelle.

"Good, because this is the least of your worries for today," she warned.

Having lost all strength, Nola collapsed to the floor. The burning of her neck was equally comparable to the ache in her heart. Immediately, her thoughts traveled to Gavin and how desperately she wanted him to come and save her, to see his face, and to beg for his forgiveness. Elias's influence was a constant distraction. Even before he moved to help her, Nola could feel his concern for her.

"Don't touch me." She cried out with very little strength. The instant she spoke she was aware of how her torment bothered Elias. "Take this away, please." She begged Ysabelle. "This is wrong!"

"You will get used to it," Ysabelle answered. "He has no choice but to please you now." She smiled as if she had revealed great news.

"Nola," Elias called to her. His voice trailed off in her head seeing his lips had not moved. "I could no more hurt you than myself," Elias added. He offered his hand, and she grasped it with desperation she could not have imagined. His face was perfect; he seemed to glow in her eyes. His nearness made her breathe easier and she forgot about her weakened state. All she craved was his touch and ability to control what seemed to be drowning her.

"Jarron," Elias called as he lifted Nola off the floor. "Here," he attempted to hand Nola to Jarron. "Has Luke been unlocked?"

Surprised by her own actions, she clung to Elias to keep away from Jarron.

"Yes." Jarron answered.

"It's alright," Elias's smile was entrancing as she was handed to the vampyre. "He will take you to see Luke. I will come to you soon."

"The human hasn't had time to clean up." Jarron answered, he reached for Nola. Again, she recoiled.

"Go," he ordered Jarron. "I will take her to him," Elias ordered. Relieved at both his touch and his words, Nola clung to his arm without questioning the reason.

A beautiful giggle rang through the ship. "Aren't you being generous with your new wife?" The lighthearted tone in Ysabelle's voice was unmistakable.

"Luke can care for her for the moment. I have other things to worry about." Elias lifted Nola's lethargic body and carried her to the door. "Besides, they can't go anywhere."

"Yes, and you must figure out a strategy... before my grandson arrives to remove your head for taking his beloved." The light blue in her eyes began to shine with her amusement. "You know Gavin feels her pain as readily as she does."

"Will I face your retribution in the event I should end his existence?" Elias held serious concern in his tone. "He is of your line." Elias straightened his shoulders as Nola's blood began to powerfully course through his veins.

"You were unsuccessful at retrieving my book from this child.

You failed to steal it from Gavin. And your lack of control nearly killed the first created female Absolute in over one-hundred years." Ysabelle stepped to the center of the room with a glorious smile. "Not to mention, you married his prodigy. It is not my retribution you should be concerned with." She lifted her chin with pride. "Fear my grandson. I hold no stake in the outcome of your battle."

Closing her eyes, Ysabelle inhaled deeply as tiny white particles of shimmering dust and sand began to lift from the floorboards and collect around her feet. The slight tapping sound was barely audible. Within a moment, pale fragments were hopping up around her like droplets of snow in reverse. "And Elias," she called, opening her light blue eyes once more. "Should Joslyn or Nola receive even a scratch from anyone of your creatures ... I will end all of you." She offered a brilliant and honest smile. "Go on," she waved her hand at him to leave the room. "You have very few hours before sunset and not nearly enough humans to feed an army of this size. She looked around the ship as if she could see the passengers. "Once night falls, they will sail into port, and you will face Gavin's wrath."

"I'll be ready," Elias spoke without a doubt.

"Then, I shall see you again." Ysabelle lifted her head and closed her eyes as the particles of dust began to whirl around her skirts. Elias turned toward the door and covered Nola's eyes as the sound of a sandstorm filled the room.

Chapter Fifteen

Chaos

At first, her vision sought out Gavin. Quickly, she understood no emanation was near and all connection was vacant. The man before her had familiar dark eyes. His hair fell gently over his eyes, and he held her as if she were the only woman in the world. However, when he caressed her cheek, her vision cleared.

"Luke?" Her hand went right to her neck. Spoken words were torture through the deep gaping wounds Elias left in her flesh.

"It's not bleeding anymore," he whispered. "One big guy brought you in here and the other's scattered. They haven't come withing twenty-five feet of us."

"How long have I been asleep?"

"I don't know," he answered. "But those things have brought some food and fruit. I wouldn't eat the meat," he whispered. "There is no way of knowing where it came from."

"What have they done to you?" she asked, realizing for the first time that he had removed his shirt to soak up her blood. His entire body was covered in bruises. It looked like he had been whipped with a cane.

"They wanted to know everything about that book from Graelohr." He cast his eyes downward in shame. "It wasn't worth it to keep quiet. If I hadn't told them what I did, they would have..." He nodded his head to Nola's neck. "But I swear, I never answered a single question about you. I wouldn't."

"It's alright," Nola couldn't move her head enough to nod. "This is all my fault."

"What in the world made you come here?"

"I had to find you." She brushed the hair away from his face to inspect the cut at the edge of his eye. "I came to bring you home."

"Home?" He shook his head. "I don't think either of us are ever going home now. These things are everywhere, and they drink our blood." Glancing at the opposite entrances to the front of the room he made sure no one was coming. "Did you find Davey? I don't remember how it all happened." Luke checked her wounds and looked behind him once more. "Mum... she hit the wall so hard... tell me she's alright." As if remembering the night, Luke looked away for a moment.

There was no choice, she was forced to give the news despite his obvious agony. "I am so sorry, Luke." Nola held his face and looked into his eyes. "Her wounds were..." His body had been beaten and tortured endlessly. However, it was the news of his mother that brought the glistening effect to Luke's eyes. His agony was deep.

Reaching out to him, Nola held him as her own tears streamed down her face. As if she had bumped into a wall, she felt a rush of consciousness, an awareness that Elias was feeling the sum of her pain. Afraid he would sense her deep emotion for Luke; she quickly left his tight embrace.

"Did they find Davey?" With the back of his wrist, Luke wiped his eyes.

"No," she answered. "He knows you are missing and I'm sure he is out looking for you." Nola took his hand despite Elias's constant intrusion within her. "Now, you have to listen to me. We are not here alone. Lord Graelohr knows where we are. He's only a few miles away and will be coming for us as soon as the ship heads to shore."

"That's exactly what they want," he admitted. "There is something about him being stronger than the others. More and more Vampyres arrive every night, trying to form an army just to fight him." He repositioned his legs and looked at the doors once more. "Nola, how are you involved with him? I've heard them say things about you. They don't know if you are like Graelohr or if you are like me. Tell me. Tell me you aren't one of them."

"I've taught children for years and I can't stand the sight of a dead chicken, Luke. How could I be one of them?" Her reasoning satisfied him easily. "But" she offered a warning tone. "There have been changes in me that I don't understand, and I can't explain." Feeling the wounds on her neck, she glanced into his dark eyes. "Still, they have proof that I am human." Amazed that a single puncture wound was as large as the tip of her finger, Nola felt the sting once more. "There is too much to explain right now. Just believe that Gavin and his sister will come for us, but we have to be ready for whatever they need us to do."

"Jarron will turn me into one of them first," he whispered.

"Don't say that." Nola held her hand against his cheek. "We will get you out of here." Rubbing the raw abrasions on his wrists, Luke continued to look around.

"Our only chance is if they make me as strong as they are." He spoke nearly in her ear. "They can't let me go after what I have seen, and with their speed and strength, I can get us out of here."

"Shh," Nola warned. "They can hear us." Pulling her attention back, she explained. "You can't exist like that... surviving on human blood? You would have to hide in the shadows for the rest of your days. Give up every chance at ever having a family and being happy?"

"It's either everlasting power or death. Believe me, Nola, I have done nothing for the past week except marvel at their capabilities. These people may be vicious and horrifying, but they are smart. Many of them have been around the world several times." There was a thought-out sense of excitement in his voice. "Just think of the things I could learn... of what I could do."

"You could murder someone every night, if you weren't careful," she answered. "Gavin will get us off of this ship without you becoming the same as the creatures that did this to us!" For a moment, Luke considered her words. Then, as if seeing her point, he slowly nodded his head.

"Alright, do you know his plan?"

"No, I wasn't supposed to come looking for you alone."

"Then, he doesn't know where we are?" Luke began to panic.

"He can find us," she assured him.

"Do you at least know where we are?"

"This ship is just outside of Port Chatsworth," she answered as the stabbing pain in her neck caused a tear to roll down her cheek. "Elias will have to keep the ship as far away from land as he can until nightfall. Then the Vampyres are strong enough to fight." A feeling of desperation fell over her, but as quickly as it came, she could sense Elias's frustration. The simple reminder of their bond forced tears to well up in her eyes.

Seeing the rare emotion, Luke reached for her. "It's going to be alright." He pushed back her hair and held her face. "We will get out of here."

"It won't matter if I do," she whispered sadly. "I can't leave anymore."

"There is no time for this. Nola. This isn't like you. You're never one to get worried or afraid." He tried to smile, but it didn't last more than a second. "Tell me, what you can. Where is Lord Graelohr? I heard them talking about him, how he walks in daylight and how they can sense if he is close. They say he will be very difficult to kill."

"That's right," she answered, finding new hope. "He's far more powerful than anyone on this ship. Even more powerful than Elias."

"Who is Elias?" Luke looked up at the entrances to be sure they were clear. "Is he the tall one?" Nola nodded, following his gaze to the doors. "He doesn't come too often, but they all treat him like he's a bloody king."

"He's Elias Percy. The very reason you and I were brought here."

"And you think Graelohr can take care of him?" Luke asked. "I think so," she answered softly. Her mind recalled the two people Gavin murdered in the alley and how fierce he had been. The image stayed with her for more than a moment. "Yes," she answered again. "I have no doubt that he can manage Elias."

Having only a small idea of what Elias was capable of, Nola let the free recollection of Gavin enter her mind. As if someone had closed a door on her internal vision, Nola was stopped from viewing him. It was unclear exactly how the event happened. At once, when the memory was clear, it became foggy with images of Elias, images she had never seen. As if a hard wind blew in, washing away any memory of Gavin, the ship below her began to hum. It was a lot of sound.

The humming increased as he drew near. Luke seemed completely unaware of both the sound and tremor, but as if burned by a brand Nola shot across the floor as far away from Luke as she could get. Instantly, she felt remorse. The displeasure she felt from Elias at that moment was as if she had committed an ultimate sin. Her mind being on Gavin and her body touching Luke's filled her with far too much guilt for someone not used to emotions.

"Nola?" Luke asked before he could finally hear the heavy footsteps. The fear in his eyes was more than Nola could bear.

"Do you have such little faith in your new husband?" Elias asked, stepping through the small door. The blood that he had taken from her was enough to make his body react in a similar and foreboding manner. His shoulders seemed broader, his neck thick, and his arms as solid as steel.

"Stay away from me," Nola warned, ready to kick at him if she needed to. She scurried back in the straw in front of Luke.

"Husband?" Luke asked in the background.

"How can I possibly stay away?" Elias crossed the floor in a blur of motion, hauling her up to her feet. "Your blood is in my veins. A six-hundred-year-old Absolute has bound you and I. You could be on the other side of the country..." He pulled her straight up against him before she could imagine recoiling. "...and still feel this close." He stared down at the terror in her eyes and watched them slowly begin to return to normal. As long as he was holding her, Elias could suppress whatever she felt. Rational thinking was still with her, but the useless emotions were gone. Inhaling gently, she completely understood that he had no desire to hurt her.

However, he was furious with being charged with her emotion and forced to endure it.

"Let go of her!" Luke yelled, grabbing a crate from the side of the room.

"Luke, no!" Nola yelled as he raised the crate far above his head. Though she was unable to read his thoughts, she was aware of Elias's rage upon sight. "Stop!" Nola slid under Elias's arm to put herself between them. "He'll kill you," she whispered.

Sheer terror marked Luke's face as he slowly put the crate down. Looking back over her shoulder, Nola could see that Elias had drawn fangs, both top and bottom. Feeling his energy, she knew that it was her fresh blood that fueled his animal tendency, and he had little regard for Luke. "Stop!" Nola instinctively took hold of the beast's forearm. "Please!" Ignoring the plea, Elias tilted Luke's head to the side, visualizing the pulses of blood in his veins. All the while, Luke struggled for air. Fear controlled Nola just enough to give her courage. Reaching down to the crate, she took the wooden cover and hit Elias on the shoulder hard enough to break one of the boards.

Dropping Luke like a wet rag, Elias threw his arm outward, sending Nola across the room.

Everything went yellow. Nola blinked her eyes a few times, but the room continued to fade into the golden hue. In a moment, she could see, but not through her eyes. The vision was brought on by the hit to her head. She could see large hands sliding an oiled stone over a silver blade. The sword was much longer and thicker than any she had ever seen before. The hands were male. The words 'away from stern sunset' stained in ink on the back of one of the hands. Polished to perfection, the sword tilted just enough to purposefully reveal Gavin's reflection. It felt as if the words had meaning, though she did not understand. A rush of hope soared through Nola as Gavin lifted his sight to Levi, Joslyn, and the early evening sun. She could feel herself being lifted physically, but it wasn't until she heard Elias's voice that Nola came away from the golden hue.

"Damn," Elias lifted her head, checked her hands and arms. He gently felt her calves through her skirts. "Are you alright?" She couldn't answer at first. Nola was overcome by a strong feeling of guilt and concern from Elias. A single wound on her body would send him into devastating misery. "Nola, look at me?" His amber eyes seemed more golden for a few minutes as she tried to shake the images. "Tell me where you are hurt," he cupped her chin in his hand and pressed his forehead to hers. The intense regret he felt was incomparable to anything Nola had ever experienced before.

"I'm alright," she answered, not only for his benefit but to rid herself of the agony.

"You had a vision?" Elias asked, trying to regain his hardened composure. It was obvious to them both that the bond they shared was complete and powerful. "Never touch an Absolute while they are feeding," he warned. "We cannot control our actions all of the time."

"Luke?" Nola looked around Elias's broad shoulder to see him hunched over and chained back on the floor. He didn't answer her, but she could see that he was moving and there was no blood on him.

"What did you see?" Elias asked. His regret and curiosity flowed into her deeply. "Tell me." He commanded, leaning her away from the wall and touching the center of her back to assess any injuries.

"No," Nola answered with a blank stare. "I didn't see anything."

"It is not in us to lie," he reminded her. "I am bound to you. I know you saw Gavin." Helping her to her feet, Elias bowed his head slightly. "I did not mean to harm you."

"You meant it very much," she corrected him.

"Tell me what you saw." Elias' eyes were dark and intense.

Nola wanted to ignore him, but the bond was too insane for her to comprehend. "Nola, we will share everything." The words were a promise more than a warning or request.

"He sent me a message," she answered slowly. "He is preparing his sword."

"He is not alone?" he asked, as Nola again looked back to her frail cousin. "Joslyn is with him?"

"Yes," she answered, carefully. "What are you not telling me?"

"Please let go," she whispered, pulling her arm away from him. The constant distraction of his anger made it impossible for her to think.

"He's given you hope and confusion," Elias retained his hand on her arm. "What is the confusion?" The inquisitive way he stared at her, and the intrusion of her private feelings exasperated her. She tried to pull her hand away again, but he held firm. "Tell me."

"I don't know," she answered. Holding her under her arms Elias helped her to stand.

"It won't matter." Bringing Nola to her feet, he looked over at her once more. "There are only a few hours of daylight left. I need to rest." Taking Nola's hand, he began to head out of Luke's prison. "It will take endurance to survive the night and keep a watchful eye on you." Nola's head still whirled far too much to argue with him.

"Wait!" Luke called through a strained voice. Elias stopped short. "Make me whatever they are." Even knowing as little as he did, Luke knew by view that Elias and Jarron were not the same creatures. Nodding his head to the room of Vampyres, Luke strained his voice for volume. "Don't leave me here."

"These men fight for me, Mr. Ellis. You will not be given their strength and speed to betray me," Elias laughed before he moved toward the door again.

"Who will protect her?" Luke's voice became stronger as his bravery grew. "What will you do if she is killed?" Nola could see scars on his back as he curved forward on his knees. "I swear to keep her safe." In his tortured state, both Elias and Nola could see that he meant every word.

"Luke, no! You don't know what you're saying!" Nola argued, filled with fear.

"I told you I have thought about this every day I've been locked down here," he reminded her. "I'm dead either way," he nodded to the space around him. "...they will not let me go."

"You're right," Elias agreed honestly. "I will not let you off of this ship alive."

"Then kill me. Kill me to make me ...what they are ... for Nola's sake." He nodded toward the woman Elias held like a rag doll.

"Please Luke," Nola broke free of Elias's hand and knelt before him. "I can't let you do this."

"I have watched over you for as long as I can remember." Luke's eyes were deep and revealing. "I can't leave this world knowing you are in danger."

"It's not worth hundreds of years of suffering," she whispered as a tear rolled down her cheek.

"None of them look like they are suffering." Returning his attention to Elias, Luke lifted his head as high as his sore neck would allow him. "Give me the ability to protect her."

"Even if I do, you will never be as powerful as I am." Elias forewarned. "You will feed nightly; women and children will taste the best. Sunlight will burn your skin instantly, and common punishment for disobedience is being locked in a vault for decades at a time, unable to end your own life." He turned to Nola, feeling her awe and fear. Shaking as much of the irritation as he could, Elias continued, "Do you still desire eternity?"

"Yes," he answered without hesitation. Keeping his eyes on Nola seemed to cement his decision.

"If you betray me or my wife in the slightest way, I will tear your limbs and send them to the far corners of the world," Elias warned.

"You have my word." Luke held direct eye contact with Elias as proof of his sincerity.

"Very well." Elias held out his hand as the humming sound rose and the floor began to shudder. Though Luke had no idea what was happening, Nola knew that he was calling Jarron Tempest.

"No!" Nola called, pulling Elias's hand. "You can't do this!"

"Consider it my gift to you." Taking her by the shoulders, Elias lifted her in front of him. "He will be yours. In a year's time, if you cannot give me what Ysabelle wants, you will be free to take him as your lover." Nola glanced at Luke and wondered what it would be like to share the emotion he had always felt for her. Just then, Jarron entered the tension filled room.

"Do you want me to kill him?" Jarron asked. "No," Elias answered. "Turn him."

"Now?" Jarron looked around with surprise. "It will make one hell of a mess."

"Luke," Nola whispered, filled with dread.

"Take her away," Luke whispered, lowering his head, coming to terms with what he had subjected himself to.

"Get him a human," Elias tried to make the request as silent as possible. "He will need to feed as soon as life purges from him. Then, clean him up."

"Of course, we could always use another scholar in our midst."

"No, No!" Nola cried.

"It's alright." Luke tried to reassure her.

Taking Nola by the arm, Elias pulled her out of the room despite her resistance. Her agony was intense, and she fought against him so much that in the end he simply lifted her in his arms and carried her through the decks of dirt and lurking Vampyre's.

At the opposite side of the ship, he climbed the stairs to the top deck and set her in front of him to ascend the hatch. The sunlight sprawled over every inch of the deck. It seemed like two entirely different worlds to Nola. The dark and demented were kept below while hope remained above. Over the water a tiny strip of land to the east held attention. Somewhere, Gavin was sharpening his steel and watching the ship. Still, the waves of burning salt lapped around the ship, reminding Nola of how trapped she truly was.

"Let him go," Nola turned to Elias. "Please!"

"How can someone so small have so much damn emotion?" Elias looked at the sky, completely annoyed. "Will you at least try to control yourself? I am starting to wonder if killing you would be easier than being aware of every little sentiment you have!" His annoyance turned to anger, and it overwhelmed her. Nola stepped away from Elias still feeling as if he were touching her. No matter how far she backed away, his anger coursed through her. "Stay there," he warned her as she took another step. "Watch the rail!" As soon as the warning was called out, Nola reached back to touch the wooden railing. Immediately the water soaked into the skin of her palm boiling under the flesh. Shaking her hand vigorously, Nola wiped the water on her sleeve and winced in pain. "I said to watch the rail," Elias warned again, suddenly there pulling her back to the center of the deck.

"Why can't I get away from you?" She called out, pulling her arm out of his.

Unintentionally, her wet sleeve slid across his forearm below his folded sleeve. His groan was immediate. Elias held his arm out as if it were on fire. His face distorted and Nola watched as his wet skin began to smolder and crack open just below his elbow. A growl came from his chest as he endured the burning salt. Like drying clay his skin fractured along the wound. Some of it fell like dust, but most of it simply vanished into many layers of tissue. The wound did not go deep, but it showed Nola exactly how fortunate she was for her little blisters.

Feelings of fear, regret, and an immense amount of satisfaction filled Nola until Elias grabbed her shoulder and pushed her towards a cabin below the raised quarter deck. All the while, he kept his arm away from him still feeling the pain. Opening the door, he shoved her inside before closing out the sunlight.

"Enough!" Elias raised his voice more than she was prepared for. "If you don't control yourself, I swear I will strip off every ounce of your clothing and smother you completely so I can!" His eyes were wild with pain and anger. "I will not suffer your ridiculous sentiments any longer!"

"Then undo this... this... connection that woman made!" Too angry to be afraid, Nola yelled back. Elias reached for a pitcher of fresh water and dumped it over his arm, spilling it to the floor.

"Sit down!" He ordered pointing to the bed with the pitcher in

hand.

"No!" Nola yelled back. Before she could say another word Elias disappeared in a blur of motion. Nola could see the color of his white shirt and dark trousers as they moved, but he was too fast to see any detail. In an instant, she was seated on the bed, hands tied before her waist. A strip of cloth covered her mouth. Her scream was muffled as he came to a stop before her. His fangs bared as he leaned over her face.

"Pay attention," Elias warned as he grabbed onto the back of her neck gently. "You have one minute to control everything you feel." He had tilted her eyes up to his but then let go of her neck and slid his fingers to the back of her dress. "Stop the fear, stop the anger," his hand slid to the first button above her shoulders, "stop the worry and the panic ...before I show you just how powerful this bond between us really is."

The memory of his fangs in her neck was terrifying, but the possibilities of what he was going to do was intensely distracting. Nola wriggled against the rope at her wrists and tried to back away from him, but her panic angered him more. Instantly, Elias plucked off the top button. Shoulders squared; Nola sat upright trying to avoid his touch. She closed her eyes and fought the urge to cry out as the tip of his finger slid to the next button. She could feel the bed press in as he leaned against it to bring himself closer, but she wouldn't open her eyes. The closer he came and the further into her dress he moved his hand, the more she panicked. A second later the next button popped off her dress.

"Ignore the irrational feelings and think of a solution." His breath was warm and heavy in her ear. Elias slid his hand under the satin material of her dress and let his palm lay flat below her neck. "Control your breathing." His words were as smooth as silk.

Noticing that his speech was different than when his fangs were born, she opened her eyes to see that he had withdrawn them. The touch of his hand was intoxicating as it manipulated every mad emotion she could experience. "Focus on what you can do instead of what you feel." Slowly, Nola found herself thinking more clearly. She found herself thinking with his assistance of control. Though she hated it, she realized that letting Elias touch her was more beneficial than trying to escape him. Sighing heavily, she lowered her head knowing that he would remove his hand from her dress as soon as she relaxed. "See," he whispered, sensing her calmness. "That wasn't so hard." Elias slid his fingers back up to her cheek and pulled the gag away from her mouth.

"If Gavin kills you, will this be broken?" Nola asked with her first breath.

"I don't know," he answered honestly. "Under normal circumstances you would mourn the loss of me for ten years of more, but since you are still mostly human, it may not affect you at all."

"If I were to die?"

"Let's just say that I have my work cut out for me, since you are so fragile." Elias noted. "I suggest we work together."

"I'd sooner throw myself over the railing." Her words were bold, and she almost meant them.

"I had another set of chains brought up here, in case you had any ideas." He grabbed onto the rope at her wrists and pulled them loose. "Would you like to try them on?" Nola's cold expression was enough of an answer. He stood up and unraveled his sleeve to cover the wound on his arm. Moving over to the curtain on the window, Elias slid them open and checked the sun's position in the sky.

"Why are you risking your life for this?" Nola asked, still aware of a tingling sensation on her back where his hand once was. "Gavin will kill you." When the words escaped her mouth, she felt an awareness from him. "You fear it, don't you?" Knowing that she had touched on a sensitive subject, she closed her mouth. Elias glanced at her with a warning glare. At that moment, a quiet thud came from the deck below. It brought Nola's concern back. "Was that Luke?" she asked unaware that she had given into her fear. "What will Jarron do to him?"

"Exactly what he asked for." Elias was suddenly before her. Still surprised by his speed, she sucked in her breath, but his hands were on her too quickly. "Jarron will take him by the neck, much like I did." Lifting her chin, he silently conveyed her safety by touch and view of his perfect honey eyes. "He will tilt the boy's head and bear the thick vein," Elias drew his finger along Nola's skin, "...just about here." The tip of his finger added more pressure to her artery. His touch thrilled her skin. It was uncontrollable. "Then, he will empty the boy of all but his last drop of blood." His eyes seemed to darken as he leaned forward. His square jaw held her attention. His lips were thin, and his smile was maddening.

"Stop it," Nola insisted at the way he spoke with the liberties he took.

Elias ignored her plea, feeling her wave of unintentional curiosity. "When his heart has nothing more to pump, Jarron will infect him with his own black blood." His voice was deep in her ear, causing Nola to shiver from the unsettling sound. "The poison will spread like wildfire through his body, killing his organs and forcing him to wretch out whatever life he had left. And then," Elias trailed his finger up Nola's arm. "He will die." The answer was flat and cold.

"Jarron will then feed him human blood. The process is a little difficult, trying to feed the dead, but it is done."

"Enough," Nola hissed.

"You wanted to know," Elias whispered. "Once the blood enters, his body will either accept it and function with rapid success or be denied life of any kind."

"Please, stop this!" Nola grabbed onto his arm. Her pain was readily passed on. "He is everything that is good in this world! You can't do this to him."

"You will thank me for it should we fail in our duty." Holding onto her hand, Elias lowered the tone and volume of his voice. "If you do become Absolute and all you know of this time is gone, he will still be with you."

"A Vampyre," Nola whispered. "How could I ever want that for him?"

"You will see," he answered gently rubbing his thumb over the back of her hand. His words were honest, and his tone was kind, but the feeling below her skin proved that he only wanted her contentment to give him a child. Nola pulled her hand away, but the cheap and shallow feeling was still apparent.

Elias walked around to the bed and flopped down on the pillow. Just then, Nola heard the hatch open from the center of the deck, nearly thirty feet away. Turning to the window, she watched Jarron step out into the sunlight as a wave crashed against the bow sending a very light sprinkle of sea water over his skin. Filled with hate, she watched the detestable creature wipe the water off his face and silently wished it had burned him to ash for what he had done to Luke.

"Why doesn't it hurt him?" Nola asked, the venom in her eyes looked black.

"The sunlight?"

"The water?" She clarified.

"The best of our understanding is that because they are dead, their skin does not absorb the salt that sucks the fluid from living flesh." Elias repositioned his head on the pillow.

"They can swim in it?" Nola kept her eyes on the small plot of land on the horizon.

"Yes," he answered. Elias tucked his arm behind his head. "It is a vast boundary for us. We never travel across the open sea unless there is no other way."

"But Gavin said there were many of you in other countries," she wondered out loud.

"Yes, and most have traveled with a woman like Ysabelle or Joslyn." Elias stated calmly, encouraging the conversation.

"Can all Absolute women travel like that?" Nola refused to look at him in bed.

"I can't say for sure. I haven't met them all." The inflection of his voice had a lighthearted tone. "No," he answered honestly as he crossed one foot over the other. "Like any other ability it differentiates."

"How can you even think of sleep at a time like this?" Finally looking at him, Nola saw that he had unbuttoned most of his shirt. It was the first time she ever thought of him as Gavin's equal. Elias may have appeared tall and lanky, but beneath the shirt he was as solid and trimmed as Gavin. At the same moment, he looked down at his chest and then smiled at Nola.

"Would you like me to take the binds off?" He teased until Nola turned away. Her face flushed fully and for a first, she experienced embarrassment. "I'm tired," he answered, a twinge of guilt passed through him. The bond between them was not only new to her. He felt much of her infantile knowledge and experience. She was filled with negative emotions. He could barely withstand her aura. Wanting to ease the fight inside of her, he sought to ease her fear. "I need rest. There will be a long night ahead of me."

"I doubt that." Nola sneered. "Gavin will come for us."

"Good, then I won't have to wait long to be rid of him." Pressing his head into the pillow again, Elias sighed gently. "You're Lord Graelohr lacks my youth and fighting experience."

***

At last, her vision turned to the golden haze she had been seeking. The rain rolled in from the west and tapped against the windowpane. It seemed to take forever, but as soon as the sun set Nola was finally transported into her first true vision.

For over an hour, she held concentration near the window of the cabin, listening to Elias's deep breathing, and recalling every image of Gavin that she could. At last, while Jarron paced the deck in the pouring rain, the golden haze she had been waiting for finally encased her gifted view.

Far across the water to the sails of a small ship, Nola could see a pair of hands holding onto the ropes of a tall mast. Through the yellow hue she could see his dark colored skin and knew it was Levi. He was holding onto a lantern. The light was so bright it nearly blinded them both. Nola controlled her breath and stayed with the vision as Levi lifted his head and glanced across the water to the tall ship anchored in place. Impossible to be certain, she felt as if Levi were implying, she should stay with his view. The haze was confusing. It was shifting and left widely to interpretation.

Suddenly, Levi's keen tracking sight vaulted her past the ship, far to the cliffs near a harbor. There, in a rain drenched pink gown, Joslyn waited. Her auburn hair hung heavy with the rain, but her eyes were piercing blue, and her body had the appearance of a newly fed Absolute. Just as quickly, Levi turned his attention to the opposite side of the harbor.

There, Gavin stood with his sword at his side. Nola inhaled, welcoming the sight of him, his dark hair slicked back from the rain and his dark eyes scanning over the ocean waves. The words written on his hand came to her eyes. However, she could not read them clearly.

Without cause, her stomach hurt, and her chest tightened. Guilt of disloyalty to Elias was physical, still Nola forced onward with the vision. Gavin's brow was furled, his shoulders squared, and his eyes never left the water. However, Levi turned back to the lantern in front of him, causing Nola to blink her eyes from the intense light. All too soon, the vision faded.

"Where is he?" Elias asked directly behind her. Still blinded by the golden haze, Nola jumped away from his voice and held her hands out in front of her.

"Stay back," she warned.

"I can help," he took her hand. A sigh of relief came over her as the haze subsided and human vision returned. "What did you see?" Returning to look out the window, Nola realized that many of the men from below deck had awaken and made their way out to the darkening sky above. Without barely any conversation at all, some of them had placed wooden beams into the cylinder at the front of the ship and began to turn the winch. A few moments after they were done, the vessel began to move with the waves. "Nola," Elias called again. "What did you see?"

"Gavin," she answered honestly, knowing he would sense a lie. "He is waiting for you." The image of Gavin's handsome face stayed in her mind and Nola began to smile.

"You will mourn his death before the night is out," Elias warned her. "I've promised every man on this ship prime hunting grounds with Graelohr out of the way. I doubt I could stop them if I wanted to." He watched her closely for several moments, but her smile did not fade. "You don't believe me."

"No," Nola proudly shook her head. "I have every faith that Gavin will succeed."

"Then, I feel sorry for you," Elias whispered, lifting her chin with his fingertips. "Your pain will be that much greater when I prove you wrong." Jerking her face away from his hand, Nola turned to the knock at the door.

"You should see this," Jarron warned through the thick wood. "It won't be long now," Elias whispered.

Moving to the side of the room he picked up a long scabbard beside the bed. Withdrawing the blade inside, he checked the hilt and slid it back into the sheath. A few moments later the belt was fastened, and he exited the cabin with Nola following behind.

"She's been coming up for a few minutes now," Jarron stated. She's pretty light and I haven't seen a single man on deck except the helmsman." Elias looked at an approaching ship as if he could see every detail without a telescope. It would have been an impossible feat to imagine if she had not just seen Levi's advanced sight.

The small vessel had two masts and sailed gently toward the harbor from behind their ship. At the top of the first mast, Nola noted the extremely bright lantern that nearly blinded her in Levi's sight.

Her chest swelled with the thrill of hope but just as quickly Elias became aware of her anticipation.

"It's not them," Elias whispered from directly behind her. "I can feel Joslyn's heat more than I can feel the rain." Droplets of water pelted her shoulders as she listened to him. "She's still on land and very close."

Nola held her eyes on the ship, still staring at the bright lantern. There was no way for her to conceal her hope, and she knew that Elias would soon get suspicious. Using what he had taught her; Nola slowed her breathing and turned her focus as far away from Levi and Gavin as she could. Looking at Jarron, she concentrated on her hatred for him.

"What have you done to Luke?" She hissed at him.

"He has no one to blame but himself," Jarron answered, letting his wild blue eyes smile at her. "I gave the bloke three chances to die an honest death."

"Honest death? You should have never offered him death at all! You should have never had him!" Nola screamed at Jarron, ignoring the smug smile on his face.

"Ah, you would have been mad at me either way, little sister."

"Don't call me that! Never call me that!" Shaking off Elias's controlling hand, she stepped away from Jarron. "I want to see him," Nola demanded moving toward the hatch.

"I wouldn't do that if I were you, ...little sister." Jarron took every opportunity to infuriate her.

"Let her go to him," Elias ordered taking another quick look at the ship still looming in the distance. "We are nearly in the harbor.

"Man your stations and keep your eyes open. Joslyn grows nearer on every wave. I have no doubt Graelohr isn't too far off."

Ignoring Jarron's warning glare, Nola descended into the hull of the ship. Three steps down brought her to a complete stop. The decks were filled with Vampyres draining whatever they could find from their human captives. Nola had only believed that the four from the village had been taken onto the ship but like Luke, many more had been transported.

"This is a gruesome sight," Elias agreed from right behind her.

Her disgust was almost amusing, given her situation. "If you're insisting on seeing Luke you had better prepare for worse than this. He will be filthy, sickly, and desperate for blood."

Frozen to the step, Nola knew that she had to continue. Her boots were not so easily convinced. With the courage of a lion, she stiffened her shoulders and stared at the passage before her. He was through one large narrow room, and she set forth to walk through the line of disgusting Vampyres.

The first of the rooms was sheer terror. Though the humans did not argue or complain as they were being drained, Nola could still see the wish for freedom in their eyes. At least twenty Vampyres stood waiting without enough blood to go around. Aware of their concern, Elias nodded to all of them.

"Soon," he assured them. "But you will have to be quick about it once we reach land. There is at least one very powerful Absolute waiting for us. She is not happy and will burn you from the inside out. To make matters worse, you are forbidden from harming her in any way." Elias warned them all with a steady glare. "Use the water to keep her away from you." He continued along the deck as they turned to listen. "Lord Graelohr will not be far off. He will use metal to shock and distract but can only defeat you with his fangs or his sword. Take off his head before he gets to use either one. Then, bring it to me."

Elias, without being touched, found himself shoved up against the frail wooden railing. Nola had no idea what had happened, until she saw his body move forcefully against the railing again, as if being hit by an invisible wave. Aware of Nola's fury, Elias grabbed her quickly. Any emanation that pushed him away was instantly subdued by his superior touch. With her in hand, Elias guided her into the second part of the room by her shoulder.

The smell of wet dirt filled her senses. All the mounds of dirt had been disheveled, leaving the wooden planks beneath her feet almost impossible to see. From the end of one of the mounds two young women stood wiping the dirt from their naked bodies and stepping into fantastically colored gowns. Both glared at Nola, however, took their time dressing as Elias passed by.

"How could Luke ever want to be a part of this?" she asked, hurrying into the next room where he lay on piled up straw.

"Stay away." Luke's voice was a strained groan as he curled up on the floor and turned his face away from her. A black tar-like substance surrounded him, hidden within the piles of straw.

"What have they done to you?" Nola asked, too afraid to get any closer.

"The worst is over," Elias spoke gently as Jarron followed them into the room with a terrified woman in tow. Luke eyed the woman dangerously. "At the brink of death, when Jarron gave you his blood your body took in the poison." Kneeling, Elias spoke in a grave tone to Luke. "You are no longer human, having died the moment this..." he kicked a pile of straw with the black tar-like substance. "...left your body." Nola's tears ran steadily down her cheek as she looked at Luke's horrid face. His eyes were wide and darkened, his skin was pale and bruised, and the entire time Elias spoke Luke watched the woman with hunger in his eyes. "If you drink from her, you will live forever. If you deny yourself the thirst ...I will grant you death." Turning away from Luke, Nola bowed her head in her hands and cried silently. "If it's any help," Elias wrapped his hands around Nola as she melted into his embrace. "Nola wants me to kill you."

"No!" Nola turned to face Luke. "I don't want you to die, but you can't exist like this." Her desperation was impossible to hide.

"There really isn't anything in between," Elias explained callously. "His pain is over. His suffering is over." Grabbing the human woman by the neck Elias hauled her in front of Luke. "This is your chance to do everything you have ever wanted. Women will love you just by the way you look at them and no human man will ever be more powerful."

"Nola, get out of here," Luke warned as he staggered to his feet, eyes staring at the woman's neck.

"No, Luke," she cried out, as Elias held her arm. "Think of what you'll become." Looking up at him, Nola held her hands together and begged him not to go on. Luke had never seen Nola cry. The outpouring of emotion from her had been so rare, there was no precedent for the occasion. It was all she could do to not fall to the floor.

Luke reached out for the woman, ignoring Nola. There was little sentiment in his eyes, except for a moment of fear when the two sharp fangs tore through his gums and grew beyond the confinements of his lips. Nola lowered her head, unable to believe what she was seeing.

A sharp pain took over his stomach and Luke buckled for a minute, but as if the woman's blood would rid him of the pain, he leapt for her. Turning her away from Nola, Luke thrust his new sharpened canines into the delicate neck. The sound of her scream forced Nola to cover her ears. At that moment, Elias and Jaron fell back against the hull of the ship, moved by an unseen force. Luke and his victim also swayed with the uncontrolled invisible wave. The Absolute knew Nola was the sudden cause of the instant affliction.

"Get her!" Elias ordered, holding his hand to his chest. Jarron grabbed Nola off the floor and hurled her across into Elias's arms. As if every muscle in his body contracted all at once, Elias felt her pain as physically as Nola did and held her firm. "I have you," he called, grabbing her face with his hands, and soothing her any way that he could. Unable to avoid her inflicting pain, he held her against his chest and hurried out of the room.

"What do you want me to do with him?" Jarron called as Luke let the dead woman fall from his arms.

"Clean him up. Then, bring him directly to me." Elias answered.

"No!" She cried. Her agony raged through her at a crippling pace. Elias was immune to none of it and had to force the air to constrict his lungs.

"Nola, stop!" Elias ordered. Clutching her to his chest he climbed the stairs two at a time until the vision of the water halted him completely.

"They're heading right for us!" One of the Vampyres called from the sails above. "They should have turned off by now if they were headed into the harbor!"

With their vessel nearly in the harbor, Elias watched as the two-masted fishing ship sailed directly for their stern. He could barely concentrate on what to do with Nola's vivid anguish tormenting him. The changeling was a monstrosity of new and unhinged emotions.

She seemed to be feeling everything at every moment without a hint of control. She could barely breathe without a new sentiment causing an annoying push and pull to the undead aboard.

"Board that vessel!" Elias ordered, motioning four of the men at the rail to attack the approaching ship.

"Go!" Jarron yelled as the fishing ship grew even closer. The only light was the one attached high on the top of the mast and it seemed ominous to all. Silently, the four hungry men dove into the water and hurled themselves through the waves to the oncoming ship. Still, with Nola completely hindered by what Luke had done, Elias could not handle the problem.

Cradling her in his arms, he hurried back to the cabin and set her down on the bed. Once the door was closed, he took her hand in his and pressed his forehead to hers. She persistently tried to escape but he was overwhelming. All reassurance was impossible to transfer. No matter how hard he tried, her grief was more painful than he had felt in decades. He was nearly desperate to kiss her, to tempt her sensually to bypass her shock. Had there been any indication it would not have made matters worse; he would have tried.

"Jarron, bring me the boy!" He called so loudly that Nola covered her ears with her hands. "I'm sorry." He focused on her completely, realizing how the loss of Luke's humanity was the last piece of the poor woman's heart to break. "Nola, you will have him forever. He is still the same."

"He's a demon!" She cried out, her words spanning into moans and tears. "You've made him a monster..." Her voice was almost lost as he clutched her hands.

Just then, a sudden loud snap and crash caught their attention. His hearing sharpened as well as hers and they both turned toward the door. An explosion rocked the night and a scream from the deck drew Elias away from Nola. Opening the door of the cabin, Elias hurried to the back of the ship to see the oncoming vessel all ablaze and set on a collision course with their stern. The fishing ship was a floating bomb bearing down on their vessel.

"Get to the boats!" Elias ordered. Three of four Vampyres that had been sent to attack the small ship disintegrated in the flames. One had made it to the water, but his burns were severe and there was no time to save him. A large wave hurled the fiery ship forward, aiming straight for their bow. The smell of dynamite in the wind warned Elias of what was coming. With a keener sense than the others he moved with the speed of light back to the cabin and threw himself completely over Nola as the explosion hit hard.

Time moved as slow as a growing blade of grass. Nola felt speed and power as Elias hurled himself over her and safely to the floor. Grabbing the mattress from the bed, he covered their bodies. The room lit up and the sound was so loud it hurt their ears. Nola felt his weight for a moment as something came through the door and hit the mattress, but Elias recoiled from the force and braced himself for any further impact.

A second explosion, the sound of unmistakable cannon fire, came from the back of the ship along with a third bomb. The windows shattered as wood and flaming debris hit from every direction. Nola cowered beneath Elias as the sounds of screaming surrounded them.

"The hulls been breached!" The call rang throughout the deck. Immediately, Elias and Nola both felt the same fear of the salt water.

"We have to go!" he shouted, tossing off the mattress and hauling her to her feet.

Nola followed him out of the cabin realizing fire had engulfed the entire stern of the ship. Finally, the words she had seen written on Gavin's hand in her vision made sense, 'away from stern sunset' was his way of warning her about the fire. Screams of terror and pain surged through the vessel.

The waves put much of the fire out. However, some of the wood had been coated with oil from the fishing ship, spreading devastation instead of dousing it. "They waited too long," Elias almost laughed as he looked to the docks around the harbor. "You can swim ashore from here." He ordered what was left of the crew.

"Nola," Luke called, as Jarron brought him up from below deck.

"Jarron, get the canvas." Elias stood between Nola and the flames as he assessed the surroundings.

All at once, a smaller explosion came from the sinking ship. It was minute compared to the others but powerful enough to hurl a large broken spar straight at Nola's head. With lightning-fast reflexes, Luke caught the wooden spar in his hand just inches away from her face. Neither of them knew who was more surprised by the reaction.

"Alright," Elias looked at Luke. "Stay with her! Keep her away from the fire and not a drop of water can touch her."

"The ship is sinking!" Luke reminded him. "How in the hell am I supposed to keep her out of the water?" In the lower decks smoke and ash billowed free; taking with it the screams of the Vampyres being burned. Those that made it to the water swam as fast as they could, but there was no accelerated speed like they had on land. Only those that fed were strong enough to jump over half of the distance to shore. "There is fire everywhere!"

"Then you'd better be on your guard," Elias replied leaving them both on the deck. He began to climb the mast directly in front of him and quickly began to slice the canvas from the yard. Wary of the surroundings, Luke placed a protective arm in front of Nola and watched as the flames danced their way along the railing.

"Can you swim?" Luke asked them both toward the cabin. Everything about him had been the same as the day of the Egyptian opening. His skin was clean and healed with no bruises of any kind, his hair was wet, but clean, and his eyes were as dark and calming as they could ever have been.

"I can't touch the water," she explained taking in the perfect sight of him. "Seawater burns my skin."

"Then we will think of something," he stated clearly. Nola clung to his shirt and pulled him back into the cabin.

"How could you do it?" she asked, knowing it was not the right time to question.

"Damn it, Nola. We are both getting off this ship and getting away from here. I couldn't make that happen chained down in the hull!" He watched as the Vampyres sought out the high rigging and jumped from the ship. Their intense strength and speed hurled most of them to the shore. Some fell short and landed in the water but were able to swim to the docks. "Why is it that you can't touch the water, but they can?"

"It's complicated," she answered, feeling the hull begin to pull down into the water even faster.

"Because you are dead," Elias explained, coming toward them with a large piece of canvas, "the water will not affect you. Nola has never died, and the salt will pull every ounce of moisture out of her skin, leaving ash." Grabbing onto his sword, Elias showed him the polished blade. "If I were to slice your arm, the skin would repair itself as quickly as I cut it. Nola and I take days to heal. The water won't kill her," he glanced down into Nola's eyes and lifted her chin to assess any damage. "But if trapped in the water she would be immobile with pain as her skin slowly burned... until the waves carried her to shore."

"Then swimming is definitely out of the question," Luke whispered. "What is the canvas for?"

"You have a choice," Elias spoke to Nola as he looked over the water. "You can be dragged through the water and risk getting wet or thrown fifty feet and risk breaking a few bones."

"Give me a boat!" Nola stared at him as if he were insane. "There isn't time, and I don't know what else Graelohr has planned. We need to get you on land, now."

"Either way, she will heal in a few days." Jarron said as he tossed another large piece of canvas down to the deck. The ship began to tilt as he held on tight. "A broken bone will keep her from moving too fast if we lose her on land."

"Help me." Elias handed an edge of the tarp to Luke. "Wrap her tight."

"What?" Nola asked.

"I'm going ashore," Elias stated. "Jarron will take you to the top of the rigging and jump as far out as he can. Before he hits the water, he will throw you to me."

"You're insane!" She nearly screamed at him from inside the canvas.

"Not as insane as Graelohr for putting you in a position like this." With a thick piece of rope, Elias tied the canvas around her. "Look there," Elias spoke to Luke, motioning to the small cliff at the side of the harbor. "Do remember that woman?"

"She's one of you?" Luke noted the sword in Joslyn's hand, accepting his intense visual perception with ease. "That is Graelohr's sister."

"Stay away from her. She is powerful and will kill you regardless of who you are to Nola." Hoisting Nola up onto his shoulder, Jarron positioned her as comfortably as he could.

"You can't do this!" Nola screamed inside the canvas packaging.

"Go," Elias ordered Luke. "Get to the shoreline and catch her if I'm not there. As soon as I get there, I am going to need someone to guard her."

"Right," Luke said as he judged the height of the flames and the distance of the water.

"Trust your instincts, boy. Newborns are strongest in their first year," Jarron called from above. "Take a run at it and then jump."

Following the advice, Luke felt the ship begin to slow in the waves as it succumbed to the water. The fire had begun to smolder, but much of the top deck was still engulfed. Glancing up at Nola wrapped in the canvas one last time, he took off at a full run and jumped over the railing of the deck. Expecting to land right away, he pulled up his legs and watched the water. It seemed to never get any closer. The rain had diminished so much that the speed at which he spanned the water almost dried his hair. Having jumped nearly fifty feet over water, the wood of the dock cracked where his feet landed.

Standing upright, Luke stood in awe. He was the first to reach the dock. Most others had ten to fifteen feet left to swim. Pride swelled in him as he looked around. At least twenty men were beginning to pull themselves up on the docks when a snap caught his sensitive ears. Luke looked down the dock, noticing for the first time that the entire wooden fixture and the boats around it were blanketed with kerosene-soaked straw. Using keen sight, he could see that some of the boats held crates of dynamite with the words 'Chatsworth Mines' written on them. The snap that caught his attention was the pop of a fuse in the center of the rounded dock.

"Stop!" Luke held out his hand to the undead that were climbing up on the platform.

All too quickly, the dynamite ignited, lighting the straw and kerosene. The wood from the boats became deadly projectiles flying into the chests of several Vampyres. Luke barely turned in time to see a stake flying toward him, an instant before he was tackled down by an unseen force. The powerful hit sent him over the dock and slammed him into the grass just behind the spreading fire.

"Who did this to you?" Gavin asked, his hand around Luke's throat, eyes lit with silver and fangs protruding from his lips. His rage was more than expected, before him stood the remnants of Dottie's son.

"I had to," Luke answered. "I couldn't leave her with them!"

"The name of the man ...who did this to you?" Gavin shook him firmly. The fire erupted throughout the dock, pouring burning kerosene and other oils into the water. Screams of death and agony surrounded the harbor. Gavin looked up just as the people from the village began to flee. Beyond the flames, Joslyn stood with her sword at the ready attacking anyone that came through the fire. The surrounding bay had become an uproar of terror and flame. "Tell me!"

"Jarron... Jarron Tempest," Luke answered quickly with a rise of panic at the sight of the true Gavin Graelohr. "Don't kill me. Nola needs me! Jarron is about to throw her to the shore. I have to be there!" The fear and honesty were as pure as the rain. Gavin stared at him a moment longer before noticing a few of the stronger Vampyres break through the fire.

"Tell her I will find her," Gavin commanded Luke as he let go of his neck. Before Luke could move, a man with his fangs bared, threw himself at Gavin. His speed and accuracy brought him within an inch of Gavin's shoulder. Reacting, the enormous Absolute lifted his silver blade. The speed of the Vampyre inadvertently slit his own throat. "Go!" Gavin yelled at Luke. Returning his attention to the bay, he readied his sword to extinguish anything that came from the water or the burning boats.

The oil spread well into the water but those that survived the explosions were doing well to avoid the flames. Their rate seemed unmatched as one by one the Vampyres left the water and scurried around the flames. Most fled right by, looking for their next feeding. However, those that took captives on the ship made their way straight for Gavin.

His sword was deadlier than the fire. Three hundred years of experience made Gavin clearly undefeatable. Twirling the hilt of his blade around his hand, he thrust the razor-sharp edge through the air and lopped off any head that he could reach. He did not directly aim at any single individual; he simply placed his blade in their unfortunate path. As they attacked, his block was their death.

Many older Vampyres stormed the docks, each of them determined to kill the ancient Absolute. Just when it seemed like they would swarm over him, another formidable force arrived from above. Descending on them, Levi withdrew his own blade, choosing his victims one after another. Young and very much an islander, Levi waited for his attackers with his knees apart and his sword straight up in the air. For every man that came toward him, he offered one damaging blow that would leave their neck vulnerable. No Vampyre that came near him lasted longer than two blows.

Watching the battle rage on without him, Elias could stand the carnage no longer. From the rigging of the ship, he hurled himself through the air, knowing that if he were older, he would have been able to move instantly. There was little room at the rocky outcrop near the end of the docks. However, as surefooted as a wild cat, he landed on the flattest part of a raised rock.

"Now!" Elias yelled to Jarron.

Being the last Vampyre on the dying vessel, Jarron judged every wave and tilt of the burning ship. When the order was given, Jarron hoisted Nola higher onto his shoulder, steadied his feet, and jumped as far away from the ship as he could. The extra weight was impossible to calculate. Still, he waited as long as he could in midair before thrusting the canvas package through the night sky, a mere second before he hit the water.

Feeling her stomach merge with her chest, Nola screamed at the top of her lungs. The flight seemed to last forever as her weight carried her down further and further. Without knowing how far away she was or what was in her path, she pressed her hands against the canvas and continued to scream. Her voice was so loud that she didn't hear the pebbles and sand hitting the canvas. Then, she felt a familiar presence and heard Elias call out.

"Joslyn, no!" Elias yelled as Nola and the canvas disintegrated into the twilight. The storm of pitch-black dust and pebbles lasted less than a second, but it was enough to enrage Elias. Climbing off the rocks and onto the land behind the burning docks, he looked out over the village for a likely place that Joslyn would take his wife.

"Nola, it's me," Joslyn whispered once Nola's feet touched the ground. Untying the rope and pulling the canvas off Nola, Joslyn continued to ease her mind. "You're safe."

"Where is Elias?" Nola asked immediately.

"Gavin will take care of that little arrogant problem." Continuing to unwrap the rest of the canvas, she tossed it aside.

Nola couldn't focus for a moment. Looking around her, she could tell that she was in a warehouse with crates and barrels everywhere, but something inside of her felt torn. It was as if being so far away from Elias made it difficult for her to function. His anger, his concern, and his anxiety raged through her body as readily as her own emotions. However, not being able to see him or touch him made her tolerance that much worse.

"Nola, what is it?" Joslyn asked, touching her face, and looking for any wounds. "Who did this to you?" Her voice rose when she saw the fang marks on her neck. "This isn't Vampyre." The shock in her voice could not be concealed. "Elias is too young to have done this. Who put their teeth to you?"

Nola could barely feel Joslyn's relief or worry. The touch of her hand was calming, but little more than Dottie's or Luke's would have been. She couldn't pass her feelings on to Joslyn either. The loss of such a connection brought a tear to her eye.

"It was Elias," she answered. "He had to find out if I was still human or not."

"For pity's sake, girl. You've been bonded to Elias, haven't you?" Joslyn touched her face, her arms, and her hands to try and get any emotional connection from her. "I dare say, it serves you right for running off without us!" Her comment was cold and irritating. "Trust me, it won't be this intense forever. We will sense each other again. This is the overbearing power of the binding. How could this happen?"

"A woman named Ysabelle." The tears came quickly as Nola thrust her arms around Joslyn's neck.

"Ysabelle... you can't mean... the Ysabelle?"

"Yes! She was beautiful. Small, light blonde hair, and the largest eyes I have ever seen!" Nola continued to look around the room for intruders. "There was nothing I could do." Holding onto her with as much strength as she had, she wished Joslyn could ease her pain. "They turned Luke into ...one of them." Her emanation picked up and emotional control seemed to waver fiercely. Now, I am trapped with Elias for at least a year!"

"Listen to me," Joslyn held her cheeks and stared into her terrified eyes. "It's going to be alright. This can be broken, especially if you did not enter it willingly. For years, our women have been forced to marry men."

"I'm not one of your women," Nola argued. "Ysabelle made me! My parents were not Absolute. That is why Gavin could not find them. I am something Ysabelle created, the same way she was ...made."

"You were born to human parents?"

"Yes, and orphaned," Nola whispered as she shook her head. "At least that's what Ysabelle told me." Again, a torn feeling welled up in her. She needed to find Elias. She could sense his frustration and concern. All of his emotions coursed through her veins. She could feel his desire to touch her hand and stop the intense sentiments.

Suddenly, the idea of being with him seemed like the only possible end to her suffering. "I have to go!"

"No!" Joslyn held her shoulders firm. "If I have to tie you to this room, I will! "You will not seek him out!" Joslyn glanced down at the rope near the canvas. "I know what you are feeling, and I understand the intensity. Elias's cruelty has done this to you, not adoration, kindness or even duty!"

"I don't care," Nola bowed her head. "I have to go."

"Nola, think of Gavin. Think of all the nights you sat outside just waiting for a glimpse of him. You love him. You've loved him for a very long time now. This connection with Elias will end, but only if you stay here and stay quiet!" Just then, Joslyn cupped her hand over Nola's mouth. She heard something in the distance and Nola tuned in her senses to listen carefully.

"Nola?" Luke called from the doorway of the warehouse. Grabbing onto Joslyn's wrist, she pulled her hand away.

"Luke!" Her excitement was impossible to hide. "It's Luke."

"I don't find that as fortunate as you do," Joslyn added.

"Are you in here?" He asked.

"Stop right there." Releasing Nola, Joslyn stepped to the center of the warehouse and faced him. Her emanation was slowly inflicted, causing Luke to stay where he was and feel the intense warning heat.

"What is this?" He asked.

"This is what will kill you if you come any closer," Joslyn warned.

"Where is Nola?" Luke asked, watching his hands turn red from under the skin and feeling as if he were catching fire. "Nola, where is she? I have to know she is alright."

"You're the impressive Egyptologist, Dottie's son." Joslyn added as she watched him willingly suffer for Nola. "So, you want to become a part of history instead of just studying it?"

"Just tell me Nola is safe and I'll leave." Luke doubled over in agony as his hands began to blister and boil from the internal heat.

"Joslyn, stop!" Nola grabbed onto her arm, feeling the same intense power, that Luke felt.

"Alright," she agreed, lessening the incredible discomfort. "What do you want with her?"

"To keep her safe and get her away from here." Luke stood up and watched his hands as they instantly healed themselves. "But I need to know where I can take her."

"You can't take her anywhere, Newborn." Joslyn called him the name as if it were a title. "Elias can feel everything she does. You may be stronger than before, but you're still a pup in this wolf-fight." Aware of Nola's history with Luke, Joslyn considered all of her options. "Can you keep her here? Defend her against any Vampyre and hide her from Elias?"

"I can," he agreed instantly.

"Get back!" Joslyn stated with a firm tone as the door at the end of the warehouse opened. Nola ducked down as Luke hurried to her side. Both of them watched Joslyn in sheer amazement as she jumped straight up to the ceiling and held herself suspended on all fours behind one of the braces. As suddenly as it came, Joslyn's emanation dissipated to a simple sweet smell.

"I know I heard you in here, little one. There is no sense in hiding," a male Vampyre called. "Someone is waiting for you."

"Elias isn't exactly a patient man," another creature added.

In a blur of silent motion, Luke left Nola's side. She had no idea where he went, but as the two men approached her, she resorted to facing them, head-on.

"I'm not hiding," Nola stepped into the clearing.

"Maybe you should be," the tall bald man stated with a fang-filled sneer.

"Maybe you should mind your own business," Joslyn stated from the braces above. Dropping down directly behind him, her stunning eyes and beautiful red hair did nothing to hide the horror of fangs as they descended on the man's neck. With both top and bottom teeth bared, Joslyn ripped half of the man's neck wide open.

The second man had no defense as he watched his partner be brutally murdered. Like a snake in the grass, Luke pounced on him from behind, grabbing his head and twisting it clean off.

Nola hid her eyes from the slaughter. Again, the desire to find solitude in Elias's arms filled her. Holding her face in her hands, Nola did her best to hide her tears. The disgust and horror surrounded her constantly. She felt all of the vulnerabilities and none of the strengths.

"Your squeamish tendencies will make you a very complicated Absolute," Joslyn wiped the blood from her mouth. "How you intend to survive is a mystery to me." Looking back to Luke, she nodded her head in approval. "You may be just the kind of fighter we need on our side."

"Let's hope so." Luke shook his head, enamored by her beauty. "I would hate to be your enemy."

"Get her to the roof," Joslyn ordered. "She's tied to Elias and will want to get to him." Joslyn pulled a small dagger from her sleeve and handed it to Nola. "Take this and go with Luke. Up there, it will be more difficult for them to find you, and less likely for you to try and reach Elias." Joslyn turned to Luke and gave him a warning stare. "If either happens, I suggest you defend her with your life." Joslyn touched Nola's cheek and smiled gently. "Gavin will end this soon," she promised.

"Where are you going?" Luke asked.

"Why should I let my brother have all of the fun?" She smiled with a glimmer in her eye. Before Nola could argue, Joslyn disappeared into a streak of light tinted pink from the color of her dress.

"How do I get you up there?" Luke asked, still unaware of how his new capabilities worked. Looking at a hatch in the roof, he judged the height and distance. "Stand back," he warned, readying himself for the jump.

As graceful as a bird, Luke nearly took flight, jumping the fifteen-foot ceiling with ease and hauling himself up through the hatch without breaking a sweat. Nola could hardly believe her eyes to watch him perform such a task, but Luke loved every minute of it.

"Can you believe this?" he asked, jumping back down and landing in front of her, bending his knees to absorb the impact. "Can you do this?"

"No." She shook her head. "And I don't want to!" Luke picked up the rope that was tied around the canvas and wrapped it under her arms and around her chest. "Look, I know you can't understand this, but I have to find Elias." Her desperation did not affect him at all. "Luke, I must." Fully aware that she didn't make any sense, Nola pleaded with him. "My heart is pounding. My body aches. I feel every bit of his fury and outrage. My chest will not let in air... I have to find him!"

"To what end?" Luke asked, looking up at the ceiling again.

Before she could answer, he made the jump a second time. Then, with the strength he had acquired, he hoisted her up in a matter of seconds and set her on the roof of the building. Once safe, he closed the hatch and looked around them. All sunlight had faded. The only light came from the fire below. "Do you see that?" Quietly, Luke laid down on the roof and pointed to the fire and piles of bodies below. "The man you are trying to get to, is responsible for all of this."

Nola laid down and scooted as close as safety would allow to the edge of the roof. Below them, the fire was slowly burning what was left of the docks and filling the entire harbor with smoke. Mack Banit and Hugh Pattlow had joined the fight, using every bit of their strength in what seemed like an endless battle. Both kept their eyes on Gavin and Levi, watching their backs in between defending themselves. Their methods were crude and merciless. However, it was the carcasses in their wake that held Nola's attention.

The bodies on land solidified to coal and burnt flesh. The bodies in the water did not disappear as quickly. They decayed slowly, appearing slimy and grotesque until finally sinking under. Still, several of the Vampyres remained. Nola caught the gleam of a blade below, and for the first time, her eyes viewed Gavin.

"It's him," Nola almost scurried to her feet, fearing the vicious attack he faced. Gavin held his place in the harbor, guarding the water and the streets around him.

"Stay down," Luke demanded, pulling her back to the roof with more force than he intended. "Can you see like we can?"

"No," Nola answered, barely able to control her fear for him. "He's too fast," Luke explained. "The men are coming at him full force, but Graelohr moves at twice their speed."

Closing her eyes for a second, Nola concentrated on everything about Luke. He was safe. He was there, and no matter what Jarron had done to him, he was still the same man she loved throughout her childhood. Opening her eyes, Nola watched Gavin in the battle, through Luke. As easy as falling asleep, Nola found the golden hue within Luke's newly sharpened sight. Reaching out blindly to hold his arm, she focused on the vision before her.

As an undefeatable force, Gavin turned his blade to every opponent the moment they moved toward him. His eyes shimmered in the night, catching every hint of movement. Even when three attacked him at once, only one was able to sink his teeth into Gavin's flesh.

The other two were sliced through the neck before they knew what happened. The one that tasted Gavin's blood fell backward as if having acid poured into his mouth. A second later, Gavin swiped his sword through the air and ended his life instead of letting him die in agony. However, when he turned to face his next opponent, Nola had a clear view of the large gash bitten out of his upper arm. It wasn't a fatal wound, but severe enough to slow him down. To make matters worse, there seemed to be no end to the Vampyres attacking him. It wasn't long before Gavin began to slow down.

"Are you alright?" Luke asked, feeling Nola clench onto his arm. A few seconds of silent blindness passed before Nola nodded her head.

"He's hurt," she whispered.

"I thought you said you couldn't see like us?" Luke took a moment to glance at the world around him with new eyes and keener hearing. While Luke was admiring the night, Nola took advantage of his distraction. Coming to her feet, she took off in a full run back to the hatch. "Stop!" Luke called rising to his feet and chasing after her.

As fast as she could, Nola hurried to the hatch. She did not have a plan but knew that she had to get to Gavin. However, Luke was not about to fail in his task. Unaware of how strong he was, Luke grabbed her hand and pulled her back to face him. The snap was loud and clear as the bones in two of her fingers broke. He released her immediately, shock and regret covered his face.

"I'm so sorry," he stated clearly, reaching out to her again. "Let go of me!" Nola screamed, shoving him away from her as hard as she could. Her hands were a blur as they moved. Inhuman strength soared through her body. The force was so powerful Luke flew backward, clearing the rooftop and falling to the ground. Nola looked down at her hands, disbelieving what she had just done. "Luke!" Her scream went out through the night, drawing the attention of everyone in earshot. Knowing that she then possessed more power than ever before, Nola hurried to the edge of the roof.

Closing her eyes, she found the courage to risk everything. With a leap of faith, Nola left the rooftop feet first and hurled to the ground below. Her knees bent as she landed, but somehow there was incredible grace to the event. Her body responded as if the twenty- foot drop was no more than a small step. Opening her eyes, she turned to Luke.

"Are you alright?" she asked, just as stunned as he was.

"I think so," he stood up, amazed at his ability to brush off the intense fall. "What was that?" He asked. Ignoring his question, Nola looked down at the harbor and started off toward the water. "Nola, stay here." Luke argued with her. "You can't go to Elias."

"I don't think you can stop me anymore, Luke." Her pace was quickening, but she did not run. There was too much fighting at the harbor and although she knew for certain that she was becoming Absolute she did not yet know how to fight. Fortunately, she did know that none of them could touch her if she was bonded to Elias.

She had not felt his presence, since being on the ship. Being away from Elias left her constricted and confused as if trying to control a bad dream. However, as Nola made her way to the harbor the awareness of him brought clarity. She could not see him, but there was no doubt he was nearby. To make matters worse, she knew that he had spent his time hiding from the battle and feeding on the villagers that did not flee.

"What is it?" Luke asked as Nola stopped suddenly.

With her eyes on Gavin, Nola felt how strongly her mind wanted to seek out Elias. She knew he was close and that he was coming for her, and she desperately wanted to call out for him. Tears welled up in her eyes as Luke placed his hand on her shoulder.

"Get me to Gavin," she cried quietly.

"I don't think now is such a good time." Luke watched as Gavin continued to fight one of the larger and stronger men from the ship.

"Luke, just take me to him!" She grasped his arm for support. It was an unbearable pain not to turn around and find Elias. "I cannot say it again." The desire for Elias was pulling her heart from her chest.

"Carry her," Joslyn ordered, suddenly at their side. "You're going to get a little hot under the collar," she added.

Stepping in front of them, Joslyn began walking toward Gavin. Slowly, every Vampyre in her path cleared the way. Unable to stand the internal bonfire Joslyn possessed, most of them moved as far away as they could. A few of the older ones stood the blisters on their skin, knowing they would heal. However, none of them tried to step any nearer to the three-hundred-year-old beauty as she pushed her emanation outward like a fiery barrier. Dropping his sword, Gavin turned to see them approach.

"Nola," Gavin called out of breath and exhausted from the long fight.

Luke could barely stand to walk behind Joslyn but took every agonizing step until he could place Nola in front of Gavin. The large Absolute's eyes were hollow and black, his skin covered in blood and ash, and his fangs drawn and fierce. Yet, his face was still the most handsome of any she had ever beheld.

With a single hand Gavin took Nola by the arm, sheathed his fangs, and pulled her into his embrace. Luke, having done as promised, escaped the wrath of Joslyn's heated circle. No one dared to come near Gavin with Joslyn at his side, not even Mack and Hugh. However, the moment between Gavin and Nola was cold and heartless.

"Nola?" Gavin looked down at her as she stepped away.

"I'm sorry," she cried. Tears streamed down her face as every bit of hope was lost. There was no solace in his arms and no chance of feeling anything for him ever again. "I'm so sorry." Gavin's brow furled as he realized what Elias must have done. No matter how he touched her, she would not feel his influence.

"No!" Without warning, Joslyn screamed at the top of her lungs. All of them turned to see the scarlet haired beauty fall to her knees. Across the harbor, Levi had just sliced his blade through Jarron Tempest's throat, reveling in the satisfaction of the Vampyre's death and letting his head roll to the water's edge. In retribution for his oldest friend, Elias slashed a gaping wound down the islander's back. Joslyn felt the pain of the gaping wound. Thus, the fiery protection around them gave way. Gavin was halfway to them when Elias held up his hand.

"Stop!" Elias warned with his sword held to Levi's neck. "You will not take my best Vampyre and my wife!" His body pulsed with fresh blood. The young Absolute was more than ready for a fight. "Joslyn, if you can't bear the loss of your husband, I suggest you return Nola to me."

The gash down Levi's back was debilitating and he had no way of defending himself. Gavin stood still, knowing the pain Joslyn was enduring. For several moments, Gavin stared at Levi, trying to devise a solution.

"Don't hurt him." Nola begged, walking toward Elias.

"I won't," Elias agreed too easily. "All Joslyn has to do is leave. She has interfered enough for one night." His stern countenance left no doubt of his fury.

"Go," Gavin called back to his sister in a voice deep and dark. "I can't," Joslyn whispered, unable to take her eyes off her wounded husband. Elias held Levi by his hair and pressed the edge of the sword against his neck hard enough to draw blood. As if the clouds above were shattered by Joslyn's pain, a heavy rain began to fall.

"You don't have a choice," Gavin growled to her. "He's right," Elias agreed. "I now know what kind of connection the two of you have. I don't envy you the pain you will feel if you disobey." Nola stepped next to Gavin and glanced at him one last time. In a strange, glorious sadness, she turned to walk toward Elias.

"Go!" Gavin ordered Joslyn one last time.

In that moment, from her crouched position on the ground, Joslyn welcomed the storm that formed around her. It was fast and furious, and instantly she was gone. However, it was several more moments before the scent of spices left the air.

"How ironic, Graelohr" Elias let Levi fall to the ground as Nola came to his side. "You guarded her for all these years, just to lose her in one day."

"After I kill you, I'm going straight for the person responsible for this," Gavin warned, pointing the tip of his sword at him.

"You would kill your own grandmother?" Elias smiled devilishly as he took Nola's hand.

A dangerous grin spread across the elder's lips, "I will without pause," Gavin answered, twirling his sword around by his side. "But you will be first."

The clash of steel filled the air as Gavin attacked. Though she was fast, Nola still did not possess the sight needed to understand what was happening. All she knew was that her heart ached for Elias as her mind tried to think of a way to protect Gavin.

Elias's sword was quick and brutal. Each slice was made within inches of Gavin's wrists, bound to disarm his opponent. He was quick and sure footed, keeping Gavin moving backward.

With a large gash out of his shoulder, Gavin had no choice but to fight without raising his left arm. His movement was only slightly restricted, but his power was more than Elias had prepared for. The two were thus equally matched, Elias quick, and Gavin strong. Their blades clashed constantly as they moved through the debris at their feet.

"Nola!" Levi called to her, unable to move. "Get me up!" Though the fight was almost impossible to look away from,

the truth was that they weren't safe. There was no way of knowing how many Vampyre's still lurked in the village or if they would finish off what Elias had started.

"Help me," she begged Luke. The rain pelted the ground as they rushed to Levi's side.

"Get me up," Levi instructed through his ragged breath.

"Right," Luke agreed before setting his eyes on the gash that spanned the length of his back. "This is bad," he admitted.

"Wrap it." Levi looked up at Luke and then down to Nola's dress. "Hurry!"

Unable to stand the sight of his blood, Nola turned her attention to her dress. Nothing more than rags, she began to recall all the reasons it had shredded. Alas, there was no other choice, tearing the tattered material, she handed it to Luke.

"Put your hand here," Luke instructed. Nola could barely stomach the thought of touching the gaping wound, but there was a complete lack of option. Gently, she pressed his skin together and held the gash closed as Luke wrapped the material around Levi's chest.

A sudden groan caught her attention and Nola felt as if her world was about to end. Turning around, she saw that Gavin's sword had pierced Elias's shoulder.

"No!" Nola screamed just before Luke caught her by the arm. "Do you hear that?" Elias asked Gavin, flaunting his ownership of his prize. "She will blame you for every wound you inflict on me." Gavin glanced at Nola, unable to ignore the severe pain he was causing.

"She'll survive," Gavin growled, raising his sword again.

Elias blocked the blow and continued to fight. That one little pierce of his shoulder set the battle on a different course. Elias began to slow, while Gavin grew stronger with intensifying satisfaction.

"What is happening?" Nola cried out, trying to watch the blur of motion as the constant clanging of steel filled her ears.

"Get her out of here," Levi used his sword to come to his feet. "No matter the outcome, she is safer with us," he said to Luke.

"Where do I take her?"

"North," he answered. "Joslyn is waiting on the hilltop."

"No!" Nola cried. "I'm not leaving!"

Elias stopped when Gavin took a slice to his chest, but the battle was quick to resume. Another pause showed blood pouring out of Elias's shoulder, but he countered with a blow to Gavin's forearm. There seemed to be no end to the bloodshed and Nola felt the panic rise with every second.

"You can't stay here." Levi took her hand and pulled her closer, nearly the same height on his knees as she stood.

"No!" Nola shook him off. "I'm not leaving!"

When Nola turned back to watch the battle, her sight somehow changed. The war before her slowed to a pace she could see. Elias held his sword with two hands, countering every blow Gavin made, visibly weakening. Boldly, Gavin flipped his sword around his side while Elias backed away. His stamina was nothing compared to the three-hundred-year-old Absolute. Readying his sword for another blow, Elias watched as Gavin's powerful strike descended. The hit was so hard, the harbor echoed with a sound of thunder. Only then could Nola see the blue light that ricocheted off Gavin's sword and into Elias's hands. Using the static from the storm around them, Gavin had been slowly galvanizing his opponent. At last, Elias fell to his knees before Lord Graelohr.

"Stop!" Nola ran straight toward danger with her new unnatural speed. All emotions raged like a river wild as Elias filled with doubt and perpetual fear. Gavin pulled his sword to the side, preparing to strike the final blow. However, before he could let his power fly, Nola stood before him. Turning his steel blade upward, he barely missed removing her head. "Please," Nola begged. "Don't do this!" Grabbing onto his wrists, she held his sword with him. "You can't do this to me." Touching his face, she stared into his eyes, proving her pain with constant tears. Her terror was real, and Gavin couldn't kill Elias with her bound to him. Releasing his sword, he let it fall to the ground. Inhaling freely for the first time, Nola believed it all to be over.

Just then, Luke moved behind her in a flash. The sound of slicing flesh rang in her ears. In that second, Nola's eyes widened, her mouth fell open with intense physical pain. Gavin reached out to her, seeing what had already happened. Behind them, Luke stood with the bloodied sword in his hand and Elias's head rolling away from his feet. Shock held his face for a moment before Luke furiously kicked Elias's head far away from its body. Pride soared through him as he faced Gavin. It had been his pleasure to destroy the manipulative monster that killed his mother and controlled Nola.

"No!" Nola screamed again. Gavin's massive arms engulfed her, turning her away from the scene. "Let go of me!" she cried, feeling her chest swell with an agony sure to kill her. "How could you?" she screamed into Gavin's solid chest.

Her tears streamed down her face as he held her. Silently, Gavin nodded his appreciation to Luke. He then motioned for the young Vampyre to drop the sword and help Levi. He would not let Nola see the way Elias's body turned to ash and wash away with the rain. For several minutes he held her firmly stroking her hair as she cried.

Finally, when it seemed like she would run out of tears, Nola raised her hand to his neck and pulled Gavin closer. From the base of her palm, a slight calming sensation flowed into her. Nola was so distraught by Elias's death; she barely felt the tranquil serenity from Gavin's touch sashay through her flesh. First, it moved through her hand, followed by her arm, and then her entire being. Fully aware that she was free of Elias and the bond they had, Nola turned up to Gavin in confusion. The feeling of emotional control made her grateful for Gavin's nearness. It was not as intense as it had been. However, she allowed her hand to remain firm, reveling in the peace he readily supplied.

"We have to go," Gavin whispered, sliding his hand over her hair. Nodding her head, Nola agreed. However, as he released her and reached down to pick up his sword, the devastating emotions of Elias's death raged through Nola once more. To silence the unyielding pain, she grasped Gavin's arm and held it tight. "I've got you," Gavin promised, squeezing her hand. Yet, the small effort wasn't enough for Nola. As soon as he put his sword away, she returned to his embrace, unwilling to let him go. "Maybe you should stay close for a day or two." Ignoring his wounds and wrapping her arms around his neck, Nola silently agreed. "You did not enter the binding, Nola. It was forced on you. You will not mourn him for long at all." Gavin did not force her attention to his black eyes and bloodied features. "I expect you to be very angry sooner than you realize."

"What do you want to do about the town?" Levi motioned for Luke to return his sword as he spoke. "Should we burn it?"

"Leave it," Gavin answered, still holding Nola. "Discard the bodies elsewhere. Port Chatsworth has suffered enough. Hugh, I need you and Mack to get the carriage and make sure there is nothing of ours left behind."

"I'll get him to the carriage," Luke offered once Levi was on his feet. The gigantic islander placed his arm around Luke's shoulder, and they started back toward the town. As the distance between them increased, Gavin took a moment to focus on Nola.

"Are you alright?" He whispered the words into her hair.

"I don't know," Nola admitted honestly, concerned that if Gavin were to let her go for just a moment, she might feel the ache of Elias's death. Gavin looked around at the deserted harbor and the desolate town behind it. An enormous sense of responsibility ran through him as he assessed the destruction. To her surprise, Nola was aware of his conscience. "This is not your fault," she whispered.

"Isn't it?" He asked. Gavin wrapped his arm around Nola's shoulder and started back toward the road to wait for the carriage.

"No," she insisted. "They planned this! Elias and that woman... Ysabelle! They set all of this in motion. You were just trying to save Luke and me."

"Ysabelle?" Gavin stopped walking and let go of her. He pushed his wet hair away from his eye. "Ysabelle married you to Elias?"

"Yes," Nola answered. Though she did not fall under the intensely crippling sadness she felt immediately following Elias's death, she still reached out to take Gavin's hand. "She came to the ship." Her voice contained the sound of relief as she relayed what she could to him. "She told me that I was not born Absolute. Gavin, she said she had me created... like she was." Gavin remained silent, repressing his anger as Mack drove the carriage toward them.

Suddenly, Nola filled with a sense of trepidation. "Will she come for me?"

"No," he stated firmly with a shake of his head. "You're safe with me." His words were honest and firm as the carriage came to a halt in front of them. "Let's get you and Levi back to the house. We will make more sense of this once you are both taken care of."

Chapter Sixteen

Change of Heart

Each curved step led deeper and deeper into the tomb below Graelohr Manor. Though the walls were painted white, there was no mistaking that many men and women had lost their lives in the dark recesses of the catacombs. Nola picked up her full rose-colored skirts and watched the tips of her satin slippers as she made her way to the cobblestone floor. She had not actually been in the chambers beneath the manor before but having seen them in her visions she knew right where to go.

A single torch on the side of the wall always remained lit. Though Gavin was renowned for his electric lighting, the rooms below the mansion were very much a relic. Following the light past the large sofa in the center of the circle, Nola made her way to the individual cells far away from the staircase. There, she peered in at the marble slab behind the iron gate that protected Luke while he slept.

The sun had not set, but Nola was determined to be there when he awoke. With her back against the stone wall, she stared at the center of the room. Curiosity led her to wonder how long the mansion had been there and how long the tomb had been in use, but before she could dwell on the matter the sound of footsteps on the stone drew her attention.

In front of Gavin a servant of the house made her way to the cellar. Dressed in her uniform she seemed very unconcerned about treading in the darkest part of the house. Gavin walked behind her, silent yet somehow reassuring. Nola knew that he did not need to feed, so the woman's presence was a little concerning. As she grew near, the scars on her neck and wrists suggested that she was no stranger to the habits of Vampyres.

"It will be alright," the woman whispered, touching Nola's arm before opening the gate and entering Luke's chamber. Curiously, Nola looked up to Gavin. Still, he remained silent yet reassuring.

The sound of cloth sliding across the rock let Nola know that Luke was awake. Tuning in with perceptive ears, she listened intently to the sound of his fangs as they descended and the slicing of skin as he quickly thrust them into the woman's neck. Inhaling an uneasy breath, Nola waited with her back against the wall, refusing to look into the room.

"Enough," the woman whispered as Luke fed eagerly. Unable to quench his thirst, he ignored her quiet plea. "Please, enough," she called again. Casting a nervous glance at Gavin, Nola considered entering the room to save the woman. However, before she could move a steady static charge began to build in the air around her.

Continuing to feed, Luke sunk his teeth into the woman's neck a second time. Her gasp of fear was unmistakable. As a result, a charge of energy caused the iron gate of the cell to hum with invisible power. Luke released the woman, feeling the electricity run through his skin. A few seconds went by before the air stilled, and the iron was silent when the woman stepped back out of the cell. Exhausted and pale, she made her way to the stairs where Gavin took her hand. Passing a quick nod to Nola, he helped the servant back to the main floor.

"I hope you learn to control that soon," Nola whispered as she entered the chamber.

"Did you feel that?" Luke asked as he pulled off his bloodied shirt and reached for the clean one hanging on a pin in the wall. "It was like I had spent an entire day running my feet across the rug in front of a fireplace."

Not realizing that Nola had let her mouth fall open, she looked at the drastic change in the man she considered her closest friend. For all the times she leaned on his shoulder and hugged him on holidays, Luke had never looked as broad and muscular as he did at that moment. The transformation between human and Vampyre crossed every threshold of morality, but the physical differences were easily as noticeable. Not a woman in Thedford would see him as average any more.

"Yes," Nola stuttered through her answer until his shirt was replaced. "Gavin is very powerful. You will feel that sense of thickness to the air whenever you are around him. Once you leave the city it tends to diminish."

"So, it's almost like his calling card?" Finishing the top button of his shirt, Luke smiled at Nola.

"I imagine so," she answered.

"And you make me feel like I am standing in a strong river current," he added. "Do I put off anything like that?" He wiped a small drop of blood off his hand and ran his fingers through his hair a few times.

"No," she answered. "Only we have that trait, I understand."

"I figured as much." Tucking in the bottom of his shirt, Luke motioned for Nola to lead the way out of the chamber. "Hugh and Mack have been filling me in on some of the details."

"About that," Nola paused just outside of the small stone room. "There is something you have to do, Luke." The depth of her voice was concerning.

"I know." Reaching out to take her hand, Luke gently slid his thumb over the back of her hand. "I have to leave, don't I?"

"It's the best way." Her answer was more difficult to say than she imagined. "You can't go back to the museum and returning to any kind of life here in Thedford City would only bring more questions." Luke glanced down at the floor and kicked a small piece of broken stone with his boot. "Joslyn has offered to take you with her."

"With her?" He looked back up with playful curiosity. "With her where?"

"Back to Egypt, of course," Nola answered. "She and Levi still have a ton of work to do in the field and your knowledge of ancient artifacts really seemed to impress..."

"She's going to let me go with her?" His excitement was unyielding. "I get to go to the ruins?" Letting go of Nola's hand he rustled his own hair gently. "I get to see the pyramids?"

"Well, yes... if you want to." For some reason, Nola imagined Luke having a tougher time leaving the city of his childhood. "You have to tell Davey though," she explained. "Go see him and Miss Bram and let them know that you've received an offer you can't refuse."

"That is a little understated, don't you think?" Luke smiled, surprisingly able to keep his sense of humor. Turning away, Nola lowered her eyes and began to walk toward the staircase. "What is it?" he asked.

"Nothing really," she answered. "I just imagined you would want to stay a little longer, that's all." The heel of her slippers clicked gently on the stone as opposed to the deep thud of his boots. At the top of the stairs a young male servant stood with a tray of two glasses of wine. Nola immediately took a glass, but Luke shook his head silently at the offer. Once the servant walked away, Nola lifted her glass to the light to inspect the thin transparent liquid.

"Wait a minute," Luke came before her and forced her attention with his stern voice. "Don't you think I would stay with you ... if you wanted me to?"

"You are rather eager to go," she admitted, seeing the familiar adoration that he had always shown her before.

"I would stay here forever, Nola," he admitted quietly before lifting her chin with his fingers. "But it wouldn't make a difference."

Releasing his hold, he placed his hands in the pockets of his trousers. "Would it?"

"I doubt it." It took a few seconds before she answered honestly. "But it doesn't mean you get to disappear forever."

"Alright," He smiled with a chuckle. "I'll come back every now and then and check on you. Who knows, maybe one day things will change."

"Maybe," Nola whispered, hiding her serious doubt.

"I don't mind going." Looking down the hall at the large window, Luke could see the purple hue of the night cast a shadow. "Mack is teaching me to hunt."

"I don't want to hear about it." Shaking her head, Nola wished he hadn't said as much as he did.

"Alright, I'll find Joslyn and Levi and find out when we are leaving."

"You may want to wait," Nola warned him. "They've been hidden away since yesterday morning." She viewed the floor, hiding her smile. "The wound to his back must not have been as severe as we thought. I only wish they could be a little quieter with their reunion."

"Alright, your point is conveyed." Luke smirked and scratched the back of his neck. "Until then, I had better learn everything I can." His unwavering optimism nearly made Nola smile. However, as soon as he reached out to touch her, he stopped. "Your Lord is warning me not to touch you," he whispered, looking at the tips of his fingers. "I hope he is always this protective of you." The gentle gleam of his playful eyes filled Nola with a sense of peace she could never have imagined.

"Go on," she almost chuckled as Luke made his way down the hall.

Slowly following behind, Nola took a few moments to enjoy the feeling of the clean, soft satin of her dress. It was a simple pleasure to be fully rested, have her hair washed, and a new gown to wear. Though the stress of the last few days had left her without much of an appetite, her thirst for wine was endless. Life's little pleasures had all been lost on her before. However, she was not likely to take them for granted anytime soon. Turning toward the stairwell that led to the second floor, Nola raised her eyes to Gavin as he stepped out of a nearby study.

"He took the news slightly better than you imagined," Gavin stated. Her silence proved her slight sadness. "He will be restless like this for the first few years. Honestly, I'm surprised Joslyn is willing to take on the responsibility. As far as I know, she's never kept a Vampyre." Tilting his head to the side, Gavin shrugged his shoulders gently. "She did take to him immediately at the museum. Maybe this will work out better than we imagine."

"Luke will be fine wherever he goes," Nola stated.

"I've never doubted that." Gavin's comment ended with a small pause of silence. An awkward glance passed between them just before Nola placed her foot on the stairs. "Can I ask where you are going?"

"I don't know really," she whispered glancing at the wine glass. "I was thinking I would read a book."

"You were going to look for the journal," Gavin stared at the beads in her gown.

"I wasn't going to rummage through your things," she confessed.

"But you would read it if it happened to be laying around," he finished her thought. Taking a few steps ahead of her, Gavin beckoned for her to follow. "I gave it to you once already. Why would I keep it from you now?"

"I'm not certain, in all honesty." Nola answered, climbing to the small wooden railed balcony overlooking the hall below. "I am uncomfortable to ask for it."

"That's a shame," he whispered, leading down the hallway to his chambers. "I hate to think I still make you uncomfortable."

"It's not you." Her voice was quiet and unsure. "I'm not even sure I want to know what I haven't read yet."

"Your knowledge of the world has grown significantly these last few months. At this point you may as well gather as much information as you can."

Stopping at the open door to his bedroom, Gavin reached into his pocket and withdrew a match. Nola stood still as he entered the large room and lit the nearby candle just before the mirror. The ivory walls came to life with the light. At the side of the room, the large thin veils hung from the ceiling at the end of his bed.

"I thought you would have kept it someplace under lock and key," Nola stated as Gavin entered the room and walked to his bedside table.

"Normally I do," he added as she leaned ever so gently into the room. "I've studied it a little further these last few days."

"Because of Ysabelle?" She entered the room.

"Yes," he answered. Pulling open the top drawer of the dark wooden table, he looked at the leather binder. "This book has been handed down through my family's generations. Once it is read and understood it is then passed on to the next generation to teach their children." Looking at the dry cracks in the cover, he ran his hand over the hide. "Ysabelle has been asking me to return it to her for centuries," he admitted. "I was reluctant at first, thinking I would need it again someday. She offered me money, trinkets, and a handful of priceless artifacts. However, when she offered me a woman that had just turned Absolute within the last year, I knew there was something within these pages far too valuable to hand over." Holding out the book, he waited for Nola to enter the room and take it from him. She hesitated at first. Then, she set her glass on the dresser before coming to stand before him. "Ysabelle is not welcome in my territory and knows to stay away. She will not come after this again. I can guarantee my reluctancy has kept you safe all these years." He placed the book in Nola's hand. "It will be far easier for her to steal one of the other copies."

"She can't come here at all?" The desire to feel safe had become a constant companion.

"She won't," Gavin answered, peering into her dark eyes. "I'm sure that Ysabelle seems heartless and evil. For what she did to you, I can't disagree," he whispered softly as Nola flipped the book on its side to assess the spine. "But she is a living legend." Reaching out to touch Nola's sleeve, he judged how well she was receiving his explanation. "All but one of her children are dead, and I am one of five direct descendants left from her line. Ysabelle has outlived all of her family," he whispered. "Although it was wrong and unforgivable, she was trying to continue our existence without the loss of any more of our women."

"You condone what she's done?" Nola could not believe her ears. Turning on her heels, she walked back toward the dresser.

"No," he shook his head quickly. "But she will always have my respect and obedience. I am certain that once she hears of what happened in Port Chatsworth, she will not come to you again. You are too frail for her to risk upsetting any further."

"You believe she will just leave me alone?"

"I do. You are becoming exactly what she wanted, Nola. Her time will be better spent trying to recreate whatever it was that worked with you. Your lifetime is but a season to us."

"Recreate what happened to me?" Looking at the book, she considered the tell-tale entries it held. "By kidnapping more infants and draining their blood?" The words made her mouth dry. "Forcing women to bond to Absolutes to bear children," she directly thought of her unwanted commitment to Elias. "Could you stop her?"

Though he shook his head, Gavin could not answer. In truth, Ysabelle's theory was not altogether unimaginable. The idea of a new line of Absolutes had a positive aspect. For three hundred years he had felt loneliness when it came to thoughts of their species. His hesitation was enough to infuriate Nola. She turned on her heels and left the room. Her hair fluttered over her shoulders and trailed behind her as she made her way down the hall.

"Wait," he called, suddenly behind her. Gavin gently grasped her arm and pulled her around to face him.

"I can't believe you," Nola raised her voice to the hollow hallway. "You would turn a blind eye to what she is doing for the chance at a few more women? How many children have to die?"

"A moment of thought does not equal a solid judgment!" Gavin argued. "You of all people should know that silence and observance can give you an advantage in nearly every situation."

Taking a moment to consider what he was saying, Nola had to agree that he was right. Even Dottie had mentioned that she wished she had the ability to remain silent when she did not know the right words to say.

"I'm sorry," she replied quietly. "The thought of anyone else going through what I have survived is frightening." She glanced up at Gavin with a calmer demeanor. "What if the next woman is not lucky enough to have someone like you watching over her?"

"I have given this thought," Gavin agreed, reaching out, feeling her concern through the sleeve of her dress. "My decision is unclear."

"What would have happened to me if you wouldn't have been here?" Nola shook her head as memories of Elias inflicted a familiar pain.

"There are a few elders that I should be able to contact and deliberate with. One of them might be able to help," he added.

"Good," she sniffled gently, adjusting the book in her arms. "Will these senseless sentiments ever go away?" The emotions brought on by Elias's bond and death still washed through her at inconvenient moments. It was visibly apparent that she still felt loss and grief.

"If you want," Gavin answered. Reaching his thumb to her cheek he gently trailed it over where the tear had just fallen. His eyes held a small glow to them, but Nola found herself focusing on the deep enchanting chocolate color. The longer his skin touched hers, the less she felt the sadness. The immediate relief reminded her of the constant uncertainty with him. Pulling his hand away, Nola lifted her chin boldly.

"I want to stay with you," she stated as clearly as she could.

Startled, Gavin stared at her soberly. "We are too close already," he argued looking down at the book. "You have no comprehension of what else is in this world."

"No." Nola reached up to his face and felt the strong firm lines of his jaw. "You don't understand." Closing her eyes, she concentrated only on her affection for him. "I want to stay with you." Every unsure feeling, every scared notion, and every ounce of fear was given willingly to Gavin. Nola wanted there to be no confusion of how she felt, even if she didn't fully understand it herself. His features changed subtly. His eyes darkened, his brow furled slightly, and he reached his arms out to hold her waist.

"You are too young for any of this," he whispered. "For any of this, or just you?" she asked daringly.

"Not for me," he shook his head as he answered. "If our connection gets any more powerful, you will be blinded to everything else in this vast world. There is still so much for you to learn." Nola could feel the ache in him as he tried to keep himself away.

"Then why can't you be the one to teach me?" She moved closer to him, lifting herself up to her tiptoes. Unnerved by his steady reserve, Nola pulled on his neck until she could reach his lips.

His kiss was held back by his desire to protect her. Still, Nola was not about to give in. She pulled him closer, tilting her chin more and letting her lips linger longer with each kiss.

His hands held her firmly, slowly pulling her closer. Nola felt him give in slightly, but he maintained his reserve. Ignoring the book between them, Nola unfastened the collar of his shirt and felt his warm skin beneath. Still, she could feel his reluctance and intent to let her go. Desperate and unsure, Nola kissed him again, this time more slowly and seductively. He tolerated it for a moment until a deep growl came from his chest. Quickly, Gavin stood up and held her waist away from him. Still, the sound she had heard, and the touch of his skin made her keenly aware of how close he was to losing control.

"Do you need help with that?" Gavin asked as he looked down at the book in her hand.

"No," she answered, letting him go and realizing how close he was to ending the moment between them. Glancing behind him, Nola noticed the candle still burning in his bedroom. She then held out the book and eyed the cover slowly. Then, as if completely at a loss, she knelt down and placed the book on the floor of the hallway. Lifting the bottom of her rose-colored skirts, she pulled off her slippers and set them aside next to the ancient journal.

"What are you doing?" Gavin asked. When she stood up, she was nearly an inch shorter than before.

"Whatever I have to," she answered softly. Removing the delicate silver necklace from her neck, Nola held it over her shoe and dropped it inside. "I don't want to see the world. What I have seen of it so far scares me to death." She unhooked her earrings and dropped them in her shoe as well. "All I want is to be with you. I think it's all I've ever wanted." Nola sighed a ragged breath, unsure if he would reject her still. Lifting her arms behind her head, she unfastened the top two hooks of her gown. Gavin watched her intently as she then reached up and removed the single comb from her hair, letting it cascade around her shoulder. Then as she had done with everything else, she dropped it in her shoe.

Standing tall, Nola walked directly past Gavin and made her way to his bedroom. Reaching the door, she placed her hand on the frame and turned back to see if he would follow. With a slight dumbfounded grin Gavin bent down to retrieve the book and her shoes. Then, silently he followed. The closer he came, the more intense her sense of fear was. She glanced down at her hand, seeing that there was a slight shake to it.

"Your emanation is making me unsteady," he stated. Closing the door behind him, Gavin put the book and her shoes on his dresser. "You're pushing me away almost as quickly as you're pulling me toward you."

"This is what I want," she answered calmly, standing at the end of his bed.

"I know," he whispered. Gavin joined her near the bed and reached out to touch the gently falling ringlets of dark hair. "I won't be able to let you go after this." His warning sounded more like paradise to her ears. Nodding her head, Nola reached up to his shirt and unfastened another button. His chest was warm and firm beneath her hand.

Gavin reached his arm around her shoulders and unhooked her dress, letting the front gape open more as the weight of the skirts pulled it down. Her thin petticoat revealed the curvaceous physique hidden beneath. Sliding her arms out of the sleeves, Nola reached up to him, eager to experience his mind-altering kiss and his erotic primitive growl.

Before she knew what was happening, Gavin had swept her over the bed and pressed her to the pillow, letting his lips trail over hers. There was no reserve in his touch, only the deep satisfaction of surrender. His hand felt every curve of her body, savoring the taunting design of her petticoat.

Nola loved how his hands ran over her waist, gripped her thighs, and pulled her leg to bend around him. She closed her eyes to the sensual emotions that filled her as Gavin tasted the skin of her neck and shoulders. There was no fear at all when her shift slid up her leg, revealing more of her than any man had ever seen.

Everything felt so natural that she let herself read his silent instructions. Nola lifted her shoulders as he untied the thin white petticoat. She arched her back as the material was drawn over her head, and she pulled him to her breast as his fascination with her was unleashed. Uninhibited in every way, Gavin somehow managed to remove his shirt. The connection between them caused the candle to flicker near the dresser. Nola pulled him to her, letting her lips roam over his skin, until he finally came to her.

Fearless and desperate, Nola urged him on, drunk from the exhilarating thrill of his massive body. When Gavin lifted his head, his long white fangs had protruded completely. Still, she urged him on. Bowing his head to her shoulder, he drew the sensitive canines over her skin. It was a strange thrill for Nola. Never had she imagined that the feel of his fangs being drawn across her skin could be more seductive than his kiss. Nola welcomed the growing addiction, arching her back to meet his every touch.

With a flick of his fangs, Gavin nipped gently around her neck. The skin never broke, but the sensation thrilled her like no other. Nola inhaled with the complete feeling of Gavin. His body, his heart, and his soul were one with hers.

It felt like hours had passed as he loved her. Exploring her body and becoming familiar with every response she gave. Gavin listened to her breathing and carved his movements into every way she deemed necessary. He watched her inhibitions vanish as she ran her hands over his muscles. Nola couldn't see his smile but was aware of how sensitive every move she made pleased him.

Gavin rolled over the bed and pulled her body to span the length of his. Unwilling to let her go, he pressed his nose into the locks of her hair, taking in the scent of the woman he loved. Her body was weak, but she still explored his perfectly firm muscles as she lay next to him. All too soon, the silence was broken by the loud ring of the doorbell.

"Are you expecting someone?" Nola asked, pulling the blankets up under her chin.

"I am," Gavin answered, moving from the bed, and retrieving his clothes with incredible speed. "I'm sorry, but we have to get dressed."

"Tell me it's not Davey!" Feeling her knees buckle from the instant anticipation, she came to her feet with his help. "You did not invite Davey, did you?" Her gown was over her shift long before the bell rang a second time.

"It's not Davey," he assured her. "Your hair..." Handing her back the single clip, Gavin hurried to fasten the closure of her gown as she fixed her hair in the mirror. "Miss Peetz inquired about you this morning. I thought it was only fair to give her a chance to see you."

"Miss Peetz, from the school? Whatever for?" Nola asked. "It would be more adequate to assume she is wondering when I'll be returning to work, than to assume she is genuinely concerned about me."

"Either way, I wasn't going to let her worry about you any longer." Aware of her disappointment and desire to go back to bed, Gavin lifted her chin and sighed heavily. "I'm sorry," he whispered. "There was no way I could have prepared for this." He nodded back to the bed.

"It's alright," Nola stated, letting her hands fall to her sides as Gavin started to the door. Before it was opened, he turned around one last time and captured her lips in a surprisingly powerful kiss. "You do realize that I'm bringing you back up here the moment she leaves."

"Good, now let's go." Nola instructed, hoping a second glass of wine would calm her nerves enough to get through the brief visitation.

Descending the stairs quickly, Nola felt the comb in her hair sliding gently out of place and paused at the bottom to refasten it. Off in a distant open room, two of Gavin's servants stood over a silver tray with a bottle of wine. Unaware that the silent Absolutes were in the hallway, one of the young women held her hand over an empty glass. As Nola checked the security of the comb, she watched the young woman let several drops of blood run out of her hand and into the glass. Before Nola could see any more Gavin turned around and noted her attention.

"Miss Peetz will be waiting in the foyer," he stated, reaching out to hold her hand with reassurance. Moments later the second servant pleasantly brought Nola the large glass now filled with wine.

"Would you care for a drink?" The lady asked, handing Nola the single glass, and curtsying to Gavin before moving on. Lifting the glass to the light above, Nola realized for the first time that every glass of wine she had consumed over the last few days had become thicker in consistency.

"Thank you," she whispered. Unable to stop herself from drinking. The thought of the blood nearly made her stomach churn, but the taste of the wine was delectable. Aware that she ingested the full glass in a single breath, Nola stepped over to a nearby stand and set the vessel down. She wanted to ask Gavin a hundred questions, until he reached out and took her hand. Then, everything seemed to fade into a wave of null importance.

"Your employer is waiting," he reminded her. Releasing his hand and straightening her gown, Nola nodded her head and began the long walk down the hallway.

Careful not to walk too quickly, Nola smiled as she came to greet Miss Peetz in the foyer. There was no doubt that the electric lighting held the schoolteacher's attention as she admired the strange luminescent glass bulbs.

"This is fascinating!" Miss Peetz beamed. "Nola, you simply must allow me the grand tour." Her elation was a little more than Nola expected. Her voice was too high, and her smile was too wide. At first, Nola was only annoyed by her feminine countenance.

However, when Miss Peetz turned her gleaming smile towards Gavin, Nola felt an annoying twinge of jealousy.

"There are more rooms than you could imagine," Nola spoke slowly. "I'm not sure we could fit them all into one visit."

"Oh, well I would be more than glad to stop by as often as it takes." Again, her sharp beak-like nose was turned up toward Gavin. He smiled at her kindly, but Nola was irritated by her brazen countenance.

"That isn't necessary." She licked her lips, realizing how the glass of wine still left her mouth dry. "I'm sure you have a lot to keep you busy with schoolwork and all. Perhaps we should just see a few rooms for now."

"Oh, I would love that." Miss Peetz clasped Nola's hand and started to follow her down the hallway. The moment she realized that Gavin was not following, the narrow-headed woman stopped short to address him. "Of course, you must join us, Lord Graelohr. You wouldn't deny me the pleasure of your company, would you?" she asked with her eyes roaming over Gavin's broad shoulders.

Something snapped within Nola's train of thought. A quick piercing pain shot through her inside lip and the slight taste of blood perked her senses. Her vision was keen. Her hearing increased to a level of intricate identification, and everything in the room smelled like the wine that had grown thicker over the past few days.

"Did you notice the chandelier?" Nola asked, aware of how strange her voice sounded with new and foreign teeth to speak through.

"I did," Miss Peetz answered as she lifted her head to take in the decorated view. "What an interesting form of lighting," the schoolteacher added, again smiling to Gavin. As she lifted her head up and down to view both the chandelier and Gavin, Nola could not help how easily her eyes perceived the thick blue vein that ran down the length of her neck. "I would love to have this kind of lighting in the schoolhouse," Miss Peetz continued. Nola moved her focus to Gavin's eyes, almost asking him if she should follow her instincts. "Do you think I should take it up with the board?"

"Definitely," Gavin answered, gently nodding his head toward Nola. As soon as the word left his mouth Miss Peetz glanced up at the lighting once more.

The display of the bright blue vein was too much for Nola.

Lifting her upper lip, she felt the smooth easy soreness of her teeth as they extended to their full length. Her eyes stayed on Gavin as Miss Peetz watched the brilliant lights above. Holding out his hands, Gavin filled the room with a slight static charge, causing the lights to flicker, distracting the poor entranced woman.

"You can try," Nola whispered as she inhaled deeply. Like the strike of a viper, Nola leapt forward. Jerking the schoolteacher's head to the side, she eyed the vein once more before fixating her eyes on Gavin. The thirst was too intense. Flexing her jaw muscles, Nola's fangs pierced through the schoolteacher's skin, accepting her scarlet delicacy as quickly as it flowed over her lips.

A special thanks goes out to Diana Taylor, Matt Ready, and Heather Falkenstein. This book would not have been possible without the support of my friends and editors. These people have polished this story several times to help create a vibrant and exciting adventure.

For more amazing stories of forbidden romances and distant lands, check out my website Ladybooks.life. There, you will find adventures including my own memoir/self-help story. Once bedridden and wheelchair bound, I currently live an exciting life surrounded by peace and tranquility. However, for those who need to be whisked away, Naylene Caulder might be a fun story to try. Check it out – and again, thank you for reading Novallia. I hope to hear a comment or review on your thoughts.

Not every woman craves adventure.

Having a semi-feral little sister is exhausting and expensive. Naylene Caulder is at the end of her rope with Josey. Fighting, stealing, and running away have become common for the twelve-year-old.

Unfortunately, it was the rock Josey smashed through Captain Ridley's office window that became the catalyst for Naylene's dangerous adventure.

Though Josey is brave to the point of being reckless, a rare moment of fear finds her accidentally loaded onto a merchant ship. Naylene will not stand by as her little sister sails across the Atlantic. Heartbroken and terrified, she strikes a bargain with Captain Samuel Ridley.

In the midst of his own conniving plans, the Captain agrees to assist the beautiful woman manipulating his empathy. Catching one of his own vessels and returning the ladies to Port Lorne sounds annoying, but simple. Samuel is used to managing small-town catastrophes. After all, he owns half the businesses surrounding the harbor.

Naylene did not plan on Evan Kerrick complicating her entire life. As a navy deserter, Evan spent years amassing treasure for his crew. It didn't matter that his cousin, Samuel Ridley, felt the brunt of his attacks. When Kerrick seizes another of Ridley's ships, the pirate has no choice but to kidnap the feisty girl hiding among the crew.

However, instead of fear, Josey sees an unsung hero in the pirate.

Through every meal and each storm, Naylene begins to falter beneath Samuel's advances. Still, Captain Ridley has dangerous business to conduct while Evan Kerrick is the key to his fortune or downfall. Despite the passengers he's meant to reunite, Samuel's plans are already in motion. With no other option, he sets sail for the Caribbean.

For Captain Ridley, it's business.

For Evan Kerrick, it's revenge.

For Naylene, it's a terrifying adventure she would rather avoid.

Now, with a maritime battle looming, she must choose between the lesser of two devils. One way or another, Naylene is bound to bring her little sister safely home.